DANNY HANUMAN AND THE QUEST FOR THE ANCIENT SEA KINGS

THE RAMA TRILOGY

P J ANNAN

Danny Hanuman
and the
Quest for the Ancient Sea-Kings

P J Annan

Design and Artwork by Patricia Moffett

Table of Contents

THE SECRET TRAINING MANUAL

You're in shock. Your head is reeling and your heart is pounding. Your life is being ripped from its moorings like a boat on a stormy sea.

Outside his bedroom window in the suburbs of Manchester, Danny Hanuman observed pewter grey thunder clouds gathering. A grey car cruised past. A black raven flew down and landed on the roof of the house opposite. It was an unusual sight in the city. Was it an omen?

Danny sat in dumb disbelief as he grappled with his feelings. It was an awful thing to discover about your father. Someone you'd looked up to for the last sixteen years as a truthful person. The betrayal was revealed by accident. It started with the discovery of a secret manual in his father's study. It had a weird title, *The Application of Remote Viewing in Field Situations*. Like, whatever that meant. But it was the words stamped across the page that did it. *Central Intelligence Agency*. It took a few minutes for the significance of this to sink in. He'd heard of the CIA in the movies.

With unseeing eyes, Danny thought back to his father's many absences over the years when he was growing up. His father had to go on a tour of duty with his Army regiment, he said. He was serving King and Country, he said. All very well. But *which* country was he actually serving? The awful truth dawned on Danny. His father was a spy and he'd fooled everyone. Including his own son.

Painful memories came flooding back to Danny from three years ago. He'd been told by the policeman on his doorstep that his mother had been killed in a car accident. At first he couldn't take it in. He'd ended up being cared for by his neighbours down the road, the Mithil family, until his father arrived home on leave from the Army.

To say he was devastated by the news was an understatement. His mother was the most honest, sincere and caring person you could ever wish to meet. She couldn't have known about Dad. She wouldn't have kept a secret like that from her son.

At first his father had considered sending Danny to boarding school. He thought it would be the best solution then he could go back to the Army on another tour of duty as soon as possible. The alternative was to arrange for a distant relative, Millicent Harper, to come and be house-keeper for him.

Danny knew how much he would miss the rambling old Victorian house that he called home. It used to belong to his grandparents and it gave him a connection to them. He would miss the attic where he kept his train set and all his old games. He would miss the mossy smell of the woods at the end of the street where he'd climbed trees and collected conkers as a kid. He'd miss the wildlife he'd nurtured and made friends with.

And most of all, he would miss being close to the Mithil family. They treated him with kindness and respect. They knew things that helped him make sense of his crazy world. Especially Sita.

A floorboard creaked outside on the landing and jerked Danny back to the present. It was a regrettable fact that Aunt Millicent had come with baggage. It took the form of her eleven year-old brat, Coral-Jane. Danny could hear her shrill voice now, on the other side of his bedroom door.

'You in there Danny-boy? You better let me borrow your computer or I'm gonna make a lot of noise.'

Danny's fists clenched. He knew from bitter experience what was coming next. Sure enough, the pulsating beat of her terrible music thwacked through the closed door at top volume. You'd think Aunt Millicent would put a stop to it, but no such chance. Her porky offspring could do no wrong.

Aunt Millicent was a tough cookie at the best of times, with her flint grey eyes and set, humourless mouth. She found fault with everything Danny did or said. So much so, he gave up trying to talk to her unless he had to.

A few minutes later he heard Aunt Millicent's stentorian tones booming out from downstairs.

'Are you ready to go to the Trafford Centre, my little angel?'

Danny rolled his eyes at the misnomer.

The music stopped abruptly. Coral Jane issued her ransom demands.

'I want some new shoes.'

'Yes, of course, poppet.'

'And a new dress. And ...'

Her voice faded as she went through the vestibule to the front door. Minutes later Danny heard the car start up. The house fell silent and he heaved a sigh of relief. His first thought was to see what Aunt Millicent had left him in the kitchen for his lunch. Bread and cheese. No surprises there. And *they* were going to be having a slap up meal in the shopping mall. Still, it was worth it for a bit of peace and quiet. Danny took a deep breath and savoured the moment.

Suddenly, there was an imperative knocking on the front door, followed by an insistent ringing of the doorbell. Danny ran down the hall and flung open the door but there was no one there. Instead, he spotted an unusual package resting against the step. His eyes widened. Who was delivering mail with no postmark and on a Sunday, too?

He looked along the street and saw a motorbike rider wearing a satchel. He was waiting at the kerbside looking over his shoulder at Danny's house. When he saw the occupant open the door and pick up the package, he revved up his engine and disappeared round the corner. It could have been a military courier, but the bike had no distinguishing features. The rider was wearing a brown leather outfit with a dark brown helmet and visor, which hid his face.

Danny came back in and closed the door. He examined the object more closely, turning it over in his hands. It was slightly bigger than A4 size, wrapped in stiff brown paper and roughly tied up with string. It had some squiggly writing at the top that could have been Arabic. Danny couldn't see a sender's address or any further clues. It didn't even have his name on it. It merely said, *'For the Attention of D.H.'*

Intrigued, Danny untied the string and removed the first layer of brown paper. Inside was another, more securely wrapped parcel, taped all over with old-fashioned sticky tape. Danny noticed a crumpled piece of white paper tucked into a fold and carefully drew it out. It revealed a hastily scrawled note in his father's handwriting.

Do not open this parcel any further. Keep the inner part intact. Take it immediately to the study and hide it securely. Make sure that you lock the door again. Do nothing until you hear further from me. It is imperative that you tell no one about this, for your own safety.

Mike

Mike? His father? Why did he not say *'Dad?'* Danny scanned the note again. Could it be that his father was creating a smoke screen to protect his son in case the parcel fell into enemy hands? Danny had a sense of looming danger and his heart started beating like a metronome.

He put the parcel down on the granite worktop in the kitchen. A cuppa, that's what he needed, to steady his nerves. He switched the kettle on while he weighed up the instructions. *Don't open this parcel any further.* Danny's fingers itched to rip the parcel open and see what was in it.

His father had always maintained Danny's besetting sin was his curiosity. He thought back to the time when he was four years old. He'd taken his parents' old-fashioned alarm clock to pieces to see where the noise was coming from. His father had found his son busy playing with clock gears all over the carpet. He'd given him the sharp edge of his tongue, reducing the little boy to tears. In contrast, his mother had responded by buying him books on science and technology to teach him how things worked.

Danny toyed with the idea of opening it. The problem was he'd have to use scissors to cut the tape and then it would be obvious he'd looked inside. What would happen if his father found out? A moment's reflection reminded him of his father's caustic tongue. No way did he want to face that again. It would be more prudent to follow instructions.

He quickly nipped up to the attic and retrieved the key from the key safe. The study was located downstairs along the back hallway. It would have led to the servants' quarters in the olden days. As he entered the room, he locked the door carefully behind himself.

He looked with interest around the hallowed precincts. He'd never been allowed in here on his own before. There was only one window in the room, and it had bars on the outside. There was an oriental rug on the floor and though worn, the beauty of its pattern was still visible. He sniffed the air. Bit musty. Hardly surprising really, considering how long his father had been away.

The walls were covered in maps. There were some modern political and geographical layouts, which was what you'd expect from a soldier involved in military reconnaissance. But there were also many replicas of medieval maps. They had names such as *Piri Reis, Bouache, Mercator, Dulcert Portolano.*

High-resolution photo images from modern satellites were neatly stacked on the oak desk in the middle of the room. On the top was a NASA image of Antarctica. Beside them stood a digital magnifier. A framed photo of an attractive woman sat on the desk to the right.

Danny meandered over to the bookshelves that covered one of the walls. His father had an impressive collection of books on topics that ranged from science, politics, and geography, to strategies of warfare and tactics in the modern army. None of it surprised him. He was aware his late mother's research had something to do with the medieval maps. He also knew his father was an expert in geographical and physical topography. It was a shame that when he came home he couldn't say much about where he'd been.

From Danny's point of view, what else did you do in the Army apart from fighting? When she was alive, his mother had seemed to bear the separations with fortitude, but Danny knew inside she suffered. It led him to hate the whole notion of war.

He was just about to place the parcel in the desk drawer when he had a feeling of his mother's presence. He picked the photo off the desk and held it close to his chest for a moment. Tears stung his eyes.

I miss you, Mum.

As he replaced the photo, an idea came to him. A better hiding place for the parcel would be in amongst the books on the bookshelves. He went over and pulled an autobiography of a great general off the shelf intending to hide the parcel behind it. But as he did so, his attention was drawn to the space at the back where the book had been.

Just peeking out was a spiral bound manual. As he reached in and touched it with his fingers he felt a frisson of danger. It had a strange sub-title, *'How to Develop Remote Viewing Capabilities.'* It was obviously some sort of training manual, well used and thumbed through by the look of it. Danny scratched his head as he puzzled over it. But it was the words stamped across the front that caused his jaw to drop. *'Central Intelligence Agency.'*

CIA? What connection did his dad have with foreign Intelligence Services? Maybe he was even a double agent? Danny was appalled.

Just because someone wears a uniform and you called him Dad for the last sixteen years, doesn't mean you know him. What else has he hidden from me?

With a sense of hot injustice, Danny remembered occasions when his war-hardened military father had ridiculed Danny's interest in the workings of the brain and the hidden potential it might have. But as Danny flicked through the pages his anger evaporated and curiosity got the better of him. The authors wrote in quite matter-of-fact terms and Danny was struck by the rationale they gave.

Our military trainers have coined the term 'Remote Viewing,' to express the ability to cognise that which is beyond the here and now.

He rang Sita. If anyone could explain this to him, she could.

Sita Mithil was his neighbour's twenty year-old daughter. She was incredibly bright and had just passed all her exams to become a doctor, the youngest person in the country to do so. They had become very close after Danny's mother was killed in the car accident. Sita's kind and caring nature had provided much needed comfort to the teenager. Danny found her supportive and wise beyond her years and had learned much from her. He remembered the many times she'd listened sympathetically while he poured out all his woes. She was the only person he could really talk to about things. She was like the big sister he never had.

He dialled her number.

'Hey, kiddo, how are you doing?' came Sita's dulcet tones.

'Sita, hi. Do you know anything on the topic of Remote Viewing?'

'I believe it's the term they coined at Stanford for the telepathic ability to 'see' that which is normally hidden from our sight. They did a lot of experiments I believe, in the 1970s and 80s.'

'Do you think it's real?' Danny asked.

'I would say the mind has a much greater potential than we normally give it credit for,' Sita replied. 'The difference is between the East and the West's way of thinking about that potential. Back in those early days, a number of countries wanted to know about it for military applications. In the East we regard *extra sensory perception* or ESP, as a by-product of higher states of consciousness. We don't regard it as an end in itself.

'As you know, Danny, I'm interested in the science of how the brain functions. We are now able to pinpoint some abilities that the mind is capable of. I'm involved in research to do with its application for paraplegic victims.'

Danny felt he couldn't say any more without revealing his source and betraying his father.

'Okay. Thank you very much for that, Sita. I'd better go now.'

He went back to reading the manual.

Scientists tell us we are only using 5-10% of our full potential. The brain's apparatus can be likened to a prism. Just as invisible white light is refracted into the colours of the rainbow, so the range of human consciousness, can be expanded by holistic training.

The vast majority of people can be trained to have some level of greater awareness. However, there are certain talented individuals who are born with a gift for 'inner sight.' Our military trainers are keen to work with these gifted few.

Danny's eyes caught on this passage and for some reason it resonated with him. He decided he needed more time to study the information. Tucking the manual under his arm he locked up and trundled upstairs.

He had just seated himself at the desk in his bedroom when his phone rang.

'Hey, Danny, it's me again,' came Sita's voice. 'I forgot to ask you how the *'Kids for Peace'* website is doing?'

'I'm just about to check it,' Danny resplied.

When they first started *Kids for Peace* online, they posted protest songs. It wasn't just Danny's guitar playing and Sita's melodic voice that attracted attention. It was the combination of a good-looking boy with chestnut hair and hazel eyes, and a dark-eyed girl of outstanding natural beauty, that proved to be a winning combination.

They'd recently started singing Beatles songs together and it appeared to have struck a chord with young people around the world. Danny looked at the number of views to date.

'Wow!' He checked again. 'Sita! It's gone viral. There are over two million hits!'

'Fantastic!' she agreed. 'We'll have to record another song soon. Must dash now though as I've got a medical paper to read for work tomorrow.'

As she rang off, Danny added a quick post to the page.

Thank you everyone for your support. Next step will be to organise the first Peace Rally in the park – and we'll invite the press. Watch this space!

Minutes later however, a new message flashed up.

Mr Hanuman. A word of advice – stop the peace campaigning. Such things can be bad for your health.

The writer had signed himself only as, *'The Aculeata.'*

A dark shadow passed across his window. Danny stared into space, oblivious. Who were *The Aculeata?* They must be a sinister organisation if they were against the idea of world peace. And why were they were issuing threats – *bad for your health?* What did that mean? Were they going to harm him?

Danny nearly jumped out of his skin as the front door unexpectedly slammed. But it was only Aunt Millicent returning home with Coral-Jane. She sailed along to the kitchen like a battleship in full flow. She always seemed to wear military style clothes, khaki coloured and severe. With her cropped hair and her habit of barking out orders, she might as well have been a sergeant major.

Behind her swaggered Coral-Jane, triumphant at her own success.

'I've got a new computer of my very own, wimpy-boy,' she bragged. 'So *there!*'

As his aunt was putting the shopping away in the kitchen, she spoke in her abrupt way.

'Danny. I've had an email from your father. He'll be home some time in the next two weeks. Get your room tidied.'

The hint of a smile crossed Danny's face.

'Okay, Aunty.'

But Coral-Jane wasn't suited. She shook her head and her highlighted locks bounced to one side. She put on a pout.

'I won't have to give up my bedroom, will I, mummy?'

'No. Don't you worry, my little popsicles. Uncle Mike can have Danny's room and Danny can go into the attic.'

Danny turned away and clenched his fists. Coral-Jane was in *his* parents' room. His father might not sleep there any more as it held too many painful memories. But nonetheless, the fact that Danny was going to have to move out of his room and go into the attic with its bare floorboards and camp bed, rankled.

Coral-Jane gave a sly sideways look at Danny.

'Mummy, does Uncle Mike know that Danny's a pacifist?'

Danny scowled at her.

Typical! What a blabbermouth. Anyway, I won't let her cause trouble between dad and me. I'll explain it to him properly when he gets home. Then he'll understand what we're doing and why.

Coral-Jane prattled on. 'Mummy, did you know that Danny and Sita have launched a website – ?'

Danny looked down at her. 'Oh, sorry … was that your foot?'

He sighed. Hopefully his dad would be in a better mood this time when he came back. The last few times when he was home on leave he had told Danny he should join the military so he could *'be a man'* and *'tough up.'*

I bet he got Aunty M to treat me mean on purpose. Not that she ever needs any encouragement. And she keeps me on starvation rations. Says I cost too much to feed.

Danny made excuses for his dad knowing he was still grieving, but he couldn't escape the conclusion that dad's personality had changed since mum died.

MONDAY 6:00 am

Danny got up early, keen to give the training a go. The manual recommended doing it while you were fresh, first thing in the morning. He sat cross-legged on the bed and read the instructions out loud.

'Let your mind become like an empty rice bowl. Rid yourself of thoughts, ideas, impressions. Have no pre-conceived ideas. Just simply be.'

'That's easier said than done,' Danny screwed his eyes as he tried to concentrate on the given coordinates.

But try as he might, unbidden thoughts crept in to dominate his awareness. *I wonder where his regiment is stationed right now?* His fingers strayed to the bedside table. He picked up his phone and read the message from his father once more. It was short and to the point.

Danny. My tour of duty is to end shortly. I'll be home on leave some time in the next week or two. I'll come as soon as I can. I hope I'm going to get a good report about you from Aunt Millicent.

Danny grimaced. Fat chance of that!

He pulled himself back to the task at hand.

'Clear your mind. Describe or draw the surprising images that appear in your awareness. Some thoughts are just imagination. Don't let them dominate your consciousness. Let your mind float free.'

Danny closed his eyes and managed to clear his mind as directed. He began to feel the silence, the peace. So much so, he was taken unawares by the experience when it came.

Whoosh! It was as if a veil had lifted from his inner sight. Danny found himself transported to the outskirts of a battle zone. He gasped as acrid smoke stung his nostrils and he coughed for air as it filled his lungs. The ground beneath his feet shook and his ears hurt with the deafening explosion of mortar bombs.

Now, he was moving far beyond the war zone to a remote desert region. He could see the barren, sandy wilderness stretching for miles in all directions. The only sign of habitation was a sprawling compound surrounded by 12-foot-high fencing and rolls of barbed wire. As he got closer Danny could make out mercenary soldiers in scruffy uniforms languishing about in the shade of a number of pre-fab buildings, which included a couple of large aircraft hangers.

Danny's attention was riveted by a group of Bedouin traders who were setting up their stalls inside the camp. He watched as the Arab merchants used large machetes to skilfully cut through whole water-melons and set the slices enticingly on their stalls.

A tall Bedouin took a prepared tray and slipped away from the rest of the group. Danny felt there was something familiar about him. He watched him carry the fruits across to the main headquarters building. On entering, he set them down on a table in the entrance hall. The Bedouin listened outside the main office door for noises within. The only sound was a loud snoring coming from a room at the end of a corridor. It was the searing heat of midday and most of the compound occupants were taking a siesta.

As the Bedouin lifted his headgear to wipe the sweat from his brow, Danny got the shock of his life.

'Dad!'

He gasped. What was his father doing there, disguised as a Bedouin? Why wasn't he in his uniform?

Major Hanuman silently opened the office door and slipped in. There was no one in the main office, but a loud snoring came from an adjacent room. Papers were left scattered carelessly over the desk. The Major drew out a micro camera and clicked furiously as he snapped page after page.

With expert efficiency he checked the rest of the room. He opened the filing cabinet and after a quick rifle through, he pulled out a dossier. He swore under his breath as he read the front cover. He slipped it into the capacious inner pocket lining of his robes and left.

Danny's heart began to beat fast as he watched his father hastily re-join the tribal people. What he was doing was obviously very dangerous. The Major spoke a few words in fluent Arabic to their leader who then gave curt orders to his people. They all quickly packed up their things and left.

What did it mean? Who was his father working for? What were those people doing out in the desert? Danny didn't have any time for further reflection however, as the vision faded into mist and he found himself in a different environment altogether.

He was immersed in the cool, dappled shade of an ancient forest. There was a subtle change in the atmosphere, which now felt sublimely peaceful. A fragrant breeze rustled through the branches and melodic birdsong could be heard. The forest floor was carpeted in bluebells and wild flowers and little woodland creatures scampered about.

Over to the east, Danny noticed a blue light moving through the trees towards him. As it grew closer, he was able to make out the form of a well-built warrior. He wore a metal breastplate and helmet. There was a long sarong type garment tucked into his belt. He carried an ornate bow slung over one shoulder, and a quiver full of arrows on the other. In one hand he held up a lantern, which emitted an incandescent blue glow.

As he drew near, Danny could make out the handsome stranger's face, the most striking feature of which were his luminous, brown eyes. He had a clear, penetrating gaze and his manner was calm and measured.

'Danny,' he said, without introduction. 'Your destiny is decreed. You have a special Gift that you must use for the good of humanity. At the appointed hour, I will be waiting for you.'

Danny wanted to ask how he knew his name. What did he mean, destiny? And how was it decreed? But as he opened his mouth, he found he couldn't speak. No matter how hard he tried, no words came out. And to make matters worse, as the image faded he became aware of a dreadful pounding coming from somewhere outside his head.

Bang! Bang! Bang!

Was it a bomb going off? Fear gripped Danny's heart like a frozen fist. For a moment, he was suspended in time and space. Then he came to, with his pulse racing and a thudding in his ears. With a jolt, he realised he was back in his bedroom and someone was hammering on his bedroom door. In a confused state, he called out.

'Eh? What? Who is it?'

'Wakie wakie! Rise and shine. Get up, lazybones!'

Aunt Millicent flung the door wide open and strode into the room. She carried a clipboard under her arm, from which she unclipped an A4 sheet of typewritten paper.

'It's 7.35am. You're late. You'll barely have enough time to get through your chores as it is. Here's your job list for today.'

Danny watched in sullen silence. He knew better than to voice his grumbles.

As he got ready his phone rang. It was Sandeep Mithil, his best friend.

'Hey pal! Have you forgotten your invitation? Get yourself over here without delay. Breakfast is getting cold.'

Danny needed no further urging. He picked up his backpack and headed off down the hall, avoiding the kitchen. When he reached the front door, he turned and called back to his aunt.

'Just remembered, I've got a meeting at Uncle Janak's house and I have to go right now. I'm going to do some work before school with Sandeep and Urmila.'

The mention of Uncle Janak would usually get him a pass on the chores. Aunt Millicent was in awe of such an eminent medical man as Professor Janak Mithil, and anything he said was sacrosanct.

It was only a few doors down the street to Sandeep's house. Danny sauntered along taking deep lungful's of the fresh morning air. At the far end of the street was a row of shops, including a chemist, a convenience store and a chic café. There was hardly anyone about. The only people Danny saw were a store owner putting a sign out, the café proprietor unwinding a stripy awning and a grey Audi pulling up at the kerb and parking outside.

Sandeep, immaculately dressed in his school uniform and not a hair out of place, was standing on the top step of the imposing three-storey residence. He was holding the door open for Danny.

As the two boys made their way into the house, the occupant of the grey Audi removed his sunglasses and spoke into his phone.

'I have located the subject's house as per your command ... I see ... You want to arrange for a little *accident*?'

2

UNDER SURVEILLANCE

OAKDENE AVENUE WAS A WIDE leafy street in one of the quieter residential quarters of Manchester. The houses reflected the faded Victorian grandeur of a bygone era. Some had been converted into apartments but many, like the Mithil's family home, retained their original imposing features.

Sandeep ushered his guest through to the high-ceilinged dining room with its elaborate cornice and marble fireplace. As they sat down at the dining table Danny's face lit up with appreciation at the sight of the appetising breakfast dishes laid out before him.

Granny Mithil, a plump little lady with bright, kindly eyes, bustled about them. Her grey hair was tied in a long plait down her back and she wore an apron over her sari. An indulgent smile spread over her face as she watched Danny tuck in to his food with relish.

Of the two friends, Sandeep was of medium height, and precise in all things. He was smartly dressed, as he always was, whether it was in his school uniform or casual clothes. In contrast, Danny, who was tall for his age, gave little thought to his appearance or his attire, unless Urmila told him off for being unkempt.

Sandeep's precision was part of a character that was gifted in mathematics and computer sciences. Sandeep was a computer whizz, just like his father, who had been headhunted to work in Silicon Valley in the US. But Sandeep's parents had wanted him to remain at his prestigious school in Manchester so he could finish his education. The arrangement suited Sandeep and he now lived with his grandmother and the extended family consisting of his Uncle Janak, Aunty Devaki, and his two cousins, Sita and Urmila.

'Hi, Danny,' Urmila acknowledged him whilst absently picking up a plate from the table. She was wearing an apron over her school uniform and her long dark hair was tied back in a ponytail. She delicately brushed a stray curl from her cheek.

If anyone had said to Danny that Urmila was a pretty girl, with her fine bone structure and dark, lash-fringed eyes, he would have been astonished. As far as he was concerned, she was just one of his best pals from as long as he could remember. He felt comfortable when he was with her. If he had thought about it at all, he would have said romance was what happened in trashy novels, it was nothing to do with liking your mates.

Urmila untied her apron and made her way over to a big squashy sofa at the far end of the room. The TV was on and she leaned in close to hear an interview on The Good Morning Show. The camera panned to an earnest looking young man in his early thirties. He wore a checked shirt with a mis-matched tie and jacket as if sartorial considerations were beyond him. He had a thatch of light brown hair that he had a habit of running his hand through absently as he talked. The TV presenter introduced him.

'We have with us in the studio today, Dr Richard Greenwood, the eminent science historian. He is the curator of the Science and Culture Museum, here in Manchester.

'Richard, I believe you have made some amazing discoveries that are leading you on a quest for an ancient civilisation. Can you tell us more?'

The curator's blue eyes lit up with boyish enthusiasm.

'We have explored some anomalies on a number of medieval maps,' he said. 'We have examined ancient sites worldwide, including a 13,000 year-old site in ancient Turkey. We are seeing mounting evidence of the existence of an extremely ancient civilisation who were more advanced than our current view of history can account for.'

'Advanced?' said the interviewer. 'In what way?'

'They had sophisticated mathematical and astronomical knowledge,' Richard replied. 'They were great travellers, too.'

'What are your team currently working on, Dr Greenwood?'

'We are currently searching for missing pieces of the historical and geographical puzzle. We are working closely with the documentary film maker, Dr Kirsty O'Donnell, who is calling her new series *Quest for the Ancient Sea Kings*.'

The interviewer raised an eyebrow.

'Wasn't Professor Eissen working on that ancient culture in Turkey before he disappeared? What happened to him?'

'Yes, my colleague, Dr O'Donnell, spoke to him only last week about his excavations at the Gobekli Tepe site. He said he'd made an important discovery, but he disappeared on his way home from work that same day. We don't know where he is. A rumour was spread about that he'd defected to the Eastern Bloc.'

'So it's a mystery,' the interviewer shrugged. 'However, I'm sure it won't stop your research at the museum, Dr Greenwood. It sounds absolutely fascinating. When can we expect to hear more?'

'We'll keep you posted,' promised Richard. 'And of course, you won't want to miss Dr O'Donnell's documentary series when it comes out.'

'Watch this space, ladies and gentlemen,' the interviewer said. 'I shall look forward to bringing you details of this project as it unfolds.'

As the interview ended, Urmila chewed the end of her pen thoughtfully, and then jotted down a few notes.

Danny had little interest in anything other than the food on the table before him. He zoned in on one of the delicious dosas, savoury stuffed pancakes, which were Granny Mithil's speciality. He was onto his third one before he managed any conversation.

'Did you know, mate,' he said to Sandeep. 'That the CIA sponsored experiments in Extra Sensory Perception at the Stanford Research Institute back in the 70s and 80s?'

'Is that so?' Sandeep was incredulous. 'ESP? Why did they do that?'

Danny suddenly realised he shouldn't reveal his source.

'Er, well. Like, this book I'm reading tells you that the Russians were researching possible applications of mind power back in the days of the Cold War.'

Sandeep buttered a piece of toast.

'The Russians eh? I'd have thought they would have been more interested in science.'

Danny filled up his bowl with muesli as he replied.

'And the Chinese were doing it too,' he said. 'When the US found out, they wanted to keep abreast of the situation so they created a department to study it and see if it worked.'

'I didn't think the Yanks would go in for esoteric stuff like that,' said Sandeep. 'But the science interests me. I'd like to read this book you mentioned, mate.'

Danny was floored, so it was much to his relief that Urmila came and joined them at the table at that point.

'I wish you two had watched that interview with me,' she said. 'It was brill. Dr Greenwood says they're looking for a lost civilisation. I thought it would interest you, Danny, what with your mother - ' She stopped and clapped a hand over her mouth, adding awkwardly,

'Oops! Sorry, Danny.'

'Because my mother was an archaeologist?' Danny shrugged. 'At least she was before she had the fatal car accident. It's okay. I'm all right talking about it nowadays. It's just school history that I've got problems with.'

'Right on,' Sandeep agreed. 'I can't relate to modern history, either.' He adopted a teasing tone. 'But Urmila loves it, don't you coz?'

'No I don't!' Urmila retorted. 'I love *ancient* history, but not the stuff we have to learn in school, with dates and British victories, and stuff. It's boring. My father says it's biased and Eurocentric.'

'The thing that gets me,' Danny said. 'Is that they tell us we can learn from history, so we don't make the same mistakes again. Yet you switch on the news and what do you see? More wars and fighting, all over the place.'

'I know,' Urmila sighed. 'At least in Rama's day, you had honourable knights and champions to fight for noble causes, and stuff like that.'

Danny looked puzzled. 'Who is Rama?'

'Don't you know?' Urmila raised incredulous eyebrows. 'He's just the greatest hero *ever*! The epic legend of the Ramayana is all about his stirring exploits. We're studying it at our Bhavan evening class.' Suddenly an idea struck her and she clapped her hands. 'Why don't you come along to the rehearsals this week, and find out for yourself? Sita will be there and she'd be delighted to see you.'

After breakfast they all went their separate ways. Sandeep and Urmila headed off in one direction to get the school bus. Danny went to collect his bike and cycle helmet.

He sent a quick text message to Sita, although he knew by now she'd be assisting in the operating theatre at Manchester Royal Infirmary. As an exceptionally gifted child, Sita Mithil had been coached by her father, the eminent neuro-surgeon, Professor Janak Mithil, from an early age.

Whereas other children had simply played with their dolls, Sita had used a marker pen to draw the major organs of the human body on her dolls. She would tend their injuries and dress wounds; she could reel off the names of all the bones in the human body by the time she got a skeleton for her sixth birthday. Now, having passed all her exams with top marks, she was in the first year of her foundation programme and undergoing her internship.

When Danny got to school, his phone rang. It was Sita.

'Hello, kiddo,' she said. 'I'm having a break in the staff canteen. What's up?'

'We've had a threatening message come in via our site.'

'I wouldn't worry about it too much,' Sita reassured him. 'Bear in mind there are trolls everywhere these days. Or do you think it could it be Sycker? You said he's always looking for ways to torment you at school, didn't you?'

'Yeah,' said Danny. 'You're probably right. By the way, I returned your book this morning. Got to dash. See you later.'

'Hang on a minute, Danny. A message has just pinged into my inbox.' There was incredulity in her voice as she read it out loud.

Dr Mithil. A word of warning. Desist from further peace campaigning. It could be bad for your health.

'How strange!' she exclaimed. 'It's signed, *The Aculeata.*'

OVERLOOKING the River Seine in one of the smartest quartiers of Paris was a sumptuous penthouse suite. The interior was a combination of opulent designer chic and priceless antique collectables. Expensive hand-woven Persian silk rugs covered the parquet floor, which was inlaid with exquisite marquetry.

The long windows were festooned with swags of silk brocade, yet had remote controlled blinds and one-way glass. On the walls hung original masterpieces of fine art, Chagall, Matisse, Velasquez, Rubens. This was a person with enough wealth to indulge every whim of eclectic taste.

A large glass and chrome desk stood to the side of the room. In stark contrast to the soft furnishings, it faced a recessed area bristling with high tech equipment. Banked from floor to ceiling were smart TV and computer monitors. Positioned at the top was a computer system showing all the major satellite systems orbiting the earth.

On the desk was a computerised monitor displaying a world map. It showed the position of dawn as a bell curve moving through all the earth's time zones. It was 8 o'clock in London.

Some displays played muted news channels, showing headlines from around the world. Others had images of hacked CCTV footage, including the interiors of government buildings, museums, streets and landmarks in major cities. The central monitor was currently playing *The Good Morning Show* on British television.

The only occupant of the room was a darkly brooding figure. He sat in a cream, tooled-leather office chair surveying the monitors. A scowl twisted his heavy features. He tapped his foot impatiently then leaned over and with one be-jewelled finger, pressed the intercom on his desk.

'I want the data on all the high net worth individuals, the wealthiest, who have their own private collections. And send it in with General Maricha.'

19

Minutes later, the door opened. A swarthy man wearing military fatigues entered the room. He was above average height with a hard, muscular, stocky build. His face bore the signs of battle with its broken nose and ugly scar running down one cheek. His deep-set dark eyes were sharp and alert, taking in every detail of his surroundings, including the selected programme on the smart TV monitor.

On entering the room, he saw it was empty. The only signs it had been occupied minutes earlier, was the slight swivel of the office chair and the lingering smell of outrageously expensive perfume.

Bowing low, General Maricha placed the dossier in front of the desk monitor that merely showed the black silhouette of the Parisian skyline at night.

'The High Net Worth Dossier, as you requested, sire. What is your command?'

The General held a privileged position in *The Aculeata's* organisation. It was he who had helped stage many a successful military coup. His was the practical hand steering the ever-expanding network of influence and power.

From the monitor on the desk, the voice fired questions at him.

'What information have you got on Dr Richard Greenwood?'

'He's a Cambridge graduate with a good reputation in his field. He believes there is a more ancient world history than is currently known. He's putting it about there's evidence of a lost 10,000 year old civilisation. He is sticking his neck out, challenging prevailing theories.'

The printer on the desk spewed out a long sheet of paper.

'Maricha, take a look at that,' the Dark One instructed. 'It's the price list for our catalogue. We do not want the scarcity value of our artefacts to be reduced by some meddling academic. There's too much at stake for that to happen. If he gets too close ... this curator may become - shall we say - a little tiresome for our plans.'

'Understood, sire,' General Maricha nodded. 'My agents were not able to find any adverse history. But I'm sure we can manufacture some, if required?'

'Monitor him carefully. He must be stopped, one way or another, from finding any evidence that an advanced people lived on the earth over 10,000 years ago. Inform your Agents.'

Maricha jotted down notes as the Dark One continued,

'They must promote *our* version of the past. It is imperative that we corner the market on world history.'

'Can you clarify, sire?'

The Dark One tapped the screen for emphasis. 'Listen carefully Maricha. History has become a valuable political tool in our hands. By manipulating a country's history we can control the minds of a nation. Tell your agents we want them to promote only the most Eurocentric theories. We do not allow any *ancient* cultures to have been 'civilised'. It's only the westernised view of civilisation that must prevail.'

'Understood, sire,' the general replied.

'We can use history to shape mind-sets,' the Dark One continued. 'We can use it to destroy traditions. We can use it to manipulate prevailing theories into what *we* choose them to be. When we wipe out the cultural history of a nation we undermine the people's national identity, rob them of their sense of pride in who they are.'

'Masterly, sire,' agreed Maricha. 'And we can control whole populations by implementing our own ideas of culture?'

'It is vital that we also destroy the evidence buried in their archaeological sites.'

'So the wars have a dual purpose?'

'Of course. The media must be manipulated to tell the populace what we want them to believe.' The Dark One warmed to his theme. 'It is imperative that people don't identify with an *ancient* legacy. You are to direct international government departments as to the acceptable theories of mankind's history. Civilisation began 4,500 years ago. Before that, they were all nomadic savages, and ignorant, primitive cave-dwellers.'

'Understood, sire.'

'Maricha. Keep that curator under observation. Do whatever you have to do in order to discredit his work.'

The General clicked his heels. 'And the boy? You asked for information about Dr Anjani Hanuman's son.'

very easily and wander around the room disturbing others. They are so knowledgeable that they argue points with their teachers in front of other class members. And the worst thing is, they are often right.'

Richard raised his eyebrows.

'As you can imagine, Dr Greenwood, this shows the staff member up in front of the other pupils. These particular pupils also have a tendency to be over-assertive, demanding and lacking in social skills. They have little awareness of how to work in a team. To be quite honest, Dr Greenwood, the school can't keep up with their need to be stretched, intellectually.

'So when I read about your research project, I knew it would suit these five young people down to the ground. It would give them the challenge and intellectual stimulus they crave. They have already been working independently on their own research topics of interest for quite some time. I believe they will have a genuinely worthwhile contribution to make to the museum.'

'Interesting,' mused Dr Greenwood as he listened to the names the Head teacher read out. 'Well, I must say from our side, Dr Ashburn, they sound just what we are looking for. Particularly that last boy.'

AS THEY WAITED OUTSIDE in the corridor, Danny suddenly felt a violent shove in the back. It sent him off-balance and he fell heavily against the wall. As he picked himself up, he saw the thick-set, tattooed neck of Sycker topped by his close shaven head, swaggering off down the corridor.

Silvio Sycker was the son of a very wealthy school governor. His father had donated a new science lab to the school. But Sycker had also secured a place due to his outstanding rugby talent. He had helped the school win many prestigious cups. Some said that he was on performance enhancing steroids. But it was only whispered. No one would dare say it out loud.

As usual Sycker was accompanied by his two cronies. They were all sniggering as they walked on.

Danny winced and picked himself up.

'Hey! Leave-off, will you!' Sandeep shouted after Sycker.

'Sticking up for our friend are we?' Sycker called back. '*Pakkie-boy!*'

Everyone heard. Danny caught Izzie Dalton's look of disdain, as if to say, *he can't even stick up for himself, let alone his friend.*

At that moment, everyone started filing into assembly. Once the pupils were all seated in the hall, the headmaster, Dr Ashburn, addressed everyone in his commanding voice.

'Now that your exams have finished you'll be going out on work experience.' He ignored a few mutterings, as some of the pupils reacted to the word *work*. 'I will now read out the list of names and work placements pupils have been matched with.'

Danny was only half listening. But his ears pricked up when he heard Sycker's name mentioned.

'Sylvio Sycker, has been offered a place at Taddakka Solutions.'

'That's great,' Sandeep whispered. 'We won't have to deal with *him* again, thank goodness.'

As he neared the end of his list, Dr Ashburn said,

'We have a special placement for five fortunate students. Here to tell us more about it is Dr Richard Greenwood, curator of the Science and Culture Museum in Manchester.'

For a moment many pairs of curious eyes swivelled onto the curator. There were one or two snide remarks as people started guessing who the five might be. Words such as *swots, geeks* and *nerds* were audible.

Dr Greenwood cleared his throat.

'I explained to Dr Ashburn that the Museum is willing to offer up to five work experience places but only to the right people. The placement will involve a high level of research. The project we are engaged in requires highly innovative thinking. We may possibly change the perception of history, as we know it.

'These five will get an opportunity to work with the celebrated documentary film-maker, Dr Kirsty O'Donnell on the research for her new series. This may involve field trips and visits to interesting locations at home and abroad.'

Izzie Dalton nudged Urmila. 'Oh, I think Dr O'Donnell is amazing. I've been following her work for *ages*.'

'And the five students I am offering places to are, Urmila Mithil, Hugo McCloud, Isabella Dalton, Sandeep Mithil and Danny Hanuman.'

'Congratulations,' Dr Ashburn shook their hands in turn as they came up to the stage. 'I'm sure you will all be a great credit to Lindale Academy. We're very proud of you all. Good luck.'

As the bell went for the end of school, Dr Greenwood handed each of the five new recruits a folder containing a sheaf of papers.

'I'd like you to read this background information to bring yourselves up to speed on the work that Dr O'Donnell and I are currently engaged in at the Museum. You will find web sites to refer to for further research.'

Richard paused.

'Please bring your current research with you when you start work at the Museum next week.' As he closed his briefcase, he looked serious. 'I want you all to remember this: some aspects of your research work will involve highly sensitive data.

'You will have to sign a Confidentiality Agreement to keep information private, or strictly within your group. This applies to everything unless you have express permission from myself or Dr O'Donnell to the contrary.'

Dr Greenwood closed his briefcase. He looked searchingly at them.

'One final thing I want to emphasise. This is a cooperative effort. I'm expecting you all to work together as a team.'

Danny and Sandeep exchanged horrified looks.

'Work as a team with that control freak, Izzie Dalton?' Danny muttered.

'Fat chance of *that!*' Sandeep whispered back.

At the end of school, Sandeep and Urmila hurried off to their bus stop. Danny went to get his bike and helmet. He carefully positioned his iPhone in his rucksack and set off.

He was so preoccupied that he hardly noticed the journey home. He didn't notice the grey car tailing him. He forgot all about avoiding certain routes close to where Sycker hung out.

John Lennon's voice broke into his thoughts:

'Imagine all the people, living in the world ....'
Danny sang along with the refrain:
'You may say I'm a dreamer .... but I'm not the only one ...'
Unfortunately, Danny saw that he wasn't the only one. With a shock, he spotted the bulky figure of Sycker up ahead. He wasn't with his usual school cronies, but was talking to a gang of older youths, some of whom Danny recognised as belonging to a local street gang. They seemed to be having a very intense conversation over a package.

On the spur of the moment, heart thumping, Danny swung left down a side street.

Phew! He didn't see me.

His relief was short-lived. The dazzling sunlight was now straight in his eyes. He couldn't see the road ahead properly. He didn't see the grey car that cut in on him until it was too late. He swerved violently out of the way.

He was aware of skidding ... a sickening thud on hard ground ... voices calling out ... trying to hold on to consciousness ... a swirling mist ... an inky-black void.

Darkness. Silence.

DANNY GRADUALLY BECAME aware of a long, black tunnel. A pinprick of light pierced the dark at the very end. It was faint at first but as he moved forward it became brighter and brighter until it almost dazzled him.

As his vision cleared, the most astonishing sight met his eyes.

3

A VISION OF DESTINY

As Danny drifted into semi-consciousness he felt light-headed. His fingers touched what felt like grass, but something was different. Hazy thoughts flitted like butterflies across his mind. He listened to the rippling of a river, a breeze rustling through trees, some hauntingly beautiful flute music.

Other senses were kicking in. Incense, spices and rosewater wafted on the breeze. The temperature was hot and humid. Not your average Manchester weather. Danny opened his eyes to find he was lying on the banks of a wide river in the shade of a banyan tree. Not far away, he could see the polished granite walls of a huge fortified city, shimmering in the glare of the sun. Had he gone mad? He shut his eyes again.

Suddenly, to his horror he felt a sharp point pressed up against his neck. His heart skipped a beat and he could hardly breathe. A voice spoke in a language he didn't understand. Danny's eyes flew open to behold a stranger standing over him. He wore a dirty turban and tunic; he had a barbaric, pock-marked face, and there was no mistaking the menace in his cruel eyes. He wielded a sword which had its point pressed firmly up against Danny's throat.

The bandit spoke again, this time more insistently. Now he had his knee on Danny's chest, pinning him to the ground so Danny couldn't move. This is it, Danny thought. It's the end. But as he waited for the sword to fall, a thudding sound rent the air.

Thwang!

The man's face contorted in pain. The sword dropped out of his limp fingers and fell to earth with a clatter. The man toppled over. It was then that Danny saw the arrow sticking out of the man's back, from his right shoulder blade.

Minutes later three men came running over to them from the direction of the citadel. One of them reached Danny first.

'Are you alright? Have some water.' A young warrior held out a water flagon to him.

'Thank you,' Danny suddenly realised how thirsty he was.

The other two men had reached them by this time and were dealing with the bandit. They looked as if they were soldiers at arms. They led the ruffian away in the direction of the city.

Danny raised himself onto one elbow to see his rescuer. He was clad in strange garb, adorned with jewelled armbands and necklet. He had an ornate bow slung over one shoulder, and a quiver of arrows held by diagonal ties on the other. There was something vaguely familiar about him.

As he sipped the cool water, Danny continued to weigh the stranger up. He looked to be in his early twenties, with the well-honed physique of a man at the peak of physical fitness. He was dressed as Danny imagined an ancient nobleman would be. He wore a golden helmet and breastplate; he had fine silk cloth gathered from the waist with a jewelled band around; there was a diagonal piece of silk cloth, which was placed across one shoulder to his waist. Danny was puzzled as to why he should seem familiar. He was sure they had never met before.

'Who are you?' Danny asked.

'I am Lakshman,' the stranger replied. He slung the water bottle over his shoulder as he checked Danny for injuries. Satisfied the boy was fit to walk, Lakshman straightened up.

'Please follow me. I have been sent to get you and bring you to the palace.'

Danny got to his feet.

'Where am I? What river is that?'

'It's the River Sarayu. You are in the mighty city of Ayodhya. Now, please come with me.'

As they entered through the city gates, Danny felt disoriented and confused. There were busy streets with strange market stalls, people wearing colourful costumes, unusual sounds and smells. His feet followed but his head lagged behind, full of burning questions. 'How ... Where ... Who ...?'

Lakshman ignored all attempts at conversation and walked quickly up the main street. It was a wide boulevard paved in smooth cream marble. There were stalls lined all along the sides, where traders and artisans were making and peddling their wares. Narrower streets ran off at right angles. Each had yet more stalls and interesting looking goods.

Danny wanted to stop and take it all in. There were potters at work, craftsmen were carving wooden boxes, or making candlesticks. Some formed brightly coloured beads into necklaces and adornments. There were stalls selling incense; embroidered shawls; bales of rich fabrics. There were stalls selling brightly coloured fruit and vegetables.

Danny noticed there was a queue forming at a stall selling flowers woven into long garlands. Lakshman saw Danny's curiosity and paused. He went over to the stall and came back with an orange flower garland in his hand. He offered it to Danny.

'This is for you. It is our custom to greet visitors in this way.' He placed it around Danny's neck and set off again. He slowed down from time to time in order to point out sights of particular interest.

'See that street off to the left down there? Where you can see all the decorated flags hanging out on poles? Those are our Merchant's Guild quarters. On the other side to the right, you can see the Overseas Traders' quarters. The fine houses up ahead are where the Ambassadors from many foreign lands stay when they are in residence with us.'

A delicious smell of cooking floated over from one of the street market stalls. Danny was reminded of the Indian shops in Manchester. Fragrant curries bubbled away in pots; a boy walked past pushing a handcart laden with pyramids of sweet treats.

As they walked on, Danny was astonished to see that there was a covered area with what looked like a dentist's surgery in operation. It looked very clean and clinical with white polished marble floors and surprisingly similar dental instruments to those his dentist had at home.

'Why are all the streets laid out in this regular grid pattern?' Danny asked.

At this Lakshman stopped. He led Danny to one of the larger houses and as they entered the coolness of the interior, Danny saw studious gentlemen with long beards, pouring over charts of mathematical configurations on a large table.

'Here are our city architects who are highly skilled in their art,' Lakshman explained. He addressed the senior of the group, who was wearing a blue turban.

'Greetings, honoured Sage Ganapati. Would you explain to this young visitor the reason for our city's layout in the grid pattern?'

The elderly gentleman pointed to the blueprint. Locations of drainage and water-courses were clearly marked. The most striking feature of the plan was its orientation to the cardinal directions. The chief architect replied.

'The alignment to the east is like a tuning fork. Everything is made up of vibrations, and the sun generates a massive magnetic resonance and vibrational force on the earth. It makes sense to harness this energy.'

When they came back out into the dazzling sunlight, Danny sensed a buzz of excitement in the air. Everyone seemed to be preparing for some special event. There was bunting, floral decorations and embroidered pavilions spread around the marble streets. Craftsmen were making jewellery and Danny saw pieces in fine filigree gold, polished precious gems, exquisite settings and mounts. One of them greeted Lakshman who replied.

'Greetings Nagaraj. I can't stay and talk today. I've been sent to bring this warrior to the palace without delay.'

Warrior? Danny's heart sank. He tried to find the words to tell his rescuer he'd got it wrong but Lakshman only quickened his pace.

Danny could now see that they were heading up an incline, straight towards the ornate white marble entrance of a magnificent palace. But Danny couldn't take in the splendour of the carved stone figures and gilded decorations. He couldn't enjoy the spectacle of the horses and richly decorated elephants as they waited for the procession to begin.

The burning thought in his mind was what they were going to do to him when they found out he was an imposter. He searched for words to explain the terrible mistake.

'Er … Lakshman. There seems to be some sort of misunderstanding. I don't think you've got the right person. You see …'

'It's fine,' Lakshman didn't turn his head or break step. 'You can explain it all to my brother.'

They arrived at the eastern gate of the palace. This main entrance had magnificent columns ornamented with carved reliefs and inlaid with gold and precious gems. There were two sentries in full ceremonial dress holding long spears and guarding the access.

But to his horror, Danny saw there were also two full grown male lions lying on either side of the gate. The beasts were motionless except for the occasional flick of a tail. As Danny and Lakshman approached, the lions emitted a low rumbling growl and half rose to their feet.

Danny recoiled in horror, but Lakshman was unmoved. He raised both his palms towards the beasts in a gesture of command. He said something in a language Danny didn't understand. The lions were instantly obedient and lay back down, but they kept a watchful eye on Danny.

'How did you … I mean … You can control lions?'

Lakshman nodded as if it were quite normal.

'Of course. All the Kalari warrior elite are trained in the management of ferocious beasts.'

'Wait here. Sage Vasishta has commanded your presence. He will be here shortly.' And with that Lakshman was gone. Danny didn't have long to wait. The curtains over an arched doorway parted and in stepped an elderly gentleman with long hair and a silver-grey beard. He was dressed in flowing white robes and held a staff in his hand. His erect posture belied his great age. Danny felt an unmistakable aura of wisdom and authority from him.

Sage Vasishta studied Danny in silence for a moment, looking deep into his eyes. When he finally spoke, it was as if he knew everything about Danny.

'Your destiny has brought you here, Danny Hanuman. You have a gift, a special quality that draws on a higher state of consciousness. The time is coming when you will be severely tested, but you are not yet ready. Rama will undertake your training.'

Danny was now certain they had got the wrong person but he was completely at a loss for words as the Sage continued.

'There are negative forces which are at present dominating and corrupting the earth. They will try and stop your attempts at peace through many means. Rama will be your mentor. He will teach you how to discriminate between what is Truth and what is falsehood.'

Danny must have looked as bewildered as he felt, for the wise man continued in rallying tones.

'Do not lose heart when you return to your own time and space. Now, you are to wait downstairs for Prince Rama. You will commence your training under his guidance shortly.'

Training? Danny opened his mouth to speak but Sage Vasishta had already left. A servant appeared, and escorted Danny down to the courtyard.

Danny was left standing there, feeling utterly alone and afraid.

Who is this mysterious Rama that everyone is talking about? He's bound to see through me. What will he do when he realises I'm nothing but an imposter?

He put his hand on his forehead and groaned out loud.

'Oh, this is absolutely terrible!'

A voice came from behind him.

'Greetings. We meet again, Danny.'

Danny looked round at the speaker. He recognised him at once as the tall, handsome stranger in the forest from his first Remote Viewing experience. Now, without any introduction, he knew he was looking at Prince Rama. Although he was wearing ceremonial warrior garb on his well-built frame, Rama nonetheless had the refined features of a nobleman.

Danny finally plucked up the courage to speak.

'Look. Erm ... Your highness. There's been a misunderstanding. I'm not who you think I am. You see, I don't aspire to being any kind of a warrior. I'm not a fighter at all. Quite the opposite, in fact. You see - I'm a pacifist!'

Danny waited for the ridicule that usually followed this announcement. But Rama just smiled. He had a way of looking that held no hint of judgment, only an acceptance of who Danny really was. Danny began to feel better. He found himself blurting out,

'You see the thing is - my dad thinks I'm a wimp. Or worse still - a coward!'

Rama shook his head.

'No misunderstanding on my side. Only the lack of proper training in your case. A man of peace is most certainly not a coward. Don't worry. You will learn fast. I will teach you.'

Rama took a bemused Danny out of the courtyard to an outside practice arena. There were many groups of boys of varying ages in training. Some were engaged in combat with long wooden staffs. A group of older boys had curved swords and were engaged in ritual swordplay with high leaps in the air and clashes on shields.

A group of girls were practising graceful moves in what seemed like slow motion karate to Danny. Another group were practising advanced yoga holding extraordinary postures that almost defied the limits of what the human body was capable of.

'What's this system called that everyone is practising?' Danny asked.

'This is the noble art of Kalari Payattu, the most ancient of martial arts, handed down from Master to disciple in a long unbroken line over thousands of years. It is a profound training for self-development. The individual cultivates his or her *Shakti* power and over time, gains mastery of the Self.

They passed a group of men and women practising an extreme form of archery. They were aiming at targets that were like tiny specks in the distance. It seemed an impossible feat, yet they were hitting them time and time again. Rama waved to his brother, Lakshman to joint them.

'How are they able to do that?' Danny was astounded.

'That is the training we undergo,' Rama said. 'It takes years of discipline and dedication. The most potent Kalari methods cultivate *Shakti power*. But the technique is not given out lightly. It is withheld until the Master deems the student is worthy of being initiated. All weapons are useless against those who possess mastery of the *Shakti* power.'

Rama gestured to one of the groups engaged in stretching postures

'All students must pass physical endurance tests and extreme yoga training for the ultimate in strength and flexibility of body. All must be disciplined and show respect for their teacher, who we call Guru. Seeking his blessing is vital for those who wish to be given the secrets of the Shakti power.'

'This is a unique system of martial arts,' continued Lakshman. 'Because it integrates within it a system of healing arts, called Ayur-veda. You see, Danny, our Kalari Code of Honour dictates that we may only fight in self-defence, never as the aggressor. And even then, those who cause harm in the course of combat must also have the ability to heal the injuries that they inflict.'

'*What*? Even give healing to their enemies?' Danny's brows snapped together in disbelief. 'Surely they don't deserve to be healed?'

'Yes, in principle they do, for to a Kalari Knight, all life is sacred,' Rama said. 'The true Kalari warrior rises to the rank of Knight, only after having perfected both the art of disempowerment and the art of re-empowerment.'

'What about if a bad person gets hold of the Shakti power?' Danny asked.

Rama and Lakshman exchanged significant glances over Danny's head.

'That is a good question, Danny,' said Lakshman. 'If the Shakti power is abused by a person of evil intent, they can wreak havoc and devastation with it. There will be wars and destruction of the environment on a global scale.'

Rama looked grave. 'If such a person is in a position of power, they will try to destroy others who have this system of knowledge so no one else can rival them. They will lead many people astray.'

Lakshman said, 'If an evil person develops partial Shakti power whilst still led by his ego, he will seek only to destroy, and will kill without remorse. That is something you will have to face in the future, Danny, once you are trained.'

Danny gulped and his eyes bulged like a meerkat on guard duty. He was now absolutely certain they'd got the wrong person. He didn't have an opportunity to speak however, as Rama took Danny over to the shade of a large banyan tree and motioned for him to listen and watch. Sage Vasishta was talking to a class of student novices.

'What is the Kalari Knight's mission?' Sage Vasishta asked.

'To uphold honour and chivalry; to uphold dharma and respect in society,' the students chorused.

'What is *dharma*?' Danny whispered to Rama.

'It means doing your duty or following your rightful calling in life.'

Sage Vasistha surveyed the students.

'Out of all the weapons at our disposal,' he asked. 'Which is the most powerful?'

The students offered a number of different answers.

'The wooden staff, sir.'

'The sword, sir.'

'The spear, sir.'

'The bow and arrow, sir.'

'Bare handed martial arts, sir.'

Sage Vasishta shook his head and looked over at Rama.

'Will you tell them Prince Rama, what is the source of the most powerful weapon?'

Rama bowed and said,

'Respected Guru Vasishta, it is the *mind,* which is the true source of power for every weapon. Real power lies within - it's not external. Outer shows of strength depend on contact with the inner Shakti power.

'A mind that is attuned to the energy source of Shakti gains invincibility in combat and in battle. The greatest combat of all is within each one of us. Anger and fear are our inner demons. We have to win that battle in order to gain true victory.'

'Well said,' approved the Sage. 'Rama, truly you have mastered this inner battle. Know this, all of you,' he surveyed the students and Danny.

'He who fights in the grip of anger, or fear, or greed, he is weak. But he who fights with a calm, steady mind is strong and victorious.'

Vasishta indicated that he wanted to speak to Danny, alone.

'When the time is right, Danny Hanuman, you will learn what you need to know. But you must be on your guard. Dark forces have been unleashed on the world, and they will stop at nothing till they gain supreme power. The Dark One, who led the demonic armies in times of old has been reborn in this Kali Yuga era.'

Danny gulped. 'What does he want?'

'He wants *you*, Danny,' said the sage. 'You are the one that will ultimately stand in his way. The prophecy says that the son of the wind will bring about his downfall under the guidance of Rama. Keep your gift of inner sight to yourself or it will put you in mortal danger. You have been given this vision of Rama's Age for a purpose. Hold fast to it. They will try and wipe it from your mind if you are captured. Do not let them win.'

A million questions seared through Danny's brain that he couldn't ask. He was being transported inexorably from the scene, moving back from a height, floating, weightless, down a tunnel of light. There was one thought uppermost in his mind.

They've got it all wrong. The prophecy can't possibly be about me. I'm not a warrior, and nothing is ever going to change that.

4

THE MEDIEVAL MAP MYSTERIES

Five brand new recruits gathered in a little cluster outside the Museum of Science and Culture to begin their work placements. The museum was an imposing building, several storeys high, constructed of red brick. The chrome and tinted glass doors were presently closed until the curator came to let the students in and give them security clearance.

Danny was wearing a jacket that Aunt Millicent had got for him in a sale, but the sleeves were too short for his long limbs and he felt awkward and uncomfortable in it. He would have worn his old anorak if Aunt Millicent had let him. Danny glanced around the group and wondered if they were all as nervous as he was. His stomach was doing back flips on a trampoline.

The others were also wearing brand new, smart work clothes. They were trying to look confident but Danny spotted little giveaways. Urmila, the smallest of the group at five foot two, was wearing a pale blue floral dress that made her appear younger than her years. Her brows were slightly drawn together and she nervously twisted the ring on her finger round and round.

Hugo, usually the most placid of the group, was wearing a brand new beige duffel coat and looked self-conscious. Danny observed him biting his lower lip and glancing repeatedly at the entrance.

Sandeep wore a smart navy jacket and tie and looked like he was already an efficient member of the workplace. But Danny saw him check his watch for the umpteenth time and noted he was avoiding eye contact, as if he didn't want to make small talk.

Then there was Izzie Dalton. She looked all smart and grown up in an expensive green tailored dress with tan coloured ankle boots. She carried a shiny new briefcase and looked outwardly nonchalant, as though starting work was no big deal. But it soon became apparent that she'd transferred all her nervous energy into aggression. She glared at Danny with open hostility.

'*I* heard what you said about me at school, Hanuman.'

Danny gave an indifferent shrug. Izzie flicked her newly coiffed hair and turned her back on him. She spoke to Urmila in deceptively sugary tones.

'Hi, Urmila. This is going to be a wonderful opportunity in spite of having to work with *some* people.' She gestured as if she regarded Urmila and herself as separate entities. 'Anyway, us girls must stick together.'

Urmila looked decidedly uncomfortable. She said in her gentle way,

'Remember what they told us, Izzie. We have to work together as a team.'

Hugo clapped his friend on the back.

'Danny! Glad you're here, mate. I was worried you might miss the first day at the Museum. Did you suffer from concussion after the accident?'

Danny was nonplussed. He had been dreading any questions about his experience.

'He wasn't a typical case,' Urmila reported. 'Sita told me he recovered remarkably quickly but he had unusual brain functioning while he was unconscious. He was exhibiting Alpha brain waves, which indicate a different level of consciousness. She wants to study him for her research project.'

Danny tried to deflect the topic of conversation away from himself.

'Anyway, Uncle Janak wasn't worried about me. He said I could go home the next day - '

Sandeep interrupted, a big grin on his face.

'Yeah! He saw how much you ate for breakfast and said the NHS budget couldn't stand the strain if you stayed for lunch!'

The general laughter that greeted this was quickly subdued by Urmila's next comment.

'One of the witnesses said there was someone going through your backpack while you were out for the count. She thought he went off in a grey car, but there was too much commotion going on for her to be sure.'

'Scumbag!' Hugo was disgusted. 'Thieving from an accident victim.'

'That's strange,' said Danny. 'There was nothing missing from my backpack. Wonder if they were looking for something in particular?'

'You okay, Danny?' Urmila looked concerned. 'You're a bit pale.'

Danny was spared the task of answering any more questions as just then, the front door of the museum opened and Dr Greenwood appeared on the threshold. They all trooped up the paved driveway that led to the main entrance to meet him.

'Welcome to the Museum, everyone,' came his cheerful greeting.

He held the tinted glass doors open and they all entered the building into the spacious foyer.

Izzie dived straight in, her manner full of the self-importance of a student who has passed her entrance exams to read law at a top university.

'I would like to know the background of this building, Dr Greenwood. It is my policy to acquire the history of a place before I begin.'

The curator gave her a cool appraising look.

'I was about to tell *everybody* its history, Izzie!' He glanced round the group. 'As you might guess, this edifice was built during the industrial revolution. It was once part of the cotton mill industry that Manchester was famed for. When it was converted, the eight storeys were redesigned and renovated to retain many of its architectural features, representing its gritty industrial past.'

He led them through various areas on the ground floor as he spoke.

'You can see we now have a modern, functional design with chrome, glass, and stainless steel used throughout, including our glass elevators on the outside of the building. I'm sure you will all be interested in the hi-tech interactive computer displays relating to many of the exhibits. You'll be given an opportunity to explore those in our quiet times later on.'

Dr Greenwood seemed at pains to put everyone at their ease.

'Any questions, so far?'

Danny raised his hand.

'Er - can I ask something? Is there anywhere to get food and drink, Dr Greenwood?'

Richard's lips twitched but he answered gravely,

'Important question, Danny. Follow me.' He led them through a set of double glass doors. 'This is the self-service cafeteria, where you can eat your meals while you work here.'

The students saw tempting displays of cakes and desserts. They sniffed the air appreciatively as delicious smells of fresh coffee and baking wafted over to their nostrils. A blackboard listed the day's menu specials for lunch.

A plump lady in a checked overall behind the counter waved at them with a good-natured smile.

'Good morning, Dr Greenwood,' she called over. 'Aren't you going to introduce me?'

'Of course! These are the students I was telling you about,' Richard gave an inclination of his head. 'This is Mrs Buzowski, head of catering, and a very important person on the team.'

He winked at her in a conspiratorial manner, and she beamed widely at the students.

'You just come to me, dearies, and I'll look after you on the food side. Okay?'

Dr Greenwood led the way back through to the entrance hall. He stopped at the reception desk and collected a set of laminated badges hung on ribbons. He handed one to each of the students.

'Here. Take your individual Identity Card and put it round your neck. You must wear it at all times while you're here. It shows you're authorised personnel. I'll now give you a whistle-stop tour of the public areas, so you can get your bearings.'

As they followed along behind the curator he said,

'I want you to get a flavour of the exhibits and what the visitor sees. After this, if you wish to visit any particular exhibit for your own interest, I'd appreciate it if you did it in your own time.'

They passed through various rooms, Richard all the while giving a running commentary on the objects of scientific and historical interest. He was obviously proud of the role Manchester had played in the early days of computer development, a fact that impressed Sandeep greatly.

Finally, he led them back down the stairs to the ground floor.

'Straight ahead of us through that series of rooms are the exhibits of ancient weapons.'

It was Hugo's turn to be impressed. He gazed up at one of the huge wooden structures that dominated the area.

'I'm very interested in technology, Dr Greenwood. And I must say, that is a very good reconstruction of a Ballista firing machine.'

'Yes,' agreed Richard. 'It's from Roman times and the technology was surprisingly sophisticated for those days. You can see the same level of skill in the structure of that Siege Engine too.'

'Can we look in that room off to the side, Dr Greenwood?' Danny asked.

'Sure. That room houses some of the oldest exhibits in the Museum,' said Richard. 'Over there you can see one of the oldest known artefacts in Britain.

Urmila read the label in front of the glass case.

'It says it's a longbow made of yew tree wood. It was found at Clacton on Sea in the UK. It has been dated to around 450,000 years old. Wow! That's incredibly ancient.'

'It certainly is,' agreed Richard. 'And it goes to show that humans were involved in technology long before most people realise.'

'What's that grey object in the other glass case, Dr Greenwood?' Danny pointed to a dimly lit area of the room.

They all gathered around the exhibit. On a wide, reinforced stand was a dull glass cabinet. It contained an object that looked as if it might be a kind of bow. It was hard to distinguish it clearly because it was covered all over in grey ash. The frame that held the glass case together was made of a dull, greyish-black metal. There was nothing remarkable about it that the students could see. Izzie read the card in front of the exhibit out loud.

'It just says, *Exhibit 108. A Bequest from Mr Parashuram.*'

She frowned. 'That's not much to go on.'

'No,' Dr Greenwood agreed. 'We have classified it as being a bow of some sort and we believe it to be very ancient. We can't get at it to carry out dating tests because the casket that houses it is locked. Unfortunately, no one knows the whereabouts of the key. And we don't have any reliable information about the object to give us any other clues to go on.'

'Why don't you break it open?' Danny asked.

Richard shook his head.

'We can't. There was a strict legal covenant attached to the object when it was donated, which said that the casket must not be forced. Only when the key is found, is the casket to be opened. There's not much more we can do so it doesn't figure largely in the museum's plans.'

After their tour of the public parts of the museum, Dr Greenwood led them to a door with a sign, which said *Private, Staff Only*. He pressed his thumb against a digital recognition display to the side of the door. A robotic voice intoned,

Identity confirmed. Authorised personnel. Dr Richard Greenwood.

The door gave a click and opened automatically.

'You've all been given clearance by Eddie Salter, our Head of Security. Now, let's go behind the scenes. Follow me.'

Richard escorted the students through a dizzying maze of corridors and up several flights of back stairs. He finally stopped to open one of the doors on an upper floor.

As they entered, Danny saw before him a spacious room with high ceilings and long windows that let in the bright sunlight. In the centre of the room was an enormous pine table.

A projector screen hung on a wall at the far end. There were rows of shelves against one of the walls upon which lay intriguing looking artefacts and dusty boxes of exhibits. The wooden floorboards were shiny and smelt of years of old polish and disinfectant. In one corner was a kitchen sink and worktop with a kettle on it.

Richard leaned on the table.

'Welcome to your workroom. This will be your base during your placement here.'

He hesitated as the sound of voices carried in from the corridor outside. A pompous male voice could be heard speaking in distinctly patronising tones.

'I'm telling you, Dr O'Donnell, I don't care how clever these kids are supposed to be. I don't think there's any point in pursuing the medieval map mysteries. It's a controversial theory that we'd do well to forget about. And as for those kids, I am certain they won't come up with any worthwhile contributions to the museum's research. You're wasting your time with them.'

A female voice was heard, sounding exasperated.

'Really, Darius! You can't go by their chronological age. The Headmaster of their school says they are all exceptionally gifted. They've already produced some outstanding research, which is why they were brought to our attention. And my TV producers are very keen to involve this younger generation in my new documentary series, *The Quest for the Ancient Sea Kings*.'

'Well, I'm not convinced, Dr O'Donnell,' the male voice continued in disparaging tones. 'You'll never find out who that ancient civilisation was, if indeed it existed at all. And as for those kids, they might be bright, but I doubt very much if they will be able to work together as a team. These types never can. It'll be like herding cats. You'll see.'

The students listened to this interchange with mounting indignation.

'Ruddy cheek!' said Hugo.

Izzie adopted a superior expression as she looked at the others.

'Have you lot done your background research set by Dr O'Donnell? I don't want to be shown up by any of you.'

'What a cheek! There's no need to be like that, Izzie,' snapped Sandeep.

'We've all done our research, so don't you go insulting people!' Danny retorted.

'We talked about this on the phone, Izzie,' said Urmila, her brow creasing. 'It doesn't bode well if we can't work together. And whoever he is, that man is obviously going to be looking for faults. If we fall out, it will play right into his hands.'

Minutes later, the door opened and two visitors entered the room. The first was a rather short man in his late forties. He had a long face and a long nose that he had a habit of looking down haughtily. His greying hair was combed over from one side to the other. He wore a charcoal grey suit with a silk cravat carefully tied at the neck. Under the jacket was a floral waistcoat. The overall impression was of a dandy with an ego to match.

He surveyed the students with a disdainful expression. But his prim-lipped disapproval became marked when he eyes alighted on Danny. Danny had the feeling this man had taken a dislike to him for some reason.

A muscle worked in Richard's jaw as he assimilated his colleague's outspoken comments.

'Good morning,' he said, forcing a level tone. 'Students, I would like you to meet the museum's finance director, Dr Darius Merrick.'

Dr Merrick gave a curt nod, but his expression remained set and aloof, as if not deigning to offer friendly greetings to those who were beneath him. Richard introduced the second visitor whose attitude couldn't have been in greater contrast.

'And this is the celebrated documentary film-maker, Dr Kirsty O'Donnell.'

The students saw before them an attractive woman in her late twenties, with china-blue eyes and a warm smile. She was dressed simply but stylishly in a white silk blouse, pale turquoise jacket and navy trousers. Her blond hair was scooped back and held with a jade clip. She came forward to greet the students with her hand outstretched in a friendly gesture of welcome.

'I'd like to commend you all on being selected to work with us here at the museum. We're looking forward to having you on board the research team. Your fresh approach will be of value in the task of counteracting prejudiced versions of history.'

She glanced sidelong at Dr Merrick as she spoke.

'OK, everyone,' Richard's tone was brisk. 'Let's get down to business! Please take a seat.'

Everyone sat round the table as instructed, except for Dr Merrick who made a point of refusing. He went to the back of the room and stood there with a notebook and pen, as if he were assessing them. He made Danny feel as if he were a specimen under a microscope.

'Dr O'Donnell and I,' Richard began 'would like to hear your research on the medieval map mysteries.'

Kirsty O'Donnell went to the shelves at the side of the room as if she was looking for something. She became incredulous as she searched in vain along the lengths.

'Richard, have you seen the rolls of replica medieval maps? I left them all here last night in readiness for today's session.'

'No. I haven't seen them. It's not like you Kirsty, to lose them, you're normally very efficient. Are you sure that's where you left them?'

'Yes! Absolutely positive,' she looked worried. 'I've had them specially reproduced for the documentary series. I thought they'd be a help with this morning's session.'

Dr Merrick shook his head and spoke in disparaging tones.

'Tut, tut, Dr O'Donnell. My time is too valuable to waste, searching for missing items.'

Richard's brow furrowed. 'Let's leave it for now, Kirsty. We'll have a good look for them later. We can manage using computer projections of the maps.' He used a remote control to lower a projector screen at the end of the room. 'Have you students got your presentations ready to show?'

Izzie Dalton's hand immediately shot up.

'Yes, shall I start?' She hustled on without waiting for an answer. 'After I read your fascinating research on the topic of the medieval maps, Dr O'Donnell, I examined the evidence presented by Professor Hapgood. His team were intrigued by the fact that many medieval maps contained some elements of unexpected accuracy.'

'That's rubbish!' butted in Dr Merrick. 'Medieval cartography is just a load of wild guesswork.'

'Dr Merrick, I agree that some of it is guesswork,' Danny countered. 'But I also think it's wrong to dismiss other people's painstaking research without giving it due consideration. If you study the research on these maps with an open-mind, you'll find there is something mysterious about them. And although the medieval maps contain a lot of inaccurate cartography, the truth is, there are inexplicable segments which are very accurate indeed.'

'Give me an example then!' sneered Merrick. 'I don't believe you lot know what you're talking about!'

'Let's look at this replica of the Piri Reis map,' Izzie said. 'The year was 1513 when Admiral Piri Reis drew this map of the world - as it was then known. But one of the remarkable facts about it is that it shows Antarctica.'

'So? What's wrong with that?' Merrick blustered.

'The medieval cartographers simply couldn't have known about the continent of Antarctica because it wasn't discovered until the 1800s!'

'You've just proved my point!' Merrick gloated. 'It must have been a lucky guess!'

'No, it couldn't have been simply guesswork!' Sandeep argued. 'The outline of Antarctica is too accurate. To make sure of its accuracy I checked it against NASA's modern image of the continent and it matches much too closely for it to be chance guesswork.'

'But there is an even greater mystery which reveals something even more extraordinary than that!' said Danny. 'The truly remarkable thing is the Piri Reis map shows Antarctica *without any ice build up* on it. The ice there nowadays is nearly two miles thick. How could anyone have known the topography of the land under the ice unless it was drawn at a time when it was once ice free? That would be logical only if it was drawn up *before* the last ice age. In other words, the cartography was drawn at least ten thousand years ago, before the last ice age had begun!'

Merrick's lip curled derisively. 'So would you mind telling me how Piri Reis managed to produce this accurate depiction of Antarctica even though he didn't know of its existence?'

Urmila replied. 'We know Admiral Piri Reis got his information from much, much earlier source maps that dated back into antiquity because he tells us that on the notes he made on the side of his map.'

'What I tried to bear in mind when I considered the Medieval Map Mysteries,' said Izzie. 'Is that the medieval cartographers had to use second hand sources a lot. They also depended on intelligence gathered by spy networks.'

At the mention of *spy networks*, Danny's cheeks flushed and he shifted in his seat uncomfortably. Izzie noticed and gazed at Danny curiously. She made a mental note to get to the bottom of that one and see if she could needle it out of him.

'You have to bear in mind, Darius,' Kirsty O'Donnell explained. 'That cartographers had privileged access to secret information. The medieval cartographer was in effect part of the spy agencies, very much equivalent to the CIA and the MI6 of today. Dating back from antiquity, maps were always handed down as Top Secret to the highest ruling elite of their day. It was extremely valuable information in terms of warfare and trade.'

'And it was very useful in medieval times when piracy on the high seas was a lucrative business for unscrupulous governements,' added Sandeep.

'You're not going to tell *me*,' Dr Merrick gave a mocking laugh. 'That you're taking Hapgood's work seriously are you? You can't surely believe there are clues in some medieval maps to an ancient civilisation of sea-farers?'

Richard Greenwood frowned at his colleague.

'There have been snide attempts to undermine Hapgood's credibility on certain online websites. But the fact is that Professor Hapgood was a highly respected academic and a Harvard University graduate.'

'It's interesting to note,' Sandeep added. 'That he worked for the CIA at one time. But he fell out of favour when he started revealing the mysteries of the medieval maps.'

'Strangely enough,' said Hugo. 'Professor Hapgood didn't die of natural causes in his old age. He was killed in a car accident.'

'Well, it seems curious to me,' said Dr Merrick. 'If his investigations were as thorough as you say, Hapgood's research findings weren't taken seriously by the establishment.'

'Oh but they were,' Hugo assured him. 'As a matter of fact, Hapgood's work was taken seriously by the genuine experts he consulted.'

'Yeah?' Merrick's lip curled. 'Like who?'

'Like the expert cartographers of the US Air Reconnaissance Division,' Hugo retorted. 'There's a letter from their commanding officer, Lt Colonel Ohlmeyer, who agrees with Hapgood that the maps show accuracy in places, which simply can't be explained away as "accidental".'

Danny noticed a red light on Merrick's mobile, which was sitting on the counter beside him. Was he recording their session? The finance director looked disgruntled.

'Bear in mind, Darius,' said Richard Greenwood. 'That scientific research of core samples has revealed that Antarctica was once a temperate climate with trees and plants.'

'You're basing a lot on one isolated map.' Merrick continued to be dismissive.

Izzie jumped up and pointed to a large landmass on one of the onscreen projector maps. She spoke in her assertive manner.

'It's not just one map! Look at this map that was compiled by the cartographer, Turk Hadji Ahmed, in 1559. He had access to *the most extraordinary source maps*, because he clearly shows a land bridge nearly 1,000 miles wide, connecting Alaska and Siberia.'

'That shows it's a mistake then!' The superior smile that formed on Merrick's lips didn't reach his eyes. 'The region that you are showing is under the sea – it's called the Bering Straits.'

'It is *now*,' said Hugo. 'But the remarkable fact is Turk Hadji shows it as a *land* mass called Beringia, a huge geographical region connecting Russia and Alaska. No one knew about this ancient landmass in medieval times.'

'The original map,' Danny said. 'Was obviously compiled by a people who had surveyed the land *when it was above sea level*. This could only have been done before the sea levels rose at the end of the last ice age. Turk Hadji himself didn't know or understand this. He only faithfully copied his map-work from much more *ancient* source maps which had been handed down to him.'

Sandeep had done his homework. 'Geologists confirm there was a land bridge where the Bering Strait is nowadays. They called the land Beringia, and it's possible we could be talking about a people who lived more than10,000 years ago.'

Richard Greenwood patiently tried to explain to his colleague.

There is mounting evidence of a civilisation in very ancient times who were great sea-farers and travellers. Our mission is to find evidence of them.'

'My new documentary series will chart our Quest of discovery,' Kirsty O'Donnell said.

Merrick raised exasperated eyes to the ceiling. But he then urged persuasively.

'Surely Dr O'Donnell, you aren't going to use this controversial material about the medieval maps in your documentary series?'

'Well, of course I am, Dr Merrick!' she retorted. 'I am challenging outmoded Eurocentric views of world history.'

'Such as *what?*' Merrick stuck his chest out in a pompous manner. 'Surely, you must agree it is thanks to the historical rise of *Europe* that we have advances in science and industrialisation today.'

'By historical rise,' Danny blurted out, unable to stop himself. 'Do you mean that invading the lands of India, Africa, and the Far East, on every continent of the world, and stealing their resources, counts as *progress*? Because that's what this supposed 'progress' in European terms is founded on.'

'The problem is,' Kirsty had a militant gleam in her eye. 'There has been a continual academic bias towards labelling non-Europeans as *primitive*. This has filtered down the education system to the man in the street and is the root of racism, even today.'

'Indeed, it has,' agreed Richard. 'Dr Merrick, do you realise that nineteenth century schoolchildren were being indoctrinated in geography class, that the native people of the Colonial Empire were all *savages* unless they were taught to be "civilised" by the West?'

'And it wasn't just Britain,' Kirsty added. 'This attitude was pervasive throughout all the other European countries. On that basis, it enabled them to justify invasions and wars from which they benefitted at the expense of the indigenous people.'

Sandeep thought back unhappily to his own experience at school.

'Racist attitudes are still being perpetuated in some areas of society, to this day.'

'Bias was evident in legal circles, too,' Izzie recalled. 'Their view was that non-European, non-Christian countries were *inferior*. So they excluded them from contributing to International Law.'

Dr Merrick shook his head as if he was listening to a bunch of anarchists plotting treason. He gave them all a cold look before spinning on his heel and leaving the room, banging the door behind him.

When it was time for the tea break, Hugo, in his rush to get to the biscuit tin, knocked a cup of tea all over the floor. Danny quickly ran down the corridor to Twyson's storeroom. It didn't take him long in the janitor's domain to find a mop and bucket. He was just about to leave the room, when he spotted a black bin bag near the door. Ever curious, he opened it and had a quick look. His jaw dropped. Inside, were several rolls of parchment paper. Danny realised he had stumbled upon the missing medieval maps.

Richard Greenwood immediately got on the phone and summoned the caretaker to explain. But when Twyson, with his stubbly chin and brown overall, shuffled into the room, his explanation was simple.

'Last night I found that black bag beside the waste paper bin. You knows the rules. If it's in a black bag beside the bin, whatever it is gets taken away. I wouldn't be doing my job proper if I didn't removes rubbish. It's not *my* job to inspect the bags to see what you're throwing out.'

Kirsty and Richard exchanged glances. Who had put the maps in the black bag?

LATER THAT AFTERNOON they all dispersed to begin work on their various topics. Danny wanted to research astronomical instruments. He went off to study the reference books in the museum's extensive collection.

There were hundreds of them, lining the walls of an anteroom adjacent to Dr Greenwood's office. Danny found an informative book on astrolabes and sat on the floor to read it. He was tucked away in a corner between some bookshelves and out of sight of the office door.

He was so engrossed that the shrill ring of the office phone startled him. But before he could move, the door flew open and Dr Greenwood shot in from the corridor. As he answered he pressed the speaker button. Danny inadvertently overheard the whole conversation as it unfolded.

'Hello?' Richard said, slightly out of breath.

A voice with a guttural foreign accent spoke.

'Dr Greenwood?'

'Yes. Speaking,' said Richard.

Danny tried to place the accent. Eastern European? Middle East?

'I have an offer for you, Dr Greenwood,' said the voice. 'My client has a very valuable Assyrian relief panel, which he is willing to offer to you, personally. It is so rare, that it is considered priceless. You could sell it to your museum for a fortune.'

He hustled on without giving Richard a chance to speak.

'In return we would like to come to a little "arrangement". A simple exchange of artefacts, that's all. Money is such a dirty subject, is it not? My client would like to acquire an object in your museum.'

Danny saw Dr Greenwood's shoulders stiffen and he held his breath.

'The item in question is worth very little, Dr Greenwood, but my client is willing to make you this generous offer: the valuable Assyrian relief for this little trifle you have lying around somewhere in your museum.'

'Eh? What are you talking about?' Richard said. 'And who are you?'

'Ah ... Yes. You can call me Mr Smith. My client is interested in acquiring that casket, Exhibit number 108.'

Richard frowned, 'You mean the one with the ash covered bow in it?'

'Just so. Exactly. The ash-covered object. It is a worthless trifle of no significance, but my client likes the rock crystal casket that houses it.'

Richard's tone was firm in response.

'I'm afraid that none of our exhibits is for sale!'

The caller's tone instantly changed. Whereas before, it was wheedling and persuasive, now it became downright menacing.

'Then you will have to suffer the consequences, Dr Greenwood. And you will regret it! Don't say I didn't warn you!'

And on that note, he slammed the phone down.

When the call ended, Richard sank down onto the office chair. As he did so, it rolled backwards on its castors. Suddenly Danny and the curator were eyeball to eyeball.

Richard's jaw dropped.

'Danny Hanuman! What on earth are you doing there? Did you over-hear that phone conversation?'

Danny nodded, dumbfounded.

Richard's brow furrowed.

'I wish you hadn't for your own sake. If these people are who I think they are, they are ruthless. You must not tell anyone what you heard. For your own safety. Understood?'

Danny nodded solemnly. The curator went on.

'All calls into the museum are recorded. Eddie Salter will be onto it. He's in touch with the Police Department who are monitoring sales of stolen or looted war goods.

'But what puzzles me is, why are they so interested in that dusty old exhibit?'

5
TSUNAMIS AND THE BIG DELUGE

4:00 am

Danny's visions often occurred in the early hours of the morning. This one came with alarming clarity. He'd spent the evening researching the ancient landmass of Great Britain as it would have been when it was joined to mainland Europe. He wanted to see how it looked before the last Ice Age. He plotted the coordinates, as they would have been over 10,000 years ago. Britain was joined by land to mainland Europe, to Ireland, and Norway.

Danny was fascinated by ancient Dogger Land, and what it was like before sea levels rose and submerged it. Even to this day, he'd heard of trawlermen in the Dogger area regularly pulling the skulls of mammoth and sabre-toothed tigers out of their nets.

The only trace of Dogger Land nowadays was a name on the shipping forecast.

IT WAS daybreak and Danny arose full of excitement. The gathering of clans for the big hunt was to take place this day. He gathered his things in readiness, his trusty bow and quiver, his spear and his cloak against the early morning cool, although later it would get too hot for comfort. He set off through the lush verdant plains along the ancient well-worn tracks.

He was in his element, smelling the dew on the grass, listening to the calls of the wild birds and holding his spear at the ready. He knew these lands well. Many of his family members were spread out in villages dotted across the lowlands between Gaul and Dogger Land. In the far distance he saw the white-flecked chalk downs of the lands inhabited by the Breton folk. They were mirrored in the chalk downs on his people's side.

Danny waved excitedly to his Gallic cousins as he travelled towards their village of Kalais, up the hill not far distant. They waved back. Today they were all going hunting together, the men of his village and theirs in a cooperative hunt for the bison that roamed the plain. It only happened like this once a year. It was the big occasion he looked forward to.

Tonight there would be feasting and dancing, songs and stories by the campfire. The travelling musicians would come all the way from the Swabian Alps. They would play their ivory flutes and it would melt your heart. Betrothals would be arranged between families, too. Maybe even his if he proved his valour today.

In the distance, Danny suddenly noticed the herd had begun to behave very strangely. He knew these animals, had tracked them many times, but this behaviour was something he had never seen or heard of before.

The bison herd leader stopped grazing and the whites of his eyes rolled. The rest of the herd lifted their heads and sniffed the air. Then as one, they started stampeding, first this way then the other. They finally headed en masse in desperate panic towards the highest ground ahead of them. Herds of deer did the same, and mammoths trumpeted in terror, following the same pattern of escape, *away* from the lowlands. Even moving amongst them, also on the run, Danny spotted the fierce sabre-toothed tiger. He was mystified. It was unheard of. What could possibly have spooked them like this?

In the distance he could hear a faint rumbling sound. The ground beneath his feet began to tremble and quake. The noise became louder and louder, until it turned into a deafening, thunderous roar. There were crashing rocks and trees tossed high aloft as if the earth and air were being ripped apart by a gigantic pair of hands.

And then Danny took in what he was seeing. It was a towering 50-foot wall of blue-green water tearing through the land. It was moving faster than a hundred galloping horses. The people in all the lowland villages had seen it too. There were screams of terror and people tried to flee for their lives. They were too late. The water overtook them.

Only those villages on the very highest ground would survive the devastating onslaught of the tsunami. Only they would live to tell the tale to their grandchildren.

Teenage Danny stood rooted to the spot as the wall of water rushed towards him. *He was done for!*

Danny awoke, gasping for breath. He had to sit up to take in his surroundings. It had all been so real. He knew he was back in his bedroom at home, but he felt as if he were drowning. It took him a full ten minutes to be able to breath normally and make sense of what he had witnessed. It was as if he'd just relived another lifetime.

At breakfast time he phoned Sandeep.

'Mate, do you know if there is factual evidence of a major flood event, that could have started with a tsunami around ten thousand years ago? And could it have created the English Channel?'

'Yeah, deffo, there was,' Sandeep confirmed. 'Flood water from melting glaciers was unleashed with such massive force that it bulldozed through the lowlands to create what is now the English Channel. You could say it was the defining event which cut us off from Europe and created the island nation that came to be known as the British Isles.'

Danny was left to reflect on this. What cultural records would the indigenous people have passed on to future generations to tell them of this massive flood event in their history. And more importantly, to warn them of its potential future occurrence?

· · ·

'I've called a staff meeting this morning,' Richard looked round the assembled company at the workroom table. 'And I'm including you students as trainee staff while you work here. Today, I need to warn everyone to be on their guard.

'We have reason to believe that some of our exhibits - well, one in particular - is the subject of criminal interest. We would like you to keep your eyes peeled and report any suspicious activity you see in and around the museum.'

'Is there anything in particular the criminals might be interested in, Dr Greenwood?' Izzie asked.

Richard glanced fleetingly at Danny. 'It seems that the old, unidentified bow downstairs has some appeal. We don't know what, as we haven't been able to put a monetary value on it.'

Mrs Buzowski was there as Head of Catering and Hygiene. She piped up,

'Gives me the colly-wobbles, that thing. Spooky, it is. You can feel its vibrations.'

Richard gave her a look of indulgent tolerance.

'Now then, Mrs Buzowski! We've had this conversation before, haven't we? That floor polisher your cleaner uses whizzes around so hard, it makes everything around it vibrate.'

But Mrs Buzowski was adamant.

'I felt it vibrate and I know what I feel.'

Izzie raised her hand.

'Could we go and examine the exhibit more closely, do you think, Dr Greenwood?'

'It will have to be in your own free time if you do. You are going to be very busy with your work here from now on. We are answerable to the Museum Committee and they want results.'

'Yes, indeed!' said Kirsty O'Donnell. 'It's essential that we concentrate on our research to discover the identity of these ancient *Sea Kings*. My producers also want to see results.'

When the meeting ended all the staff members left the room, apart from Dr O'Donnell who remained behind to talk to the students.

'I'd like to hear your research so far,' she said. 'Who'd like to go first?'

Izzie preened herself, and sifted through her papers, as she got ready to put herself forward. The three boys exchanged knowing looks. Danny whispered behind his hand.

'I don't know where she keeps her prerogatives, but she sure exercises them a lot!'

The boys sniggered.

'You lot should be grateful,' chided Urmila, overhearing. 'Izzie's a born organiser, and whilst she might be a bit bossy, she at least keeps us all focused and on task – which is more than we'd do on our own!' She looked pointedly at Danny and Sandeep.

But as Izzie patted her shoulder length sandy bob and prepared to speak, Dr O'Donnell interrupted in a firm tone.

'Urmila. Would you like start? Please tell us about your research.'

Urmila looked slightly surprised, but her eyes lit up as she spoke.

'I researched ancient Flood Mythologies to see if I could find any common factors between them. Obviously, there's the well-known biblical version of Noah and his Ark. But there are also many other widespread legends of cataclysmic floods in the ancient world. They are preserved as traditional tales in indigenous cultures on every continent. The stories might vary in detail, but in general they all tell of a world-wide deluge and rising sea levels in the ancient world, which caused huge landmasses to be submerged.'

Kirsty jotted down notes.

'Interesting. Go on.'

'Some experts,' Sandeep said, determined that Izzie shouldn't dominate the proceedings. 'Now believe these stories, which have been passed on in an oral tradition over millennia, may be a valid human record of actual events -'

'They are just *stories!*' a sarcastic voice rudely interrupted from the door. 'They are not factual evidence.'

Danny's heart sank as he recognised Dr Merrick's long face. The finance director had entered the room unannounced and behind him came Richard Greenwood. He was accompanied by an older man they'd never met before. The stranger looked stern.

'Students,' said Richard Greenwood. 'Let me introduce you to the Chair of the Museum Committee, Professor Plendergarth.'

The students weighed up the elderly gentleman before them. He wore a brown tweed jacket and an orange bow tie. Behind his half moon spectacles were shrewd grey eyes, which seemed to take everything in as he looked around the room. The lines at the corner of his eyes were like corrugated cardboard but hinted at a sense of humour. He had a habit of cocking his head to one side as he listened, which gave him a curious, birdlike appearance as if he was permanently questioning the world around him.

When he spoke it was in a deep resonant voice.

'I must inform you that Dr Merrick has filed a complaint that you are wasting your time looking at what he calls mere *'stories.'* So, I wanted to hear about your work for myself and see what your response is to that criticism.'

Kirsty O'Donnell's eyes flashed fire at Merrick. But Richard played it cool as he answered the professor's question.

'What I would say, professor, is that we are often quick to disparage the histories of indigenous people, as if they are *'mere stories.'* But let me ask you this, Dr Merrick. What else is 'history' other than the academic study of a collection of 'stories' of events of the past? No one has a monopoly on history.

'I see where you are coming from,' Professor Plendergarth nodded. 'If you ask a hundred people to watch a show, you'll get a hundred different versions of the same event they've all just seen. So, what you are saying is that history is recorded by the victors. The defeated will tell a very different story of the events. And it will be valid to them from their point of view.'

'Kirsty O'Donnell elaborated.

'We would like to think of archeology as a science, yet really it's all about constructing 'stories' around an artefact or a discovery. It's educated guesswork and theorising. We can't be sure if it is absolutely true. We need to try and cross reference it somehow.'

'So that's why we've used a discipline called Archeo-mythology,' said Izzie. 'It scientifically analyses indigenous people's folk stories and cross-references them with science to see if they contain any elements of factual truth.'

'Our hypothesis follows from the study of the medieval maps,' said Danny. 'If there *were* people living pre-ice ages, would their histories have recorded any flood events that might give us clues as to their identity?'

Professor Plendergarth looked pleased.

'Good work, young man. D'you know what Dr Merrick? It seems to me the students' are doing valuable research on this topic. I'd like to hear more from them.'

Merrick looked piqued, but he had no option but to listen.

'There are many examples of flood myths,' said Izzie. 'They have been preserved by just about every culture on every continent of the world. For example, an Aztec story sees a devout couple saved while the divine storms drown the wicked of the land. Creation myths from Egypt to Scandinavia, from India to South America and the South Sea islanders, have all involved cataclysmic floods of various sorts, devastating the land and remaking the earth.'

'You can't surely believe *oral* histories are accurate records of events?' Dr Merrick said in his prim-lipped way. 'They are just *tall tales* passed on by uncultured, primitive people.'

'That's what we've been led to believe,' said Danny. 'But it is a very Eurocentric viewpoint, Dr Merrick.'

'But it's not really evidence,' Merrick persisted in dismissive tones. 'Unless there are *written* accounts that could be validated in a western academic sense.'

'As a matter of fact,' said Hugo. 'There *is* a written account which is over five thousand years old. It is from an ancient and very advanced culture called the Sumerians. Their description is called the *Epic of Gilgamesh* and it was written on clay tablets in an ancient writing called Cuneiform.'

Merrick pursed his lips in annoyance. Two red spots appeared in his cheeks and he glared at Hugo.

The professor noted Hugo's hesitation.

'Finish your story, young man.'

'The Sumerian written account tells of the following events,' Hugo said. 'There was a wise man, called Utna-pishtim, and he is warned of an imminent flood about to be unleashed by wrathful gods. He takes the warning seriously and he builds a vast oval-shaped boat. It's reinforced with tar and pitch, and is big enough to carry all his relatives, grains and animals. After enduring days of unprecedented storms, the Sumerian wise man, like Noah in Genesis, releases a bird in search of dry land. They all land safely on a mountain, there to begin life anew.'

Professor Plendergarth nodded.

'Interesting. You know what I think, Darius? I think we need to keep an open mind. *What if* we entertained the idea that it was a true history? As a written account it has a wealth of detail. And furthermore, it has the proven antiquity of being over five thousand years old.'

'Yes, sir,' Danny said. 'And it is a legacy from a highly sophisticated culture that had an advanced system of writing. How did they have that when mankind was supposed to have been primitive in those days? How does such an advanced and cultured society fit into our current conceptual model of history?'

The professor's sharp eyes bored into Danny.

'Oh my,' said Merrick with a little sarcastic titter. 'He is wanting us to re-write history now, eh, professor?'

Professor Plendergarth ignored him and said,

'What I would like to know is, have any of you cross-referenced Flood Mythologies with other disciplines? For example, have you carried out scientific or geological research that might verify ancient floods actually happened on a wide scale?'

Sandeep said,

'Yes, we have, sir. We found there is scientific and geological evidence of devastating floods, tsunamis, and ice cap melts, over ten thousand years ago and more. For a start, there was a series of mega flood events, sixteen thousand years ago.'

'There is further scientific evidence,' said Izzie. 'Of a geological event, called the Younger Dryas, which took place around 11,000-years ago. It caused world-wide floods and devastation over many areas. The world map then would have looked very different to the way it looks today.

Many landmasses that were joined to each other back then, are now under water.

'If you look at this map of ancient Britain around 10,000 years ago, for example,' Hugo said. 'You can see it was joined to mainland Europe by a wide stretch of land called Dogger Land -'

'Which was submerged by a super-massive flood event,' Sandeep said, turning his screen round for them to see. 'I've created a computer simulation on my laptop. It shows how the rising sea levels of various ice ages melted and re-formed, and how it is likely to have affected ancient land masses.'

The professor looked impressed.

'In anthropological terms,' said Urmila. 'How would the native people *not* remember such massive events as these, nor pass a warning of it on to succeeding generations? And what better way to do that, other than by stories?'

'The Greeks such as Plato spoke of such events,' said Izzie, with a nod to Dr Merrick's interests. 'And he was a highly intelligent person.'

'Are you relating this submerging of landmasses to the medieval map mysteries?' queried Professor Plendergath.

'Yes, because it is our hypothesis,' Urmila said. 'That even if they were in the minority, there were highly intelligent people living in those ancient societies. There would have been a range of intelligence amongst people, such as one would get on a standard distribution curve, scientifically speaking.'

Hugo continued.

'In other words, there were at least *some* people who were highly intelligent in the ancient societies and there were those who were less bright. Similar, when you think about it, to nowadays in today's world.'

Izzie added, 'If we can find an ancient civilisation who were cultured enough to understand maths and astronomy for navigation, it would give weight to our theory.'

'They were too primitive for those disciplines back then!' Merrick blustered.

'Who says they were too primitive?' challenged Danny. 'Our research shows evidence there were advanced cultures over ten thousand years ago who were just as intelligent as we are today.'

Merrick's attitude changed from that point onwards. He stopped putting objections forward and instead, started making notes on his iPad as if composing a dossier. He then sent an email to someone.

'So you students are proposing,' Professor Plendergarth mused. 'That the mythologies of the indigenous peoples may possibly reflect a true collective memory of these ancient past events?'

'That's right,' said Richard. 'Another point we have to consider is the different attitude towards oral histories between the cultures of the east to those of the west. The east has a tradition of passing on the oral history of their epic stories as a sacred tradition. They are preserved verbatim in a language called Sanskrit.'

'And Sanskrit recitations have been given special status by UNESCO,' said Kirsty. 'Who have classed the oral traditions of the east as one of the priceless heritages of mankind.'

'I studied the cave paintings at Lascaux in France,' Danny said. 'They show horses and other animals as if they are running wildly. What if the animals they depict are fleeing from a natural disaster? What if the paintings were being used as a teaching aid by the older generation to tell stories to the younger ones. The message might have been about what to do if they ever see the animals running away en masse like that. *Follow them, because it's a sign there's going to be a tsunami!*'

The professor's bushy eyebrows shot up in surprise.

'That's an interesting interpretation, young man. Those cave paintings are dated around 26,000 years old. And you are saying, if they are intelligent enough to render a lifelike reproduction of an animal, they have the brains to tell stories to their young ... Fascinating. It remains to be seen what other evidence you can come up with to support your hypothesis.'

'The question is,' said Kirsty O'Donnell. 'Were any of those ancient cultures advanced enough to qualify for our *Sea Kings?*'

Just then the door opened and in came Mrs Buzowski wheeling the tea trolley. She called out with her cheerful smile.

'Tea break!'

Everyone gathered in clusters with their tea and biscuits, with the exception of Merrick, who quickly left the room. The students stood around near the window.

'Don't you think,' said Sandeep, out of earshot of the adults. 'Professor Plendergarth with his wiry build and bushy beard looks like someone out of *The Lord of the Rings*?'

Professor Plendergarth, meanwhile, was in deep conversation with Richard and Kirsty. He had an arrested expression on his face.

'So *that's* Danny, Dr Anjani Hanuman's son? It was tragic, her passing so young. Dreadful car accident wasn't it? She had been on the phone to me only the day before, telling me that she'd made a breakthrough. So sad she never made it to that conference in Oxford to reveal her findings.'

'It was very tragic,' agreed Richard. 'Who knows what she might have revealed had she lived?'

'It was awful,' said Kirsty O'Donnell. 'Her brakes failing when they did.'

Richard agreed. 'It was a shame that her computer was so badly damaged in the car wreckage that nothing could be retrieved from it. It was rumoured there was a Notebook too, but that was never found. '

Professor Plendergarth glanced over at Danny, who was laughing at a friend's joke. The professor's bright eyes bored into the curator.

'Do you think he knows anything?'

'Probably not,' said Richard. 'But time will tell.'

IT WAS when Danny got home later that evening that his world was rocked on its foundations. He was pottering about in the attic, putting finishing touches to preparing it as a bedroom. He made up the folding guest bed with fresh linen and found a bedside light.

Next, he decided to look for a rug to cover the bare floorboards. He thought there was likely to be one in the cupboard under the eaves where many objects d'art from his mother's travels were stored.

Danny found a huge antique painted chest, which creaked as he opened the lid. He lifted out a few carved African statuettes and set them to one side. Underneath he noticed a photo album. He ended up getting completely side-tracked, sitting cross-legged on the floor as he leafed through the album.

Memories flooded back of family holidays, times when they had all been so happy together. He felt a surge of nostalgia.

'Me, mum and dad at the beach. Oh yeah, the zoo trip! Me on my first bike – oh, hello? What's this….?'

There was a photograph of a stepped pyramid at the back of the album. It seemed out of context in amongst the family snaps. Danny was puzzled. It wasn't like his mother. Normally, all her work was neatly catalogued. What was even stranger was that there were words written in his mother's handwriting to the side of the photo.

'Cherchez la!' An arrow pointed to the side of the photo.

'Search there?' Danny was mystified. What did she mean? Did his mother expect him to make a trip to some pyramid or another?

As he gazed at the photo, he noticed it wasn't quite mounted in the same way as the others. They were all mounted on card, covered with an adhesive film. But this photo seemed bulkier. Danny ran his fingers over the surface. Was there something beneath it? He carefully peeled back the film and removed the photo.

There, underneath, nestled an envelope. It was one of those light-weight types that people use for airmail. It was blue with a red striped border all around the edge. On the front, in his mother's handwriting, were the words:

'For Danny. To be opened in the event something has happened to me.'

With trembling fingers Danny pulled out the folded A4 sheet of thin, flimsy paper and read the contents. His mother had written:

5:30 am.

'Danny, dearest, I don't want to worry you unnecessarily and I am just being a bit over-cautious, I'm sure. All being well, I should be home tonight as expected and you may never get to read this. But just in case …

I'll be setting off in a few minutes for The University of Oxford to give the presentation I told you about. But if you are reading this and I'm not around, something may have happened to me.'

Danny's eyes filled with tears, and it was a few moments before he could read on.

It is probably just my imagination, but I feel there are shadowy forces at work. I am sure my phone is tapped, and I received a very strange message via email yesterday. It said:

"Dr Hanuman, stop investigating these ancient mysteries. We strongly advise you not to give this report at Oxford or it will be bad for your health. We urge you to stop your research while you still have time. Otherwise you will reap the consequences. Signed, 'The Aculeata.'

Danny's heart was thudding like a boxer's punch-bag as he forced himself to continue reading.

'Danny, I have made a big breakthrough in my work. It could revolutionise everything, not only in archaeology, but also in our very understanding of ancient history and civilisation. Many theories will need to be revised if I am correct.

Your father is on a far distant tour of duty and I can't get a secure message to him. I don't know what to do about the threats.

I have heard of a number of eminent archaeologists who have died or disappeared recently. One of my colleagues in India, Professor Haldiki, is said to have committed suicide, though his body was never recovered. He was an expert on the Indus Valley Culture, one of the most ancient cultures in the world so he is a great loss to the world.

It's probably all just coincidental and I'm being a bit over-cautious. After all, why would ancient history be a cause for controversy to that degree?

I am determined not to give in to these threats. But just in case anything does happen to me, I'd like someone to finish my work. It's so important it gets out to a wider audience. Once it's out there, I feel you will be safe. You already know a great deal from the work we've done together, more than you think.

Although my research is on my laptop it is also backed up on the Cloud. Strangely enough, someone tried to hack into my account a couple of days ago.

I have also kept notebooks containing insights based on my research. What I have discovered about ancient maths and astronomy I believe is revolutionary. You are the only person I know that can I can entrust with them ...

Unfortunately, the flimsy paper had disintegrated along the fold and the only part that was intelligible were just a few words.

Uncle Janak's reference book ... More clues in my notebook ... safe place ....
Seek out the Noble Ones .... They hold the key.

Danny stared into space. His brain was numb. It wasn't the clues, or anything to do with his mother's work, that was uppermost in his mind. All his feelings, his pent up grief, his sense of loss, merged into one intense emotion. He felt incandescent rage erupting through his psyche like molten lava.

'They made it look like a car accident - but it was no *accident.*'

He clenched and unclenched his fists. Overcome by powerful emotion and without knowing what he was doing, he punched the cupboard door hard. The power in his fist had such force it went clean through the wood. It left a big hole and splintered pieces all over the floor. Danny was oblivious. He made a vow there and then.

'The cowards! I will find whoever did this to my mother - and they will pay for it.'

6

CASTLERIGG STONE CIRCLE

DR GREENWOOD PARKED the hired minibus in the lay-by up the old lane near the ancient stone circle. It was a few miles outside of the town of Keswick in the Lake District.

There was a smattering of tourists, a beaten up old camper van, a professional photographer alighting from his white van, but otherwise they had the place pretty much to themselves.

'What a great day for a field trip,' enthused Hugo, alighting from the vehicle and savouring the warm sunshine.

'So *this* is the mysterious Castlerigg Stone Circle!' Urmila exclaimed, hoisting her backpack over her shoulder.

The rest of the students gathered their things and walked across the lane. The iron gate that gave access to the ancient monument squeaked as they opened it. Ahead of them was a grassy slope and as they walked uphill they could see a structure silhouetted against the skyline. Grazing sheep were dotted around the huge field with its dry-stone walls. Woolly lambs were plaintively bleating or skipping together in gangs at play. It could have been a rural scene from anywhere.

Except for the fact that near the top of the hill stood a cluster of massive monolithic boulders placed in a wide circle.

'When you are actually here,' Danny turned three-sixty degrees to take it all in. 'You can't doubt that this construction is a work of careful deliberation by some ancient hand.'

'Wow!' Sandeep glanced at the surrounding fells. 'What a great setting for an ancient stone circle.'

'They sure knew how to pick the spots,' agreed Urmila. 'You can see for miles.''In the distance is the lake of Derwentwater,' Izzie spouted as if she were a tour guide. 'And Borrowdale Valley is said to be the wettest valley in England and ... ' She prattled on in this manner, but everyone ignored her and set off exploring by themselves.

Danny was happily in his own world, taking it all in. He breathed deeply, enjoying the warm smell of sunlight on grass, the scent of the meadow, the mother sheep tenderly nurturing their growing lambs. It was a good weather day in the Lakes, the sort that tended to happen in late spring. A black raven alighted on the wall at the top end of the field. It remained there, motionless, as the students began their field work.

'OK, guys,' Izzie set off at a jog all round the perimeter of the site and ran up and down the steep hill for good measure. She wasn't even out of breath as she rejoined them. 'I've sussed out the lay of the land.' She produced a tape measure and compass. 'Let's take some measurements.'

'It's alright,' said Danny. He'd decided the best way to deal with Izzie's bossiness was to be firm. 'I've got my own compass.'

Urmila pointed to a cluster of smaller stones set on the edge of the circle. 'Right. So over there, which direction is that set of inner stones facing?'

'That's east,' said Danny, taking a compass reading. 'I wonder if it's the entrance?'

'It says in my guide book, it is probably where they had some kind of altar,' said Hugo.

'When you think about ancient people,' said Sandeep. 'We've been taught to think of them as if they were illiterate savages. And yet, their stone circles were oriented to the cardinal directions. How could they do that unless they had a working knowledge of mathematics?'

'*And* astronomy,' Danny emphasised. 'If they accurately calculated the compass points, and the solstices, we can be sure they had a working knowledge of astronomy.'

The raven flew overhead, unnoticed, and circled for a minute or two near the stone circle.

'How do you work that out, *Einstein?*' said Izzie, raising a supercilious eyebrow.

'Because, *Miss Clever-cloggs,*' Danny retorted. 'If I asked you right now to show me precisely where due north was without any instruments, you would have to know which direction the sun was in to even hazard a *guess –*'

'Yeah, *yeah!*' Izzie always played a provocative game of Devil's Advocate. It came of her father being a leading QC. 'The way I look at it, these ancient people just got a bunch of boulders and put them in a circle because of their pagan beliefs. They probably thought the sun was a god to be worshipped. But it doesn't mean they knew about constellations and astronomy.'

'That's where you're wrong!' Danny was emphatic. 'You're thinking from the point of view of a lay-person in ancient times. As such, you wouldn't have a clue any more than a non-specialist person would have nowadays. Only a *specialist* would know as to when or where the solstice was to occur and where to put these massive stones. The fact that so many stone circles have placements oriented precisely to where the sun rises on the equinox or solstice, could *only* have been done by a class of trained and skilled astronomers.'

'Yeah,' agreed Hugo. 'They must have observed and calculated the phenomenon over many decades to be sure of accuracy. It was very skilled work.'

'And therefore,' said Urmila. 'They had to have had distinct roles in their ancient society. The Celts had a priestly class, called the Druids and they were the astronomers. But they must have also had a class of skilled engineers who had the technology to move the stones as well. And labourers, and cooks to feed the workers.'

Izzie bit her lip as she concentrated on her phone's search results.

'Your point could be of interest, Urmila,' she conceded. 'It says here, there's another stone circle in Cumbria called *The Druid's Circle* at a place called Birkrigg Common. And there are others in Wales and England.

The Celts were in Scotland and Ireland, as well as Brittany and the continent.'

'Yeah,' said Hugo. 'The Druids were hounded by the Romans because they offered them too much resistance. You know the problem with history? The most war-like people always give themselves the gloss of conquerors, like the Romans did. Even when they're stealing peoples' lands and resources and turning them into slaves, they paint themselves as brave conquerors.'

'And the Druid culture had the respect of the locals,' Urmila said. 'The Romans wanted to break the strength of their cultural identity and were at pains to spread misinformation about them.'

While they were talking, the raven flew down and landed out of sight behind one of the largest stones. It cocked its head on one side as if listening. The photographer appeared to be the only one that noticed it.

'Coming back to astronomy,' said Sandeep. 'There were many cultures that knew about the planets and constellations thousands of years ago. There were the Sumerians, the Incas, the Mayans, the Indus Valley Culture, the ancient Greeks, to name but a few.'

'But you've no proof they understood *mathematics*,' Izzie insisted. 'Which would be absolutely essential for a detailed understanding of astronomy. Without that proof, your case is weakened.'

'As a matter of fact,' Danny said. 'I'll shortly have an Almanac on loan which, I've been told, will prove the ancients had knowledge of mathematics. And it will show the ancient cultures had extremely sophisticated astronomical knowledge because they could calculate such data with precision.'

The photographer, who was setting up his tripod nearby, paused and weighed up the angle of the light with his meter. He moved closer to examine one of the nearby stones.

'Not only that,' said Hugo. 'What about their ability to move large monoliths into exactly the right position to catch the first rays of the sunlight on the solstice or equinoxes?'

'Yeah,' agreed Danny, giving a mocking look at Izzie. 'If you want to catch the first rays of the sun at the summer solstice, you can't just say to the Neolithic workers, 'Oh excuse me Ethelred, I've made a mistake on the plan. Can you just move that megalith a few feet to the right? Back a bit. To me. To you. And shift all the other large stones along while you're at it. We're just using guesswork to make sure we catch the solstice in the right place. Oh dear, you've taken too long. The sun's gone now.'

Sandeep grinned at Danny and put on a posh voice.

'Oh, I say, you prehistoric fellows. The sun has just moved. Can you reposition all those fifty-ton stones ten feet to the left?'

Izzie frowned at the general laughter.

'I don't see why it's funny,' she whispered to Urmila, a puzzled expression on her face. 'Are they being humorous? *Now* what have I said to send you into a fit of the giggles?'

'Let's analyse this, guys,' said Sandeep. 'If we accept they had an understanding of astronomy, they must also have had a sophisticated understanding of mathematics. We need to challenge our assumptions about ancient people –'

'Like, what proof have you got to challenge our assumptions with, then?' Izzie always needled with her questions. Without waiting for an answer, she suddenly broke off and yelled at the top of her voice at a group of children who were climbing on the stones.

'Oi! *You lot*! These are important archaeological remains! GET OFF THOSE STONES! RIGHT NOW!'

The two mothers had been gossiping together, standing idly by while their brood had been climbing, jumping and generally messing about on the ancient monument. They glared at Izzie. A couple of the younger kids burst into tears and ran to their parent. The women gathered all the children together and with a further dirty look at Izzie, left the field.

Izzie looked triumphant. The others turned away, mortified.

'Now, where were we?' she said.

'Open your mind, Izzie,' Hugo retorted. 'These ancient people had knowledge of geometry and could calculate the cardinal directions. They took a fixed point on the horizon at the equinox to accurately calculate which direction was east. And from there they calculated intersecting right angles for the other directions.'

The photographer took a panoramic series of shots, ignoring the fact the students were in the way.

'Archeologists found evidence,' Sandeep said. 'Of many small carved stone crosses at the Indus Valley sites which appear to be talismans. They were crossed at right angles. That would make them thousands of years old.'

'And,' said Urmila. 'In the cultures of the east from time immemorial, the four-armed cross was sacred because it represented the laws of nature which guarded the four cardinal directions.'

'Now I come to think of it,' Hugo added. 'The well-known statue of the ancient Sumerian king is wearing a pendant in the shape of a cross around his neck. So that would make it at least five thousand years old.'

He broke off and rubbed his stomach.

'Is it lunchtime yet?' he appealed to Danny for moral support.

'Too right, mate!' Danny agreed. 'Let's find a good spot for our picnic.'

Izzie got her camera out of her backpack and took careful photos of the stones. She called out commands to the others.

'Everyone! Before we have lunch, you must each take loads of photos so we can evaluate them on our return home.'

They pretended not to hear her and chose a spot near the top of the slope. They sat down and pulled out their packed lunches. Danny looked disappointed.

'Just look what Aunty Sergeant's given me. Bread and cheese. Again. And the bread is stale. Ugh!'

'Well, guess what I've got for you here?' Urmila produced a plastic picnic box. 'Granny and I made an extra packed lunch for you this morning.'

Danny gave her a grateful smile. He unwrapped the food and sunk his teeth into a vegetable samosa.

Izzie made rather a forlorn figure sitting a little distance away, all on her own. Kind-hearted Urmila took pity and went to sit beside her to eat her own packed lunch.

After she'd finished eating, Urmila flicked through the notes she'd made in her sketchbook.

'Do we have any further evidence that the ancient circle people had knowledge of mathematics?' she asked the others.

'Yeah,' Sandeep nodded. 'I looked at the work of Professor Alexander Thom-'

Urmila's pen poised over her notebook.

'Isn't there some controversy about his work? What do you know about his academic credentials?'

'They are excellent,' said Danny. 'He was -'

'Alexander Thom was a brilliant scientist and inventor,' Izzie cut in, drawing on her eidetic memory. 'He was Head of Engineering Science, at Brasenose College, Oxford. He designed the first high-speed wind tunnel which our aircraft designers needed in WW2 and helped us win the war.'

Hugo added,

'Actually, Alexander Thom is one of my heroes. He took painstaking measurements of hundreds of stone circles in Britain and France. He concluded there was a standardized mathematical measure evident at many of the stone circles and prehistoric sites. It was this standardized measure that Thom coined as the *Megalithic Yard*.'

'And amongst his other achievements,' said Danny. 'He founded the discipline of Archeo-astronomy. My mother told me there was a concerted effort to discredit Thom's work in certain quarters, but she found it a mystery as to why.'

The professional photographer pulled his black beanie hat up over his ears. He unzipped his grey cagoul and moved closer to one of the stones with his tripod. He lingered, his camera taking close-ups of the stones, studying them intently. The raven was nowhere to be seen.

Danny mulled it over.

'Coming back to the quest for the *Sea Kings*. If you can orient an ancient construction like a stone circle to the cardinal points, you would presumably be able to apply your astronomical knowledge to navigation. Should we work on the hypothesis they had an understanding of the alignment of lines in relation to latitude and possibly even longitude?'

Richard Greenwood strode up to the students at this point and over-heard Danny.

'Try and find me some evidence of longitude if you can, Danny. It would be very valuable in terms of our Quest -'

As he broke off to check a message on his phone, Danny saw a van drive quickly past on the road. He couldn't be certain, but it looked as if the writing on the side read *Taddakka Enterprises*. He shrugged it off. Probably imagining it.

'Message for you all from Dr O'Donnell,' Richard called out. 'She says, while you're out on field visits, can you take a note of local place names as they can often give additional clues as to the history of a place.'

'Like this stone circle is called, Castle*rigg*', said Urmila. 'I wonder what they meant by a *rigg*?'

'And that mountain over there is called *Latrigg*,' said Hugo, consulting his guide book. 'Like a 'ridge' maybe.'

'Or the *Rig* Veda,' said Urmila. 'It's from Sanskrit.'

'You can discuss it with Dr O'Donnell,' said Richard. 'When we get back to the hotel. She's preparing for the visits of some of the cultural exchange delegates, this evening.'

'I wonder what they'll be like,' said Hugo.

'Probably dead boring and don't speak a word of English,' said Danny.

He couldn't have been more wrong on both counts.

BACK IN HIS van in the layby, the photographer uploaded his digital images to his laptop computer. Somehow, as well as the monolithic stones, he had managed to get images of each of the students in with his shots. And once they were on his computer he went on to activate his Facial Recognition software.

He dialed a number and spoke into his mobile.

'They are using mathematics as evidence. And it appears they will shortly gain access to the Almanac.'

THE MINIBUS SET off for the country house hotel where they would be staying the night. It was situated in one of the Lakeland valleys. The road twisted and turned and ran alongside one of the lakes for a long while. It was very scenic though tricky and narrow in places. But Dr Greenwood seemed to know the way.

An hour later, they entered the gates of an extensive holiday complex. Its grounds had been skilfully landscaped to retain specimen mature trees, and the path to the main hotel building ran alongside a picturesque stream. It had once been a mill-race and the original waterwheel had been cleverly incorporated as a water feature so the diners at the hotel could sit and watch it of an evening.

As well as the main hotel building itself, there were also a great many attractive wooden holiday lodges spaced at intervals throughout the grounds. Each one was detached and screened from its neighbour by mature hedges and trees.

It was early evening by the time Dr Greenwood pulled up in the hotel car park. The students were in high spirits as he led them through the entrance of the building into the swish dining room.

Kirsty O'Donnell came rushing over to welcome them, clipboard under her arm. She wore an elegant blue jacket and skirt, and looked very professional.

'This is an important event that we're hosting. I want you students to mingle and be friendly to the cultural exchange delegates who have arrived. They are here to take part in our series of conferences entitled, *The Heritage Cultures of the World*. 'When you get the opportunity I want you to chat to them. Take note of their indigenous customs and traditions.'

Danny could see people of all nationalities, standing about, chatting. They were resplendent in their national costumes. A tall Zulu gentleman in traditional robes, accompanied by his wife in equally colourful attire, smiled and nodded a friendly good evening to the students. They didn't have much time to chat however, as before long, the sound of the dinner gong reached their ears.

'Come with me,' Kirsty reappeared and led the students to a table. 'I've arranged for you to sit here by yourselves. Tomorrow, you will have the chance to mingle with the delegates.'

And with that, she bustled off to greet a group of Sikh visitors.

Danny and Hugo beamed with delight as they saw enormous wood-fired pizzas and fries begin to arrive. The conversation soon became a relaxed, background chatter.

At the end of the main course Danny was staring out of the dining room window, lost in thought. He noticed a battered old Land Rover pull up in the hotel car park. The door opened and a black and white collie jumped out, closely followed by its owner, a local farmer by the look of him. Danny heard another couple of doors slam, as if there were other occupants to the vehicle, but his view was obscured by the trees.

After that, he lost interest as his attention was claimed by the arrival of dessert. Without further ado, he started digging into a large chocolate ice cream sundae.

Sandeep posed a challenge to the table at large.

'Which do you think is the most powerful - light sabres like in Star Wars, or phasers, like in Star Trek?'

'No contest!' Hugo promptly replied. 'Light sabres, without a doubt!

'But what if you needed to stun someone without a fight?' said Sandeep.

'Well, I can see the merits of both,' said Danny.

The girls exchanged glances and rolled their eyes.

'Like any of that stuff is *real!*' said Izzie, scornfully.

'Well much *you* know!' retorted Sandeep. 'Like, the science was real because nowadays they are using tasers in police forces to stun people. So that proves that Star Trek was way ahead of its time. So there!'

'Yeah,' Danny said, turning to Izzie. 'And in Star Wars, *The Force* uses, like, people's energy field, see - '

He broke off, suddenly aware that the conversation at his table had come to an abrupt halt. Not only that but everyone else in the dining room had stopped too, mid-spoonful, to gawp at something behind him.

All eyes now seemed to be riveted in his direction. Danny had his back to the door and had no idea what could have caused such a show-stopper. Suddenly he felt a firm hand on his shoulder and a familiar voice spoke.

'Hello, Danny. We meet again ...'

Danny swung round and found himself face to face with Rama and Lakshman, the two illustrious brothers from his Remote Viewing experience.

Although the two tall, good-looking men were an impressive sight, it was more than their national dress that caught the eye. There was something about them, some aura, which drew people's attention like a magnet.

Kirsty O'Donnell rose to greet them. She seemed very surprised at their familiar greeting to Danny.

'Oh my. I didn't realize you knew each other. How did you meet?'

Danny was taken completely off-guard. He couldn't think of a plausible answer. He was trapped like a burger in a bap. He turned bright red and stammered,

'Er. Well, you see...'

But how could he explain it? They wouldn't understand. He couldn't give details of his Remote Viewing experience with all the further questioning that would entail. Fortunately, Rama came to the rescue.

'Oh, Danny observed one of our training classes, didn't you, Danny?' Danny gulped and managed to nod agreement, wondering what was coming next. Rama continued.

'And Danny has enrolled on the Kalari warrior training course.'

'I have?' Danny looked bemused. The other students all looked at Danny, astonished.

Sandeep however, turned rigid with anger. His eyes bulged and he looked thunderstruck.

'You did WHAT! And you didn't mention a word of it to *me*? Your best mate! How *could* you?

Danny shifted uncomfortably in his chair wishing the floor would open up. But Kirsty O'Donnell didn't seem to notice anything was amiss. She clapped her hands and spoke enthusiastically to the two princely brothers.

'How splendid! Is this part of your cultural heritage?'

'Yes, ma'am,' Lakshman nodded. 'Kalari Payattu is the most ancient system of martial arts in the world. It has been practiced for centuries in our country. It is unique in that it not only incorporates a system of self-defence, under a strict Code of Honour, but also an ancient system of healing.'

Rama added, ' For it is said by the Masters of Kalari, that he who dis-empowers an enemy, must also be able to re-empower him, too.'

'Fascinating!' exclaimed Kirsty, beaming. 'I hope you will allow me to include this in an episode of my Cultural Heritage documentary series?'

She turned to the students.

'And do you know what? It would be great if you could *all* take part in the training so we can show how it's done.'

Sandeep murmured in a reproachful under voice to Danny,

'Mate. Why did you not tell *me* about this? And anyway, I thought you were supposed to be a pacifist?'

To Danny's relief, before he could think of a response Richard Greenwood appeared and ushered them all through to Reception to collect the keys to their rooms.

'That's it for tonight, folks. I want you all to go and unpack and settle in for the night.'

Their rooms were in wooden lodges spaced around the landscaped grounds of the hotel complex. But once outside, Sandeep waylaid Danny.

'Why did you not tell me you'd met Rama before?'

'Because –'

'Because *what?*'

'You wouldn't have believed me,' Danny shifted his feet uncomfortably.

'Try me.'

'Well, it's hard to explain. I've started having these, like, visions. They call them Remote Viewing experiences. And that was when I met Rama, in one of those episodes.'

'Like, any of that stuff's *real*,' Sandeep scoffed.

'But it *is* real and I've got a book that tells you the US military trained people-'

'Oh, pull the other one! If you can't see it, it's not real.'

'Oh yeah?' Danny could feel himself getting heated. 'Why don't you go and stick your fingers in that electric socket and see if electricity is real or not? You'll get a hell of an invisible shock!'

'Let's face it, Danny,' Sandeep's jaw was clenched and he was beside himself with anger. 'You stole a march on the rest of us so you could be top dog.'

Danny gazed in horror at Sandeep.

'How could you even *think* such a thing of me? How could you believe I would behave like such a lowlife?'

But Sandeep was done talking. He stormed off to his room with a parting shot.

'Don't you speak to me *ever* again, Danny Hanuman. You're no longer any friend of mine...'

Little did either of them know, the repercussions from this incident were to place both of them in mortal danger.

7

AN UNEXPECTED VISITOR

5:00AM

After tossing and turning fitfully all night, Danny got up early and had a shower to clear his head. Rama had arranged for the group to meet at 6:00am at his lodge for the first training session. Armed with the hotel's plan of the extensively wooded grounds, he wound his way through the leafy glades in search of the noble brothers' accommodation.

While Danny walked he thought he heard a twig snap behind him. He looked round quickly but couldn't see anyone. But as he moved through the forest he couldn't shake off the uncomfortable feeling he was being followed. When he got to the brothers' lodge the door was open and no one was about. The TV was blaring forth and he heard the news anchor say,

There has been another killing in the notorious gangland Dandaka District of Manchester. Police believe it has been carried out by the infamous Taddak Gang, and that it's drug related.

Danny's brows knit together. There had been rumours of Sycker's involvement with the shady side of Manchester's night-life. His father owned a chain of nightclubs. He wouldn't put it past him to be involved with a dangerous gang. *At least now that Sycker's left school he's not my problem any more, thank goodness.*

Danny's attention was suddenly riveted by strange sounds in the distance, some way off from the log cabin. There were blood-curdling yells and the clash of metal on metal. It seemed to be coming from the wild, uninhabited area of the forest beyond the complex. Danny ran through the trees, crushing bluebells underfoot, oblivious to their wafting fragrance. He followed a gurgling brook until he came to a sunlit clearing.

There, a most unexpected sight greeted him ...

IZZIE DONNED her track suit and set off for an early morning jog, making the most of the beautiful surroundings. She overtook Urmila, Hugo and Sandeep, who were walking at a more leisurely pace, enjoying the birdsong and fresh morning air.

Suddenly they too, heard the unmistakable sounds of a skirmish going on. They froze in their tracks like startled deer and then began to run through the woodland glade in the direction of the noise. Izzie was the first to arrive at the clearing, closely followed by Sandeep and Urmila, with Hugo wheezing along at the rear. Danny greeted them portentously.

'Guys,' he said in awed tones as he led them to the clearing. 'Just look at this.'

Their jaws dropped as they observed a mock battle take place between Rama and Lakshman. The two warriors were engaged in a ritual demonstration of swordplay with shields. They rotated around twirling their curved swords above their head with practiced ease as if they'd been made of gossamer threads instead of heavy-duty tempered steel.

The swords clashed on the metal shields with such force, the reverberation rang throughout the woods. But what caused the students eyes to start from their heads, was the astounding leaps and turns the warriors made in the air. At each leap, the brothers gave a blood-curdling battle cry, which sent shivers down the spine of the onlookers.

'Look at that,' Danny whispered to Urmila. 'They're leaping so high, it's like they're defying gravity.'

The brothers' focus was intense. Their faces registered no emotion. They were oblivious to the onlookers as they performed their set practice routine. Danny began to be concerned in case any more people heard. Someone might think it was a real fight and would surely call the cops.

'Er, Rama. Lakshman,' he called out. 'Hi there. We're all here like you told us. When do we start our training?'

Izzie was mightily impressed.

'Great demo of Kalari Warrior skills,' she said, as the brothers came over to greet them. 'You don't even seem to be out of breath.'

'Yeah,' said Hugo. 'You were like, almost levitating!'

Lakshman shrugged. 'Mastery over our bodies is taught from an early age. Our disciplined training works in a similar way to ballet dancers in your culture. The high jumps we use are to evade and confuse the enemy.'

'We're ready to start,' said Danny. 'Can't wait.'

'We sure are,' echoed Izzie, flexing her muscles.

Hugo was more dubious.

'Will I be able to train with my weight problem?'

'Don't worry, Hugo,' said Lakshman. 'We will keep within your individual capabilities and work from there.'

Sandeep was the only one who remained silent. Although he joined in the training, he refused to look at Danny and kept as far away from him as possible.

'OK,' said Rama. 'Let's start the training with an exercise called *Salute to the Sun*. It's the best warm up for the next level of training.'

It was an hour later when their session ended. The students were ravenous after what had turned out to be a strenuous workout with the brothers.

'If that was 'basic,' Hugo muttered to Danny. 'I can't imagine what advanced is going to be like.'

As they walked back to the hotel for breakfast they were joined by a venerable white-haired gentleman. He wore long orange robes and carried a wooden staff covered with a cloth. His eyes were dark and deep and had a penetrating gaze that missed nothing.

'Let me introduce you,' Rama said. 'This is Master Vishwa-mitra, our highly respected Guru.'

'What's a Guru?' whispered Izzie to Urmila.

'It's a wise and knowledgeable teacher,' she whispered back.

Vishwa-mitra's learned countenance surveyed the group.

'So fate has decreed we all should meet. The opportunity to learn from one such as Prince Rama, the noblest of all Kalari Knights, does not come around very often. Use this gift wisely and learn all you can from him.'

'Could you tell me,' asked Hugo. 'What exactly is a Kalari Knight?'

'It is a practitioner of Kalari Payattu which is our ancient system of martial arts,' said Lakshman. 'You will learn more about it during training.'

'Ooh, I'm looking forward to learning a system of martial arts,' said Izzie, her eyes lighting with a militant gleam. 'I'd like to kick some butt ends.' She glanced at Danny.

'I'd like to learn, too,' said Hugo. 'I've been wanting to get fitter now I'm not in the rugby team anymore. I hope it'll help me lose some weight.'

'Yeah,' Danny's mouth was set in a grim expression, absorbed in the thought of the task he'd set himself to find his mother's killers. 'Let's hope this helps us overcome our enemies.'

Unfortunately, Sandeep took this tactless utterance personally. He already felt hurt and betrayed. Now he was being identified as an enemy. He stared at Danny through narrowed, suspicious eyes. What had happened to make Danny behave like this?

Urmila, for her part, wore an anxious expression. She was a gentle soul who couldn't bear to hurt a fly.

'Is it just like, all about *fighting*?'

'Not at all,' said Rama. 'It is much more than that. It's primarily a system of holistic training for self-development. We practice yoga and meditation to develop and train the power of the mind, not just the body. We follow a strict Code of Honour which dictates we must always act in self-defence, never as the aggressor.'

'What marks the Kalari system out from the others?' Danny enquired.

'It's the fact that our training includes a system of healing called Ayurveda. Our code stresses that if we inflict injury on an enemy, then we must know how to heal him, too,' was Lakshman's response.

Urmila's brow cleared.

'Oh yes,' she said. 'I've learned about the noble art of Ayurveda from my father.'

The three foreign visitors looked at her in surprise. Vishwa-mitra said,

'Who is your father, child?'

'He is Professor Raja Mithil,' said Urmila. 'He's a consultant neuro-surgeon in Manchester.'

The sage nodded wisely.

'I would like to meet your illustrious father, Urmila. We will have much to talk about.'

They made their way along the path towards the hotel, pausing a while at the brothers' lodge for them to change into the more conventional tunic, gilet and trousers.

When they entered the dining room it was beginning to fill up. People were making their way to the self-service breakfast buffet that was laid out with sumptuous-looking food.

After loading up their plates up the teenagers made their way towards a long table where Richard and Kirsty sat with several other conference delegates. Rama and Lakshman took their seats near the curator and began to eat their meal. The two good-looking brothers were attracting a good deal of attention from the other delegates. Richard chatted to them over the meal.

'Please excuse me, but I didn't catch which country you were from?'

'We are from Sapta Sindhu,' Lakshman replied.

'Let me see if I can work it out,' said Kirsty. 'I have a rudimentary knowledge of Sanskrit. *Sapta*, means 'seven' and *Sindhu* means a river. It must be the Land of the Seven Rivers?'

Rama nodded. 'Correct.'

There were surprised comments from many round the table.

'Are you not from India?' an African delegate enquired.

'You see,' Rama explained. 'The land we are from doesn't exist anymore - at least not as it used to be in days of old. All of us are reborn in many times and places. We await restoration of the Old Ways in the land of our fathers to come to our own true birthplace.'

'How mysterious,' said Kirsty. 'I hope to learn more of your culture during our conference.'

A sharp-featured individual with a pallid white skin, and sparse mousey hair, was listening intently to the conversation. His curiously hooded eyes were half hidden as he leaned forward and spoke authoritatively.

'Oh, you must mean you're from the Punjab, I take it?'

'Oh, good morning, Dr Zeuber,' said Kirsty O'Donnell. 'Everyone, let me introduce the delegate from the Institute of Foreign Affairs in Moldova.'

'In answer to your comment,' Lakshman said. 'We are not from the region you call the Punjab. The land we are from is the land of the ancient Rig Veda.'

A scowl deepened the grooved ridge between Dr Zeuber's eyebrows.

'That is surely a *mythical* land?' he said scornfully, looking down his long nose at the two brothers.

'The lands of the Rig Veda are not mythical and the rivers which the ancient texts speak of are real,' said Rama. 'The River Indus, and the Saraswati River in particular are important to our culture.'

'Well, the Saraswati doesn't exist, it's merely a mythical river,' insisted Dr Zeuber.

His manner was confrontational and aggressive. Danny was mystified by it. Why was this delegate being so provocative to Rama? He seemed to have a hidden agenda.

Dr O'Donnell picked up on the undercurrent, too. She spoke firmly to Dr Zeuber.

'It has been confirmed by aerial surveys and also the Geographical Survey of India that the now dried up River Saraswati existed in ancient times. And we must give credit to the ancient Vedic texts that speak of an ancient historical time when the River Saraswati did indeed '*flow to the sea.'* We believe it may have relevance to the quest for the ancient *Sea Kings.'*

She put her hand up to stop Zeuber who was about to argue the matter further.

'That's enough for now, Dr Zeuber. Let us leave these matters to be discussed in the later conferences. For now, let our honoured guests eat their breakfast in peace.'

Dr Zeuber gave a curt nod and got up to leave the table. As he passed Rama's chair, he leaned over to say pointedly,

'I shall see you again no doubt, *Prince* Rama.'

After he left, Kirsty O'Donnell looked puzzled.

'That's strange,' she said in an aside to Richard. 'I didn't mention that these two delegates were royal princes. They're supposed to be incognito. I wonder how he knew that?'

'I didn't much like him, or his attitude,' said Richard.

It was late morning when the conference ended and the students were headed out of the hotel to the minibus. They were to have another field trip before heading back home to Manchester. Danny paused to get his phone out of his backpack and check for messages. The others went on ahead to the car park.

From a corridor to his left, the door of one of the rooms was slightly ajar and Danny could hear talking. It sounded very much like Dr Zeuber's thin, nasal whine. Danny was instantly curious and pricked up his ears. He tiptoed closer to see if he could overhear the telephone conversation that was taking place.

'I'm telling you, he's going to be talking about the antiquity of the *Sea Kings*, and then before you know it, it'll be an all-out cultural revival ... Yeah, that's all very well you saying he has to be stopped, but how? ... And just why is the Dark One so keen to get his hands on the Primordial Energy Source? ... You think he needs it to recruit his strength to take the Kalari warrior on? ...

At this point the door was pushed shut and Danny couldn't hear any more.

What did it mean? What was the *Primordial Energy Source*? And was Rama the *'he'* that Dr Zeuber referred to who had to be 'stopped'?

When they got back home that evening, Urmila invited Danny back to her house for supper. But any hopes she might have had of the two boys being reconciled were speedily quashed. As soon as they got in, Sandeep shot up to his bedroom and refused to come down while Danny was still in the house.

After they'd eaten, Uncle Janak popped his head round the lounge door.

'You got a minute, Danny? I've got something that might interest you.'

Danny eagerly followed him into his study. Uncle Janak was usually too busy for idle chat so this must be something important.

Professor Raja Janak Mithil was an eminent scientist and a highly respected professor of medicine. He had an air of quiet wisdom about him with his keen, perceptive eyes set within a round, pleasant face. Everything about him was neat, from his neatly trimmed grey hair to his neat, precise movements.

He exuded calm assurance which inspired confidence in his staff and patients, alike. He was used to command over a large team at the Royal Manchester Hospital and his style was to lead by example. He earned the respect of all who knew him through the indisputable depth and breadth of his knowledge and experience.

He looked over rimless glasses at Danny and his gaze softened.

'I heard you were looking into mathematics and astronomy for your project at the museum, son. Is that correct?'

'Yes, that's right, Uncle,' Danny said. 'I'm looking for evidence that the people of long ago might have had a mathematical understanding of astronomy. And if they did, I wondered if I could find any evidence to indicate that they had an understanding of longitude, too?'

'Interesting question, Danny,' Raja Janak's expression was serious for a moment. 'It's gratifying that you are interested in these matters.' He sighed deeply. 'I wish you could get Sandeep to be interested. He has no respect for his own culture.'

He shrugged in a resigned way and spread his hands. His expression gave way to a gentle smile.

'Anyway, be that as it may. I'd be delighted to help you, Danny. I think I have the very book for your needs.'

Danny looked around the room. Books crammed the shelves on either side of the ornate fireplace from floor to ceiling. Without hesitation Professor Janak pulled down a large book and handed it to Danny.

'Here we are. I think you'll find this useful. It's the Almanac that your mother borrowed from me a few months before she passed. Your mother and I had many in-depth conversations about its implications. She used to come and ask me questions about mathematics, Sanskrit, astronomy, science and culture amongst other things. It was always a pleasure to discuss these subjects with her. Take some time to study this work, and then come back to me. I'll be happy to answer any questions you might have.'

He looked at the volume in Danny's hands and was struck by a thought.

'Actually, son, this is a very old and rare, first edition of this book. It is extremely valuable and although it has been reprinted, I don't know of any others like this original one. What's more, it has some of your mother's notes in it. I wouldn't normally let it out of the house.

'So on second thoughts, by all means have a quick look but then I think it will be best if it goes straight to the Museum. There it can be kept safe and secure. I'll ring Dr Greenwood about it in the morning and arrange to drop it off. But I'm putting you in charge of keeping it safe while it's out of my house. Okay?'

'Yes. Absolutely. Thank you, Uncle, for the loan of it. I'll take great care and make sure nothing happens to it.'

As Danny walked down the street back to his own house, he saw something that caused his heart to skip a beat. There was a Land Rover parked in his driveway. It was a vehicle he recognized. He started to run towards home.

Major Hanuman was an imposing figure in his green and ochre fatigues. At six feet four inches tall, with a lean, muscular soldier's physique, he was not a man to be trifled with. His weather-beaten face had been baked in desert climates for many years resulting in deeply etched lines, which made him look older than his forty-five years. A certain world-weariness clung to him, as if he'd seen more than his fair share of human suffering.

He greeted Danny with a reserved handshake, not the hug that Danny used to get from him when his mother was alive. Worse was to come. An awkward silence hung between them at supper. For most of the time, this was punctuated by Aunt Millicent prattling on about how much work she'd been doing. How economical she was. How much she cared for Danny, the dear boy. Did Mike like the food she'd cooked? His favourite roast dinner? Danny could see she'd gone to a lot of trouble to impress his father. There was more food on the table than he'd seen in a week.

Major Hanuman was a man of few words at the best of times. He glanced at her occasionally but didn't waste his breath in reply, except to say, *Yes. No. Oh really?* He studied Danny from time to time under frowning brows. The boy had grown even more like his mother since he last saw him.

Danny could see his father was more preoccupied than usual. When the meal ended, he said,

'Come through to the study, Danny.'

He led the way through to his office and opened the desk drawer. Danny mentally thanked his lucky stars he'd put the parcel back in the desk drawer after all. There was no way he wanted his father to know he'd discovered his secret.

Major Hanuman pulled out the brown paper parcel and studied it for a moment.

'This is Top Secret, Danny. It contains clues that could revolutionise our view of history –'

'Is it my mother's Notebook, Dad?' The words blurted out of Danny's mouth before he could stop himself.

The major frowned.

'I don't want to say it. Oh what the - yes, it is. It was stolen from the wreckage of her car –'

'And you recovered it from somewhere?' Danny knew he was treading dangerous ground, but he needed to know if his vision was true.

The frown turned to a puzzled look.

'Don't ask me any more questions, Danny. All I will say is this. Your mother had discovered evidence of a long lost civilization. She noted it in cryptic clues in her notebook. However, all the artefacts she mentions have disappeared one way or another. There have been staged wars, which 'accidentally' destroyed the ancient archaeological sites she was studying. Many important artefacts, which 'disappeared', have mysteriously turned up in a catalogue of valuable items for sale to private collectors. We know there is an international gang involved who are very powerful and have the ear of many influential people –'

'*The Aculeata?*' Again, Danny couldn't stop himself.

Major Hanuman paused, an arrested expression on his face. He spoke sharply.

'What do you know about *The Aculeata?*'

Before Danny had a chance to reply the major's phone rang. He went out of the room to take the call but Danny heard a few words.

'Urgent? I see. Yes, I'll be ready in the morning.'

When he came back into the room he said,

'The less you know about the Notebook the better for your own safety. Listen to me, Danny. I don't want you to try and carry on your mother's work – it's too dangerous. Look what happened to her. And others have met the same fate. Leave well alone, son.'

His voice tailed off and he gripped the table so hard his knuckles turned white. After a minute he gathered himself. He spoke to Danny with a forced attempt at light-heartedness.

'Let's go and relax in the lounge for a bit. Fancy a game of chess?'

Danny nodded. His father chatted as they played.

'We've got a real international problem on our hands, and you'll never believe this, Danny –'

Danny's stomach suddenly felt queasy. His intuition told him something unpleasant was coming ...

'I've heard that some kid is promoting a web site for peace at all costs. Says he's going to organize peace rallies to stop the war. Never mind that some of us are putting our necks on the line to sort out this war on terror for *their* benefit.'

The dark clouds loomed over him again. Danny felt sick. This wasn't the moment he'd have chosen.

'About that, Dad –'

Coral-Jane had been sitting watching TV with Aunt Millicent. They had a whispered conversation and Aunty nudged her offspring. Danny didn't think they'd heard his father's comments. But he soon realized his error.

'Uncle Mike,' said Coral-Jane with wide-eyed innocence. 'Did Danny not tell you that he's a pacifist? And he's the one who's doing the Peace web site with Sita.'

The Major visibly blanched under his tan. He fixed Danny with a steely glare that would have pierced an armoured tank at fifty paces.

'I can hardly believe my ears! Is this true, Danny?'

Danny felt his cheeks flame.

'Yes, but please let me explain it to you. Sita is right behind it – '

He didn't get a chance to finish the sentence. His father was angrier than Danny had ever seen him in his life. He almost bellowed.

'Don't try and hide behind Sita. She's a wonderful, kind-hearted girl. It's part of her culture to be a pacifist. That's her right, and I respect her for it.

'But *you* were born to a military family. I expected you to follow in my footsteps. How can you let me down like this?'

Before Danny could respond, a thought struck him. His face darkened.

'Oh no! Don't tell me you're a *coward?*'

Danny opened his mouth to speak but his father raised his hand to stop him. He rose abruptly from the table, sending chess pieces flying. His lips were pressed tight together and his eyes were hard as quartz.

'I'll tell you this, Danny. I'm leaving tomorrow on a mission. But by the time I get back, you had better have sorted your ideas out. And you will take down that *Website for Peace*, or you'll no longer be a son of mine!'

Danny sat there stunned. How could he explain everything to his father now? It was all falling apart around him. First the fallout with Sandeep, and now this. Who could he turn to for help?

And how could he ever prove to his father that he wasn't a coward?

8
THE STRANGE CASE OF
EXHIBIT 108

10:30AM

Something black shot past Danny's ear as he sat in the workroom, missing him by millimetres. He looked up from the book he was studying, startled.

'Oops! Sorry, mate.' Hugo lumbered after the object.

As he bent down to pick it up, Danny looked rueful.

'That was close, pal. I see you haven't mastered that drone technology yet?'

'It's early days,' Hugo grinned. 'But I'm getting there.'

He fiddled with the controls of the sophisticated drone and it hovered in the air for a few minutes. He turned the screen so Danny could see the camera action. Izzie realised he was hovering over her work.

'Will you stop playing with that thing, Hugo, and get down to some *real* work!' she said crossly.

'One of these days, it'll come in handy,' he prophesied. 'You'll see. And how am I to master the technology if I don't practice?'

'Well, do it outside, Hugo,' Urmila urged. 'It's dangerous to mess with it indoors.'

Hugo shrugged and packed the drone and the controls away in its carry-rucksack.

'Dr Greenwood says it will be very useful,' Sandeep reported. 'When we go out on field trips 'cos you can do aerial surveys from above.'

Urmila raised her head from the workbench where she was busy, arranging photographs of ancient sites.

'Isn't Dr O'Donnell filming in front of a live studio audience today?' She sounded anxious.

'Better than a dead one!' quipped Danny. 'Yeah, OK. Terrible pun. Sorry!'

Izzie gave Danny a scathing look.

'Where is Dr O'Donnell?' demanded Sandeep, wishing she were there to give them instructions instead of Izzie.

'She said she was going to give the cultural delegates a guided tour of the museum,' Hugo said.

'I'd like to know more about the history of this Kalari warrior tradition,' said Hugo, conversationally.

'Oh, yeah?' said Sandeep, a sarcastic edge to his voice. 'Well, Danny's our resident expert, or so it seems. Maybe *he* can answer your questions?'

Hugo sensed trouble brewing and tried to change the subject. 'Er, anyway, it must be time for our tea break, surely?'

At that point the door opened and in walked Rama, Lakshman and Dr O'Donnell. The students' faces brightened. All except Sandeep, who looked away.

'Greetings,' said Lakshman. 'Dr Kirsty suggested we call in to make further arrangements for your training sessions.'

'And we thought we'd see if you had any questions for us,' Rama said.

When Rama smiled at them, the tension lifted and Danny instantly felt better. They all did apart from Sandeep, whose forehead was still grooved in an unhappy frown.

'Great,' said Izzie. 'I wondered if you could tell us more about the tradition.'

'In a nutshell, Izzie,' said Lakshman. 'The root of our ancient Kalari tradition is a system of integrating mind and body which develops the individual's Shakti power. This is something you will learn more about as we go along.'

'The Kalari Knight,' said Rama. 'Behaves honourably. They act in self-defence, or if they fight it's to protect and defend the innocent, or vulnerable members of society. They never act as the aggressor and always seek diplomacy rather than war.'

Sandeep didn't ask a direct question. Instead he pulled a face and glanced sideways at Danny. He muttered under his breath.

'Well, I'd like to ask about the bad *karma* for people who deceive others?'

Rama heard. His face remained impassive as he said,

'In Sanskrit *karma* literally just means 'action' whether good *or* bad. 'Karma' refers to the Law of Action, a scientific principle that governs forces throughout the universe.'

'Think of gravity, for example,' said Lakshman. 'For every *action*, there is an equal and opposite *reaction*. If you bounce a rubber ball against a wall, it will bounce back at you. *Karma* is like a letter. Once posted, the universe will make sure it's delivered. It will catch up with you somewhere in time. That's the law of nature.'

He glanced at Sandeep, whose cheeks flushed. 'But we can't act as judge and jury for anyone else's karmic actions.'

Just then, Rama's mobile phone rang.

'Greetings Vishwa-mitra,' Rama moved closer to the window to take the call. Danny saw his expression change. A muscle in his jaw worked and he sounded increasingly grim.

'Just a moment Guru, sir, while I pass this on to Lakshman.'

Rama cradled the phone while he relayed the message to his brother. 'An hour ago the priest downtown had a brick thrown through his lounge window with a message tied to it. It said, *'Go home pakkies!'* His wife and children were in the room with him and they were terrified.'

The students looked at each other, shocked. Urmila's eyes filled up, her ready sympathy aroused.

'It sounds like more racist bullying of the priest,' she said in a scared whisper. 'They regularly torment him and his family.'

Rama glanced meaningfully at Lakshman.

'The priest says these thugs are intimidating him with demands for money.'

'I believe it is called a *protection racket*,' brother,' Lakshman looked grave.

'I see,' said Rama speaking into the phone. 'Honoured Vishwa-mitra, please tell the priest that Lakshman and I are on our way over there.'

Even as Rama turned to speak to the students, Lakshman was already on his way out of the door.

'It seems there are evil forces at work,' Rama explained. 'A gang leader working for someone called Taddak, is demanding money from the peaceful priest and his family. The gang are from the notorious Dandaka District. Vishwa-mitra wants us to go and deal with the situation.'

About ten minutes after the brothers had left Danny happened to be looking out of the top floor window. He noticed a blue Toyota Yaris pull up in the street below. It parked outside the museum and the occupant got out. Danny gave a startled yelp and to the others' surprise he shot out of the room.

He rushed down the stairs and arrived at the car just as the driver was opening the rear hatch door.

'Hey, Sita!' Danny exclaimed. 'What a nice surprise.'

Sita's smile lit up her lovely face when she saw who it was. She put the box she was holding down in order to give him a hug.

'Great to see you, little bro,' she said.

'Here,' Danny said, motioning to the car boot. 'Let me help you with those.'

He lifted the heavy storage crate out of the boot. It seemed to be full of wires and technical equipment.

'Sita, I thought you were busy at the hospital. What are you doing here?'

'Well,' Sita said, as they walked towards the museum entrance. 'I've got a day off – first in three weeks. I've been awarded a grant to carry out research into brain wave functioning. The museum is kindly letting me use their laboratory, in return for me setting up an exhibition for them at a later date, on *Harnessing the Power of The Mind*.'

Her eyes twinkled.

'I'll need some guinea pigs, you know. I thought you lot would be good people to start with for my experiments.'

'You've just missed Rama,' Danny said. 'He had to leave in a hurry. I was hoping you two might meet each other. I know you would like him. And I'm certain *he* would like *you*.'

'Rama?' Sita said, playing with the word. 'Rama. Raama. That's a nice name. I hope I'll get to meet him one of these days.'

Danny spotted a book in the box. 'Oh great! Is that the Almanac?'

'It is, yes. Father asked me to drop it off for you. Though he gave me strict instructions to lodge it with Dr Greenwood for safe keeping.' A thought struck her.

'Why don't you have a quick look now, while I'm setting up my things?'

They had arrived at the fourth floor, where both the labs and the students' workroom, were situated. Danny hadn't been in the laboratory area before. He was struck by the smell of antiseptic mingled with bleach and floor polish. It contrasted with the scent of roses that wafted from Sita as she set up her things.

The counters were shiny white and immaculate with various test tubes and technical equipment scattered around. Sita arranged two chairs in front of one of the benches. She carefully placed a machine and connected it to her computer. There were wires with various electrodes coming out of it. There was a close fitting cap attached to the wires.

Sita chatted as she prepared her equipment.

'I'm looking forward to seeing your brain waves, Danny. When you were out for the count, they were rather unusual. I'll let you know when I'm ready to begin the experiments later on.

'For now, why don't you show me where your meeting room is and introduce me to your work colleagues? I haven't met Hugo or Izzie yet, and I'd love to meet Dr O'Donnell and Dr Greenwood again.'

But when Sita and Danny entered the workroom everyone was tidying up. They were just in time to hear Hugo call out,

'Lunchtime, everyone.'

'Hang on a mo!' commanded Izzie. 'Not so fast. Don't forget we're meeting Dr O'Donnell down at Exhibit 108. She wants us all to look at the old bow before we make our way to the canteen.'

'Hey, Sita why don't you join us?' Danny said. 'You might understand some of the symbols on the casing.'

Downstairs, they crowded around the dusty exhibit looking for clues or maker's marks. Dr O'Donnell joined them and commented on its appearance.

'There's not much to go on in terms of what might have prompted a foreign buyer to show such an interest in it.'

'It's not much to look at either,' said Sandeep. 'I mean from what Dr Greenwood said, I thought it would at least be made of precious metal or something. But it's just a dusty old bow, housed in a long glass box with a dirty metal frame and a lock.'

They became aware of a clanking of metal behind them. It was Twyson with his stubbly chin and brown overall, shuffling along pushing his cleaning trolley. He produced a scraper and bent down to remove some chewing gum off the slate floor.

'Huh!' he grunted. 'If it were up to me I would have taken a hammer to that thing and smashed the casing long ago.'

'Whaaat! That would be vandalism!' Danny glared at him. Twyson goaded further.

'Not for an old bit of rubbish, like that, it ain't. It's just a bit of worthless glass.'

'As a matter of fact,' said Kirsty O'Donnell. 'We believe it is made out of a single piece of rock crystal and that would make it quite rare.'

'The thing is we're looking for clues as to its cultural history,' Urmila explained.

'Wasting your time!' was Twyson's parting shot as he trudged off. 'I bet you don't find anything!'

Izzie studied the casing intently.

'Hang on,' she said. 'I can see some kind of patterns engraved on the metal work.'

'I've got a magnifying glass,' said Hugo. 'Let's take a closer look.'

He and Sandeep produced their mobile phones and took a few photos for good measure.

'I can see some spirals, and some funny squiggles which might be writing,' Hugo said.

'If you look at the ornate design of the escutcheon round the keyhole,' said Izzie. 'It's a kind of fancy circle.'

'That's not just a circle,' said Kirsty. 'It's an Ouroboros.'

'A what?' said Hugo.

'Oh, yes' said Urmila. 'I can see it. At the top it's got a snake's head with an open mouth. Then the tail comes round in a circle and goes into its mouth. As it joins up it then forms a circle.'

'The Ouroboros,' Izzie read out from her phone. 'Is a symbol they used in ancient Egypt to represent infinity. It appears in the Book of the Netherworld, in Tutankhamun's tomb.'

'That is correct,' said Kirsty O'Donnell. 'There is an illustration in that ancient book depicting two serpents holding their tail in their mouth, coiled around the head, neck and feet of an enormous deity. The figure is said to represent the beginning and the end of time.'

'So it's an illustration of the cycle of time,' Sandeep mused. 'Where the end goes back to the beginning.'

'That's interesting,' Danny said. 'Now you mention it I've seen that in Celtic art, too. They made torque neck decorations out of gold with an Ouroboros snake eating its tail.'

'And Plato,' Izzie said. 'Described the self-sufficiency and perfection of the created cosmos as an Ouroboros. So the ancient Greeks knew of it too.'

'Others have interpreted it in scientific terms,' said Dr Kirsty. 'As in physics, such as the Law of Thermodynamics where no energy is lost, it is just recycled and reappears in different forms.'

'Interesting,' Sita peered to get a closer look. 'It's also a symbol in the Vedic culture. It is said to represent the Shakti energy. When the energy is at rest at the base of the spine, the snake is depicted as holding its tail in its mouth, and likened to a dormant seed. It's part of the cycle of reincarnation. The seed grows, flourishes, and dies, then is reborn again. It is the cycle of life, death and rebirth, over and over again. It is called the wheel of karma.'

'How d'ya get off the wheel?' said Danny. 'Sounds like a big dipper at the fair.'

'You get off it when you gain enlightenment,' said Sita.

'Huh!' said Sandeep. 'You have to earn enough merit to get off it, so that's *you* out.' He cold-shouldered Danny pointedly.

'Hah! And you too, then,' Hugo retorted, sticking up for Danny.

Delicious smells were wafting through from the restaurant reminding them it was lunchtime. Hugo sniffed the air and voiced their thoughts.

'Hey, guys. It's curry on the specials menu today. I'm off to get my lunch.'

Everyone legged it out of the room. Except for Danny who hung back and went over to the case to listen intently. Nothing. But when he put his hands on the case it seemed as if there was a subtle vibration emanating from it. He put his ear closer and was sure he could hear an audible hum...

As they ate their lunch in the canteen, Urmila said,

'Tell you what, guys, I propose we have a night out tonight to cheer ourselves up.'

They all perked up.

'Yeah,' said Sandeep. 'Why don't we go to see the latest Star Wars movie that's playing at the big complex in town?'

'Good idea,' said Hugo. 'Afterwards we can go to that restaurant in Main Street.'

When the movie finished it was late evening. The students set off in the direction of the restaurant discussing the plot animatedly.

'Drat!' Izzie announced suddenly. 'It's starting to drizzle and I haven't brought a brollie.'

'So what?' said Danny. 'You won't melt.'

'It will play havoc with my hair,' Izzie groaned. 'It'll be about twenty minutes walk at this rate in the rain.'

'Tell you what,' said Hugo. 'I know a shortcut. Follow me.'

He led the way down a side street. It came out into a run-down area with tall, red brick warehouses along one side of the street. On the other side were dark and forbidding railway arches. The area wasn't very well lit, and there was no one about. The shadows cast by the street lamps seemed to be moving as they walked. They all began to feel uneasy. Hugo was apologetic.

'Sorry, guys. I've only walked down here in the daylight. It all seems so different at night.'

Suddenly they could hear the thrumming deep bass of heavy rock music in the distance. As they drew nearer, they saw bright neon lights spilling out onto the pavement from a basement venue. There was a queue of youths waiting to be let in. Giggling girls were walking straight up to the door and the bouncers were admitting them first.

'Look,' said Izzie. 'Isn't that the new nightclub?'

'Yeah. The Nightmare Tavern,' frowned Sandeep.

'Ugh, it's got a terrible reputation,' said Urmila, eyes wide in alarm.

'It was touted as *the cool place to hangout* in its adverts,' said Hugo.

'Yeah, if you're into binge drinking and drugs,' Danny retorted.

Urmila looked pale.

'We should get out of here as quick as we can.' But even as she spoke, rounding the corner further down the street, came a gang of drunken louts, beer cans in hand. They were obviously looking for trouble.

Danny stopped. 'Let's go back the way we came.'

They turned in the other direction only to see yet more youths coming towards them the other way. They looked even more menacing with their tattoos and chains hanging from their belts.

Danny's heart was pounding like an electric jack-hammer. He had noticed a white van parked a few yards down the street from the night-club entrance. The rear doors were open and two men were doing a surreptitious trade. People were furtively coming to the back of their van and collecting white packets before going into the nightclub. One of the men turned and Danny saw his tattooed neck and profile.

'Sycker!' he exclaimed, horrified.

All the dreadful incidents that had taken place at school flashed before his eyes. Sycker had always mocked him for being friends with the Mithil family. *The Pakkies*, he called them. Danny had once rashly tried to explain they were an illustrious Hindu family and were from India not Pakistan and, regardless, it was wrong to use insulting words about people from Pakistan. Danny had paid a high price for that attempt at being brave.

Sycker was clever enough to avoid direct physical contact with Sandeep, which would have incurred instant expulsion. Instead, he'd used Danny as a means of furthering his racist bullying. There were many times Sycker had stolen his dinner money as part of his 'protection' racket.

And once, when Danny had plucked up courage and reported him for racism, the bully had to appear before the Headmaster. Of course he'd denied everything very plausibly. The upshot of it was Sycker had lain in wait for Danny on the way home and beat him up so badly he was in bed for three days. Danny had told Aunt Millicent he'd fallen off his bike.

The brutish lad was now with an older man, who was obviously no stranger to this kind of activity.

'Guys,' said Hugo urgently. 'Let's beat it out of here.'

But they were too late. There was nowhere to go.

'We're trapped!' said Urmila, in a scared whisper.

The drunken louts spotted the students. Their leader yelled out.

'Oh lookie here, what have we got? A couple of girlies with some wimpy boys.'

As the gang advanced, the students instinctively huddled together, terrified. They knew the reputation of these street gangs. They were hopelessly trapped and outnumbered.

But then the strangest thing happened. From out of the shadows on the other side of the street, two tall, well-built figures appeared. It was Rama and Lakshman and they were wearing their traditional warrior garb with breastplates and helmets. Their bow and quiver were slung over their shoulders.

Rama motioned for the teenagers to get down a nearby alleyway. They watched in amazement as the two Kalari warriors squared up to the thugs. As the drunken louts spotted the noble brothers, the ringleader let out a derisive yell.

'Hey, look! Guys in fancy dress,' he bellowed at the top of his voice.

'Yeah, with gold hats on,' said another, waving a bottle of plonk around.

'I wanna sh-try on a gold helmet-sh,' said the first lad, staggering from side to side.

'I'm gonna take it and sell the gold. It must be worth a fortune,' said the second lout. 'Here, you! Givuzz your gold bonnet.'

That was the wrong thing to say to Lakshman. His mouth curled contemptuously.

'*You? A weakling?* Look at the state you're in! You couldn't take a feather off a kitten. You are a disgrace to mankind. You are not even a worthy opponent for me to fight. Now be on your way, before I teach you a lesson you won't forget.'

The first lout stood swaying on the spot, a puzzled expression on his face. This wasn't the response he expected. But the second, stockier lad squared up to Lakshman.

'You looking for a fight?' His tone got more aggressive. 'C'mon. Make up your mind. You askin' for a whuppin'? Well, you is gonna get a beating anyway.'

He pulled out a huge Bowie knife. Lakshman shrugged indifferently.

'As you will.'

With deft footwork, and lighting speed, Lakshman's hand shot out and touched the yob on the side of his arm. He yelled in pain and the knife fell to the ground with a clatter.

'Ouch!' he complained, rubbing his arm. 'He's dead-armed me. He's given me, like, an electric shock.'

He backed off as he spoke, but several others moved in menacingly to take his place, surrounding the noble brothers. They brandished chains, knives, knuckle-dusters and other assorted weapons. It was beginning to get ugly.

Worse still, a couple of the most ruthless members of the gang set off down the alley, looking for the two girls.

All the while, Rama remained impassive. Danny watched as his mentor took an arrow and put it on his bow. As Rama fired it into the air it split into a thousand tiny shafts. Within seconds, what had been a mild drizzle turned into a torrential downpour. It created chaos. Everyone started yelling and legging it for cover, soaked to the skin in minutes. The street was miraculously cleared.

All except for the white van. Sycker slammed the rear doors shut and ran round to the driver's side. *He had spotted Danny.* A malevolent smirk spread over his face. He pushed the older man out of the way and yelled at him, motioning to the passenger seat.

'Get in!'

The man jumped in, panicking to escape the deluge. Sycker started the van with a clash of gears and a roar of the engine as he slammed the accelerator pedal down hard. The van lurched and headed straight for Danny who was now standing in the middle of the road.

Rama stepped in front of Danny and held his palm up, facing the direction of the oncoming van. Without warning, an oil slick appeared on the road and spread across the path of the speeding vehicle. Its wheels skidded and the van spun around several times, out of control. Danny saw Sycker's face through the windscreen, his mouth open as if he were yelling in terror.

The van smashed into a nearby lamppost with an almighty crash. The students came out to have a look. Sycker was slumped over the steering wheel, blood trickling down his face and onto his t-shirt. His companion was paralysed by fear, looking as if he was about to be sick.

Lakshman strode over and wrenched open the driver's door. He looked under Sycker's eyelids and checked his pulse. Then he closed the door and reported back to Rama.

'He'll be alright,' Lakshman pronounced. 'Mild concussion and a nosebleed. We'll let the police deal with them.'

Danny looked in the back of the van. He noticed on one of the cardboard boxes was printed the words, 'Taddakka Solutions.'

Rama spoke briskly as if nothing out of the way had happened.

'We're going to escort you all straight home, it isn't safe to be wandering around the streets of this area at night.'

On the way Danny reflected on the incident. It seemed it was only him with his gift of sight that had seen a ball of light leave Rama's arrow prior to the oil slick. It seemed as if he was the only one that saw Rama fire the ball of light into the air immediately preceding the monsoon downpour. Questions buzzed round his mind like bees on steroids. *Just what kind of powers do these Kalari warriors have?*

That was also a question the occupant of a black limousine was asking. It had been parked out of sight under a railway arch while these remarkable events took place. The observer had seen everything. As the students disappeared round the corner, the vehicle with its blacked out windows, slid into the street. On its number plate were the letters 'TADDAKKA.'

9

TREASURE IN THE JUNGLE

It was late afternoon and the students were beginning to pack up their things ready to leave the museum. But Danny was missing. Suddenly there was thud outside the door and a muffled exclamation. Urmila ran to open it and found Danny picking up a pile of heavy books at his feet. She helped him deposit them onto the workroom table.

'Dr Greenwood found these hidden away in an old chest,' Danny explained. 'They're the museum Log Books from the nineteenth century. He thinks they may help us with clues as to the mystery of Exhibit 108.'

'I don't see why we have to stay behind,' Sandeep grumbled.

'Shut up, Sandeep,' Izzie snapped at him. 'This is an important mystery we need to solve.'

'I agree,' said Hugo. 'But I need a cup of tea and sustenance before I can begin.'

'Yeah,' said Danny. 'Me, too.'

'It won't take us long if we all chip in,' Urmila spoke to her cousin in soothing tones, pouring oil on troubled waters as usual.

'Right, c'mon,' Izzie handed them a volume each. 'Remember that all donations, bequests, and purchases will be recorded in these logs. While we trawl through them, look out for an entry that mentions the old bow.'

The next hour saw them scouring the heavy, leather-bound volumes examining the neat, copperplate handwriting. There was a focused silence punctuated only by the crunch of custard creams.

'*Bingo!*' The piercing shout made them all jump. Urmila jabbed with her finger. 'I've got it. Look!'

Izzie grabbed the Log Book off her.

'Gimme! Let me see!' She read out the entry.

'*October 15th 1851. The donation of an antique bow has been made today by a gentleman named Shri Parashuram. He states he is the guardian of the object known as 'The Great Bow of Shiva.' It has been on loan to the Crystal Palace Exhibition, since it was sent over from colonial India.*'

'It states,' said Izzie. 'That Mr Parashuram accompanied the exhibit all the way from India and guarded it until it arrived here.'

Hugo looked over her shoulder and read out,

'*It is kept in a rock crystal casket and it is an object of untold antiquity. The donor states the object must be kept in its case at the Manchester museum, where it will be on loan, until such time as its rightful owners come to claim it.*

'*When asked for an estimate of its value Mr Parashuram stated it was to be put at a value of "priceless".*'

'That's weird,' said Urmila. 'Considering it's an old piece of ash-covered wood.'

'And look at this,' Danny said. 'He told the curator it could emit a kind of electro-magnetic energy. And it is of such an extreme weight that even 20 men couldn't lift it unaided.

'That explains why it was lodged on the ground floor in the building adjacent to the modern museum. I guess because of its extreme weight, once it was placed there no one could move it again,' Sandeep deduced.

Hugo agreed. 'So they just knocked through the adjoining walls and that's why it appears to be off the main museum.'

Izzie carried on reading.

'*It was reported in the Victorian Times daily newspaper that it wouldn't budge even an inch until Mr Parashuram began to utter a rhythmic chanting. Only then could the object be lifted onto a horse drawn carriage. Eyewitnesses who were present at the time reported the chanting also had a remarkably calming effect on the four skittish horses, which were harnessed to the carriage.*'

'Are there legal conditions attached to it, Izzie?' Danny asked.

'Yes. It states a binding legal Covenant has been placed on this donation to the effect that its lock must never be forced. The Covenant Conditions state that *The casket may only be opened by the proper key. However, no key was given at the time of the donation.*'

Urmila grimaced. 'Drat! What a pain.'

'That's not all. Listen to this,' Izzie said.

"Whosoever claims that they are the rightful owner must bring with them two proofs of ownership: the first will be in the form of an Ouroboros key. This is the only key that will open the casket.

The second proof will take the form of a Last Will and Testament, detailing their lineage, and their ownership of the bow. From then on, the Great Bow of Shiva shall be theirs, to do with, as they will.

'What puzzles me,' said Hugo. 'Is what on earth could it be made of, that causes it to be such a tremendous weight? It's frustrating that it's covered in ash, so we don't have any visual clues to go on.'

'Well, it looks like it's going to remain a mystery,' Urmila looked disappointed. 'I wonder why that foreign man was after it?'

Sandeep shook his head. 'An even bigger mystery concerns me. Namely, whereabouts is that special key that will open the casket? It could be anywhere in the world.'

'Let's face it guys. The likelihood is it's lost forever somewhere between the ocean and the Indian sub-continent.' Danny looked glumfaced. 'It would be like looking for a grain of sand on Brighton beach.'

It was a dejected group who picked up their things ready to go home. Izzie gave them all a reminder before they left.

'Don't forget that tomorrow Dr O'Donnell wants to see our research on that ancient culture of South Asia.'

That evening Danny studied the map coordinates of the area before he fell asleep.

*4:00*AM

It was unbearably hot and clammy in the humid jungle heat. Danny's clothes clung to him, wet through and dripping. Mosquitoes stung his face and leeches clung to his legs. He swatted at them with his hat but to no avail.

'Where are we?' he asked his guide, who was hacking his way through the dense, swampy undergrowth with a machete. The man was around forty years of age dressed in a white tunic, with a red turban on his head. He had the wizened appearance of a much older man.

'You are in Cambodia,' the guide told him. 'You Europeans are on an expedition to discover treasure. Your colleague, Henri, the archeologist, has been searching for the legendary treasure hidden somewhere in this unexplored jungle.'

They made their way through the jungle for another hundred yards. Suddenly, rising up through the trees like an apparition, appeared the massive stone towers of an ancient temple. The mellow stonework glowed like cream jewels in the early morning sun.

'What is this place?' Danny gazed in open-mouthed wonder at the spectacle before him.

'This is a sacred place to my ancient people,' said the guide. 'It is known as the temple of Angkor Wat.'

Danny's astonishment grew as they arrived at the main temple gates. Although it was almost overgrown with jungle creepers the stunning beauty of its carvings were still evident.

A wide moat surrounded the whole complex, the interior of which was accessed by a remarkable causeway. Danny guessed it depicted some kind of story because there were precisely fifty-four stone figures carved on one side of the bridge, and the same number on the other side. That gave a total of one hundred and eight in all.

'Look, Henri,' Danny said. 'Those statues all appear to be holding a rope of some sort.'

'That is not a rope,' their guide said. 'It is a giant snake. They are using it to churn the cosmic ocean in our great legend.'

'Is there a mathematical significance to the numbers?' Danny said.

'Of course not,' Henri answered. 'How could there be?'

'You are wrong,' their guide contradicted him. '*All* of our numbers have mathematical significance. The number 108 is one of the sacred numbers of the precession of the equinoxes.' The guide observed Henri's look of disbelief and chided him.

'Do not underestimate the sophisticated mathematical and scientific principles that are encoded in the structures of this place. European explorers rarely try to understand the depth of culture when they visit the countries of the east. They belittle our ancient people's intelligence. Only the learned and the wise take the trouble to study it properly.'

As Danny wandered around the site, he could see there were five huge temple towers arranged like dots on a dice. All were ornately carved with elegant figures. But the central tower was the tallest and most imposing. The guide led led Danny to a frieze carved on a long internal wall.

'Look at this,' he said. 'It's an ancient legend carved in stone. It has provided the inspiration for the construction of Angkor Wat.'

Danny saw carvings in semi-relief as if the story was emerging from its stone imprisonment to be retold time and time again.

'What story is this?' he asked the guide.

'It is the legend of the Churning of the Ocean of Milk ...'

But at that point, the voice faded into the distance and Danny experienced a swirling mist before his eyes as the vision changed. He felt as if he were travelling backwards through a tunnel of time and space to another era.

This time when he opened his eyes, he was in a bustling metropolis. There were wide boulevards and many people who were going about their daily lives. He recognised it as Angkor Wat but in a much earlier era. The original temple complex that he'd seen in the jungle with Henri was now pristine, as if it had been newly built. The only vegetation was neatly kept fields and lush gardens. The temple could be seen at the top of one of the widest boulevards, and there were temple dancers and priests in the grounds.

Elsewhere in the city were traders, farmers, artisans of all kinds, selling their wares. There were people arriving through the city gates who looked to be pilgrims, travellers and merchants. There were scribes and cooks and children playing and a multitude of activities to be expected from a cultured race of people.

'It's the summer solstice at dawn tomorrow,' a sweet elderly couple said to Danny. 'Would you like to join us for the celebration?'

They took Danny back to their house and introduced him to their children and pets. He felt very much at home with them. As he watched them laugh and play together, he thought wistfully of how lucky they were to be part of a happy family.

In the balmy, warm evening air, they took Danny with them when they went out for the festival. There was street entertainment, feasting, music and dancing that seemed to go on all night. Danny was struck by how safe he felt in this culture. He wouldn't have felt this safe on the streets of Manchester so late at night.

After several hours when the dark night sky gave way to the faint golden glimmer of dawn, people gathered silently in the squares and temple grounds. All eyes looked east, towards the magnificent central tower of the five towers. There was a hushed and expectant atmosphere.

As the sun rose in the sky a miracle seemed to occur. For the golden orb could be seen hovering exactly over the topmost pinnacle of the central tower at the precise time of the solstice.

Danny could hardly believe his eyes. Who could design such a feat of astronomical engineering with such precise timing? The priest-astronomers of the temple could be seen taking calibrated measurements of the exact position of the sun at the eastern horizon. They appeared to be keeping very exact mathematical records of the date and time.

His host looked at him with eyes that suddenly seemed to be like Vasishta's. He said,

'You must find out about the *Kali Yuga*, Danny.'

Danny wanted to ask what that was but he felt light-headed and began to drift towards the tunnel of light. When he awoke in the morning he reflected on the vision still lingering in his consciousness. There could be no doubt he had met a highly cultured people.

But how could he explain it to anyone? How could he satisfy the Museum's academic requirements and prove an ancient society possessed such sophisticated mathematical knowledge? And then he remembered the Almanac. Maybe it would contain clues to the valuable proof he needed?

'THIS AFTERNOON,' Richard Greenwood said, looking at the pile of papers on the workroom table. 'The Museum Committee want to hear your presentations. Be prepared to answer any questions they might put to you. He saw the alarm on their faces and added, 'Don't worry, they won't bite. But they want to hear any evidence that the people of South East Asia understood mathematics and astronomy.'

'There is an element of the committee,' said Kirsty, exchanging a significant glance with Richard. 'Who believe that we are dealing with a primitive culture.'

When the tutors left, an argument broke out amongst the students.

'I suggest we examine one of the friezes on the temple wall,' said Danny. 'I believe we can show it contains mathematical principles.'

Sandeep was instantly dismissive.

'Don't be so stupid,' he said. 'It's an ancient temple complex. Artistic? Yes, I'll grant you that, but mathematical? In your dreams, mate!'

'Actually,' said Urmila. 'I agree with Danny. I've been doing research along the same lines to show this culture had sophisticated mathematical understanding. Let me show you…'

1:30PM

The museum's lecture theatre had a claustrophobic atmosphere. There were no external windows and the surrounding walls were painted matt black. The lighting mainly came from the lights overhead and footlights at the front of the stage area. Without these, the room would have been in pitch darkness.

The seating was steeply raked with a central gangway down the middle. The main focus of the theatre was the stage and the huge cinema screen behind it dominated the room.

The students watched apprehensively as the Museum Committee and various invited guests took their seats. Professor Plendergarth sat on the front row and beside him was Dr Merrick, looking sour as usual. Next to him was an overweight man with several chins and a florid countenance.

He had small, beady eyes that constantly darted hither and thither. From time to time, he took out a spotted handkerchief and mopped his perspiring brow.

Dr Greenwood introduced the newcomer to the students as Councillor Hitchin, a member of the Museum Finance Committee. The councillor gave them a curt nod and instantly returned to his earnest conversation with Dr Merrick.

Danny's heart sank as he recognised the pinched features and hooded eyelids of one of the guests. It was none other than Dr Zeuber, whom they'd met in the Lakes.

Kirsty O'Donnell and Richard Greenwood sat on the stage with the students as they gave their PowerPoint presentations.

Izzie gave the introduction.

'A French explorer is in Cambodia. Who is he? And what discovery does he make? Many European countries in the 1800s were keen to visit the east to discover trade and treasures. It was the French explorer, Henri Mouhout, who in 1860 made an astonishing discovery in the Cambodian jungle. It led him to the Angkor Wat temple complex, the largest temple complex in Asia, so they say.'

Hugo displayed slides of the ancient monument, showing it in all its artistic and engineering glory as he continued.

'The overall layout of the complex shows they had a sophisticated architectural blueprint for its design before building even began. It is aligned to the cardinal directions. It has sophisticated water management systems in place. Its construction shows evidence of skilled engineering.'

Urmila described the next set of slides.

'Everywhere, on the inside and the outside of this complex, we see that the buildings are covered in beautiful carvings of epic mythologies. These epics are timeless stories that are found everywhere in the cultures of the east.'

Danny continued.

'Investigators using Archeo-mythology have suggested the legends contain encoded scientific or mathematical principles. These are the mysteries we have been investigating.'

'You're surely not trying to tell me,' Councillor Hitchin interrupted, mopping at beads of sweat rolling down his cheek. 'These primitive savages from two thousand years ago had the ability to plan cities like we do today?'

'Yes, but they were not *savages!*' Sandeep retorted. 'These were highly cultured people who were so skilled in town planning that they had sanitation, and water supplies for their living accommodation. The interconnecting web of roads and highways would rival those of any city planning today.'

'There is a further example of far-sighted planning,' said Izzie. 'We see it in way that they looked after their travellers and merchants. There were 'rest-houses' for pilgrims and others spaced at intervals of about 17-kilometres along all the major travel routes.'

'How can you possibly know details like that?' Dr Zeuber's tone implied disbelief.

'Archaeologists have used scientific equipment,' said Urmila. 'These include aerial surveys and ground penetrating radar. It revealed that there are even more extensive buildings and towns extending further afield than the Angkor Wat temple complex. We are talking about a very cultured society indeed.'

'And did you know,' said Danny. 'These ancient cultures knew about eclipses?'

'Where did you get that information from?' Dr Zeuber sat bolt upright, suddenly alert and weighing Danny up with narrowed eyes. Where was the kid getting his information from?

'I have an Almanac on loan,' Danny said. 'Which has many mathematical and astronomical calculations, including a whole section on eclipses. It gives mathematical calculations for all eclipses from 1,260 BC, right up to 2,300 AD.'

There were expressions of interest from the members of the Museum Committee, which Professor Plendergarth voiced.

'I'd like to see this Almanac. It sounds as if it contains evidence of the highest importance.'

'The students examined one of the friezes in particular,' said Kirsty O'Donnell. 'And they believe it encodes many mathematical and scientific principles.'

Hugo started the slideshow and swirling oceans appeared on the big screen. Beautiful images of the temple appeared depicting exquisite carvings over every inch of the stonework surfaces.

'In this particular slide,' Hugo said. 'You can see a stone relief carved on a long frieze. It tells the story of a cultural legend, called *The Churning of the Ocean of Milk*. This is how the story goes.'

'Long, long ago,' Izzie began. 'The universe was nothing but a watery ocean. There were two elemental forces, the god-like devas and the demons. These two represented the opposing forces of creation and destruction. They were always fighting because each wanted to gain the dominant power over the universe.'

'The key to victory,' Sandeep said. 'Lay in which side could find an elixir called Amrita, which was the highly prized Nectar of Immortality. Whosoever drank Amrita, with its everlasting life-giving properties, would become immortal and always be victorious.'

'The problem was,' Urmila said. 'The elixir was hidden away at the bottom of the galactic ocean and was totally inaccessible. The only way to get it out was to create a centrifugal force. In order to do this, they decided to have a cosmic tug of war.'

'So they used the mountain called Meru as the pivot,' Hugo said. 'And a giant snake lent by Shiva as the rope. They churned the space-ocean back and forth, much in the same way as milk is churned in a barrel to produce butter.'

'They continue their efforts for thousands of years,' Izzie continued. 'It creates a powerful whirlpool effect which brings treasures up from the depths. In the slides we see the emerging figure of Manu, the first man, the law-giver. Lakshmi, the goddess of abundance next rises up, showering wealth. And finally, the precious Amrita appears, carried by an incarnation of Vishnu in a sacred vessel called a Kalash.'

'The problem is,' said Danny. 'When the nectar finally appears, a huge battle breaks out between the gods and the demons. Each wants to drink the nectar and become immortal. The battle rages for millennia. Finally, after a long struggle, the gods are victorious.'

'I don't see the relevance of this approach,' Dr Zeuber said with a barely concealed sneer. 'You surely don't believe these 'mythological stories' have any value in terms of our civilized, *western* way of thinking, do you, Dr O'Donnell?'

'As a matter of fact,' Kirsty took a deep breath before she answered. 'This legend has encoded within it a great deal of valuable scientific knowledge.'

'My dear Dr O'Donnell,' Merrick's tone was so patronising that Kirsty had to dig her nails into her palms. 'How do you arrive at such a conclusion?' He winked at Dr Zeuber as he spoke. 'Surely you are not going to credit this primitive culture with knowledge of maths and science?'

'This *Archeo-mythology* approach,' Dr Zeuber continued in his nasal whine. 'It is fine for your TV documentary, I dare say, Dr O'Donnell. But you see, we academics need proof and documented evidence that the ancients knew how to perform detailed mathematical calculations.'

'And of course,' said Dr Merrick. 'Maths is the very basis of science, which you of all people, Dr Greenwood, should know.'

Richard Greenwood's colour rose as he struggled to control his irritation.

Danny couldn't stop himself calling out.

'Excuse me. We have evidence that proves these people were as intelligent as you or I are today. Will the Committee bear with us while we show you our research on the subject?'

Professor Plendergarth's eyes lit up.

'Yes, yes, please go ahead. We will be interested to hear your fresh thinking on this subject.'

Izzie said,

'We discussed the mysteries of Angkor Wat with Rama, who is an expert in Sanskrit writings. He told us the temple complex is based a passage from the ancient Veda describing the principle of, *As above, so below*. This is what it says,

"As is the human body, *so is the cosmic body.*
   As is the human mind, so is the cosmic mind.
   As is the microcosm, so is the macrocosm.

As is the atom, so is the universe."

'The science encoded in the legend is based on how the Churning of the Milk Ocean resulted in a spiral or vortex,' Urmila continued. 'The legend is an allegorical description of the formation of a galaxy as it appears in outer space.'

'Through our modern science we understand that our galaxy is a spiral. The function of a black hole at its centre is a storehouse of matter. We even get the name of our own galaxy, *The Milky Way*, from this ancient Vedic legend.'

At this, Zeuber looked as if he'd just chewed a slug in his lettuce. Merrick pursed his lips and studied the floor.

Danny relished their discomfiture as he continued.

'Just as in the cosmos, patterns of spirals can be seen on earth. They are found in nature everywhere. Spirals of hurricanes, patterns on a snail shell, spirals in an unfolding fern, a pineapple, a sunflower, a pine-cone. Even the leaves on a tree, unfold in a spiral pattern.

'At the molecular level the double helix of the DNA is formed in a spiral. From the smallest of the small, to the largest of the large; from the spiral of the galaxy to the spiral of the DNA, as it said in the Vedic text, there is evidence of scientific principles at work in similar patterns across the universe.'

'At Angkor Wat the main temple complex consists of five towers, constructed in an ingenious design, based on the legend,' Hugo said. 'The inner buildings rise up in a spiral towards the sanctum sanctorum at the topmost centre of the middle tower.'

'Why did they go to all that trouble?' said Professor Plendergarth, tilting his head on one side. Hugo explained.

'The ancient Khmers designed this central tower to represent Mount Meru, which is the abode of the gods. So in essence, they were recreating heaven on earth. Once an individual reached the elevated heights, they would gain enlightenment and be able to live in the heavenly abode.'

'In fact,' said Kirsty O'Donnell. 'We see that *'Meru'* is so important to their cultural identity that they take their name from it, and call themselves the Kh-meru.'

The response of the committee members to this information varied widely. Professor Plendergarth was clearly impressed. Merrick pursed his lips and Zeuber shook his head and scowled.

'This is all very well,' he said. 'But it is merely stories and conjecture. You don't have any factual evidence to back it up, do you?'

'As a matter of fact,' said Danny. 'The architects of Angkor understood the mathematics of spirals, which are derived from the Fibonacci sequence. But here's a fact for you, Dr Zeuber. The Vedic mathematicians knew this pattern *thousands of years* before Fibonacci. The trouble was, European scholars never understood these sophisticated mathematics until medieval times. The mathematical facts that prove it are all in here.' Danny held up the Almanac, triumphantly.

'Are you saying that this *Almanac* has proof that the ancient people were familiar with mathematical principles?' Professor Plendergarth queried, looking intently at it.

'Indeed, Professor,' said Richard Greenwood. 'The Almanac is based on sophisticated mathematical calculations, which even go up to nine decimal places.'

'What about this *Kali Yuga* you mentioned, Dr O'Donnell?' enquired Councillor Thompson, a pleasant faced man with a receding hairline.

'The Almanac gives calculations from the start date of the *Kali Yuga*,' said Kirsty. 'And remarkably, knowledge of Cosmic Time is also embedded in the stone at Angkor Wat.'

'You've no proof of that,' sneered Dr Merrick.

'As a matter of fact,' said Danny. 'The proof is in the Almanac. You can see on the screen, there is a column headed '*Kali Yuga*.'

'But what is this *Kali Yuga*?' Professor Plendergarth looked puzzled. 'Can someone explain it please?'

'As we are fortunate to have Rama with us today,' said Richard Greenwood. 'I'll call on him to answer your question, professor.'

As Rama stood up and bowed politely, all eyes swivelled in his direction. He looked tall and dignified in his cream tunic and blue gilet.

'There is a gigantic cycle of Cosmic Time,' said Rama, drawing a big circle on the whiteboard. 'And it is sub-divided into four epochs, or *Yugas*. Each *yuga* lasts for a fixed amount of Cosmic Time.

'The first yuga is the Golden Age, when humans are happiest and live longest. The second is the Silver Age, when human happiness declines by a quarter and negativity creeps in. The Bronze Age sees a fifty per cent increase in negativity. And finally the Kali Yuga sees a three quarters increase in negativity. People's happiness and lifespan reduces according to each age they are living in.'

'Which age are we in right now?' Professor Plendergarth asked.

'We're in the *Kali Yuga*,' Rama answered, his face grave.

'But you are surely not telling the committee,' Zeuber gave a derisive smirk. 'That these *primitive* people could calculate dates for Cosmic Time cycles, are you?'

'Of course they couldn't,' Dr Merrick agreed, leaning back in his chair. 'These ancient people can't have been familiar with mathematics, let alone come up with an accurate date for the start of this *Kali Yuga*.'

'That's where you're wrong!' Danny butted in hotly, holding the book and jabbing it with his finger. 'Not only does this Almanac calculate the mathematics of calendrical Time, but it also gives the *exact* start date for the *Kali Yuga*. It began on February 18th 3102 BC. That means their calculations go back way over five thousand years.'

He narrowly refrained from adding, *so there!*

There were exclamations of surprise from the other committee members as this sunk in.

'Well, bless my soul!' exclaimed Professor Plendergarth. 'That is remarkable! I shall be interested to study these mathematical calculations for myself.'

But Merrick's face became mask-like, and Zeuber's hooded eyes blinked and half-veiled, making him appear more reptilian than ever. These revelations could not be allowed. Minutes later, he got up and left the auditorium.

'So let's sum up this ancient culture,' said Kirsty O'Donnell. 'The real Treasure is the timeless wisdom encoded in the very stone itself at Angkor Wat. Those people who valued their cultural heritage, have preserved the values they hold dear in the form of knowledge.'

Professor Plendergarth turned to his neighbour.

'Well, now we know the proof is in the Almanac, it makes it a very valuable piece of evidence. We'll look forward to studying these mathematical calculations for ourselves, don't you agree, Darius?'

Dr Merrick gave a lukewarm nod in response. But as they broke for lunch and Danny was about to leave the auditorium, he found his way unexpectedly barred by Dr Merrick.

'Ahem. Mr Hanuman,' he said, with studied politeness. 'I wonder if I might take a look at the Almanac that Professor Janak sent in to the Museum?'

Urmila was at Danny's side.

'I'm afraid that won't be possible, Dr Merrick,' she said firmly. 'My father has entrusted it to Danny alone, with strict instructions it must not be loaned to anyone else.'

Neither she nor Danny saw Zeuber lurking in the foyer. Nor did they see the venomous look he shot after them as they left the building. Shortly afterwards he sent a text message.

THE STUDENTS SET off for their favourite restaurant along Manchester's famous Curry Mile region. The pavements were crowded with shoppers and business people, all hurrying to get to their lunch or meetings.

As the students made their way through the crowds, a man wearing a grey hooded top and sunglasses, deliberately walked in front of Danny. He separated him from the others. Danny was forced to drop back. From out of nowhere, Danny felt a violent punch in the solar plexus. He doubled over in anguish, fighting for breath. And while he struggled, he felt his backpack being wrenched from his shoulder.

The stranger was now running off down the street with the backpack. Danny tried to raise himself up of the ground. He managed to croak,

'Stop! Thief!'

The others looked round and saw Danny struggling to get up. Izzie quickly took in the situation. She looked after the retreating figure. He was shoving people roughly out of the way as he ran. Izzie gave chase.

She sprinted as fast as she could, dodging people on the pavement and nimbly weaving in and out of the crowds.

'Mate,' said Hugo in consternation, as he helped Danny up. 'Was there anything valuable in your backpack?'

Danny groaned.

'It contained the Almanac.'

'D'you mean they've stolen the evidence?'

'Yes. All our work will be lost without it. '

10

SITA AND THE DANCE OF SHAKTI

1:00 PM

Danny groaned.

'In order to prove the ancients had knowledge of sophisticated mathematics, we need the evidence contained in the Almanac. Without it, Zeuber and his cronies will have a field day and rubbish all our research.'

The students were visibly shaken. They followed Danny as he got to his feet and set off in the direction Izzie had taken. When they caught up with her, she was standing on the corner, bent over with her hands on her knees getting her breath back. She pointed down a side street and said,

'I think he nipped into the back entrance of that Asian supermarket.'

'Wait here!' ordered Danny.

He made his way down to a set of large warehouse doors, and cautiously opened one of them. He slipped inside. There was no one around, and all he could see were cardboard boxes stacked up everywhere. But something made him push his way through a narrow gap to a doorway at the back of the premises. Through a glass panel he saw people lined up on benches at the side. They were poorly dressed and huddled together as if they were tense and frightened. They looked like foreigners and it crossed Danny's mind they could be refugees or illegal immigrants.

But there was no sign of the man in the hoodie. When Danny rejoined the others, he was relieved to see that Rama and Lakshman had arrived on the scene.

'Did you see his face?' enquired Lakshman.

'No,' Danny shook his head miserably. 'He had his hoodie pulled right up and he wore dark glasses so I couldn't make out his features. There was no sign of him in the storehouse. Though I did see something strange.' And he related what he'd seen. Danny felt sick as he spoke. He wrung his hands together.

'The Almanac is vital. Without it, we're sunk.'

'Without it,' Sandeep said darkly. 'It will be impossible to solve the mysteries of the ancient *Sea Kings*.'

A pall of gloom descended on the students.

'Oh, *why* did the Almanac have to be in your backpack?' Urmila wailed.

'Go and have your lunch,' ordered Rama. 'Lakshman and I will see if we can find any clues.'

But when the students sat down in the restaurant, Danny was too distraught to even eat. Professor Janak had entrusted the valuable book to *him*. He was mortified. When the tutors joined them shortly after, they too, were aghast at the news of the theft.

'We'll inform the police,' said Richard. 'But I wouldn't hold your breath.'

'We'll postpone the afternoon seminar,' said Kirsty, noting Danny's distress. 'I suggest you use the opportunity for another training session.'

3:30PM

The local sports hall where the training took place had very good facilities. It was a few blocks away from where Danny and the Mithils lived. As they arrived at the large, airy gymnasium, Danny tried to put the incident of the theft behind him.

The warrior brothers were strict teachers. The lessons were demanding and his muscles still ached from yesterday's workout.

Izzie warmed up in her martial arts suit, raring to go.

'Rama – I mean, *Acharya*,' she said. 'Can we learn those martial arts techniques where your hands, like, become the weapon?'

'All in good time, Izzie,' said Rama noting the militant gleam in her eye. 'This isn't just about fighting. It's about personal growth and development.'

'Let me ask you a question,' said Lakshman. 'Where does a warrior's greatest power lie?'

'In his muscles,' Izzie replied promptly.

Lakshman shook his head. 'Danny, can you tell us?'

'The real power lies in the mind,' Danny replied. 'It's like, consciousness is where the power resides.'

Lakshman nodded. 'The integration of mind and body is necessary for mastery of Shakti power.'

'A true Kalari Knight,' added Rama. 'Has mastery of his or her emotions and senses. Anger is a weakness that your enemy will exploit. You have to maintain equilibrium and balance to attain true victory. This develops with practice.'

'We always begin,' said Lakshman. 'From a place of calm. We gain this through yoga and meditation. At the start of each session give respect to your opponent, obedience to your Master, discipline in your training.'

Out of all the students, Sandeep was the only one who didn't fully embrace the training. He regarded the Kalari tradition as something that people did in the olden days. People like Uncle Janak and Granny Mithil went on about its valuable life lessons. But Sandeep had always told himself he was a modern youth, living in the west. What relevance did it have to him?

He would have opted out of the Kalari training altogether to avoid Danny, if it hadn't been for Dr O'Donnell's enthusiastic support of it. She considered Kalari Payattu to be a valuable cultural heritage, and insisted that they should all train together.

Little did Sandeep know, he was shortly to learn how beneficial the

Kalari training would be in his life. But the lesson didn't come from the noble brothers. It came from much closer to home.

6:15 PM The secondary school hall was filling up. Parents and relatives of pupils in the Bhavan Class made their way to their seats for the evening's concert. Urmila, peeping round the curtains, saw her family taking their seats. She waved at Danny, Hugo and Izzie who had taken their reserved seats. She noted sadly that Sandeep had gone to sit with his relatives, rather than sit with Danny.

Sita was taking the starring role in the classical Indian dance performance. Danny had done his best to get the two princely brothers to attend, but Rama said they couldn't. They had a dinner engagement for the cultural delegates at the City Hall that same evening.

Danny couldn't explain his reasons in words. It was just a feeling he had to bring these two together. Rama, his mentor and friend just had to see Sita, his beautiful, adoptive sister. He was sure they were meant for each other.

It had taken all Danny's powers of persuasion to get the noble brothers there. In the end, they had agreed to come for the performance only, but would leave immediately it finished so they could get to their engagement on time. Rama had looked at him curiously.

'If it means so much to you, Danny, then we will come.'

Kirsty O'Donnell was there, filming for her cultural documentary on the arts. She had been asked to introduce the concert.

'Tonight,' she said to the audience. 'I am honoured to introduce this cherished tradition of classical Indian dance. The story we will see enacted, is one of the oldest cultural epics known to mankind. It is called the Ramayana. It is a story of heroism, love and friendship. It is a battle between good and evil on a universal scale.'

The performance began with a dozen dancers gracefully moving onto the stage. They were dressed in colourful saris, jewelled bangles jingling, flowers entwined in their hair. The soft swish of their silks caressed the air as they moved. But one dancer outshone them all.

Sita Mithil effortlessly glided onto the stage like a swan moving over a lake. She wore a beautiful red pleated sari with gold edging, caught up in a gold waist band. She had fresh flowers entwined in her hair, framing her lovely face and studded into the long plait which hung down her back.

Her hands and feet were painted with exquisite henna patterns and she wore bands round her ankles on which were sewn tiny bells that tinkled like silver rain as she walked.

Sita's expertise in classical Indian dance made all the demanding physical postures look graceful and easy. But it was the beauty of her expressive face that captivated the hearts of all who saw her perform.

When the performance ended Rama and Lakshman quickly made their way to the exit to keep their rendezvous. Others stayed to eat and chat with friends. Raja Janak made his way across to where Sandeep was sitting with his cousins.

'Sandeep, can you walk home with the girls? I need to stay a bit later for an interview with Dr O'Donnell and the Bhavan Trustees.'

Danny and Hugo had arranged to go to his place and practice with his drones. It was partly an excuse Danny made so he didn't have to walk home with Sandeep.

The evening sky was spectacular as the Mithil family members stepped outside. The setting sun had suffused wisps of cloud with glowing embers of gold and crimson. But the cousins were too busy chatting to observe their surroundings. They didn't notice the golden sunlight reflected on the blacked-out windows of a grey Audi parked at the end of the road as they passed. They didn't see how it glinted on the urban CCTV cameras covering the street.

A police car on routine patrol cruised past and the occupant of the grey Audi started his engine and slid off in the other direction.

'Sita,' Sandeep said. 'Do you know what Granny said this morning?'

'No,' Sita smiled. 'Tell me.'

'She said it's a shame you're going to carry on with your studies, because you're nearly twenty-one and therefore you should be getting married.'

'No worries, sis,' said Urmila. 'At least dad knows you're a career girl.'

Normally Sita would have agreed with her sister. She had focused all her energies on her studies and so far, had achieved top grades in all her exams and practicals.

But something had happened this evening, which jolted her out of the future she'd so carefully planned for herself. While she was in the wings waiting for the audience to be seated, she had observed the most handsome man she had ever seen, sitting at the back of the room. She couldn't take her eyes off him. All through the performance, she glanced at him from under her eyelashes.

His eyes had met hers, and she knew there was a spark there. It was love at first sight as far as she was concerned. But she didn't know who he was. And he'd left immediately the performance ended. Would she ever see him again?

She was lost in these thoughts as they walked along the suburban streets on their route home. She was oblivious to the long eerie shadows cast by the sun as it streamed through the avenue of trees lining the road.

Suddenly one of the tree shadows swung loose. A youth jumped out in front of them. Another couple dropped down from a tree behind them. Yet another appeared out of the shadows followed by two more.

Sandeep looked around. His heart was pounding. They were surrounded by a gang of half a dozen youths. And one of them was the thug, Sycker. There was no way of escape.

'Hello, what have we here?' said the bully. 'Well. If it isn't the *pakkie-kids!*' His manner exuded confidence he'd chosen a soft target. He gestured menacingly to Sita's shoulder bag. 'Give us yer bag.'

The response was not what he expected. Sita ignored him and said to Urmila,

'This calls for the Chakra Formation.'

The two sisters rotated in a circle like a wheel. They faced outwards observing and weighing up the enemy. Sandeep was mortified to see that they'd put him in the middle between them both.

Their hands moved in slow motion and it occurred to Sandeep that it might have been a graceful dance routine, but what good was it against these louts?

A puzzled expression crossed Sycker's face.

'Wot the -?'

Urmila spoke conversationally to Sandeep,

'You said you wanted to know more about Shakti power, coz. Well, just keep your eyes on Sita.'

Sita placed both of her hands near her diaphragm and breathed in deeply. As she breathed out she lowered her hands as if contacting an invisible energy source.

Sandeep watched, baffled and more than a little worried.

The gang of yobs were preparing for a bit of entertainment at the cousins' expense.

'Give us yer bag!' Sycker repeated, this time more menacingly, taking a step closer to Sita.

'I am not going to give you my bag,' Sita spoke coolly. She kept a firm grip on the strap over her shoulder. 'And I advise you not to try and take it from me.'

At this the lad snorted derisively and stretched out his hand to grab the bag off her shoulder. However, instead of touching the object as expected, he encountered Sita's fingers. Sandeep looked on in amazement as Sycker started yelling.

'Ow! Ouch! Get off! That hurt!' He turned to the others, face contorted. 'She sent an electric shock right through my arm.' He pulled his arm back, shaking it to get some feeling to return to his numb limb.

'I'll just have to take it off you then.' The second youth reached out his hand and tried to yank the bag off Sita's shoulder.

'Suit yourself,' she shrugged. 'Don't say I didn't warn you.'

Sita performed a quick hand movement. The lad suddenly found that his hand hit hers in mid-air. It was as if it had hit a rock barrier and he couldn't move it any further. He tried another angle and this time he got a dead arm for his troubles.

'She's got like a force field thing around her,' he shouted to the others in frustration. 'And it's like she's got electric in her fingers. I don't get it.'

Another of the thugs tried his hand with similar results.

'This is weird,' they muttered to each other. 'Trust Sycker to pick on someone who does *kung fu* stuff.'

'Spooky! That's what I call it.'

'Hey!' yelled Sycker, pointing up the street. 'There's a car coming, let's beat the hell out of here!'

The louts backed off, running down the street in the opposite direction.

Sandeep was gob-smacked.

'Sita, that was incredible!' he said. 'How did you do it?'

Sita's explanation was typically matter of fact.

'It's part of the Kalari tradition, Sandeep. We're taught to foster and direct the Shakti power. I know you've never been interested before, or I would have taught you.'

'Yeah, coz,' said Urmila. 'Like, Sita's a black belt. She knows how to use special nerve points and all that sort of stuff.'

Sandeep said,

'D'you mean like Spock?'

Sita laughed.

'We don't think about it like that. It's just part of our tradition of self-defence. We don't seek to fight anyone and we keep it private, unless someone asks if they can learn. That's all.'

From that moment onward Sandeep became the most diligent student of the Kalari tradition of them all. Suddenly a car pulled up alongside them and the window wound down. It was Professor Janak.

'Are you all alright? Were those lads I saw running off bothering you? Get in. I'm giving you a lift home.'

All the way home Raja Janak bemoaned the fact that he'd stayed behind for the interview.

'I shouldn't have let you walk home alone. What was I thinking of?'

'Father we're old enough to look after ourselves,' Sita protested. 'You've trained us in the Old Ways. That's our protection like you've always said.'

'I never intended for you to have to use it under these circumstances,' her father groaned. 'I wanted to keep our cultural traditions alive but ...' His voice tailed off.

'Yes, and it has done thanks to you,' Urmila reassured him. 'Sita is amazing!'

'Don't worry father, Sita said. 'Now you've proved how valuable and practical our traditional skills are, you can rest easy.'

But Professor Janak maintained a reflective silence. He had been dreading this day for it meant he would have to divulge the family secret to his eldest daughter. It would change her life forever.

RAMA AND LAKSHMAN walked briskly along the street in the direction of the City Hall. Vishwa-mitra would be waiting for them at the civic reception being held for the cultural delegates.

As they walked, Lakshman noticed his brother was behaving in an odd way.

'You OK, bro?' he asked.

Rama's eyes were a-glow, and a smile played about his lips.

'Did you see her?'

'Who?'

'That extraordinarily beautiful girl in the red dance costume?'

'Oh. Now you come to mention it, I suppose she was very attractive.'

Lakshman looked at his brother. He'd never seen him like this before. With a jolt, the explanation dawned on him. *He's smitten!*

Lakshman frowned. But this wasn't allowed. They were both warriors, sworn to serve their Master in the tradition of the Kalari Knighthood. They had foresworn women and personal gain while they were on this mission for the illustrious and powerful Vishwa-mitra. It would never do to anger him, for his powers were legendary.

At the same time, Lakshman knew that his brother was incapable of being fickle. If Rama's heart was given, it would be given for all time. The question arose – was this forever destined to be an unrequited love?

THE NEXT DAY Sita came home from her shift at the Infirmary to find everyone was out. It was an ideal opportunity to do some research in her father's study. She browsed through the books until she found a large tome entitled, 'Consciousness in Human Brain Physiology.'

She set it down on top of the large mahogany desk and opened the capacious drawer to find a pen and paper to make notes. She was immediately struck by how untidy it was, almost as if someone had been rummaging through it. Who would have left it like that? It was certainly not her meticulous father. Nor was it likely to have been Sandeep, who was also neat and tidy by nature.

She began to remove the untidy clutter of assorted paper clips, pens, sticky notes and various other bits and pieces and set them on the desktop in neat, orderly piles.

As Sita reached to the very back of the drawer, her delicate fingers felt something odd. A kind of carving. She traced it out. It was a circle. She drew out her mobile and switched the torch on. As she bent down to get a better look, a circular snake with its tail in its mouth was revealed. Sita was astonished.

'Why would someone go to the trouble of carving that where it wouldn't be seen?'

She pressed the centre, and to her astonishment, a hidden drawer was pushed forward. Sita carefully pulled it out and laid it on top of the desk to take a better look.

How strange. Why would someone want to hide an object so badly they had a secret drawer made for it? It must be something of great value ...

The inner drawer contained a five-metal puzzle box, the sort her grandfather had taught her to solve when she was little. It was the work of minutes for Sita to click each piece into its correct position. At once the top slid open to reveal its contents. The box was lined inside with red velvet and lying on the plush fabric was an object wrapped in yellow silk. Sita carefully unwrapped it with eyes like saucers. For she beheld, lying in her palm, an ornate golden key.

She picked it up and turned it over carefully. The handle of the key had the form of a circular snake, with its tail in its mouth. It was beautifully inlaid with gold filigree work.

'Well, I never,' she rubbed her nose, perplexed. 'What could this key be for? And why has it been locked away so carefully?' She checked the drawer for any written clues, but there was nothing. 'I wonder if Father knows anything about it?'

But later that evening, when she drew her father into the study, his reaction was not at all what she expected. As Sita showed him the object, Raja Janak frowned and shook his head. He pressed his lips tight together as if bracing himself. He took the golden key from her and held it in his hand without saying a word.

He then got up and paced the room a couple of times, lost in an inner struggle with himself. He sighed heavily as a man for whom a great weight had descended on his shoulders.

Finally, he went over to a picture on the wall. To Sita's surprise, it swung open to reveal a hidden wall-safe. Her father took out a sheath of papers. He sighed again, in a fatalistic way as he sat down beside her.

Sita's brow furrowed. What could be wrong? It was so unlike her parent, she became anxious.

'Father,' she said. 'Please tell me what the problem is?'

Raja Janak looked at his beautiful daughter, his eyes misty.

'Sita, my dearest girl. I need to tell you something. I have here your great-grandfather's Will. In it he states that he has hidden a golden key. He prophesied that you would find it one day, and when you do, he told me what had to be done next.

'*When the key is found, the legendary Great Bow of Shiva will not be far away. This Great Bow is an ancient heirloom and it will reveal itself to our family because we are the custodians of it since time immemorial. But the rules of the tradition must be obeyed.*

'Wh-what tradition father?' Sita stammered.

'The tradition that decrees when the key to the casket is discovered, I must hold a ceremony for my eldest daughter.'

'What kind of ... *ceremony*?' Her eyes widened.

'The ceremony known as the Swyamvar for choosing a husband.'

'But - isn't that only reserved for a princess, in days of old?'

'You see,' Raja Janak explained. 'There was a tradition in ancient times for noble families to ensure their daughters would be happy with whom they married. So they gave them a choice of suitors. Our royal family lineage means we are direct descendants of the kings of Mithila. We no longer use our titles here in the west and we just behave like ordinary people.

'But the fact remains, you are the noble daughter of the Raja of Mithila. 'Raja' means *king*. It is my title of kingship, therefore your correct title is, *Princess of Mithila*.'

'You're not serious?' Sita's mouth formed a wide "O". 'Are you actually saying I'm of royal blood?'

'Absolutely. Our old aristocratic way of life was eroded under colonial rule and our lands were taken over by the authorities. But they couldn't take our bloodline. And a royal princess as I said, gets to choose from a range of noble suitors. But this is where our particular family differs. Our dynasty's tradition, handed down from the Golden Age, involves the Great Bow of Shiva.'

'In what way, father?'

'It is said that the Great Bow itself, chooses the husband for the royal princess. A contest is traditionally held to determine the victor. He must lift the Great Bow of Shiva and string it. But this Great Bow is no ordinary object. It can only be lifted by an exceptional warrior, one who possesses a high degree of Shakti power. He must be integrated in mind and body. He will exhibit wisdom as well as courage.'

Sita digested this information in stunned silence. Confused thoughts raced around her mind like a dog chasing its tail. She tried to make sense of what her father was telling her. Eventually her voice came out a whisper.

'So ... Is this what you are proposing for *my* marriage, father?'

Raja Janak looked forlorn. He shook his head.

'No, my child. I cannot do it. I have been on the horns of a dilemma since you found that key. For I know it will only be a matter of time till the Great Bow is revealed.

'As you know, our family came to the west when you were a baby and you have been brought up here. In spite of that, as a family, we have tried to preserve the Old Ways from our ancient traditions. My problem stems from the fact that when you were born, I made a solemn promise to my grandfather. I told him that when the Great Bow of Shiva was re-discovered, I would hold the ceremony, which would lead to your marriage and uphold the rules of the tradition.

'But when you were growing up I observed your talent and intelligence. With the best of intentions I brought you up as a career girl. I convinced myself that The Bow would never be found. I thought that at some point in the fullness of time, you would meet someone, fall in love, and get married.'

His face assumed a resolute expression.

'So now I have come to a decision. I am going to forget about the tradition and leave it up to you to choose, if and when, you wish to marry.'

Now it was Sita's turn to look pensive. She had put all her energies into her career and had not given any serious thought to marriage. At least … her thoughts strayed … that is, until a certain person had come onto the scene the previous evening.

She had felt a spark the first moment when their eyes met. It was the stirring of an irresistible attraction that no words could explain. She had never believed in love at first sight. But now she had to acknowledge it had happened to her.

Sita had been brought up to regard marriage as a sacred commitment between two people. She had also been brought up to honour her promises. Once given, an honourable person's word cannot be broken.

Her mind was in turmoil. Tears stung her eyes at the thought of the sacrifice her father was proposing to make for her sake. Breaking his word to his ancestors would bring with it a terrible karma. She placed a hand tenderly on his arm.

'Father,' she spoke with firm authority. 'I cannot allow you to dishonour your word on my behalf.'

Raja Janak looked at her wonderingly as she continued.

'I have an idea. I think it will enable you to honour your sacred oath made to my great-grandfather in a modern way. You see, I have made a breakthrough in my scientific experiments and my equipment can show the workings of the brain. So, I propose to devise a unique Challenge. It will reveal who is the greatest and most Noble Arya of them all.'

'Are you sure, Sita?' said Raja Janak, anxious eyes searching her face.

'Yes. Absolutely,' she said. 'My mind is quite made up.'

'Very well,' said her father. 'In that case, invitations will be sent out to eligible suitors of noble families around the globe, to take part in the Challenge of the Great Bow of Shiva.'

'Father,' Sita rested her chin on her hand. 'I think it would be advisable to keep the actual details of the contest a secret, don't you?'

'Most certainly, my child,' said the wise Raja Janak. 'There are forces out there who would kill to get their hands on this priceless heirloom.'

11
MYSTERIES OF THE INDUS VALLEY

9:00PM

That evening Danny studied the notes he'd made while he still had the Almanac. He'd made a copy of his mother's flowing italic handwriting. He re-read them once more.

Seek the "arya" people. There is clear evidence they were advanced mathematicians and scientists. I am certain they hold important clues to the ancient civilizations. In particular, the Indus Valley Culture merits further investigation ...

Danny's eyes held a misty, far-away look as he recalled his mother's lively intelligence and wit. How he missed her. She used to take an interest in people of all cultures and backgrounds. She cared about them. She wanted the indigenous people to be given their rights.

He examined the map coordinates of the Indus River system on an old pre-1947 map of the Indian sub-continent. It was to the west of India, and on the border of what later became Pakistan. The Indus flowed down to the Arabian Sea in the south and the vast Thar Desert was to the east. The Himalayas were to the north and the Hindu Kush lay to the west. Further to the west was Turkey and beyond that, was Europe.

As the evening wore on his eyelids grew heavy and he fell asleep.

4:00 am

Danny became aware of the sounds of water lapping at the hull of the boat he was on. He felt it rocking gently to and fro. He could hear nearby voices giving commands and when he opened his eyes fully, he saw he was at the quayside of a bustling port. It was on a very wide river and, judging by the style of boat and the costume of the people, he had a feeling this was the River Indus.

Danny realized he was seeing the Indus Culture at a time when it was a thriving, bustling, exciting port on a busy trading route.

There were shouted instructions from the quayside as boats were unloaded and loaded. It smelt of the sea, mingled with odours of fish, incense and wood smoke. There were cooking smells from several stalls on the land. People were queuing up to buy food.

Danny looked up. Arching over him and supported on carved wooden posts was a colourful embroidered canopy. It provided welcome shade from the hot sun. He lay on silken cushions while a servant wafted a soft brush-like fan over him. Several other people were also under the canopy and Danny guessed by their rich raiment they were wealthy merchants.

'Is this the River Indus?' Danny enquired of a merchant wearing a turban and richly embroidered robes. The man looked at him curiously.

'But of course it is. There is no mistaking it. Such a cultured people who are renowned for their learning and affluence -'

He broke off as a commotion suddenly broke out at the quayside, indicated by raised voices. At one of the many stalls on the paved quay, a woman wearing a colourful red sari was embroiled in a heated argument with a seedy looking trader. She carried a basket over her arm and looked as if she was a local housewife. She seemed to be most indignant, holding some fruit up and gesticulating to those around her. She called to one of the nearby officials, a scribe in long robes taking note of goods, to help her.

'This visiting trader is using loaded weights and measures!' she complained. 'Not like Iravan from Babylon, here,' she gestured to the neighbouring stall. 'He uses the proper Indus weights and measures which are always straight and true.'

'Let me see,' said the official striding over. 'This is a serious offence if it is found to be proven.'

He produced a set of weighing scales and carefully checked the balancing weights in the pans on either side.

'They should be the standardised one gram, five grams, ten grams, fifty grams and so on.' He continued his calculations, his expression growing more and more stern. 'You spoke correctly, Aneeta,' he said to the lady. 'These weights are not the Indus weights.' He addressed the rogue trader. 'You will be reported for this, and dealt with by the authorities.'

Danny's eyes widened at this demonstration of sophisticated trading standards. So the Indus people really were honest traders as his mother had speculated. And their precision in weights and measures was another indication of their acuity in mathematics.

On the boat, Danny realized a servant was offering refreshments to the occupants. As he helped himself to little cakes from the tray, ever curious, he questioned the other travellers.

'I am a visitor to this country from a far off land,' he said. 'And I'm interested to know where you have all come from and what the purpose of your visit is?'

A wealthy merchant in an ornate blue silk tunic with a pearl clasp, answered.

'I come from Haran in Anatolia to trade with the Indus markets. They have beautiful carnelian beads and lapis lazuli for our jewellery. They have skilled goldsmiths and craftsmen. They are always fair in their dealings with us.'

'These Indus people,' said another merchant who wore pleated white linen robes. 'Are themselves great travellers and traders. They bring goods back here from many lands. I regularly come all the way from Egypt on behalf of our Pharaoh to trade with them here. See, here are the clay seals they put on my shipment. Everything is meticulously recorded by the Indus governors.'

'I come from the far-off land of Kambodia,' said another merchant.

Danny noted he had intricate patterns neatly woven into his hair and beard. 'Our horses are highly prized by the Indus citizens. We have been trading partners for millennia. This is recorded in our cultural history.'

'There are many famous trading routes o'er land and sea,' a portly nobleman stated. 'They have existed for millennia.' He was wearing a richly appliqued yellow robe slung over one shoulder. A golden pendant in the shape of a cross hung round his neck. Danny wondered where had he seen that before?

'The Indus folk trade with my people, the Su-Meru,' he continued. 'We Sumerians originally came from the Indus and are related to them.'

'Do the Indus people travel across the sea?' Danny asked.

'Why, yes,' said the nobleman. 'They visit many foreign countries overseas, travelling long distances in their fine ships. They visit the lands of Dilmun in Arabia, the lands of the Norse and the Celts, the lands of the Rus and the Olmecs.'

'Oh look!' the first merchant nudged Danny and pointed to the quay-side. 'Mahesh the Scribe is beckoning to you. He wants you to go ashore. If you're lucky, he might give you a chance to tour the city.'

Mahesh the Scribe had a neat, dark beard and his long hair was wound up and tied into a topknot. He wore a white robe, arranged over one shoulder. In his hand he carried a bound casebook.

'What is your name, young man?

'I'm called Danny,' he hesitated. 'Er. I am not from -'

'You are not from these parts, I know,' the scribe said. 'Many people come here to learn from us, not just to trade. I will take you through the city which is built on exactly the same lines as the other cities of the Indus Culture, Danny.'

He led Danny up the wide boulevard towards the temple complex at the top of the hill. As they walked Danny saw streets running off at right angles. There were many fine two-storey houses with shutters. Each had sophisticated drainage and sanitation systems. Everything was immaculately clean, newly sprinkled with water that smelt of flowers.

There were lush green communal gardens with fruit trees and fountains where groups of citizens sat and chatted and passed the time of day. Children played happily with their toys in the streets watched by fond parents. Danny was surprised to see how well-dressed everyone was and how well-fed and affluent they looked.

'This Indus city reminds me of the city of Ayodhya, Rama's birthplace,' Danny remarked. 'But strangely, it also reminds me of Angkor Wat. How can this be, Mahesh, sir, when they were built so many thousands of years apart?'

'That is a good observation, Danny,' Mahesh said. 'Do you know which direction the front entrance always faces?'

'Is it the east?'

'Correct,' said the scribe. 'You will see the front door is always placed to the east in all the cities. When you see that, you know the culture uses the principles of Vastu Veda in their architecture.'

'Why do they always face towards the east, sir?'

'The eastern direction,' Mahesh the Scribe said. 'Is the most auspicious direction. It harnesses the energy of the rising sun to re-charge the batteries of the in-dwellers of the property.'

'What is '*the Veda*'?' said Danny.

'The Veda,' said Mahesh. 'Is the eternal wisdom of the universe in which resides all the Laws of Nature. The Veda is all the knowledge that ever existed past, present or future. It exists independent of any man or woman in much the same way, as gravity or electro-magnetism exists as a law in its own right.'

'So it's not a religion?' said Danny.

Mahesh was surprised at the question.

'No. The Veda operates on purely scientific and mathematical laws. It's not a religion. A religion is a set of beliefs. The Veda is the blueprint of the universe that underpins all existence in much the same way as the sap permeates and supports all the varieties of trees in a forest. It exists regardless of whether anybody believes in it or not. It was only through their own consciousness that the ancient seers were able to cognise its workings.'

Danny blinked as Mahesh continued.

'Danny, always remember that *wisdom* is far superior to cleverness.

They had by now reached the entrance to the temple. As they passed beneath its ornately carved and richly decorated gatehouse, they entered the cool marble cloisters of the inner courtyard.

'You will learn more in the fullness of time,' said Mahesh. 'But right now, Danny, I have instructions to bring you to one who wishes to meet you.'

They rounded a corner and Danny saw a dignified figure in an orange-robe standing in the shade. He had long white hair and beard and held a tall staff in one hand. As he stepped forward into the sunlight, Danny gasped.

'Sage Vasishta! Honourable sir. I did not expect to find you here.'

'I am travelling through the lands over which King Dasarat rules,' said the sage. 'He is a most wise and fair ruler, beloved by all his people. He sent me to visit the lands of the Rig Veda, whose hymns praise the mighty River Indus as well as the River Saraswati.'

His face became grave as he continued.

'But destiny brought you here to meet me, Danny, as I have to entrust you with a key mission -'

As he spoke, Danny suddenly felt as if a lead weight had descended on him and was pushing him downwards to the ground. It was all he could do to remain upright, so great was the load he bore.

'What you are feeling now,' said the sage. 'Is the darkness, the ignorance, which typifies the Kali Yuga. It is weighing you down. It is heavy with the negative energy that the Dark One generates when he dominates the world. The era in which your people are living is only at the beginning of the Kali Yuga, the cosmic time cycle that lasts for four hundred and thirty-two thousand years. Ravana's destructive strength is growing more powerful and it will continue to grow unless he can be stopped.'

'Who could possibly stop him?' Danny asked.

'There is only one person who can lift this terrible weight and destroy the Kali Yuga,' Sage Vasishta said. 'And that is Rama. But in order to bring the light which will destroy the darkness that is Ravana, he must have Sita by his side.'

Danny gasped. 'But Rama is on a mission for the mighty Vishwamitra. Lakshman told me he is not allowed to consider marriage without his Guru's permission. There is no way they can be brought together.'

'You, and you alone, Danny Hanuman,' said the sage. 'Must find a way to achieve this difficult task. There is no one else who can do it ...'

Danny desperately wanted to ask what on earth he could do, but the swirling mist appeared before his eyes and he knew he was travelling back through the corridor of time...

The next morning Danny didn't have any time for reflection, as he had to make an early start. He set off on his bike, heading for the park. The students had agreed to meet before proceeding to the university campus for the morning's session. The rendezvous was to be the breakfast kiosk situated near one of the entrances on the far side of the park.

Danny chose to avoid the main pathway, which joggers and dog-walkers frequented. He took the minor path that led down a hill towards a wooded area, which followed alongside a stream. He breathed in deeply, enjoying the mossy smells and sounds of the gurgling brook and birdsong. As he was riding up the hill on the other side of the dell, he spotted Izzie in the distance. She was jogging along one of the pathways with her earphones in.

A raven flew down and landed on a tree ahead of Danny. He remembered some

chilling stories he'd heard about them at the Tower of London. They were highly intelligent birds, but ferocious scavengers.

His attention was suddenly riveted on Izzie. She was heading for an area of dense rhododendron bushes on her way to the kiosk. But what she hadn't seen was a dark shadow lurking behind the thicket.

With a jolt, Danny realized the man in hiding looked to be waiting for her to come alongside him. He began to pedal furiously to warn her, to get within earshot at the very least before the potential attack. Why on earth did she have to have earphones in?

As Izzie reached the shrubbery she bent over for a moment to catch her breath. At the same time, a burly figure stepped out in front of her. Her eyes widened as she straightened up and saw him. Another man came in from the nearby entrance and was now behind her. A car was sidling along the kerb in the street outside.

Danny's lungs were full to bursting as he pedalled frantically, pushing himself to reach her in time.

Izzie straightened up. Her heart beat fast as she took in the potential attacker. He was wearing a grey hoodie and was taller and stockier than her. But not only was she fit, she was a resourceful girl. As he reached out to grab her, she did a back flip. When she landed, she gave a high kick-box, landing her foot squarely on the thug's jaw. It took him by surprise, but not for long. His expression of pain gave way to an ugly look.

By now the second man had reached her. He sneaked up behind Izzie and pinned her arms to her side. She lashed out with her feet but the first man kept a wary distance. He moved quickly to put his hand over her mouth to silence her yells for help. Suddenly he pulled his hand away and bellowed.

'Ow! The bloody bitch has bitten me!'

The two men then redoubled their efforts to drag a furious, struggling Izzie, through the exit to the waiting car.

Danny was nearly there, when he saw Hugo thudding along the path. He had also seen the incident and was coming to the rescue. He reached the scene at the same time as Danny. Hugo's big frame landed a rugby tackle on the attacker at the rear. Danny rode his bicycle and rammed it hard into the legs of the other attacker from behind.

A park-keeper's whistle sounded the alarm as he spotted the incident.

The two men ran off, leaving Izzie red-faced and seething.

'How *dared* they touch me!' she demanded of the two boys. 'And they had the cheek to tell me I had to stop the research.'

When the police came, they took very little notice of Izzie's comments, viewing the incident very much in the light of a recent increase in attacks on women joggers in the park.

It was a shaken group of students that met up at the kiosk. They sat round one of the tables and discussed the increasing threat level to their project. A 'ping' on Izzie's phone made her check her messages.

'Listen to this, guys,' she said, the colour all drained out of her face.

Miss Dalton. Take this morning as a warning. Stop your colleagues carrying out further research before it is too late. Signed, The Aculeata.

'Well it's not going to stop us, that's for sure,' Izzie rallied, her belligerent tone challenging the others.

'Okay,' Danny agreed, cautiously. 'We won't let it stop us. But we'll have to be more on our guard in future.'

'But we can't let them win!' Izzie reiterated.

'It might mean we're on to something they don't want us to know,' said Urmila.

'I suggest,' said Sandeep. 'That we go into this morning's meeting as if nothing has happened. And then let's watch Zeuber and Merrick's faces.'

'Agreed,' said Hugo. 'And we'll only tell the tutors afterwards, once we're able to be on our own with them.'

THE MUSEUM COMMITTEE sat in the university's boardroom, a large airy room painted pale green with white stucco-work on its high ceilings and plush green carpet on the floor. The mullioned windows looked out onto a paved quadrangle surrounded by other sandstone and brick buildings.

Twelve committee members were ranged along the boardroom table together with Dr O'Donnell and Dr Greenwood. Rama and Lakshman had been invited as experts in the Indus Valley Culture.

Professor Plendergarth checked his watch.

'The students are late, Dr Greenwood.'

Richard frowned. 'I don't know what can have kept them. They are not normally late.'

At that moment, the door opened and the five students trooped in. They seemed a little subdued, Kirsty noted, but there was a determined gleam in their eye.

Their arrival was apparently not welcomed by everyone. Dr Zeuber's hard eyes narrowed and he looked down at his papers. Dr Merrick gave the students a disparaging look, before dropping a bombshell. He addressed the Museum Committee in persuasive tones.

'I propose,' he said, looking round the table. 'That we stop financing the *'Quest for the Ancient Sea Kings'* and instead, focus on the more well-known *European* cultures, such as the Greeks.'

Danny's jaw dropped in horror. All the students looked equally dumbstruck. They gazed at the finance director, open-mouthed at this betrayal of the curator and his work.

'I agree with my colleague,' said Dr Zeuber, smoothly. 'We must bear in mind that the people of the Indus Valley didn't have the benefit of the Europeans' *civilising* influence. A few thousand years ago, they were just primitives. As my colleague, Dr Merrick says, we should look to the classics. The Greeks after all, have influenced us right up to the present day with their language and culture.

Kirsty O'Donnell's eyes were ablaze as she leaned forward to address the chairman.

'I can hardly believe my ears, Professor Plendergarth!' she exclaimed. 'I must protest those biased remarks in the strongest terms. That is the bigoted attitude that justified the invasion of other countries and the looting of their wealth.'

'What is more,' said Richard Greenwood, steely jawed. 'Dr Zeuber is assuming superiority over indigenous people because they are from the east, as if they are less intelligent than people from the west. This is not borne out by the evidence as we shall hear this morning.'

'Learned colleagues,' Professor Plendergarth's eyes were stern over his half-moon glasses. 'We will strike Dr Zeuber's remarks from the record and members will desist from making such comments in the future.

'Dr Greenwood,' he continued. 'On behalf of the Museum Committee I invite your students to tell us about their research on the Indus Valley Culture in the context of your Quest for the ancient *Sea Kings*.'

'Let me give you some background to the discovery of this remarkable site,' Richard Greenwood said. 'Archaeological excavations were carried out in the Indus Valley region back in the nineteen twenties and thirties. Their discoveries astonished the world. They had revealed two remarkable cities of the ancient world, Harappa and Mohenjo-daro. Their dwellings displayed remarkable evidence they'd been created by an advanced civilisation, more so than anyone had believed possible back then. The likes of this culture had simply never been seen before.'

'What was so great about them?' queried Councillor Hitchin, mopping his florid countenance. He gave a dismissive wave of his hand-kerchief. 'Surely they are just another of these 'lost civilisations' that we'll never know much about.'

'Let us keep an open mind on the subject, Councillor,' said Professor Plendergarth with firm authority. 'I would like the students to report their research findings to the committee.'

The students braced themselves for what looked like being a gruelling session.

'We examined a number of mysteries,' Izzie began. 'That surround the Indus Valley civilisation. Firstly, there was its great antiquity of over 9,500 years –'

'Objection!' came Zeuber's voice from the far end of the table. His sharp weasel features and beady eyes were alert, ready to pounce on anything. 'The Indus Culture is only around 3,500 years-old, according to the history books.

'The *history books*,' Kirsty O'Donnell said tartly, putting her hands on her hips for emphasis. 'Are sadly out of date if they give such erroneous information, Dr Zeuber. Our evidence shows the Indus Valley inhabitants were a remarkable culture which flourished at least 9,500 years ago on the Indian sub-continent.'

Zeuber's lips formed a thin smile but it didn't reach his cold glittering eyes.

'Do you have any evidence to back up your claims as to this great antiquity, Dr O'Donnell? You've managed to lose the Almanac, after all.'

Kirsty O'Donnell gritted her teeth but she held her ground, knowing the committee were hanging on her words.

'The students' research,' she said. 'Shows the Indus Civilisation was a sophisticated culture with well-developed technology over 10,000 years ago. I will now call on the students to show the committee their scientific evidence.'

Danny switched on the wall-mounted projector screen. An image of a human skull with an intact set of teeth was displayed.

'This is a skull that was found in the ancient Indus Valley region,' he said. 'When scientists examined it in detail, they were astonished to discover evidence that sophisticated dental work had been carried out on it.' He enlarged the image to show a small, neat, perfectly round hole in one of the teeth.

'This tooth,' Urmila continued. 'Has evidence of a remarkable skill in advanced dentistry. In other words, it was worked on by a qualified and trained dentist.'

'If it's not been published and peer reviewed, then it's not proof,' blustered Merrick.

'Hang on a minute,' said Izzie. 'We're not finished yet.'

Merrick gave her a hostile look as she continued.

'This scientific discovery was published in the prestigious science journal, 'Nature.' The article explains they invited a leading modern dentist to examine the tooth. After close examination, he pronounced the dental work to be so skilled that it would rival any modern dentistry of today.'

'What did the scientists conclude was the age of the tooth?' Professor Plendergarth enquired, pen poised.

'Scientific dating,' said Kirsty O'Donnell. 'Revealed the age of the tooth to be over 9,500 years old. And when we consider that this medical procedure was already well established, we have to conclude that the Indus Civilisation must go back considerably further than this date. Together with other evidence, it's fair to say it is over 10,000 years old.'

'That's interesting,' commented Councillor Thompson, a genial looking man with an ample girth and a receding hairline. He looked keen and alert as he jotted down notes. 'What other evidence was found?'

'They discovered a set of surgical instruments,' Sandeep said. 'That date from 10,000 years ago. They are remarkably similar in design to those that modern surgeons use to this day.'

There were exclamations of surprise from the members.

'Extraordinary!'

'Is it possible the discipline of surgery is really that old?'

'It needs to be investigated further.'

'It merits proper funding.'

'Another Indus mystery,' said Urmila. 'Surrounds the question of writing. Surely such a sophisticated culture must have had a system of writing? There is evidence on the thousands of Indus clay seals that shows they did. And there is evidence the Indus culture had knowledge of Sanskrit, which is the oldest writing in the world. The Rig Veda is written in Sanskrit –'

Dr Zeuber's eyebrows snapped together. He interrupted abruptly.

'The Rig Veda has nothing to do with the Indus Valley Culture.'

'But I disagree,' said Urmila. 'The Rig Veda text actually refers to the River Indus and its culture over and over again –'

'You can't prove that,' Zeuber butted in again. 'Unless you are a Sanskrit scholar, as I am. That makes *me* qualified to interpret the ancient Sanskrit writings of the Rig Veda because *I* am an acknowledged authority on the language-'

'As a matter of fact,' Sandeep cut in. 'Urmila is too modest to say it, but she is an acknowledged expert in Sanskrit. She already has a degree in the subject. But the big difference is, Dr Zeuber, that in the east, we are trained to understand the depth of *wisdom* which underpins our cultural writings – a fact which the Eurocentric view totally misses.'

The dig went home. Zeuber looked daggers at Sandeep.

'Well,' Dr Zeuber persisted, doggedly. 'You can't *prove* the Rig Veda writing has anything to do with the Indus culture!'

'As a matter of fact, we can,' Urmila spoke with calm authority. 'It has a great deal to do with it, according to the expert scholars. The Sanskrit text of the Rig Veda extensively praises the Indus River. The words, *'flow Indu for Indra'* are repeated many times over. 'Indu' is the shortened form of the River Indus.'

'And what is more,' said Izzie. 'The Rig Veda identifies sophisticated divisions of labour in the Indus society.'

'Like what?' Merrick sneered. 'They were just a bunch of wandering nomads from Europe.'

'That's not true!' retorted Izzie. 'They were the indigenous people, and highly cultured. This is made clear if you read the translation of the

Rig Veda, Dr Merrick. The literature describes various occupations, such as goldsmiths, farmers of milk cows, and grain, cooks, archers, physicians and doctors, priests, astronomers and mathematicians.'

Dr Merrick gave a meaningful look at Zeuber.

'Well, the Rig Veda people didn't know about the sea so you can rule them out as contenders for the *Sea Kings*,' Zeuber shot at Kirsty O'Donnell.

'That's nonsense!' Danny snorted as he thought about his vision. 'The Rig Veda people knew about the sea very well. They traded extensively with other countries overseas and had fine sea-going vessels -'

He stopped abruptly, aware that everyone was looking at him. How was he going to explain the details? He racked his brains but nothing came.

Urmila glanced at him curiously for a moment.

'I agree with Danny,' she said. 'There are many references in the Rig Veda about rivers which flow to the sea, and to the ocean. They were well aware of the *'western sea'* and *'the eastern sea'.'*

'Therefore,' said Richard Greenwood. 'We can't rule out the Indus civilisation as contenders for the *Sea Kings*, certainly not at this stage.'

Professor Plendergarth nodded agreement. But suddenly Zeuber's face assumed a triumphant look.

'Of course,' he said. 'This is an undeniably advanced culture, because the people came from *Europe.'*

Professor Plendergarth looked surprised. 'Are you referring to the *Aryan Invasion Theory* Dr Zeuber?'

'Indeed I am,' he replied.

'Can one of your students explain that theory to the committee, please?' Councillor Thompson's pen poised over his notebook.

'It's another mystery we investigated,' said Sandeep. 'The Indus Valley excavations made world headlines in the 1920s because they had discovered a previously unknown civilization, which was extremely advanced. The problem with this was, it challenged the prevailing westernized theories of history. These held that people in the era deemed as 'prehistory' were merely primitive savages.'

'The identity of this advanced civilization was deemed a mystery,' said Kirsty O'Donnell. 'That was discussed at length in academic circles. The European archaeologists claimed that so sophisticated a culture must surely have descended from invaders outside of the Indian sub-continent. They must therefore have come from Europe rather than the so-called 'primitive' cultures of the east.

'It was a short step,' said Richard Greenwood. 'To the invention of a very Eurocentric notion called the *Aryan Invasion Theory*. This said that a cultured nomadic people from Europe, invaded the Indus Valley and created a sophisticated civilisation, ousting the primitive locals.

'This news came to the ears of a certain politician in Austria, who would later become the feared and hated fascist dictator, Hitler. He became fascinated by the idea of an advanced race. Just who were these Indus people? Could they have a Germanic origin? He stole the name that appeared in the Sanskrit writings, the *Aryans*. In his warped mind, he created a plan for a 'super-race' that would be superior to all others.'

'Extraordinary!' said Councillor Thompson. 'I had no idea that's where Hitler got his idea from.'

Professor Plendergarth addressed the two noble brothers.

'Rama, as you and your brother are both distinguished Sanskrit scholars,' he said. 'I would like to ask for your opinion of the *Aryan Invasion Theory*.'

Rama nodded graciously.

'With pleasure, professor,' he said. 'We would interpret the linguistics first of all. The word *'arya'* was used from ancient times by the indigenous people of the Indian sub-continent to refer to themselves. It applied to all those who were born in the land of the Veda which was then Greater India.'

'You see,' Lakshman explained. 'The word *Arya* means 'noble' or 'honourable' in Sanskrit. Therefore it would certainly not be the actions of a noble or honourable person to invade another's country, steal its lands, and subjugate its people. It would go against the rules of the peaceful *arya* society.'

'Moreover,' said Rama. 'There is the ancient Indian tradition of using titles of respect, with the Sanskrit *arya* root. 'Acharya,' for example, means a highly respected teacher. That is, Ach-*arya*. The highest religious office in the land of India is the title of 'Shankaracharya.' This is the equivalent of the Pope in western cultures and he is highly honoured and respected. Note it has the 'arya' root in the title, Shankara-ach-*arya*.

'I see your point,' Professor Plendergarth looked thoughtful. 'India is renowned for its long cultural traditions. So the term *'Arya'* would not be used and maintained for a bunch of marauding invaders from the Steppes of Europe or anywhere else for that matter.'

'It seems to me,' said Councillor Thompson, rubbing his brow. 'That the old *Aryan Invasion Theory* has been highly politicized. It has been used as a tool to keep the indigenous people of India in ignorance of their own noble *Arya* birthright.'

'It is not usually known,' said Richard Greenwood. 'That Hitler was so impressed with the advanced Indus culture that he resolved to recreate his own version of it. He stole the name, 'Aryan' to use for his own planned super-race. He misappropriated the Indus people's ancient symbol for 'good luck,' which happened to be the swastika. He reversed it and put it on all his flags.

'He tried to find out whatever ancient knowledge he could in order to use it for his own nefarious ends. He spread the *Aryan Invasion Theory* because he believed, as many Europeans did in those days, that *they* were the only truly civilised race and therefore must be superior by birth.'

'The irony is,' said Kirsty O'Donnell. 'The real *'arya'* people of the Indus Valley culture were a peace-loving society. There is no evidence of violent conflict anywhere in any excavated sites. As pacifists they were the exact opposite of Hitler's intended society.'

'So, are you proposing,' said Professor Plendergarth. 'The Indus Culture as serious contenders for the ancient *Sea Kings?*'

'Indeed, yes,' said Richard Greenwood. 'But there is yet another ancient culture which may bring our Quest even closer to the truth. We will be examining that civilisation tomorrow.'

The Museum Committee as a whole, looked impressed. But three of its members were silent. Zeuber, tight-lipped, was sending a text message. Councillor Hitchin with a scowl, pulled out a spotted handkerchief and mopped his perspiring brow. Dr Merrick frowningly composed an email.

'Cor,' said Hugo in an aside to Danny. 'This Hitler stuff sounds like the movie, *Raiders of the Lost Ark*, if you ask me.'

'Except, this is *true*,' Danny said. 'And it's still being carried on to this day, by *someone* out there.'

If the students had been able to see the contents of Zeuber's text message, they would have been horrified.

AFTER GENERAL MARICHA gave his report on the morning's proceedings, there was an ominous silence. He waited in some trepidation for a response. The Dark One began to fire off a series of questions.

'You have the Almanac?'

'Affirmative, sire.'

'Do they suspect our plans?'

'No, sire,' said the General.

'Yet they mentioned the Fuhrer?' said the Dark One.

'But only in a historical sense, sire.'

'Maricha, take note! That female is a person of interest to us.'

'Which one, sire?'

'The one they call, *Urmila*.'

12

THE NOBLE ONES OF SOUTH AMERICA

THAT EVENING DANNY came to a decision. With the loss of the Almanac had gone important evidence. He felt it justified a new plan of action. It wasn't just to satisfy his personal curiosity any more. He had to do what he had to do to protect his friends. He would just have to risk the consequences with his father.

He waited till everyone had gone to bed and then crept down the back stairs by torchlight. He entered his father's study and with trembling fingers took the parcel out of the drawer. He slit it open and drew out the contents.

When he saw what he held in his hands, his pulse began to race as if it had done a circuit of Brans Hatch. *It was his mother's missing notebook.*

Slowly, almost reverently, he turned the pages. It was packed full of her research data. Clues, like nuggets of gold, took the form of sketches, notes and cryptic Sanskrit words. He made a note of the map coordinates she'd given under the heading, *'The Noble Ones of South America'*. He would need them for his next, and possibly most dangerous, Remote Viewing session.

4:00 am

Hot dry winds blew across the Bolivian Plateau like a giant hairdryer. All Danny's senses were heightened as his vision soared like a bird over the land. He saw below him the world's largest salt flat, the Salar de Uyuni. It was near the crest of the Andes at an elevation of 12,000 feet above sea level. Under its briny crust were rich levels of lithium.

He recalled that it had been used as a location for the filming of one of the Star Wars movies.

He flew on over the High Andes mountain range until he saw the extraordinary sight of Lake Titikaka, the highest lake in the world. It glittered like a mirror below him.

On its banks, he discovered the City of the Ancients, known as Tiwanaku. It was still sacred to the local Aymara people. Within its hallowed boundaries his mother's notes had indicated he must seek out the seven-stepped Akapana Pyramid. He had to investigate the Kalasasaya courtyard with its mysterious standing stone figures. And further afield, he had to find the massive machine-precision stones of the Puma Punku.

In the distance he could see a tall figure walking along the coastal path. It was a route that had been laid down by the ancients with remarkable engineering skill. The man drew closer and Danny saw he had pale skin, white hair, and a white beard. He carried a staff and wore sandals on his feet. He was quite unlike the indigenous people who were small, dark skinned and dark haired.

Dr Anjani Hanuman had recorded the legends cherished by the indigenous South American cultures. They told how the sage, Viracocha, known to all as the Noble One, had come from over the seas. He brought with him knowledge of science, of mathematics, engineering, and spiritual teachings. In different regions of the continent, he had a variety of names. But always his civilizing mission remained the same. He always taught wisdom, practical knowledge of science, mathematics, engineering, and agriculture. He brought governance, which fostered a peaceful way of life for the people.

Danny was consumed by a desire to meet this fascinating person.

Many questions burned in his mind and Sage Viracocha was just the person to shed light on the mysteries of this ancient culture.

Along the wide boulevards and extensive docks on the edge of Lake Titikaka, Danny walked till he arrived at a thriving port. People in colourful robes were loading and unloading their goods from boats onto the quayside. It struck Danny that the design of their ships bore a remarkable resemblance to the reed boats he'd seen in Ancient Egypt. How mysterious. Could there be a connection?

He followed the bullock drawn wagons transporting the goods into the inner city of Tiwanaku, the city sacred to the Aymara people. He could tell it was a highly sophisticated society by its divisions of labour. There were priests, highly skilled astronomers, engineers, artists, scribes and stonemasons. They had adopted the wise system of leadership laid down by the Sage Viracocha. It led to a well-structured and orderly community where everyone prospered.

As Danny entered the city walls, he saw a throng of people. They were all clustered around the Sage Viracocha, and all clamouring for his attention. But he silenced them with a wave of his elegant hand. He looked over at Danny and gestured for him to approach.

When Danny gazed into those wise eyes, he knew he was in the presence of a great soul. Viracocha exuded an air of calm authority, of compassion, of deep understanding. It was easy to believe he knew past, present and future.

'Ask your question, young man,' he said. 'And I will answer.'

'Sir,' Danny said. 'Can you tell me more about this sacred place and how it relates to the wisdom of the ancient *Sea Kings?*'

'Come,' said the illustrious sage. 'Let me take you to see our city and I will explain.'

He led Danny through the wide streets until up ahead of them was the seven-stepped structure known as the Akapana Pyramid.

'Is there an overall plan for the city of Tiwanaku?' Danny enquired.

'Indeed, there is,' Viracocha said. 'We build our cities according to the blueprint laid down by our architects. They in turn consult with our priest-astronomers who are experts in the science of *Vastu* Veda. They model everything on the Vedic principle of *'As above, so below.'* In other words, they make a design which recreates what is known of the heavenly plane onto the earth below.'

'Why are there seven tiers to the pyramid, sir?'

'Each step of the Akapana Pyramid represents the seven states of consciousness which a human can attain on earth. There are also seven realms of the heavenly abode, each one more glorious than the last. The pinnacle is beyond mortal dreams of happiness.'

'Was an ancient legend involved in the design?'

'Yes, Danny, the whole city complex is modelled on the Legend of the Churning of the Milk Ocean, which you may have heard of. It comes from the dawn of time.'

'I know of that legend, sir,' said Danny. 'Is there evidence of spirals used in the pyramid's construction?'

'Watch!' said Sage Viracocha. He struck the ground three times with his wooden staff. Immediately from the skies above the pyramid, dark clouds began to form. Monsoon rains poured down onto the pyramid and ran in through an eight-pointed opening at the very top of the building.

Danny heard a thunderous roar as the water cascaded through this opening and down into the interior body of the structure. It got louder and louder, until it emerged from a channel at the bottom and flowed into the Kalasasaya Courtyard as a foaming mass of white water.

'How has it produced that effect?' Danny gasped. 'It looks just like the churned-up ocean would have looked in the legend, like milk!'

'It's thanks to the ingenuity of our engineers,' said the sage. 'Inside the pyramid is a series of channels which descend from the top in a spiral arrangement. As the water is funnelled through the channels, bubbles of air are forced into the water giving it the appearance of foaming milk.'

'Sir,' said Danny. 'I can see three mysterious figures which are in the middle of the courtyard. Now it has filled up with water, they look as if they are emerging from this 'milky' ocean. It seems this how they are meant to be seen, because they have fish scales carved on their lower half as if they are oceanic beings. Who do they represent?'

'They are what you might call, *Lords of the Seas*,' said Viracocha.

'Or *Sea Kings*?' suggested Danny.

But before Viracocha could describe them to Danny, there was a disturbance. A deep rumbling noise came from within the very bowels of the earth beneath him. The ground beneath Danny's feet shook violently and rocked him from side to side. Massive geophysical forces were at work.

Danny experienced the tunnel of light that led back to his normal state. However, once home in his bedroom he began to feel uneasy. His intuition told him something was out there, lurking, waiting. It would not be long before it tried to attack him. He knew he was not ready. His training was nowhere near complete …

He sat up in a cold sweat, gripped by a strong premonition. A great danger lay ahead of him that day…

8:00 am

General Maricha spoke curtly to his agent in the field.

'What do you have to report?'

The person on the other end of the phone hesitated. He answered cautiously.

'Well. You see, General. The problem is these students are revealing certain facts which are not known to the mainstream. Especially that Hanuman kid. We don't know how he is doing it.'

'It is imperative that you find the Notebook,' Maricha said. 'It contains too much valuable information, which must not be made public under any circumstances.'

'I understand,' said the caller. 'The danger is it could lead the nations concerned to take a pride in their cultural identity.'

'Doctor,' said General Maricha. 'This Hanuman kid seems to be coming up with insights that are not from any of our authorized text-books. He may be getting his information from his mentor, Rama. In which case, it is imperative that we find a way to eliminate that Kalari exponent and prevent his influence from spreading.'

'He is a formidable warrior, sir.'

'So are *we!*' the general snapped, hitting the phone for emphasis.

'Devise a way to defeat him that he least expects.'

General Maricha slammed the phone down. But he hadn't been the only one on the line listening to the conversation.

There was a pause. Then the Dark One, known also as Ravana, spoke softly, his voice laden with menacing displeasure.

'You have allowed them to get this far in their research, General Maricha? Do you mean to tell me we have gone to all this trouble to conceal the true nature of the ancient world, and you are letting a bunch of kids blow the thing out of the water?'

General Maricha shifted uneasily.

'Er, sire. The chances are their research won't go any further -'

'*What!* Are you *mad*?' The Dark One's voice rose by several decibels. 'They are already getting publicity for their 'discoveries' through this O'Donnell woman and her documentaries. And the museum Curator is promoting them. Worse is to come if that kid uncovers any more facts.'

'What are your orders, sire?'

'Maricha. You will disrupt their activities by whatever means are necessary. Do I make myself clear?'

8:30 am

Once he met up with the others that morning, Danny shook off his feelings of unease, telling himself he had an overactive imagination.

They met at the main entrance of Blackthorn Park, the sprawling green amenity belonging to the City of Manchester. It was where Kirsty O'Donnell had organised the Culture Heritage Festival to celebrate the indigenous cultures of the world.

There were colourful marquees dotted throughout the lush facility to represent the many nationalities present. Delegates from each country had been setting up their marquees from the early hours of the morning. There were traditional costumes and crafts on display, as well as food, music, dancing and re-enactments of legends and folk tales.

Sounds of the Andean pan-pipes floated on the breeze.

'I love that music,' said Sandeep.

'Never mind the music, mate,' said Hugo, sniffing the air. 'Just smell that Mexican food.'

As the students skirted their way round the manicured green lawns and neat pathways, Danny heard a 'ping' as a message came in on his phone.

He nearly dropped it as he read the contents.

Mr Hanuman. Stop the Quest for the Ancient Sea Kings immediately, or you will suffer the consequences. Don't say you have not been warned.

The Aculeata

Danny read his message out loud to the others. Minutes later, they all heard their phones 'ping.'

'I don't believe it!' Izzie stamped her foot in annoyance as she read the same sinister message. 'How *dare* they threaten us? Just who *are* these people?'

'We can't let them force us to stop our research,' Sandeep said.

'But what do they mean, *or you will suffer the consequences?*' said Urmila, her eyes wide in dismay.

'Hey, guys,' Hugo exclaimed. 'Look over there! Dr Greenwood is waving to us. Can you see him, he's by the marquee with the red and yellow bunting?'

'You're late!' Richard Greenwood tapped his watch. A deep groove ridged his forehead as they came up to him. 'Dr O'Donnell said meet at 9.30.'

'But it's only a minute past 9.30am,' Izzie protested, checking her own watch.

'What's got into *him?*' Danny said in a low voice to Kirsty O'Donnell. She looked rather pale and hesitated before replying.

'Oh, dear. We've both had one of those threatening messages again. They want us to stop today's conference. But Richard thinks it's a hoax and he's angry. He refuses to be blackmailed.'

Danny showed her the message on his phone, as did the other students.

'I'll inform the police,' said Kirsty. 'They'll step up security. You must all be on your guard. If you see anything suspicious, immediately contact security. Eddie Salter is patrolling with his men. Stick together and don't go off on your own.'

'The delegates and audience are present,' said Richard sharply. 'Don't keep them waiting any longer.'

As the students entered, they saw the interior of the South American marquee had an enormous TV monitor at one end. On it was displayed an enlarged photo of the Andes Mountain range and soaring high above the snow-capped peaks was a magnificent condor, wings outstretched against a blue sky. They watched nervously as Kirsty O'Donnell's film crew took light readings and set up their equipment.

The audience consisted of invited guests, including the cultural exchange visitors. Representatives of South America's indigenous peoples were wearing their traditional ceremonial robes and decorations. Members of the press were also present. Danny's trepidation increased as he saw individuals from the Museum Committee taking their seats on the front row of the audience.

'OK, guys,' Dr Greenwood looked grim as he addressed the students. 'I hope you're all ready for our presentation. Be prepared for audience participation. They want it to be an interactive session with questions and answers. I can't emphasise how important this is. The future funding for our project hangs in the balance.'

'So no pressure!' Danny whispered to Hugo under his breath.

The students and tutors took up their positions on the raised platform in front of the monitor. The director indicated the cameras were rolling.

Izzie took a deep breath.

'Today we will explore one of the ancient cultures of South America. Could it lead us to the identity of the ancient *Sea Kings*?'

There were a few murmurs of interest from the audience.

'We start our investigation,' Izzie said. 'In the Bolivian region of the High Andes, nearby to mysterious Lake Titikaka, the highest and most unusual lake in the world.'

'What's the *mystery* about it?' Merrick butted in. 'It's just another freshwater lake, surely?'

Izzie shook her head emphatically.

'The strange thing about Lake Titikaka,' she said. 'Is that millions of years ago, it was right down at sea level. Then massive geophysical forces pushed it up high into the mountains. The evidence is in the geology, because all around the lake there are millions of sea fossils embedded in the rocks.'

'And what is more,' Sandeep interjected. 'The lake's fish and crustaceans still feature many *oceanic* rather than fresh-water types. The fishermen of Lake Titikaka, right up to the present day, regularly catch seahorses out of the lake.'

'Many mysteries,' Urmila continued. 'Surround this whole lake area. One of the most fascinating concerns the capital City of the Ancients, known as Tiwanaku. This was built close to the shores of Lake Titikaka.'

Dr Merrick cut in.

'You have to qualify what you mean by *'ancient.'* Our current theories date Tiwanaku to be only from around five hundred to one thousand five hundred years old. This is based on pottery shards, found at the site.'

'That surely is not a serious attempt at dating?' Danny derided, his tone incredulous. 'The pottery shards are from the *superficial* layers. Giving the site such a recent date ignores the facts from the South American experts. In fact, I would say it is a very Eurocentric interpretation.'

Merrick's eyes narrowed but he couldn't seem to stop Danny, who was in full flow.

'The whole area of Tiwanaku is much more ancient than you say, Dr Merrick. It's at least fifteen thousand years old, if we go by Professor Posnansky's painstaking research. And it's likely to be even older than that, according to the mathematical calculations in the Almanac.'

At this, there were a few murmurings from the audience and several reporters took avid notes.

'We have kept an open mind,' said Izzie. 'When researching this ancient culture and it has shown us the evidence of a greater antiquity than has been hitherto allowed.'

'You can't prove those facts without the Almanac, can you, Mr Hanuman,' Merrick said, needling. 'And I understand you've lost it?'

Danny bit his lip.

'The loss of the Almanac is a severe blow,' agreed Professor Plendergarth. 'However, let us hear what else the students have to say.'

'If you study Tiwanaku in detail,' said Hugo. 'You come to the conclusion it was the pivotal city hub of an extremely ancient and cultured civilisation. Their technology was advanced -'

'Where's your proof of that?' interrupted Zeuber.

'Firstly, there is the Akapana Pyramid,' Danny answered. 'Which is a seven stepped pyramid constructed with advanced engineering technology.'

'How can you possibly know that?' said Zeuber, with narrowed eyes.

Danny hesitated, but Hugo stepped in, keen to explain the technology.

'The archaeologists,' Hugo said. 'Used ground penetrating radar and remote cameras to investigate the interior of the Akapana Pyramid. And their observations revealed what they described as the *'most extraordinary precision engineering.'* It shows a remarkably advanced skill level comparable to our modern technology of today.

'Inside of the Pyramid itself,' Hugo continued. 'Is a series of intricate water channels which flow from the top of the seven levels to the bottom. They are constructed out of rock-hard granite, and they fit together at right angles using mitred joints. All of these are cut from the rock with such precision, there isn't a chink between any of them, not even to pass a razor blade though.'

'That is indeed an extraordinary skill,' agreed Professor Plendergarth. He wore a puzzled frown. 'But why would they go to so much trouble, when no one would ever see that kind of technical virtuosity?'

'Because,' said Izzie. 'They used their knowledge of science to control the *appearance* of the water. When it hit each interior right angle, bubbles of air were forced through the liquid. This created a foaming effect. When it emerged at the bottom of the pyramid, it appeared to be a milky-white colour. This gave us a clue as to the function of the whole layout at Tiwanaku.'

'The mystery of Tiwanaku,' said Urmila. 'Has always been, what was its religious significance? The local people have their own stories of the legend it is based on.'

Zeuber's face was like a plastic mask as she continued.

'The Aymara, who are the Bolivian indigenous people, maintain a sacred mythology to this day. It is essentially the same story as the Churning of the Ocean of Milk and this gave us an important clue.

'You see, our hypothesis maintains that the ancient Tiwanakan engineers were recreating this legend in a sophisticated way, using advanced technology and mathematical calculations. There is evidence to support this hypothesis in all the structures across the whole site.'

'So when the white water comes out of the pyramid,' Danny continued. 'It flows through a series of channels and exits into the Kalasasaya Courtyard, filling it up like a swimming pool. This gives the appearance of the frothed up milky ocean of the legend.'

'The technology goes even further,' said Sandeep. 'Because under the courtyard they have discovered a sophisticated system of linked surface and underground channels which flow all the way from under the city to Lake Titikaka.'

'Our investigations,' said Izzie. 'Show this Creation Legend, to be connected to other ancient pyramid cultures around the world. The key lies in the sacred mountain, *Meru,* which was believed to be the home of the gods in Vedic times. All the world's pyramids were designed to be the abode of the gods on earth and were sacred places.'

'In fact,' said Kirsty O'Donnell. 'Most of the ancient civilisations we have studied so far, appear to have known about the legend of the Churning of the Ocean of Milk.'

'Can you tell me then,' said Councillor Hitchin, shaking his head and setting his double chins a-wobbling. 'If these *stories* have any truth in them, where is the mathematical proof you speak of?'

'We regard indigenous people's cultural history as more than just *stories,* Councillor!' retorted Kirsty O'Donnell. 'They provide us with valuable investigative tools to help us better understand the ancient culture under consideration.'

'But where's the proof,' Dr Merrick challenged. 'That these people had astronomical knowledge?'

'As a matter of fact,' Danny replied. 'There is a remarkable edifice at Tiwanaku called the Gateway to the Sun. This is a massive block of stone with an opening through it, which forms a passageway. It has carvings all over the eastern side which are astronomical calculations for a calendar system.'

'You can hardly call that culture *primitive*,' Richard Greenwood remarked, drily. 'Just because they had different religious beliefs to us, does not render them less intelligent. On the contrary, their peaceful way of life could be argued to show a greater intelligence than ours.'

'This is all very well,' Zeuber stated, at his most urbane. 'But this is an isolated civilisation. We would need more evidence, such as you claim is in the Almanac, to corroborate these hypotheses.'

'Pity it's been lost,' Merrick affected a mournful shake of his head.

'As a matter of fact,' Danny said, recalling his mother's Notebook. 'There are other clues we can use. For example, Sanskrit is a key Archeo-linguistic tool -'

A swarthy, muscular man who was sitting with the South American delegates rudely interrupted Danny. His narrowed, hard eyes seared into Danny and his mouth turned down in a mocking sneer.

'You're not telling me that *Sanskrit* has anything to do with the English language, are you?' he said.

It turned out the man's name was Pedro, and he was supposed to be representing Mexico, though the other South American delegates looked as if they would like to disown him.

'I'll ask Urmila to comment,' said Danny. 'She's an expert in Sanskrit.'

'Right,' challenged Pedro. 'Give me an example of a *Sanskrit* word being used in English.'

'OK,' said Urmila. 'The Sanskrit root word *'astra'* means 'a star.' It gives us our English words, *'astronomy'*, *'astronomical'*, *'astrology'*, *'astronaut'*. It's not hard to see the connection.'

'That word, *'astra,'* is from the Latin,' argued Merrick.

'As a matter of fact,' Kirsty observed. 'Latin came originally from the Sanskrit. The close similarities between Sanskrit, Latin and Greek, were observed by the eighteenth century Indologist, Sir William Jones.

'In a famous quote, he compared all three classical languages and concluded Sanskrit was the most perfect, more so than the Greek or the Latin, so he decided they must all three share a common origin.'

'But,' added Richard. 'Because of his Eurocentric bias – notably his father-in-law was a Christian bishop - he couldn't believe the supposed 'primitive' people of Vedic India could have possibly had so cultured a language as Sanskrit. Therefore, he proposed that it must have belonged to an 'unknown' civilisation, before their time.'

'Let's look at another English word that comes from the Sanskrit,' said Urmila. '*Manu* is described in the texts as the first man, and is also called the Law-giver. He is wise and he is the inventor of writing. We get our English words *manu*script, *manu*facture, *man*aged, *man*ifest, and *man*date from this Sanskrit root word.'

'What intrigues me,' said Danny, recalling his vision. 'One of the statues in the Courtyard pool carries a hinged and bound casebook. I believe it could represent Manu with his Book of Laws, the legendary first man, who came out of the Ocean of Milk.'

There were exclamations of surprise from all the academics and delegates in the audience.

'A remarkable observation, young man,' said Professor Plendergarth, clearly impressed. 'There is no doubt in my mind, this project *must* be pursued further.'

Pedro subsided but looked suspiciously at Danny. At the next tea break he got up and left abruptly. As soon as he'd gone, one of the Mexican delegates, a tall, dignified man called Professor Alvarez, came over to where Danny, Kirsty and Richard, were in deep conversation.

'I just wanted to say,' Professor Alvarez said. 'That chap calling himself '*Pedro*' was not one of our delegates. He arrived before us this morning, and helped himself to one of the ponchos on display. We thought you'd invited him, Dr O'Donnell. But then he started threatening us, telling us not to reveal anything about our ancient heritage, *or it would be the worse for us!*'

'Yes,' a dark haired lady called Soraya added. 'He bragged that it was *his* people who have been destroying our archaeological sites in South America. He claimed his organisation was responsible for intimidating our local guides at ancient sites, not to reveal the truth of our culture. If we give too much of our history away to you, Dr O'Donnell, he said they would harm our families back home.'

'But we will not be intimidated,' said Professor Alvarez. 'We want to let you know about our culture and how it relates to your search for the *Ancient Sea Kings*, Dr O'Donnell. For example, our temple structures, like those at other ancient sites, each have four doors that are perfectly aligned to the four cardinal directions. The main door is always to the east.

'By the way, he was asking us questions about *you*, young man.' He put a hand on Danny's shoulder. 'Do you know who this *Pedro* is, Dr O'Donnell?'

'No,' said Kirsty. 'I didn't invite him. In fact I've never seen him before.'

Danny recalled the man's stocky build, his swarthy appearance, the hard, deep-set eyes, and the scar running down his cheek. He would know him if he saw him again.

Professor Alvarez posed a question to the students.

'I was fascinated,' he said. 'Concerning the identity of the figure you mentioned in the Courtyard at Tiwanaku, as being Manu. There are three column figures that have long been shrouded in mystery. Are they the *Sea Kings* of your Quest, I wonder?'

Before Danny could answer, Richard Greenwood interrupted.

'We have to break now for lunch. Let's discuss that interesting question while we eat, professor.'

At this comment, Danny saw Zeuber and Merrick exchange meaningful glances. Minutes later they exited the marquee with Councillor Hitchin.

'Tell you what might surprise you,' said Hugo, eyes twinkling at the others. 'I'm starving!'

'Me too!' said Danny, rubbing his stomach. 'Something smells good.'

The students made their way to the dining tables that were laid out at the far end of the marquee. They had just taken their seats, when suddenly there was a loud 'bang' and all the electrics in the tent and went off.

Danny was the first one to smell smoke.

13

ABDUCTED

As the marquee filled up with smoke it became impossible to see anything. People were coughing, panicking and stampeding everywhere, bumping into each other, looking for the exit.

Over it all, Danny heard Rama's calm voice giving instructions.

'Get on the ground, and tie something round your mouth. Follow my voice. The exit is this way.'

Danny took off his zipped jacket and tied it round his mouth and nose. He crawled through the smoke in the direction of what he hoped was the exit.

Suddenly he heard someone scream his name.

'Danny!'

It sounded like Urmila. He heard it again, this time it seemed to be coming from outside the tent. He struggled through the crowd to get out.

'Danny! Help me!' There was a note of panic in her voice.

He crawled along the ground trying not to breathe in the smoke. He emerged from the tent gasping for breath. He had to lie there and take in some fresh air for a few minutes to gather his wits.

To his horror, he saw Urmila some distance away on the ground, being tended to by a couple of paramedics. An ambulance was waiting in the street outside the park. Sirens could be heard as more ambulances arrived. A couple of fire engines were on the scene in minutes. All was confusion and chaos.

Urmila raised her head as if trying to call out something to Danny, but one of the paramedics put an oxygen mask over her face and she lay back, silent and still.

Danny ran over to them. He was distraught at the sight of his friend.

'Is she going to be OK?' he tried to hold her hand but it fell limply out of his grasp. 'Let me go in the ambulance with her - please?'

'No, 'fraid not,' said the older paramedic arranging the oxygen equipment. 'We're taking her to hospital. Emergency. Rules are rules. No one is allowed in the ambulance.'

Danny watched in despair as they strapped Urmila's lifeless body onto a stretcher. They carted her into the back of a waiting ambulance, started it up and drove off, blue lights and siren blaring.

It seemed to Danny as if he was living a nightmare. He had the same sense of paralyzed helplessness he had felt before in his life. Was she going to be alright? When would he see her again?

He went back to where the rest of the students were just emerging from the marquee and told them what had happened. They hung around for a while, lost and shaken, not knowing what to do. Richard Greenwood pushed his way through the crowds to reach them. He looked anxious and disheveled and ran his hands distractedly through his tousled hair as he spoke.

'It will be safer for you students if I take you back to the museum for now,' he said. 'Stick together and don't go anywhere until you hear from Kirsty O'Donnell or me.

After I've dropped you off, I'll have to come back to the park and deal with the situation here. Eddie Salter and Dr O'Donnell are checking with the police to see if anything else has been taken.'

Izzie was agog.

'Do you mean they've stolen something under cover of the fire, Dr Greenwood?'

'I'm afraid so. The priceless Kalash Vessel on loan from Tiwanaku, the South American site, has gone missing. The police found the delegate's security guard knocked out cold while he was trying to save the artefact from the thieves. But he was powerless to stop them. It was stolen while everyone was confused by the smoke and fire.

'But that's not all. Professor Alvarez has disappeared and foul play is suspected.'

BACK IN THEIR WORKROOM, the students sat hunched around the table, anxiously discussing the day's events.

'We need to figure this thing out,' Izzie said. 'What do we know of whoever was behind the attack? It must surely be linked to that message we all had. What other clues do we have, guys?'

'Well, it must be the work of *The Aculeata*,' Sandeep said. 'And they are a ruthless organisation, that's for sure. It looks like they'll stop at nothing. To, like, deliberately start a fire that could harm dozens of people -'

'One reason,' said Hugo. 'Those Special Branch officers were investigating it as if it were a terrorist attack.'

'Yeah,' said Izzie. 'Because of those foreign dignitaries who were there. I wonder if Professor Alvarez is still alive? It seems it was a very carefully planned operation. Dr Greenwood said they were also investigating it in terms of the international theft of looted artifacts.'

'Danny, mate,' said Hugo, noticing his friend was very quiet. 'Who do *you* think was behind the fire in the marquee?'

'Well, I would say, it wasn't a terrorist attack, though it might have been made to look like one,' said Danny. 'It's got to have been the work of *The Aculeata.*'

'We need to find out more about them,' said Izzie. 'Who are *The Aculeata* and what sort of operation are they running?' She looked it up on her phone. 'Listen to this - the word *'Aculeata'* is used as a classification of a type of parasitic insect, like a wasp –'

'But just hang on a minute there, Izzie,' Danny interrupted, struggling with his feelings. 'It's *Urmila* we need to worry about right now. They wouldn't let me go in the ambulance with her, remember? She was struggling a bit at first, but then she stopped after they put that oxygen mask on her face.'

'Oh, she's in the best place to recover, at the hospital,' Izzie dismissed his worries with an airy wave of her hand.

'OK, guys,' Hugo said, noting the scowl on Danny's face at this unfeeling response. He looked at Sandeep's strained, anxious face and sensed a storm brewing. 'I've got a suggestion. First, let's have a tea break. We'll think better after a cuppa and custard creams.'

He got up and switched the kettle on. Sandeep barely heard him. He had picked up his mobile and was looking for the phone number of the hospital. At the same time, Izzie picked up her own mobile.

'I'll phone the hospital, while *you* phone your Uncle Janak, Sandeep,' she commanded in her imperious manner. 'Hugo will make the tea. I want to know when the visiting hour is so I can go to see Urmila.'

'You're not related to her!' retorted Sandeep. 'They'll speak to *me*, her cousin, before they'll speak to *you*, Izzie. You just wait, anyway, until after I speak to my uncle.'

'I'm off to the bathroom to wash up,' Danny said. 'Make mine a strong cuppa, Hugo, and don't hold back on those biscuits. I'll be back in a minute.'

ON HIS WAY back to the workroom Danny took a left turn that led onto the corridor where the staff offices were located. He stopped in his tracks and ducked behind a wall. Something very strange was happening.

Zeuber had just emerged from Dr Merrick's office and was closing the door silently behind him. He had a package under his arm and he looked decidedly furtive. Danny had a sudden intuition:

I bet he's got the Almanac.

Zeuber was obviously intent on getting away in a hurry. He hadn't seen Danny and was headed for the lift.

Danny was instantly on the alert, cat-like, curiosity aroused. He had to act fast. He waited until the lift doors closed on Zeuber and then ran down the flights of stairs as fast as he could. He observed the lift didn't stop at any of the floors. It was going right down to the basement.

When Danny emerged from the door of the lowest floor he was just in time to see Zeuber walking briskly down a corridor towards a hitherto unknown area of the museum basement. There was a honeycomb of corridors under the old building, with rooms leading off at intervals.

Danny crept along the underground passage, taking care to keep out of sight. At first it seemed relatively quiet, but as Zeuber disappeared around a corner, Danny became aware of activity up ahead. He heard voices discussing what seemed to be the consignment of exhibits of some sort.

He heard Zeuber's irritable voice snapping out orders. *'Be careful, idiot!'* and *'Not there, you fool!'*

The unseen people appeared to be scurrying about in response. Danny noticed that, at the farthest end of the corridor, the air was fresher and there was daylight streaming in. He guessed there was a loading bay leading onto the street outside.

There was a lot more commotion, banging and shouting, and the whine of some industrial vehicles. A big operation was in progress and these people meant business.

Suddenly, Danny realised footsteps were coming towards him and they were about to round the bend in the corridor.

He spotted a side door to his left, which was partially ajar. He quickly ducked into the room and closed the door, waiting till they'd passed. The room was empty except for a few large wooden packing crates and some packing materials.

The voices drew nearer until they were right outside his door. They appeared to be checking the consignment on a clipboard. Danny's heart leapt like a bag of frogs as it dawned on him - *they were about to come into his room.*

He jumped into one of the large packing boxes and crouched down low inside. The flexibility of the Kalari yoga training came in handy. He had the presence of mind to pull a big wodge of the shredded cardboard packing material over the top of himself. He was only just in time. The door opened and in walked a couple of delivery men.

'Dr Zeuber wants us to check in here to see if there are any more boxes for this shipment,' the first man said.

'I don't think so,' said a second voice. 'Oh, hang on. It looks like this one has been missed. It's all packed up ready to go. Put the lid on and let's get it loaded up.'

To his horror, Danny heard them slam a heavy lid on top of the box he was in. He heard the click on all four sides as they closed the ratchet clips in place. He was trapped.

Should he call out and tell them he was there? But if Zeuber realized he'd been followed, who knew what he might do to him? He had little choice but to stay shtum and see where he would end up.

From all that had happened, Danny was sure Zeuber was involved with *The Aculeata*. But in what way and how to get proof of it would be tricky. Zeuber was a very slippery customer who appeared to have a plausible answer for everything. Maybe this would lead to the break-through the student gang had been looking for.

Danny felt the crate being loaded onto a forklift truck and minutes later it was being hoisted up onto the hydraulic lift of a waiting lorry.

'That's the last of this shipment, Barney. You'd better get going. They don't like it if you're late.'

The low growling rumble of the diesel engine started up and the lorry jerked forward. Danny felt a mounting wave of panic. It was claustro-phobic in that small space. Where was he going to end up? And would he be able to escape at the other end without them seeing him? His heart began racing and his breathing became increasingly shallow and laboured.

Not much oxygen in here. Must calm down. I need to practice the Kalari meditation like Rama taught me. It'll regulate my breathing and use less oxygen. I've got to keep a clear head for this mission if I'm going to make it. Must stay in the quiet Shakti zone...

The lorry drove on, and judging by its increased speed and the smoothness of the road, Danny deduced it had joined a motorway.

The few minutes of calm had helped clear Danny's mind. He remem-bered reading the SAS guide that said survival was all about mental atti-tude. It was what Rama taught, too. Those who stayed positive and focused were the survivors. Rama said *the point of power is always in the present moment. Forget about the past, let it go. Stop worrying about the future. Simply* be, *in the present here and now.*

Danny could almost hear Rama's voice in his head:

'Remember, courage is always there when you truly need it. You must locate it in your solar plexus. It is the invincible power of your own consciousness.'

Danny began to formulate a plan of action. First, he checked his watch. 3:15pm. He reviewed what he had with him: his mobile phone, but it was low on battery power. He decided that the first thing he had to do was to get a message to the others while he still had enough battery for the message to be sent. He hoped that there would be a strong enough signal for it to work.

'Guys – urgent. I followed Zeuber down to the basement. I'm sure he has the Almanac. I hid in a packing crate, but it got loaded onto a lorry. I have no idea which direction it's heading in, and my phone battery's very low. I hope you get this all right. Tell Rama and Lakshman. They'll know what to do. Danny.

He wished he hadn't left his backpack in the museum workroom. It had a snack bar in it. But then it occurred to him that there wasn't much air in the space. He could suffocate if he wasn't careful. Trying not to give in to rising panic, he felt in the pocket of his cargo pants.

Whew! As luck would have it he'd still got his Swiss army penknife with him. It had been a present from his father. He settled himself down for a long journey and began to use the sharp blade of the knife to cut out a hole in the side of the box. He scraped away at a tiny gap in the wood on one side of the crate. Soon the airflow increased. He kept working it so he would have a peephole for later.

After two hours, which seemed like an interminable age, the lorry left the smooth surface of the motorway. There were now more bends in the road and it was a rougher journey altogether. Danny started to feel sick, partly with hunger and partly with fear. He realized he hadn't eaten anything since breakfast. The stress of the day was beginning to catch up with him.

It was now after 6pm on his watch. The lorry was obviously on a bumpy off-road track. It tilted and swayed, and bumped over rocks in places. Danny was severely jolted and ached in every limb. His muscles burned with the longing to stretch his legs.

After what he guessed must have been four or five miles of track, the vehicle slowed down and halted. Danny's stomach did a somersault. *Not long now till they find me.* His forehead and palms were sweating. He realized he was trembling and wished that he wasn't so scared.

Danny shrunk down, dreading the inevitable discovery. What was going to happen when they opened the wooden box? Would they hurt him? Would they -? *Stop it! Pull yourself together. Be in the moment ...*

There appeared to be some arrangements being made. The lorry slowly reversed and backed up, he guessed into some kind of unloading bay.

Danny had no idea where they could be. He was so cramped and stiff he didn't even know if his legs would hold him when he tried to stand up. He felt weak with fear and dizzy from lack of food.

He heard the tailgate being opened and the ramp at the end being lowered. There were shouts of *'careful with those boxes'* and *'keep them the right way up!'* Minutes later, Danny felt the metal arms of a forklift pushing under his crate. Once loaded it moved forward towards what seemed to Danny through his spyhole to be a large warehouse type building. It was brightly lit and they were heading for a wall of plastic slatted vertical hangings, which were pushed aside by the vehicle.

Someone spoke to the driver and said in English, but with a heavy foreign accent, 'Put it over there with 'ze others.'

The crate was set down and the metal arms withdrawn. There was the whine of the forklift as it reversed out of the area and there were more shouted instructions, this time in a language Danny didn't understand. The outer doors to the building were slammed shut and the sound of heavy metal bolts being put in place echoed around the area.

The next thing Danny knew, someone was undoing the catches, one at a time, around the lid of his box. He cringed. There was no escape. He was about to be discovered. His heart thudded like a pneumatic drill.

As the lid lifted, Danny gasped and blinked at the sudden intensity of bright light. The packing on the top that he had pulled over himself was removed and Danny found himself looking into the astonished gaze of a dark-eyed man. He was covered up in a white boiler suit from head to toe. He'd been wearing goggles, which he now pulled up over his head in order to survey the contents of the box.

For a second, they both stared at each other. Danny's scared expression noted by the stranger, whose eyes were sad but not unkind. And although he looked utterly confounded as he took in the contents of the crate, to Danny's intense relief, he did not raise the alarm.

Danny's eyes darted hither and thither as he looked around to check out possible escape routes. In those few seconds, his adrenalin-fuelled brain assessed the whole of the premises. It was an industrial style warehouse building, with a high roof held by steel girders. It was of concrete construction with no windows in the exterior walls.

The only light source was artificial, provided by dazzling overhead neon lights. The massive space appeared to be divided into sections. The one Danny was in was totally white - floors, walls, ceiling, all sterile white.

Strangely, all the people in that area were also dressed in white. They wore white boiler suits with hoods, masks and goggles. It was a futuristic scene. There were white workstations dotted around the room with expensive looking microscopes and scientific equipment on display. All the people were intent on their tasks; no one was looking in Danny's direction.

Several of the white clad personnel were studying items through a microscope. Others were studying test tubes and placing them in racks. Danny was mystified.

To Danny's amazement, the man bending over him put his finger to his lips in a gesture for silence. He then re-covered Danny with the packing material. Peeping out, Danny could see him walking over to a stainless-steel box on wheels. He lifted out a white boiler suit and mask. Minutes later, Danny felt the man thrust these and a pair of goggles into the crate. He spoke with a heavy foreign accent. Danny guessed it was middle-eastern.

'You. Put on overalls. You keep quiet. I hide you. Do as I say.'

He proceeded to draw a screen round the crate, to hide it from view of the rest of the room. When Danny had donned the white gear, his rescuer motioned to him to come and join him at one of the white workbenches.

The man gestured meaningfully to draw Danny's attention to the entrance end of the building. Danny saw the shadowy figure of an armed guard, on the other side of the plastic wall of slatted hangings. He was wearing a black and red uniform and looked distinctly menacing. The guard stopped patrolling from time to time and came to look into the room through a fixed glass panel.

Danny's rescuer observed the movements of the guard for a few moments. As soon as he saw him move away from the window and start patrolling again, the man pointed to himself.

'Me. Eissen. You? Name you?'

'I'm c-called Danny,' he held onto the counter for support as he took in the situation. 'What is this place and what are you doing here? Are you all prisoners?'

'We have been abducted,' the man gestured to the others in the room. 'And yes, we being kept prisoner. They bring us to this remote location many months ago. It's somewhere in Scotland. I not know its name.

'But the others, like those through there,' he gestured to a set of connecting doors in the middle of the opposite wall. 'In that adjoining warehouse they bring the illegal immigrants. The bad people trick them into leaving homes and leaving families. *'Get new life,'* they say. *'Give all savings to us for journey'*. Afterwards they're transported undercover to this place.'

Eissen gestured around their immediate environment.

'It is different in this warehouse. We are here for a different purpose. We were targeted because we have university degrees. Me, I am professor of archaeology and science. Others are specialists in various disciplines, including mathematics and science of DNA. For these things - .'

Eissen gestured to the white surface in front of him. All along several metres of benches, Danny could see neatly laid out bones and artefacts. Eissen had been in the process of labeling them, and he now picked up a label in his hand, to make it look to all intents and purposes as if he was still working.

He pushed a stone artifact towards Danny and handed him a pencil and a sketch-book.

'You. Draw this object. You not look so conspicuous then, while we talk.'

Danny studied the object. It had spiral marks engraved into the hard stone. The label that lay beside it on the bench said, *From Cairn holy, Dumfries and Galloway.*

Danny recalled his mother's Notebook. In it she'd mentioned the mysterious disappearance of the *Cairn holy* spiral stone. It had been unearthed at the ancient prehistoric site in Scotland and then, some time later, it had disappeared without trace. What was more, the official sign at the site, which had mentioned the archaeological discovery of the spiral stone, had also disappeared.

It had been replaced with a newer sign that had had all mention of the spiral artifact removed. Dr Hanuman was sure it had been done deliberately and was part of a plot to conceal evidence of an ancient civilization in Scotland. She had been investigating this at the time of her death, Danny recalled.

He looked along the workbenches at the other artefacts. He recognized some of the geographic place names on the labels: a sculptured stone head from Gobekli Tepe, in Turkey; a lapis beaded necklace from the Indus Valley; carvings from the Tigris-Euphrates River in Iraq; others from Syria, and Ukraine. And there, to Danny's amazement, was the stolen Kalash vessel from Tiwanaku. Danny's brain was reeling as he took in these priceless objects.

'Eissen, why are all these objects here, instead of in museums?

'They all come from extremely ancient sites,' the archaeologist said, shaking his head mournfully. 'They loot all those sites then they bomb them, like in my country of Iraq and Syria. Same for Afghanistan. They steal all our artefacts. Especially, the General Maricha. He very bad man. He force us to analyse and then catalogue all what he calls the 'exhibits.'

Danny's brow creased as he took these words in.

'But why are you all wearing white in this section?'

'In this section of the compound, he make us examine the ancient bones for DNA. He lately brings us bones from the Indus Valley Culture. He wants us to clone their DNA.'

'Is that why this is a sterile environment?' said Danny, looking round.

'Yes,' said Eissen. 'Because ancient DNA is very easily contaminated by the researchers as they naturally shed their own particles of DNA from their skin or hair. We carry out other dating tests using Carbon 14, but it not very reliable. Then it not any good for what the General or the Dark One wants.'

'Are they anything to do with *The Aculeata*?' said Danny. 'And is this 'Dark One' called Lord Ravana?'

Eissen took a step backwards, looking visibly shocked. He spoke sharply to Danny.

'*How* you know these names? You must not speak them out loud while you are here. Who *are* you? Tell me who is your mentor?'

'I am Danny Hanuman. My teacher and mentor is called Rama.'

At this, a marked change came over Eissen. He repeated almost reverently.

'Hanuman? You, Rama's friend. Always.' He said it as a statement, but followed it through with another question. 'He is here in this country?'

Danny nodded, mystified. How could they have heard of Rama?

Eissen put his hand on his heart.

'We support you, Hanuman, warrior-knight. We devoted to Rama, noblest of men.'

Why is he calling me a 'warrior-knight'? He's in for a disappointment when he finds out I'm nothing of the sort. But on the other hand, this could turn out to be a very useful intelligence gathering mission. Who knows what I'm going to find out? That is, if I survive.

Little did Danny know what awaited him in the other warehouse.

14
THE ACULEATA'S LAIR

EISSEN WALKED over to a far bench where a similarly white clad man was closely examining an object through a microscope. As Eissen spoke quietly in the man's ear, he stopped what he was doing and quickly looked over at Danny. Then he too, pulled his goggles up over his head, and Danny saw his dark eyes shining. He put his hand on his heart as if he was pledging his support. But he glanced around nervously and his expression became cautious. He gestured meaningfully towards the connecting doors.

Eissen came back over to Danny and said in a low voice,

'That is Ashwin, my friend. He say you look through there. Prisoners brought in earlier today.'

Danny walked over to look through the glass doors into the other warehouse. What he saw made him reel as if he'd had a bucket of ice-cold water thrown over him.

In a state of utter disbelief Danny recognised the diminutive figure of Urmila. She was trying to tidy her disheveled hair back into its usual ponytail and her floral dress was crumpled and creased. Although she looked pale, she seemed to be otherwise unharmed.

'So they didn't take her to any hospital after the fire,' Danny muttered.

'They abducted her. I should have guessed. Those ambulance men were working for Maricha.'

He watched as Urmila went over to tend to a huddled group of what looked like foreign immigrants. They were seated on benches at the side and they looked terrified. One young woman clutched at Urmila's sleeve as she passed and she stopped to put her arm round her, trying to comfort her as best she could.

'Is that your friend?' Eissen said.

Danny nodded, dumbstruck.

'She speak many languages,' Eiseen continued. 'She helpful. Talks with those people. We don't know why they brought her. She not like the rest of us. She brave girl.'

Eissen opened the door slightly so they could hear what was going on.

Another shock was in store for Danny. One of the guards entered the room pushing someone in a wheelchair. The seated man's head hung down on his chest, as if he were drugged.

Danny shook his head in disbelief. It was Professor Alvarez. Urmila ran to help him but the guard pushed her away. Behind the guard came another visitor. A thin figure with pallid white skin and curious hooded snake eyes, strode into view, carrying a briefcase. Danny gave an involuntary shudder.

Zeuber! What's he doing here?

Dr Zeuber came up behind Urmila and pushed her away from the immigrants towards a different area of the room. Danny could see a cordoned off section with a series of wooden examination desks. They had spotlights placed at intervals along them to illuminate a series of artifacts, some of which looked like clay squares.

Danny recognized them.

'Those look like the Indus Seals!' he muttered. 'What are those valuable items doing here?'

'They steal all those things,' Eissen said gravely. 'From many countries.'

An old man with long white hair and a grey beard sat hunched at one of the benches, examining the seals through a hand held magnifying glass.

Zeuber pushed Urmila over to the man, this time more roughly. She stumbled and the old man got up to catch her before she fell. Zeuber gave an unpleasant laugh.

'That will teach you to obey. You will help this man. Let me introduce you. This is Professor Haldiki. He is a leading authority on the Indus Seals.

'Professor, this is Urmila Mithil. She is also extremely knowledgeable about the Seals and has a theory about them. We believe you both have made unique discoveries in this field. But there's still something missing.' His features hardened as he spoke.

'Now listen up. Here are your instructions from General Maricha. You must each pool your knowledge to solve the Mystery of the Seals, which has plagued the academic community for so long.

'And this valuable resource I have here,' he tapped his briefcase. 'Will help you with dating of the artifacts including the Indus Culture.'

As he spoke, he lifted the Almanac out and laid it on the desk in front of the professor. Urmila's eyes started from her head at the sight of it.

'You lousy thief!' she exclaimed through clenched teeth. 'That Almanac belongs to my father. He lent it to Danny and you robbed him. I'm not going to cooperate with you in any way. You're nothing but scum.'

That enraged Zeuber. He raised the back of his hand towards Urmila's face, like a snake about to strike its victim. But the professor with surprising alacrity, leaped in his way and stayed his hand.

Zeuber appeared to think better of it and said,

'You mind your tongue, girl, if you know what's good for you. But you will cooperate, make no mistake! We have ways of – how shall I put it? - *persuading* you. Take a look at those people.'

He gestured to the terrified immigrants. As he did so, he nodded to the guard who took his semi-automatic from his shoulder and aimed it at the huddled group. He glanced at Zeuber for further instructions, as if ready to fire on command.

'I am sure,' said Zeuber, his voice silky smooth. 'You don't want to see these people suffer, do you? They will be shot, one by one, all because of *you!* Do you understand?'

'You are a *monster*,' Urmila turned ashen-faced, as she fought back tears of compassion. 'Just wait till your karma catches up with you. And when Rama hears about this, you will meet your end.'

Zeuber shrugged and said in mocking tones,

'Tut, tut! I'm quaking in my shoes, my dear. You don't yet know with whom you are dealing, do you? Rama has no power over me. You'll find out soon enough.'

As he listened to this interchange Danny became rigid with anger. There was a cracking sound. Without realizing what he was doing, his hand had picked up a piece of granite from a nearby bench and his clenched fist had crushed it into little pieces. Quite unaware of what he'd done, he let the crumbled dust fall from his hand to the ground.

Eissen's eyes widened as he noted the unconscious power of the boy. But Danny was oblivious. He was preparing to rush into the room to tackle Zeuber. Before he could move however, he felt a strong restraining hand clamped on his arm. Eissen's voice growled in his ear.

'You not do *anything* if you want to see your friend ever again. If you discovered now, both you and your friend will be taken elsewhere and you will just *'disappear.'* You will never be seen again. It happen to many people. You must wait and do nothing till I tell you. Ashwin and me formulate a plan -'

'But, Eissen,' Danny whispered urgently. 'I must speak with my friend in there. Can you arrange it for me?'

'Not yet. Wait you must. When it time for evening meal and dinner brought in, you will get chance. Go to behind screen. Put on these clothes.' Eissen handed Danny a long brown tunic and baggy trousers. 'It make you look like refugee. Tie scarf round your head, like them.'

When Danny had changed Eissen briefed him further.

'There is a delay when these guards change shifts,' he said. 'The evening shift not arrive till dinner is over. 'They leave cook and his assistant to supervise us until new guard arrives. It is the most lax part of their operation. Then will be your chance.'

He looked into Danny's clear hazel eyes and good-looking features.

'Keep your eyes downcast till then. Don't attract attention of the guards whatever you do.'

After about twenty minutes, Danny heard the main doors to the adjacent warehouse being opened with a noisy clanging of metal bolts. He saw an electric golf-buggy drive in towing a trailer. The driver deftly swung it round so it was facing into the room. He stopped adjacent to a dining area where tables and chairs were set up.

The man at the wheel was a short plump man wearing a chef's hat and a dirty white apron. He got out and walked round to the trailer. He lifted up the top to reveal a series of hot plates, beneath which were the various dishes of the evening meal.

His assistant was a spotty youth with a runny nose that he kept wiping on his sleeve. He started taking out plates and stacking them on a nearby table.

Danny was relieved to see the guards had done as Eissen predicted. They'd taken advantage of the dinner hour and left early to go to the cookhouse for their own dinner. The cook was left to supervise but as he scarcely glanced at the inmates, he seemed to pose little threat.

Danny quietly slipped into the room and went close to the cluster of waiting refugees. He watched as Urmila helped the professor to stand in the queue. The old gentleman had difficulty balancing as he was leaning on his walking stick and couldn't pick up a plate with his remaining hand, which shook badly. Urmila got the plate for him and held it in front of her.

She also insisted the other elderly refugees went ahead of her, which placed her towards the back of the queue. In his disguise, Danny merged into the line and stood further back so he could overhear Urmila's conversation with the professor. He kept his head down and bided his time, waiting for an opportunity to speak to her without attracting attention.

Was the professor to be trusted? Danny listened intently to the murmured conversation between the two of them.

'I have evidence,' Professor Haldiki said in a low voice to Urmila. 'Of a much greater antiquity for the Indus Seals than has hitherto been acknowledged. But I don't want *them* to know that.'

'I, too, have discovered evidence from a scientific source,' whispered Urmila. 'I would like to compare my research with yours.'

'I will be fascinated,' said the professor. 'But on no account must we talk about it while we are *here*.'

Professor Haldiki led Urmila to an unoccupied table so they could sit on their own and not be overheard. He glanced up with a frowning expression as a refugee brought his tray over and joined them.

'This table is taken, I'm afraid,' said Urmila in a firm voice, without looking up.

'*Urmi!*' Danny said in an urgent whisper. 'It's *me*, Danny!'

Urmila's eyes bulged wide and her fork slipped out of her fingers and clattered to the floor.

'For goodness sake!' Danny remonstrated as he bent to pick up her fork. 'Don't give the game away, you dipstick! Act natural, as if you don't know me.'

With a supreme effort, Urmila tried to look normal. She said in a squeaky whisper,

'What the blazes are you *doing*, Danny? How did you get in here?' She was torn between relief at seeing him and being stung by his criticism. 'And what do you mean, calling me a *dipstick?* How was *I* to know it was *you*? Whatever you're doing, it's incredibly dangerous! Do you know who these people *are?*'

'I'm guessing they're *The Aculeata?*' Danny said.

Professor Haldiki looked over his shoulder anxiously.

'Don't say those words again young man, if you value your life. No one is supposed to know this is one of their operations.'

As briefly as he could, Danny told the story of how he'd been brought there. The professor listened intently. When Danny explained Eissen's reaction, he looked thoughtful.

'I believe there is an underground resistance movement here,' said the professor. 'But you have to be very careful. There are also those who are spies placed among us and would give us away to our captors. Trust no one - except those that Eissen says you can.'

Minutes later, Eissen and Ashwin appeared with their dinner trays and joined them at the table.

'You said you wanted to know my history, Danny,' Eiseen said. 'The ancient lineage of my family can be traced back to the learned Sabians of Haran, in what used to be called the land of Anatolia. Nowadays it is known as Turkey.

'*The Aculeata* want to extract all our ancient knowledge. Afterwards, they will deny it ever existed. They have traced back the ancient history of mathematics from beyond our early Arabic scholars, way back to the original Indian sages who devised the earliest known number system from its Sanskrit origins.'

'It is dangerous knowledge,' said Ashwin. '*The Aculeata* are re-writing history and eradicating the Vedic origins and contributions to world culture. They eliminate anyone who gets in their way. Very bad people.'

Eissen checked over his shoulder to make sure they could not be overheard.

'Listen very carefully to your instructions,' he said in a low voice. 'It is all settled for you to escape later on, tonight.'

'There will be a lorry,' Ashwin continued. 'Which arrives to pick up a special shipment. It is destined for a container ship waiting at the port of Felixstowe. It will arrive at midnight. The vehicle has a secret compartment under the base of the lorry that I will show you. It is normally used for smuggling refugees *into* this country, so it will be empty on this outward-bound journey. You must both get into it and do as I tell you.'

'It is very dangerous,' said Eissen. 'The guards at the gate will shoot you on sight if they see you -'

'Hang on a minute!' Urmila interrupted. '*I'm* not going with you!'

'Whaaat?' Danny's jaw dropped. 'Of course you're coming with me, Urmila! You can't possibly stay here, it's much too dangerous.'

But Danny noted a mulish set to Urmila's mouth that he'd never seen before. Her normally timid disposition and gentle nature had undergone a transformation. She remained obdurate.

'I'm not leaving these people,' she said fiercely. 'Just think what would happen to them if I escaped. They'd torture them to get at the truth. Poor Professor Haldiki would be first in line. And then in all likelihood Danny, *both* of us would be recaptured and all would be lost.'

'Well in that case,' Danny countered. '*I'm* not going, either. I'm not leaving without you. You surely can't expect me to leave you here with that monster, Zeuber, on the loose?'

Eissen had been listening quietly to this interchange.

'She right, your friend,' he said. 'If you go alone, no one know you here. That means you can bring back help for all of us. Smash the operation and stop the bad men.'

'We look after your friend for you till you return,' said Ashwin. 'You come back quick. Bring Rama. He save us.'

In vain did Danny protest. Everyone supported Urmila and Eissen's thinking on the subject. After much discussion backwards and forwards, Danny was forced to agree to the merits of their plan.

Thus it was with the greatest reluctance Danny Hanuman found himself, at a quarter to midnight, waiting for a lorry that would lead him to his freedom. He had finally made the heartbreaking decision to leave his childhood friend in enemy hands. And he had no knowledge of how he was going to fare once he left the premises of the warehouse complex. The prisoners couldn't tell him exactly where he was because they didn't know themselves. They said he would just have to follow his instincts.

Eissen explained how to follow the constellations of the night sky to navigate by. He then took Danny to hide in a wooden cabin located near the entrance of the warehouse.

'You wait in here. You make no sound and no light put on.'

It was a good hideout, as it served as an office during the day, but was closed up and in darkness at night. It enabled Danny to see what was going on outside, from his hidden vantage point, crouched down under the desk.

At ten minutes after midnight, he heard the droning engine of a vehicle approaching in the distance. A man in a navy blue boiler suit entered through a side door in the warehouse. He looked all around as if waiting for someone.

Minutes later, Eissen suddenly emerged from the shadows. He entered the office silently and pointed to the man outside in the blue boiler suit.

'That is Igor, who I told you about. He is expert in vehicle maintenance. When the driver goes to the canteen for his supper, Igor, he oversees the servicing of the vehicle. You wait for his instructions.'

As the lorry reversed into the loading bay, other workers arrived and began to transport the shipment with fork-lift trucks. There were many wooden crates, like the one Danny had hidden in, being loaded onto the vehicle. While they waited for the loading operation to be completed, Eissen explained this branch of *The Aculeata's* activity to Danny.

'They will take this shipment of artefacts to a container ship at the port. Then it will go on to foreign museums and private collectors,' said Eissen. 'Only *The Aculeata* will know the real history and provenance behind the objects. The true antiquity of the artefacts will be changed by their political leaders, according to their various doctrines on their country's history.'

'Why would they do that?' asked Danny, puzzled.

'Many nations vie with each other over who can claim to be the *oldest* culture,' said Eissen. 'Their leaders want evidence to present to their citizens. *The Aculeata* will provide that evidence – for a price. But in reality, *they* will be the only ones who know the truth.'

'What is the truth, Eissen?' Danny was alert to hear.

'The truth is there was an ancient civilization that was widespread. It was advanced and transcended geographic boundaries. The Dark One knows this culture had secret knowledge that gave them powers, more than anyone has yet any idea of. *He* wants that advanced knowledge for himself. In addition, *The Aculeata* don't want anyone to know this ancient civilization was peaceful.'

'Why not?' Danny's brow wrinkled.

'Because *The Aculeata* thrive on war-mongering and profiteering,' Eissen pointed out. 'It suits them to have people believe that was the norm in ancient times also.'

Danny hadn't even noticed the door to the cabin opening, but suddenly the man in the navy-blue boiler suit slipped in. He had oil-stained hands and a black smudge on his face. Eissen introduced him.

'This is Igor. He lorry mechanic. He also expert in hydraulic engineering in his own land. He created the secret compartment.

Igor turned out to be a gruff but gentle Ukrainian. He listened intently to the ongoing discussion and nodded in agreement.

'Certain leaders,' he said. 'They want to control their country's history in order to gain the people's loyalty and their obedience to the state.'

By now the last of the crates had been loaded and the guards had escorted the workers back to their quarters. As the warehouse fell silent Igor and Eissen emerged from the dark shadows with Danny. They took him out to show him the rear of the lorry.

'Here,' said Igor. 'Watch this.'

He produced a remote control and at the press of a button, Danny saw a hydraulic platform being lowered from the underside of the vehicle. It was completely out of sight until revealed by Igor.

'This secret compartment is where they bring in the illegal immigrants. It is where you must hide shortly. But first listen carefully. I must warn you of its very real and present danger. The farmhouse complex where we are now, is reached by a remote track of approximately four miles to the nearest road. The lorry will travel slowly along the track until it reaches the T-junction at the main road. There the driver will pause for a few moments and set his tachometer.

'Take this,' Igor pressed the remote control into Danny's hand. 'You will need it in order to lower the trapdoor. When it drops open, you must jump down onto the road. And immediately you must then roll clear of the wheels. You will have just a few seconds to make your escape. If you leave it too late and the vehicle sets off again, you will be crushed to death by its many huge wheels.

'If you are too slow and don't get out in time, the lorry will end up in Felixstowe and you could be on a container ship by morning. Or you may have suffocated by that time from fumes and lack of oxygen. Remember no one will know you are there. You just have this one chance. Good luck!'

Danny listened intently to the instructions. But he couldn't help being mystified by Igor's role in *the Aculeata*. After all, he seemed a decent sort of man and he was taking a huge risk in helping Danny to escape.

'Why do you work for these evil people?' he asked.

Igor gave a fatalistic shrug.

'They have my wife and children back home. They use threats against them to ensure my cooperation. But I help *you*. You, Rama's friend. You bring him here. He make everything right.'

As Danny left, all he could do was hope that Igor and the others' trust in him, was not misplaced. He would need to find Rama as soon as possible. He tried not to think about how that was going to be achieved.

In the meantime, he was leaving poor Urmila to the mercy of the dreaded *Aculeata* and the monstrous Zeuber. He thought again of how adamant she had been in her refusal to leave and how fierce and brave she had become in the face of real danger. He could only hope she would be safe till he returned.

Suddenly Ashwin, who'd been keeping lookout, appeared. His voice was laden with urgency.

'Get him in, *quick*! Zeuber is on his way with the driver!'

Danny moved like lightning. He squeezed himself into the narrow shelf at the base of the lorry. He felt the hydraulic trapdoor close up behind him. He was just in time to glimpse Zeuber's hunched walk and hooded eyes as he rounded the corner with the black garbed driver.

Had he seen him?

RAMA AND LAKSHMAN strode into the museum workroom.

'We came straight from the park as soon as we got your message. What is the problem? And where is Danny?'

Izzie brought them up to speed with the events of the afternoon.

'And he went to the bathroom,' she said with a worried frown. 'And he never came back. He just disappeared! We've searched for him everywhere. But no one has seen him.'

'Eddie Salter says he must have gone home,' said Hugo. 'But we've rung his house and his Aunt Millicent says he's not there.'

'So we've no idea where he is,' Izzie, for once, was at a loss.

'And,' said Sandeep. 'We can't find out which hospital Urmila has been taken to. All the hospital switchboards are jammed for miles around as people are ringing to find out if their loved ones have been involved in the arson attack.'

'We can't find anything out yet from the police,' said Hugo. 'They say until the situation at the Park is clearer as to whether it was a terrorist attack or not, they can't rule anything out. They will keep us informed.'

Hugo stroked his chin and looked thoughtful.

'We need to see what clues we can gather.'

'We haven't got any, *bozo*!' snapped Izzie.

'There's no need to speak like that, Izzie,' Hugo protested.

'Yeah, and *you* don't know any more that the rest of us so don't go insulting Hugo or trying to boss us about,' Sandeep said, looking up from his computer irritably.

In his calm way Rama said,

'It won't help if we allow our emotions to cloud our intellect. It's essential we don't take the stress of the situation out on each other. We need to think from a calm place of equilibrium. Only then can we use our intuition. I suggest we try to tune in to where Danny is on this map of Britain.'

'And Sandeep,' said Lakshman. 'Are you able to use your computer to access certain web sites?'

'Yes. Are you thinking–'

'Can you see,' Lakshman said. 'If you can find anything out about the operations of *The Aculeata*?'

'And where they're based?' said Sandeep. 'Right, I'm on it!'

Hugo held his hand over the Ordnance Survey map.

'I don't know why, but I'm getting a feeling of Danny around here.'

Izzie looked at the place he was indicating.

'That's a remote part of Dumfries and Galloway in Scotland. Danny can't possibly be there. That's just guesswork. You're barking up the wrong tree, Hugo.'

Hugo shrugged, but he began to look at the area on a more detailed map, nevertheless.

Another frustrating half hour passed with no news or further information.

'I'm in!' Sandeep suddenly announced.

'In where?' Izzie jumped up. 'You don't mean—'

'I've hacked into the back end of the Aculeata's website,' Sandeep grinned. 'I've got their catalogue of 'priceless artefacts' for sale to private collectors up on the screen right now.

'AND IT LOOKS to me as if the server is located somewhere on an island in the Indian Ocean.'

'Oh no!' Izzie exclaimed. 'Can't you do better than that?'

'Well,' said Sandeep. 'It looks as if they have premises in Scotland somewhere, too.'

'Told you!' said Hugo, simply. 'Got a feeling. Danny is somewhere there.'

'One way or another,' said Rama. 'We need to find Danny quickly, before *The Aculeata* realises who he is. It's vital that we get to him first.'

15
THE STRANGER IN THE SERVICE STATION

As the lorry banged and bounced over the rough track, Danny felt like a sack of potatoes. He hung on tight to the hand straps to stop himself from rolling around and hitting the sides of the compartment. Every bone in his body felt bumped and jarred.

After several miles, he felt the lorry slowing down. It stopped with its engine still running.

This is it. Only this one chance …

Danny pressed the remote and the trapdoor silently lowered.

Now or never... Got to get out quick before it starts moving again -

Heart pounding, he took a deep breath and dropped through the space onto the road. He immediately rolled to the back of the lorry, keeping to the centre of the enormous pairs of wheels. He had just got to the last couple when he saw them beginning to roll forwards.

They missed him by inches, leaving him momentarily stranded in the middle of the road. Danny quickly rolled over to the grass verge and lay still. He had no idea what other vehicles might use that road, and he had no wish to be seen until he was well clear. He took note of the name on the signpost at the end of the road. The warehouse complex was apparently called Standing Stanes Farm.

Added to the dangers he faced was the possibility that Zeuber might just have caught sight of him before the doors closed. In that case, he would send out a search party to capture him. It was just too risky to hang around in the vicinity of that evil place. He needed to get away as fast as he could.

Danny checked the night sky. He needed to figure out which direction was south so he could travel across the border. Eissen told him the ancients would use the constellations, such as Orion for guidance. But Danny noticed ruefully thick cloud covered the sky, blocking his view of the stars.

What clues in nature could he use to find the compass points? Danny recalled reading books on survival from his father's bookshelf. He climbed over a gate and started to traverse a field, heading for the shelter of a belt of trees.

"Moss only grows on the north part of the tree trunk where the sun doesn't reach. So the other side without moss will be the southerly direction."

After he decided which direction was south, Danny set off at a brisk pace across fields, keeping mainly to hedgerows and dry-stone walls for cover. He looked for other natural signs to keep him in the right direction.

To add to his woes it started to rain. He only had his hooded jacket, t-shirt, jeans and trainers on. He'd removed the refugee garments and left them in the lorry.

Before long, he was soaked to the skin. He grew more and more chilled and found it difficult to walk in the clinging wet jeans. He kept going for the next half hour, growing increasingly cold and disorientated. Each step was a struggle and his feet began to feel like lead weights.

The thought of Urmila spurred him on. In desperation, he was tempted into trying his luck at hitch-hiking. He reckoned he was far enough away from the farm now. He would have to concoct a story and hope he could get to a filling station where there would be a phone he could use.

He made it back onto a road and kept his eyes open for approaching cars. A family car was likely to be a safer bet. He saw headlights in the distance, but it seemed to be a large van of some sort. Could it be the enemy hunting for him? He panicked and dived into a nearby ditch. He regretted it immediately, as he felt the chill of muddy water seeping through his trousers.

To his horror, the vehicle slowed down and stopped just up ahead. It reversed slowly back to where he was hiding, its headlights scanning the side of the road.

He heard the rear door slide open and froze in a crouching position, hoping they wouldn't see him. He didn't dare look. Was it Zeuber's men? Had they found him?

Minutes later he heard himself being addressed by name.

'Danny, mate. What are you doing in that ditch?'

He lifted his head in the direction of the voice. To his utter relief and astonishment, he saw Hugo's worried face looking down at him. It was with mingled feelings that he saw Sandeep and Izzie were there too.

Then his grateful eyes spotted Rama and Lakshman climbing out of the minibus. He was beginning to feel dizzy with cold and fatigue and could hardly move. Without further ado, they helped him out of the ditch and hoisted him into the warmth of the vehicle.

Danny stammered out questions through chattering teeth as to how they'd found him.

Rama's reply was dismissive.

'We were tipped off, let us say. More of that, later. We need to get you out of here without delay. Time to answer questions afterwards.'

'The immediate need,' said Lakshman, starting up the engine. 'Is to get you out of those wet clothes and into somewhere warm and dry before you succumb to hypothermia. We'll take you to the service station a few miles up ahead. We should be able to get you sorted out and warmed up there.'

The service station was at an intersection between a main road and one or two minor roads. Lakshman parked the minibus some distance away from the entrance to avoid attracting attention.

Inside, it felt warm and reassuring. It was well lit, though the lights dazzled Danny's eyes at first until they adjusted. Among the various shops in the mall, there was a clothing outlet.

'Danny,' Rama instructed. 'Lakshman has bought you some new

clothes. Go to the facilities and change into them. My brother will wait for you and when you're ready, come up the stairs and join us in the cafeteria.

After he'd changed into the dry clothes Danny began to feel better. But when he was walking back with Lakshman to the restaurant area, he noticed a man in the foyer reading a newspaper. Danny had the oddest feeling he was being watched. He shrugged it off, thinking he was getting paranoid. After all, no one could possibly know him here, of all places.

The smell of food made Danny feel hungry. Although it was now 2am, he ordered a big breakfast. While he waited at the table with everyone else for the food to be brought over, he saw a group of lorry drivers all sitting together. It reminded him he should be careful how much he said in case they were overheard.

Rama had come to the same conclusion.

'Let's wait till we're safely back in the minibus before we talk properly,' he said.

While they ate, Danny gazed round the rest of the room. There was that man again. He sat a little apart from the others, reading his paper. Danny was sure it was the same man from the foyer. Was he trying to overhear what they said?

Danny studied him discreetly. He wore baggy denim trousers and a check lumberjack shirt. He had a bushy beard and a dark green peaked hat, which was pulled forward, casting his eyes in shadow. On the back of his chair was slung a high viz jacket with the word *'Forestry'* on it.

As he got up to collect his order from the counter, Danny saw that the man walked with a pronounced limp. That disability didn't seem to go with someone who would work for *The Aculeata*. Reassured, Danny dismissed further thoughts from his mind and focused on the food.

On their way back to the minibus, Danny suddenly remembered he meant to buy a bar of chocolate from the machine near the entrance.

'You guys carry on, I'll catch you up in a minute,' he said.

It was after he'd made the purchase and was walking back across the tarmac to the minibus that it happened. He was passing a dimly lit area of the service station where the bins were located. Behind them was a group of trees. Out of the corner of his eye, he saw a movement. As if from out of nowhere the stranger in the check shirt stepped out in front of him. Danny turned to run, but the stranger was too quick for him.

With muscular expertise, he grabbed Danny in a vice like grip and dragged him behind the trees, out of sight. As Danny desperately struggled to get free and shout for help, he felt a firm hand clamped across his mouth. A voice buzzed in his ear,

'*Be quiet!* Don't draw attention to yourself. Danny! It's *me!*'

Danny's knees nearly gave way under him as he recognized the voice.

'*Dad?*'

'Yes.'

Major Hanuman released his grip and Danny turned to gawp at his father.

'What are you doing here?' he gasped. 'I didn't recognize you with that beard. Dad, what's going on? Why – ?'

The major cut him short.

'No time for questions now! I'm on active duty, Danny. It's part of a covert operation. There are things I need to tell you and even more you need to tell me. But it's imperative that we're not seen together. Right now, we need to get out of this place as soon as possible, and go where we won't be overheard or observed.

'Listen carefully. When you get back to the minibus, tell Rama you've seen me. Tell him to drive half a mile back along the road and then turn right down a forest track. There, he will see a green pickup truck with 'Forestry' on the side. When it flashes its lights twice, tell him to follow it.'

'Dad! At least before you go, tell me how you knew I'd be here?'

'It's thanks to Rama, Danny. He got in touch with me to let me know you'd disappeared and where he thought you'd be found. There's a lot more to tell you but it'll have to wait. You'll find out soon enough!'

And with that, the major was gone, disappearing noiselessly into the dark night.

When they left the service station, Lakshman followed the instructions given by the major. Sure enough, when they turned off onto the forest track, they saw ahead of them a green pickup truck, parked far enough along to be out of sight of the road.

It flashed its lights twice and then set off along the wide, rutted forest track. The minibus was less well equipped for the rougher terrain and bumped along behind it, shaking its occupants about considerably.

The route that took them through the vast forest was bewildering, criss-crossed as it was with many tracks leading off to left and right. The major took a left turn, then a right, then left again. Anyone venturing in by chance would have been hopelessly lost in amongst the multitude of towering trees. But the major seemed to know exactly where he was going.

After about half an hour, the trees thinned out and the forest track came to an end at a minor country road. They followed the truck for another few miles on the tarmac road, now through countryside of grazing cows in lush green fields.

Before long, they saw the streetlights of a typical Scottish village ahead. It had low, single storey whitewashed cottages with corner stones picked out in black. They clustered either side of the long main road, together with a smattering of shops and one or two pubs. At the far end of the village, set amongst mature trees, was a sprawling red sandstone building with mustard yellow quoin stones. It had high windows and a weathervane on the roof. As the pickup swept into its drive, Danny noted the nameplate on the gate read, *The Old School House*.

The minibus pulled up and the students, together with Rama and Lakshman, got out of the vehicle and stood waiting. Major Hanuman went back to the entrance they'd just come through and checked up and down the street. Apparently reassured that they hadn't been followed, he closed the gates then limped over to the front door to ring the bell. Danny noticed there were a couple of CCTV cameras on either side of the doorway.

The museum gang were all agog at this cloak and dagger behaviour. As they were driving along, they'd tried to pump Danny for information.

'Tell us what happened, Danny?' demanded Izzie. 'How come you left when you did?'

'I can't say yet,' Danny was evasive.

'Why not?' Sandeep sounded cross. 'And why are we following that pickup? What is your dad doing? Where is he taking us?'

'I haven't a clue! Can't tell you anything else because my dad told me I mustn't until he gives me permission.'

'Did he say that when you saw him at the filling station?' said Hugo.

'Yes, but you're not allowed to tell anyone that.'

'That's enough questions for now,' said Rama. 'Danny is following orders. All will be revealed in good time.'

As they waited to be let into the unknown house, questions were buzzing round Danny's mind too. What kind of covert mission was his father on?

The front door was shortly opened by a distinguished, grey-haired gentleman. He was tall with an impressive handlebar moustache. Although inclined to be portly, his bearing was upright, and he had that air of authority that marked him as a man accustomed to being obeyed.

Major Hanuman performed the introductions.

'This is Colonel Meyers, my commanding officer. Colonel, may I present to you Rama and his brother, Lakshman. They are the elite Kalari warriors I was telling you about. And these are the friends of my son, Sandeep, Hugo and Izzie.'

The colonel first shook hands with the two noble brothers. He seemed genuinely pleased to see them.

'Welcome, welcome!' he said in bluff, yet well-modulated tones. His keen eyes missed nothing as he ushered the students through the door and into the spacious hallway.

They looked around curiously, noting the polished wooden floors and rugs. There was an umbrella stand and coat hooks nearest the door. A row of chairs was ranged along one wall and it was all spotlessly clean.

'Thank goodness you are safe, young man,' Colonel Meyers put a kindly hand on Danny's shoulder. 'Your father has been very worried about you.'

As he spoke, the colonel led them through a door to the left of the hall. The students stood transfixed, gazing open mouthed at the scene in front of them.

From the outside, the building gave the appearance of a normal family home converted from a nineteenth century school-house. But once inside, it was a different story.

For a start, the original sitting room had been adapted to be the centre of a military operation of some sort. The large bay window was fitted with black-out blinds. There was high tech equipment and computers everywhere.

Satellite images were displayed on a large screen on the wall. They showed the forest area they'd passed through and the wilds of the mountainous region beyond. A large table in the centre of the room was covered with maps and plans, some of which Danny recognized as Standing Stanes Farm. He noticed they were incomplete.

As usual, Izzie was the first to find her voice.

'Er, Colonel Meyers. This is obviously a big operation of some kind. Can you tell us what is going on?'

'All in good time, young lady. It's Izzie Dalton, isn't it?'

Her eyebrows shot up in surprise that he knew her surname. But there were many more surprises in store for her that night.

Colonel Meyers said,

'Before we can proceed, you will all have to agree to be bound by the Official Secrets Act. What you are about to learn is Top Secret and of national importance.'

The students were fazed, well out of their comfort zone. What could it be about? Nonetheless, they were all duly sworn in.

On the colonel's orders, Major Hanuman then led the students and the warrior brothers through to the back of the property.

He ushered them into an extensive farmhouse kitchen. It had a reassuringly normal feel with its dark green Aga in the middle of one wall and a well-fed tabby cat curled up at its foot. Along the other walls there was a range of cream kitchen units and at one end of the room stood a huge oak refectory table. Set around it was enough seating for at least a dozen people.

A tall, elegant lady in her fifties, with her grey hair cut in a neat bob, was setting out mugs on a tray. She poured water from a kettle into a teapot, wiped her hands on her floral apron and came forward to greet them.

Major Hanuman introduced her as the colonel's wife, Elizabeth.

'Thank goodness you're all safely arrived here,' she said, in a cut-glass accent. 'We were frightfully worried about *you*, young man.'

Hugo wrinkled his brow and looked at Danny as she spoke.

'*We* were worried about you too, mate,' he said. 'When are we going to find out what happened to you?'

'When my Dad gives me permission,' Danny responded, looking at his father.

Elizabeth frowned in concern as the major sat down heavily at the table.

'Mike, are you ok? You seem to be limping.'

'I'm fine. It's nothing to worry over, Liz. Really. We've got more important things to think about.'

She shrugged and set the mugs and teapot down on the kitchen table. She took a freshly baked batch of shortbread out of the oven as Colonel Meyers came in and invited everyone to sit down and help themselves.

'I'll start by explaining something of our set-up here,' the colonel began. 'You may have gathered this is the centre of a surveillance operation involving what we believe to be illegal activity at Standing Stanes Farm. It's about ten miles away, up in the mountains. We have been keeping it under observation for quite some time. We are still gathering information. As yet, we don't have enough evidence to take action.

'Your briefing, Danny, will hopefully provide us with valuable intelligence.'

Danny looked to his father for guidance.

'Dad. Am I allowed to tell everyone now?'

Major Hanuman held up his hand.

'Hang on just one moment longer, Danny.'

It was the signal for a couple of men to slip silently into the room. Both wore camouflage outfits, but there, the similarity ended. Major Hanuman introduced the first of the men.

'Let me introduce Sergeant 'Tyger' Diggory,'

Sergeant Diggory was a man of medium height but he was broad and square built with solid muscle. His face had seen better days with its broken nose and damaged ear. He had a pugnacious air that conveyed the impression he would give Mohammed Ali a run for his money.

The sergeant gave a curt nod acknowledging the introduction, but he remained standing near the Aga, very much on the alert.

The other man was taller with the wiry, lean fitness of a greyhound. His eyes were war-hardened and he looked as tough as his comrade, albeit in his own terse way.

Major Hanuman said,

'This is Captain Billy 'Watto' Watkins. These two are my right hand men. I would trust them with my life. They are part of the crack commando force stationed here.'

The captain also remained standing, leaning casually against the wall, but taking everything in, his impassive eyes giving nothing away.

It was a daunting audience. Danny drew a deep breath and began to recount his story from when he'd left the museum. When he described the warehouse set-up, the captain drew out a notebook and jotted something down. It was when Danny reached the point where he'd looked through the glass doors into the adjoining warehouse, that he got the most dramatic reaction.

'I just couldn't believe it,' said Danny. 'When Eissen showed me the new people that had been brought in and I saw one of them was Urmila. I managed to speak to her, and she told me they'd abducted her after the fire. She's being made to work for them. She's okay. But when it came to planning the escape for both of us, she refused to go with me.'

Sandeep's face turned beetroot red.

'Whaaat?' he yelled at Danny. 'Are you telling me *The Aculeata* have abducted my cousin and you left without her? And you're only just telling me *now*?'

Hugo and Izzie were too shocked to speak. Everything was going wrong. They looked at Sandeep anxiously, as the old feud flared up anew. He seemed to have lost his rag completely.

Major Hanuman looked at his son, his eyes registering disappointment.

'Couldn't you have found a way?' he asked.

Danny's face fell.

At that point Rama intervened, turning his clear, penetrating gaze on his furious pupil.

'Sandeep. Remember what the Kalari Knighthood teaches us,' he said. 'Anger is a weakness which an enemy will exploit. Acting on the basis of strong emotion leads to irrational behaviour and will result in failure.'

'Our Code of Honour,' Lakshman added. 'States that a Kalari Knight does not turn on his own comrades. You can't judge another man until you've walked a mile in his shoes. You do not know what it was like for Danny in that situation. I will vouchsafe that Danny acted bravely, as befits a true Kalari.'

'Indeed,' Rama continued, glancing briefly at the major. 'He did the best he could, and undertook a dangerous escape so that he could give us intelligence on *The Aculeata's* operations. He was right - we *need* his information if we are to successfully rescue Urmila, not to mention the others. And it's essential that we keep a cool head on our shoulders.'

Sandeep hung his head as his teacher's words sunk in.

'Sorry!' he mumbled, sheepishly.

But the damage had been done. Danny was sure his father and the others thought he was a coward, in spite of what Rama and Lakshman had said. He'd been feeling anguished ever since he'd left Urmila behind. Had he done the right thing? Should he have tried harder to tackle the situation on his own?

Major Hanuman's mouth was set hard and his face was grim. He didn't look at Danny as he spoke.

'It's worse than we thought, Henry,' he said to his commanding officer. 'The fact they've abducted the girl means you-know-who is gaining in confidence and strength!'

'I agree, Mike,' said Colonel Meyers. 'This is grave news indeed. It forces our hand. We must make our move much sooner than we had intended. It will require stealth and intricate planning, and that must be based on our intel.'

Major Hanuman looked thoughtfully at the two noble brothers.

'Sir,' he addressed the colonel. 'I understand Rama and Lakshman are in this country incognito on a special ops mission of their own. Rama, would you mind telling the colonel what you told me?'

Rama said,

'We are on a mission to track down two dangerous leaders of the underworld. One of them is Dr Zeuber and we have evidence that he has infiltrated a number of influential positions in the city in order to manipulate financial transactions. We suspect that he may also be an assassin. The other is called Taddakka and he's the leader of an international drug cartel. As far as we know, they take their orders from one who is called General Maricha. He seems to be one of the key leaders of the global organization known as *The Aculeata*.'

The words sent shivers down Danny's spine. The other students were riveted. You could have heard a cat's paw pad as Lakshman continued.

'*The Aculeata's* plan,' said Lakshman. 'Is to infiltrate all layers of society, including governments. They model themselves on a class of insects, *the Parasitica*, which include parasitic wasps. The way the wasp operates is to inject its eggs inside a host caterpillar. The larvae grow bigger, fed by the unsuspecting caterpillar, until eventually they hatch out of its skin, killing their host.'

'Ewww!' said Izzie, involuntarily. 'How gross!'

'Quite!' Lakshman agreed.

'They have respectable fronts for their organisations,' said Rama. 'But behind the scenes they are involved in all manner of murky deals: drug running, trading in armaments, importing illegal immigrants – you name it, *The Aculeata* are involved in it.'

Danny recalled the Asian supermarket where he'd seen what he now guessed had been illegal immigrants, pending transportation.

'Furthermore,' said the colonel. 'From Danny's intelligence, it looks as if they are also dealing in stolen artefacts. Danny, what else can you tell us about this?'

'Eissen told me,' said Danny, 'that they are looting ancient archeological sites all over the world. Especially from war-torn countries. They bring the artefacts over here, to the laboratory at Standing Stanes Farm. There, they are analysed and classified by experts, who keep meticulous records of what they study.'

'Where do they get these 'experts' from, Danny?' the colonel asked.

'They target specific scholars, like Professor Haldiki, who are leading experts in their field. First they try and bribe them. If they won't cooperate willingly they are abducted and brought here along with other immigrants.

'Or, according to our research,' said Izzie. 'We believe that if they know too much, and threaten to reveal the truth about the most ancient civilizations, they are eliminated.'

'Killed, in some faked accident,' said Major Hanuman, a bitter edge to his voice.

'Yes,' said Hugo. 'Or they mysteriously drown in their swimming pool when they are capable swimmers.'

'Or they suffer a fatal heart attack when they've previously been pronounced in robust good health,' said Danny.

Captain Watkins commented.

'These are classic tactics of the assassin's trade. Make it look like a realistic 'accidental death.'

'But the pressing question now is this,' said Colonel Meyers. 'How are we going to rescue Urmila without them harming her?'

1 6

BATTLE OF STANDING
STANES FARM

'Dad,' said Danny. 'Before we begin, can I ask you a question? How did you know where to find me when we arrived at the Service Station?'

'It was thanks to Rama,' Major Hanuman said. 'After he got in touch with me, we were able to put a trace on your mobile phone. We located it at the Standing Stanes Farm complex. We already had the place under surveillance. We guessed it was one of the operations of the international *Aculeata*. We knew their activities included drug smuggling and armaments. But the illegal immigrants side of their operation wasn't clear.

'As Danny has seen,' continued Colonel Meyers. '*The Aculeata* are using Standing Stanes Farm as a processing centre for selected illegal immigrants. Can you tell us any more about it, Danny? For instance, did you learn anything that would tell us why they target specific people?'

'Eissen told me,' Danny said. 'That *The Aculeata* target top level academics who are experts in the most ancient civilisations. They force them to reveal their knowledge in order to obtain the secrets of these ancient cultures. The scholars then tend to mysteriously 'disappear.'

'Interesting,' Colonel Meyers mused.

'We believe one of *The Aculeata's* operations,' Rama said. 'Involves various strategies for removing indigenous people from their homelands. In this way *The Aculeata* are then free to exploit the land for their own monetary ends.

Danny confirmed this, adding,

'Eissen believes *The Aculeata* intend to wipe out all indigenous people from the face of the earth. With their loss would go their traditional knowledge of medicines and how to live in harmony with the environment.'

Izzie had been reflecting on the information.

'It sounds to me like a Hitler-type form of *ethnic cleansing*,' she said.

'I agree,' said Mike Hanuman. 'And that begs the question, who do they want to replace the indigenous people with? Are our young people at risk? Is that another reason they have abducted Urmila?'

The expressions of the adults in the room ranged from incredulous, to downright horrified at this catalogue of evil intent.

'This is appalling!' Elizabeth Meyers exclaimed. 'It's a form of heinous crimes against humanity we thought we'd never see again after WW2.'

Danny went on to tell them all that he'd learned from his time at the Farm complex, including conversations he'd had with Eissen, Ashwin and Professor Haldiki.

But when Danny told them how they were treating the prisoners, particularly Urmila and Professor Haldiki, Colonel Myers rubbed his forehead, looking very grave.

'It is more serious than we thought. This information changes everything, Mike. We can't delay going in any longer.'

'I totally agree, colonel,' said the major. 'But how can it be done without the girl and the academics being harmed? They will use them as human shields, given the chance.'

'Seems to me, sir,' Captain Watkins said. 'That now they've abducted the girl, Urmila, we are seeing an escalation of their operations.'

'It is *imperative* that we rescue the girl unharmed,' said Major Hanuman. 'But how is this to be achieved? It will be extremely difficult.'

'Rama,' said Colonel Meyers. 'You know the girl in question, sir. She's trained with you. Her safety must be our top priority. What are your thoughts on this situation?'

Rama spoke in his quiet, calm way,

'Sir, if I might suggest a plan of action?'

'Yes, yes, please go ahead,' said the colonel. 'I have a great respect for your ancient Kalari tradition.'

'First of all,' said Rama. 'We need to gather as much detailed information as possible about the operations at the farm.'

'Danny,' Lakshman said. 'Can you give us an estimate of how many guards there are? How do their shift changeovers work? What else can you tell us?'

'Another request, Danny,' said Captain Watkins. 'Can you draw the layout of the farm complex while it's still fresh in your mind.'

'And then,' Elizabeth intervened in firm tones. 'He *must* go to the bunkhouse and rest, as must all the students. They have been up all night and must recoup their strength.'

'Before they sleep,' said Rama. 'While we are all still together I will outline the rest of the plan to you and your men, major.'

It was while they were finalising the plans for the rescue that disaster struck. Everyone was intently studying the maps on the table, when all of a sudden there was a terrible *thud*.

Major Hanuman, his face ashen grey, had fallen sideways off his chair and hit the ground in a dead faint. Danny rushed over to help him but Tyger got there first and pushed him away.

'Stand back!' he commanded. 'Let me see to him.'

Lakshman joined Tyger on the floor to examine the major.

'It's his leg. Look!'

There was blood oozing from the major's trousers. A pool of blood had formed unnoticed on the floor below where Major Hanuman had been sitting.

Without a word, Elizabeth got the scissors out of the kitchen drawer and handed them to Tyger. He cut away the outer fabric of the major's trouser leg. Underneath was revealed a heavily blood-stained, makeshift bandage. It had been wound tightly round the right leg.

Under the students' horrified gaze, Tyger carefully cut it away and they saw a deep, gory wound running the length of the major's leg from the knee to the ankle.

Danny saw Izzie's colour change to pale green. She turned away, retching.

Urmila wouldn't have done that.

Lakshman felt the major's pulse. It was weak from loss of blood.

After a few minutes, Major Hanuman came round. He opened his eyes and tried to sit up. His voice was barely more than a whisper.

'Must make sure this Special Ops goes without a hitch. Got to go with my men.'

'The only place *you'll* be going, Mike,' said Colonel Meyers. 'Is to the hospital to get that leg stitched up! How did it happen?'

'They've got booby traps all around the farmhouse on the hillside. Maricha and his men have excavated a ring of pits and then covered them with bracken and grass so you can't see they're there. They dig the holes to a depth of about knee height. Inside the hole they've placed sharpened pieces of slate so that as you drop down it rips your leg to pieces. Then when you can't walk you're easy prey for them to pick you off when they do their rounds of the area.

'I managed to make it back to the woods where my forestry vehicle was parked. That's been my cover, so it doesn't get any special attention because it's a known Forestry Commission working forest.

'I managed to find some first aid gear in my pickup and bandaged my leg as best as I could. I needed to get to the filling station to make sure you guys were all right. You did well to escape, Danny.'

The effort of talking was too much for him, and he fainted away again. Tyger and Lakshman took the sheets that Elizabeth hurriedly got for them and ripped them into strips. Lakshman checked the wound, then skillfully bound the Major's leg to stem the bleeding, making him as comfortable as he could.

'The ambulance is on its way,' Elizabeth announced.

Danny was horrified. He'd never seen his father so helpless. Was he going to be alright? And how would they rescue Urmila without him? Who would lead the team?

'Rama,' Major Hanuman opened his eyes and summoned the Kalari warrior to his side. 'I am handing this mission over to you. You will be in charge. My men are your men. They will follow you to the death, if need be.'

Rama nodded gravely.

'As you ask it of me Major Hanuman, it will be done. I will take this on as my personal mission in your stead. And please don't worry – '

The paramedics were in the process of carefully lifting the major onto the stretcher. It was quite a procedure and the pain-killing injection had to take effect before the major could speak again.

'Rama. Please keep Danny safe for me. He's all I've got. He's not a fighter ...'

And with that, the major slipped into unconsciousness.

As the ambulance left, Colonel Meyers saw Danny's stricken face. He patted the boy's arm in a fatherly fashion and said in bracing tones.

'Don't worry son,' he said. 'Your father is made of tough stuff.'

Once they'd seen the vehicle off, the colonel commanded everyone to assemble in the Operations Room at the front of the house. As they gathered round the central table, he said,

'Rama. Would you like to talk us through the plan for tomorrow night's special ops?'

'Captain Watkins,' said Rama. 'Regarding the lorry Danny escaped from - can you give us a report on its movements after it leaves the farm?'

'According to our intelligence,' the captain said. 'It travels to the port on the south coast and the lorry's shipment gets loaded onto a container ship. Once the unloading is complete, the driver will take the lorry to a remote seaside village on the south coast.

'He will sleep in his lorry for a few hours. Once it's dark, he drives to a remote beach, flashes his headlights out to sea, and waits. Then typically, a boatload of illegal immigrants will be dropped off on the shore by the local gangmaster.

'The driver will lower the secret compartment, and the fugitives will be quickly hidden away, unseen by anyone. The lorry will drive to a holding centre in the Midlands. The immigrants will be taken and sorted according to what *The Aculeata* wants them for.

'The handful of targeted academics will then be loaded into the lorry for the return journey to Standing Stanes Farm. They are prisoners until it arrives. That will be around midnight on the following night.'

'Does the driver stop anywhere en route closer to home?' asked Lakshman.

'Yes,' said Captain Watkins. 'It stops at the service station about twenty miles away from here for the driver to have a break and refuel.'

Lakshman turned to Danny.

'Question for you, Danny. Have you still got the remote control for that lorry?'

'Yes, sir.'

'Then I think we will arrange,' said Lakshman. 'For the lorry to have a little change of cargo …'

A broad grin spread over Sergeant Diggory's misshapen features.

'If you're thinking what I'm thinking, sir,' he said. 'I'm with you all the way.'

11:45PM

Twenty-four hours later, a number of incidents took place at a service station on the Lockerbie road in the remote Scottish Borders.

First of all, a lorry drew up and parked in the shadiest area of the designated lorry parking. The driver jumped down and checked his watch. He strode over to the brightly lit facilities and entered the premises. A dark shadow tailed him with silent stealth through the trees and shrubs that fringed the site.

It watched as the driver entered the building. Then he too, checked his timepiece and gave a thumbs-up to persons unknown.

Minutes later, a dark green wagon swept into view. It parked up on the other side of the lorry and switched off its engine. From it emerged about a dozen men clad head to toe in black. They wore night vision goggles over their balaclavas.

A white transit van appeared and parked on the other side of the lorry, sandwiching it in. A number of roughly dressed individuals wearing baggy tunics and trousers emerged from it. They were waiting for something.

Then a third vehicle, a black unmarked van, pulled up and parked right across the back of the lorry, effectively blocking any casual observer's view of it.

Out of its back doors emerged half a dozen fully armed men, dressed in night camouflage. One of them lowered the secret compartment to the lorry. Five scholarly looking men were revealed inside, hunched over, scared and dazed.

There was no fight in the captives. They didn't know what was going on. They emerged putting their hands over their heads and allowed themselves to be ushered into the waiting black vehicle. They were immediately swept away to a Special Branch centre for de-briefing and protection.

As soon as it left, the substitute immigrants swiftly climbed into the lorry's secret compartment and closed the trapdoor.

The other two vehicles then speedily disappeared from the scene, leaving the lorry with no trace of anything that had happened. No one in the service station was any the wiser. The whole slick operation had taken only minutes to accomplish.

Thus it was that Danny Hanuman, dressed once more as a refugee, was on his way to an extremely dangerous assignment - to rescue his friend from the clutches of evil.

He was the only one who knew Urmila's whereabouts and the layout of the farm complex, first hand. He was to take a small detachment to rescue Urmila and escape before anyone knew what was going on.

'Remember this, Danny,' Rama ordered. 'You stop for no one and nothing. Your sole mission is to rescue Urmila and get her out of there, unharmed.'

THE LORRY LUMBERED its way down the long track to the farm. Its occupants were on high alert, poised like coiled springs. The mission had been planned with military precision, but there were always unforeseen circumstances to be taken into account. No one could relax.

For Danny, his knees bent up to his chin, it was even more cramped and uncomfortable than it had been before. There were twelve of them now, including Rama, Lakshman, himself, Sandeep, Tyger and seven more of the major's handpicked men.

Captain Watkins was in the main body of the lorry with a detail of special SAS troops. Everyone would think the lorry was returning empty. It was a classic Trojan horse manoeuvre which, if it went to plan, would take the enemy completely by surprise.

Meanwhile, a dark green Forestry wagon was driving through the thick woods that fringed the hillside above the farm. The track ran parallel to the green fields surrounding the complex but was well out of sight of the buildings below.

The vehicle finally stopped in a clearing about a quarter of a mile away from the farm buildings. It would provide a person on foot with a view through to the warehouse complex, yet would be safely screened by trees.

The driver opened the door and jumped down. He was a nerdy young man named Chas, who wore horn-rimmed spectacles and a studious expression. His co-driver was a tubby chap with a good-natured face, named Robbie. Both were dressed in dark green forester's outfits and had binoculars slung round their necks.

They went round to the back doors where steps had been lowered to access the inside. It was an unexpected sight that would have greeted the uninitiated. For instead of Forestry equipment, along both sides of the interior were workbenches and stools. Above them bristled technical listening devices and computer monitors. Remote antennae were automatically raised above the roof.

Izzie sat with headphones on. She looked at her screen and listened intently. Hugo, sitting beside her, checked his drone equipment.

'Hi Chas!' he said to the driver as he entered and took the seat beside him. 'The camera is set up and ready to go.'

'Tell you what, pal,' Chas said. 'You're a real techie wiz with those drones.' He was plainly enjoying himself, working with a fellow nerd.

Izzie interrupted rudely.

'Shut it, you two! I've got the lorry on screen. Just about to check everyone's earpieces.' She fiddled with a control panel.

'Danny, can you hear me?'

There was an anxious pause. Then Danny's voice came through.

'Yes. Receiving you. Loud and clear.'

'We haven't got a visual on you yet, mate,' said Hugo. 'We'll let you know when– '

'Hugo's waiting,' interrupted Izzie. 'Till the lorry is nearly there before he sends his message.'

IGOR WAS in the garage at the far end of the farm complex on the night shift. He tinkered with a car he had up on the ramp while he waited for the lorry to arrive for its usual service and maintenance.

Suddenly, he became aware of something hovering in front of his face. It was a drone. And it had something dangling from it. As Igor squinted in puzzlement, the object dropped to the ground. The drone then disappeared. Mystified, Igor bent and retrieved the capsule. It opened up to reveal a piece of paper. The mechanic read it carefully, his countenance impassive.

Then, very deliberately, he took the missive to a bench, produced a lighter, and burned it. After that, he wiped his hands on an oily rag, and proceeded to the warehouse where Eissen and his friends were waiting.

The lorry would be there in the next ten minutes. They had work to do.

AS THE LORRY reversed into its bay at the warehouse, the driver was surprised to see Igor waving at him from a little distance away. Puzzled, he jumped down and walked over to see what he wanted.

He didn't see the two black clad figures creep up behind him. Nor did he have time to make a sound. He was quickly overcome by the commandos, who gagged and bound him. They waited till all the occupants emerged from the lorry's secret compartment and then pushed him in and shut the trapdoor.

Final instructions were issued from Commander Rama.

'Danny. You know what to do. You alone know Urmila's location in this farmhouse complex. Get her away to safety. Do not stop for any reason. She *must* escape at all costs. We can't give them a chance to use her as a bargaining tool. Remember, stealth is of the utmost importance.

'Follow your Kalari training. Keep low and move swiftly. Lakshman and Sandeep will go with you and provide cover for you. Eissen and the others will also escape. I repeat - do not stop for any reason whatsoever. If one of you falls, you must leave it to us to rescue them and continue with your mission. Urmila must be saved from any reprisals by these evil people.'

One by one, with extreme stealth, the first tranch of black clad commandos made their way to an open sided hay barn. They took up positions behind hay bales to provide cover for Eissen and his men to make good their escape.

But as the second group traversed the dark, silent courtyard they got the shock of their life. Out of the blue, the big arc lights covering the premises flashed on, dazzling, bright as day. While the commandoes tried to adjust their night vision, there followed a hail of bullets from the Aculeata Guards, who appeared out of nowhere. Everyone scattered and scrambled for cover.

The guards fired at random at any dark shadows. If it moved, they fired.

'Who alerted them?' Lakshman wondered as he and Rama dived for cover.

Zeuber's voice came over the tannoy system. He mocked Rama above the noise.

'You didn't bargain on the lorry's dashcam, did you Rama? Not only at the front but also at the rear as well. The guards watch it as soon as the lorry arrives here at base.'

Rama was as cool as ice. He signalled to his men to fan out. Lakshman took aim with his arrow and fired at the biggest arc lights. He took them out with deadeye precision. Sergeant Diggory and his men took out the other lights. All was instantly plunged into darkness once more. The guards without the night vision were now at a disadvantage.

Danny, Sandeep and Lakshman moved quickly. Danny led the way, using his knowledge of the farm's layout from his previous visit. As they came to the shadowy building, the farmhouse was in pitch darkness. Its occupants were either in hiding or waiting for the all-clear.

Lakshman motioned to Danny to wait while he went ahead to make sure the coast was clear. He heard noises from one of the downstairs rooms at the far end of the building and went to investigate.

As he disappeared from view into the black night, Danny motioned for Sandeep to follow him round to the back of the premises. But while Sandeep was in the process of adjusting his visor, Danny saw something else.

From round the corner they'd just passed, one of the Aculeata Guards was creeping up behind Sandeep. At the same time, Sandeep heard a warning voice in his earpiece.

'Behind you!' Hugo hissed.

With lightning reactions, Sandeep whirled round and kicked the man in the groin. He followed through with a karate blow to the side of the head. The man dropped like a stone.

'*Go!*' Sandeep spoke urgently to Danny. 'I'll stay on guard and deal with any other guards that appear from this side. Lakshman is covering the far end.'

'But–' Danny hesitated.

'Just *go!*' Sandeep's voice was authoritative. 'Get Urmila out. *Don't delay!*'

Danny wasted no further time arguing. He had located Urmila's room on the first floor. Eissen had told him she was locked up in her room at night. He threw a stone up at the window. A pause. Nothing. He threw another stone. This time there was a scraping noise as Urmila lifted the sash. She put her head out and called in a low voice.

'Who is it?'

'It's me, Danny,' he said. 'I'm getting you out of here.'

'Thank goodness. Is Rama with you?'

'Yes. And Lakshman. He's providing cover.'

'I knew he would come. What are you going to do?'

'I'm going to throw you a grappling hook with a rope attached. Can you grab it when it hits your windowsill and anchor it to the bed in your room? Then I want you to climb down it.'

'No! I can't do it.'

'Why ever not?'

'I'm afraid of heights.'

Danny rolled his eyes in the darkness. Izzie wouldn't have hesitated. But Urmila was the most timid of the group at the best of times.

'Every minute we delay is dangerous, Urmi. C'mon. You can do this. I believe in you.'

Someone tried the handle of her bedroom door. Urmila had had the presence of mind to push a chest of drawers up against it. It would buy her a little time, but not much.

She took a deep breath but she was shaking so much as she climbed over the windowsill, she could hardly hold the rope. Danny stood at the bottom ready to catch her.

Inch by inch she came down, Danny uttering encouraging noises.

'You're doing good. Nearly there.' As she landed safely, he exhaled. '*Phew*! Let's get out of here before anyone sees us.'

'It's pitch black,' she complained.

'You'll have to follow me. Hold my hand and keep close. I can see thanks to these night vision goggles.'

The battle in the courtyard was raging fiercely as they rounded the corner of the farmhouse. Danny saw that Eissen and Igor had managed to open the main gates to the warehouse complex. But the guards had the exit covered. It would be too dangerous to attempt to leave on foot.

Danny hesitated. The longer they remained there, the more likelihood there was of the guards finding them. And Zeuber was on the prowl somewhere too.

All of a sudden, Danny saw his chance. There was a car parked in front of the farm building as if someone was making ready for a getaway. If only it had its keys in it. It must belong to someone important because it was an expensive Lamborghini.

Danny told Urmila his plan.

'You must be crazy!' she said.

'C'mon!' Danny grabbed Urmila's arm. They crouched low and ducked behind some shrubbery near the vehicle.

'Right! *Now!*' Danny urged.

He kept low and opened the driver's door. The keys were inside. He pushed Urmila in through the driver's side so she wouldn't be seen from the courtyard. She landed in an ungainly heap in the passenger's seat. Danny started the engine. With a throaty roar, it leapt forward like a mighty beast. He pushed hard on the accelerator, heading for the main gates. He was aware of shouts behind him.

'Stop him!'

'Head him off!'

Guards scattered to the left and right as Danny kept his foot hard down on the pedal. He blasted through the gates to the track outside and kept going.

'Danny,' shouted Urmila. 'I didn't know you could drive?'

'I learned last year when I was on holiday at Hugo's dad's farm. At least, I mostly learned on a quad bike. It can't be that much different. Hang on tight!'

The track was stony and dangerous to a vehicle being driven at high speed. Danny felt the adrenaline pumping through his veins. He was beginning to enjoy himself.

But it was short-lived. Urmila was looking behind them. She yelled.

'Danny, look! It's Zeuber. And he's catching us up!'

With a sickening feeling in the pit of his stomach, Danny looked in his rear-view mirror. Zeuber was behind them on a high-powered motorbike speeding along the track. As he caught up with them and sped alongside, he opened fire, hitting one of their tyres. Urmila yelled at Danny.

'Lookout!'

Zeuber had headed them towards a pile of rocks at the side of the road. Danny tried to brake, but they were doing about sixty miles per hour when he had to swerve sharply. The car spun out of control and did a double somersault. Its last flip landed them the right way up. But its front wheels were now grounded in the ditch.

Danny was dimly aware that he had just totalled a few hundred grand's worth of metal.

'But the main thing is,' he assured Urmila, who was sitting rigid with shock, though otherwise unharmed. 'We're both ok.'

'N-n-not, ok,' she stuttered. '*Look!*'

17

THE DEADLY ATTACK

IN THE GLARE of the car headlights, Danny could see Zeuber getting off his motorbike. His face was mottled puce with fury and he was breathing heavily. He brandished a gun as he made his way towards them.

'That is General Maricha's personal vehicle,' he bellowed. 'You will pay for that!'

'Er, don't think so,' Danny said flippantly.

He tried to open his door, but it was stuck fast. Zeuber came to the passenger door and wrenched it open. He grabbed Urmila by the hair and yanked her out. She screamed at the top of her voice.

'Get your hands off me! You *monster!*'

Danny scrambled out of the passenger door to help her but found himself looking down the barrel of a pistol.

'Back off, punk!' hissed Zeuber, his unblinking reptilian eyes glittering cold and cruel. 'Make a false move and the girl gets a bullet through her.'

Danny put his hands up.

'OK. Take it easy. Just don't harm her, right? You can take me instead, but let her go. Please?'

Zeuber's screeching laugh sent chills through his listeners.

'*The Aculeata* have been waiting for a chance to get hold of *you*, Danny

Hanuman. And the girl is a valuable commodity. They have plans for both of you. Now *move*! Get in front of me where I can see you both. And walk yourselves back to the farmhouse.'

Zeuber made Urmila walk directly in front of him with Danny up ahead, leading the way. All the while he kept the gun pointed at her back.

Danny had no choice but to obey. He couldn't think of a way out of the situation. What could he do? He felt desperate. To make matters worse, he'd left his night vision gear in the car. The only light was from a torch that Zeuber held in one hand, the gun in the other.

The Aculeata's assassin mocked them as they walked.

'If it was up to me, Hanuman, I'd have finished you off when you had the bike accident,' he sneered. 'But General Maricha's orders were to keep you alive. For now. You have information he wants. You know too much about your mother's work to be left at large.'

'You've been rumbled, Zeuber,' Danny said. 'You're finished, no matter what happens to me.'

'Oh tut, tut! How little you know, Mr Hanuman. Your people may have taken down our operations at the farmhouse here, but believe me, this is the tip of the iceberg of *The Aculeata's* operations worldwide. You have no idea what you are dealing with.'

The noise of a distant helicopter could be heard. Zeuber stopped momentarily to look up at the skies. It seemed to make him agitated.

At the same time, there was a buzzing noise round the back of his head. He swatted at what he thought was a night hornet with his torch. He kept the gun steady on Urmila with his right hand.

The buzzing disappeared but then it came round again. Zeuber swore and swiped the air. This time, the torch fell out of his hand.

Danny heard a disembodied voice in his earpiece. It was Izzie.

'Grab Urmila and get over the dry-stone wall at the side of the road. Move quick while Hugo's drone keeps distracting him.'

'Run, Urmi! *Run!*'

As they leapt over the wall, an extraordinary sequence of events took place.

Zeuber starting firing wildly into the air in the direction they'd gone.

But suddenly the darkness was pierced by a gleam of bright blue light up ahead.

It illuminated Rama's good-looking countenance. To the side of him stood Lakshman, tall and impassive. Rama had an arrow poised on his bow.

Zeuber sneered.

'Want a fight, do you?' He fired his gun, but the blue light appeared to confuse him and the bullet went wide.

Rama spoke sternly.

'It's about time, Zeuber, you met your fighting match, instead of picking on unarmed young people.'

'Let's see,' said Lakshman. 'How you do in a fair fight.'

At that, Rama released an arrow. With unerring accuracy it knocked the gun clean out of Zeuber's hand.

Zeuber ground his teeth in fury. He spat his words out.

'Rama, you have interfered with *The Aculeata's* operations once too often. They have a contract out on you and it's time for you to be dispatched. Let's see how you like these!'

And with that, he produced a Chinese throwing star from a pouch at his side. He launched it straight for Rama's throat.

Rama ducked. Zeuber threw another couple of the razor-sharp weapons in quick succession. But Rama's Kalari agility and speed was legendary. He leapt high into the air, defying anything that was thrown at him.

Lakshman cautioned his brother, as he perceived their deadly secret.

'Take care, bro! His weapons are poisoned at the sharp points. One touch and the poison kills instantly.'

Zeuber changed tactics. He began to throw the poison discs in the direction of Danny behind the wall. One scratch and Danny or Urmila would face instant death.

Rama stood firm and steady. He loaded a silver arrow onto his bow.

'Let it be. Your reign of terror ends, Zeuber. Here and now. It is finished.'

Zeuber's response was to hiss, snake-like, and crouch down. He coiled, ready to spring forward in attack.

With a twang of the bowstring, Rama released his arrow. It pierced Zeuber in mid-air, right through the heart.

The hatred writ large on Zeuber's face froze and was replaced by a look of disbelief. He fell to the ground and writhed for a few seconds. And then lay still. It was over.

'Danny, mate,' came Hugo's voice in his ear. 'Can you pick up my drone for me before you leave? It's on the ground somewhere.'

Izzie's more urgent voice came through.

'Never mind that, Danny. Tell Rama that General Maricha is grabbing all the evidence and he's getting ready to leave in the helicopter.'

As they all ran back in the direction of the farmhouse, Danny could see two figures running towards the helipad in the far field. A burly bodyguard was at the general's side, and both carried heavy suitcases. They climbed into the helicopter, which took off, swiftly becoming a speck in the distance.

'It's not over yet, General Maricha,' Rama said quietly. 'We will meet again in the future. That's for sure.'

The next thing they knew, a green vehicle was lumbering down the track towards them. As it stopped, out piled Izzie and Hugo. Sandeep came running from the farmyard to join them. They surrounded Danny and Urmila, all talking at once about their exploits.

Sandeep patted Urmila affectionately on the back.

'Thank goodness you're safe, coz.'

To Urmila's surprise, Izzie gave her a hug.

'Well done, kiddo,' she said gruffly. 'You did well, climbing down that rope.'

Danny shook Hugo's hand.

'Mate,' he congratulated. 'You were awesome with that mini-drone. It really confused Zeuber and allowed us to make a break for it.'

Urmila shuddered.

'That hateful, evil man. I'm not sorry he's dead.'

BACK AT THE Old School House, Elizabeth had a hearty breakfast waiting for them. While they were all seated at the table, she brought them up to speed.

'Danny, I phoned your Aunt Millicent. She thinks you've been on a field trip to Scotland with your museum friends. I think it might be an idea to leave it at that, don't you? The fewer people who know about all this, the better.'

'And don't forget,' said Colonel Meyers. 'Everything that has happened is classified. Even your father's injury, Danny, was incurred in the line of duty. No one need know any more than that.'

'He's had the operation to save his leg,' said Elizabeth. 'Though your father will be in a wheelchair for quite some time to come.'

Urmila gave a concerned look of enquiry.

'It's ok, Urmila,' Elizabeth reassured her. 'I've phoned your parents and let them know we've got you here safe and sound. It said on the news your father was going to call off the Tournament and Challenge if you weren't returned to him by the end of today.'

'Of course! Sita's Challenge,' said Danny. 'I almost forgot with all this going on. We'll have to get back as a matter of urgency.'

'I think we can arrange an escort to get you there on time,' Colonel Meyers's eyes twinkled.

'But Danny,' Lakshman cautioned him. 'Don't forget Rama will have to get permission from Master Vishwa-mitra to enter the Contest. And he's not likely to give it while we're both on this warrior's mission for him.'

'Rama!' Danny looked devastated. 'You simply *must* enter. All will be lost if you don't.'

'First things first, young man,' said Colonel Meyers. 'Let's get you all back home so you can prepare for what I understand is going to be a spectacular Festival and Tournament.'

AUNT MILLICENT BEGAN SCOLDING Danny from the minute she saw him on the front doorstep. She kept it up all the way down the hall and into the kitchen.

'Why couldn't you have told me you were going on a field trip? I even had the police enquiring. They had the cheek to suggest you weren't happy at home. Huh! And I wasted some food because you didn't tell me you weren't coming home for your tea. And your father's been injured in the line of duty. He'll be in wheelchair and that'll be a lot of extra work … and … and …'

She went on and on till Danny was glad to escape up to his room.

That night, he had the weirdest dream.

He witnessed a scene at the downtown Dandaka District near the Nightmare Tavern. It was late and no one was about.

Suddenly a stretch limo with blacked out windows slid into view at the far end of the street. Its number plate read: TADDAKKA.

At the same time, Danny saw Rama and Lakshman appear out of the darkness. They stepped into the middle of the road. Vishwa-mitra was there, too, his staff in his hand. He remained on the pavement, observing his warriors' prowess.

The car door opened and a tall figure stepped out. He was clad in a long black leather coat and wore a black trilby hat and sunglasses.

Danny stiffened in horror. So this was Taddakka!

As the black figure squared up to the two princely brothers, he laughed and mocked them. Then Danny got the shock of his life. Without any warning, Taddakka produced an AK 47 assault rifle from under his coat and started firing at the noble brothers.

Rama was unfazed. As if expecting something of the sort, he murmured 'Meisner kavach' and a few other words in Sanskrit. A clear, bullet-proof shield, manifested around Lakshman and himself. The bullets bounced off harmlessly.

At this, Taddakka was furious. He produced a second gun in the other hand, firing both ferociously.

Lakshman quietly placed an arrow on his bow and took aim. It went square though the very top of the hat, blasting it off Taddakka's head, but leaving him unscathed.

As the hat fell, a mass of tatted hair cascaded down to the shoulders. With a yell of fury, the figure threw away the sunglasses. Danny reeled in disbelief as he took in what he was seeing. *It was a woman!* Her eyes behind the sunglasses were red and bloodshot. She had warts on her nose and yellowed, fanged teeth.

From this hideous vision emitted a blood-curdling shriek.

'Rama! Be prepared to breathe your last. I will now destroy you!'

To Danny's surprise, Rama hesitated, as if unsure of what to do.

It was then that Vishwa-mitra stepped forward and spoke to the Kalari warrior.

'Rama, do not delay. You must kill *her*, before she tries to kill *you*. Rakshasa-demons grow stronger at night. Her strength is growing every minute.'

'But Master,' said Rama, hesitating. 'I cannot do it. She is a woman. It is against our Kalari Code to kill a woman.'

'Rama,' said Vishwa-mitra. 'Taddakka is the drug baron who has been feeding off the misery of young people and ruining their lives for years. Do not delay, O prince among men. There is no sin in this self-defence. This demon has already killed thousands of men and women and fed off their life force. It has given her enormous power.'

As Taddakka re-loaded her gun, and prepared to take aim once more, Rama took a silver arrow from his quiver. With careful deliberation, he placed it on the bow and drew the string back.

He closed his eyes and murmured some words that Danny couldn't make out. Then he let it fly. With a thud, the arrow hit the creature right between the eyes. It gave a hideous scream and fell to the ground in a crumpled black heap.

There was a moment's silence while the onlookers watched and waited.

Seconds later, Danny saw something emerging from the dark pile on the ground. A glowing white ball of light emerged and hovered in the air above the body.

To Danny's amazement, the light coalesced into the form of a beautiful, shining woman. As Rama approached her, she put her palms together and spoke to him in a soft, sweet voice.

'O Rama, thou art truly noble,' she said. 'Thou hast released me from a dreadful curse, which was placed upon me by the evil Dark Lord, Ravana. He abducted me as a very young girl and got me hooked on drugs.

'He made me his slave, so that I too, pushed drugs onto other young people. I also fed off their misery, like him. It was only *you*, Rama, prince among men, who could have released me from this accursed re-birth and the miserable cycle of destruction into which I have been locked.

'But beware! Pedro is none other than General Maricha, Ravana's right hand man. As well as being a master of disguise, he is also a ruthless killer and greatly to be feared. It was he who gave me orders to assassinate you and your brother.'

Rama held up his hand in blessing as she gave her last words.

'May you be victorious in your battle against the Dark One, O Rama. You are the embodiment of Truth. *Satyam Eva Jayate.*'

Danny's vision clouded and he saw no more.

The next morning's headline news read,

'*Gangland leader killed in rival shoot-out.*'

OVER THE FOLLOWING WEEK, plans were made to remove the Great Bow of Shiva from the Manchester museum. It was to be taken to Hartland Abbey, the country seat of the Earl of Belvedere.

Lord Belvedere was a long time friend of the Mithil family and Raja Janak felt that Hartland would be a secure venue in which to hold the Challenge of the Great Bow.

But there was one big problem. The weight of the Great Bow was phenomenal. Although there were many volunteers from the local football team who offered to move the antique object, when it came to it, no one could actually shift it, no matter how hard they pulled and pushed.

It was only when Sita led the way, reciting something softly in Sanskrit, that they were able to transport the bow onto a waiting lorry. She went ahead in her father's car, in convoy, until they reached the gates of the stately home.

Once there, the Bow was placed safely inside the Great Hall of Hartland Abbey to await preparations for the day of Raja Janak's Challenge.

7:00 am

The day of the Tournament dawned bright and clear. Hartland Abbey sat majestically overseeing proceedings, its mellow stone and turreted spires bathed in the golden glow of the rising sun.

'Good morning, ladies and gentlemen,' Kirsty O'Donnell's voice held barely suppressed excitement as she spoke to the outside broadcast camera.

'Welcome to the Finale of the Culture Festival, which is being held here, at Hartland Abbey, the country seat of the Earl of Belvedere. Lord Belvedere's family and the illustrious Mithil family have connections that go back for hundreds of years.

'Incidentally,' Richard Greenwood interjected. 'Some of you may already know Hartland from visits to the adjacent Wild Life Safari Park. It is best known for its wild animals, particularly the lions. You can just get a glimpse of its perimeter fence over there in the distance.

'Today will take the form of a Grand Tournament,' said Kirsty. 'Each country will demonstrate their long held traditions. It begins with the Tournament Spectacular, a procession like no other. Our outside broadcast team will be bringing you live coverage of the events as they happen.'

The camera panned round into the distance revealing Hartland Abbey's acres of rolling parkland, and lush green lawns interspersed with groups of specimen trees.

'Over there,' Kirsty continued. 'Is the arena where the main contests will take place. Around you are tents for guests to sit and take refreshments. Every nationality will be serving their own speciality foods and judging by the delicious smells wafting over here, there's going to be something to please everyone.'

She fiddled with her earpiece.

'I am getting a message it is about to begin. Over to you, Richard.'

Richard appeared on camera, his hair neatly plastered down, wearing a smart jacket and shirt. He stood in front of a large open-air amphitheatre.

'This is the arena for the displays of martial arts and equestrian skills which take place after the procession.' He gestured behind him. 'The ceremonial ride past is just about to start.'

The rows of wooden-tiered seats were packed with excited crowds. Raja Janak and Sita were sitting in the centre of the spectators on a raised platform under a canopied awning.

Music blared out from loudspeakers, and Richard had to shout to make himself heard above the din. Suddenly the music stopped. A royal fanfare was blown by liveried trumpeters.

'Something is happening,' he said. 'The crowd is going wild – .'

Rama and Lakshman could be seen, riding on plumed and richly decorated horses. Rama was riding a pure white stallion and with his handsome features, he looked every inch the royal prince. His loyal brother, Lakshman, rode on a chestnut bay, looking gracious and dignified.

They cantered into the arena at the head of the procession. They stopped beneath the dais where Raja Janak and his family sat, and their horses bowed low in salutation.

Rama caught Sita's eye and put his hand on his heart, as if to say, this is for you. Sita blushed and looked down in some confusion. Her heart was in her mouth as she watched.

The Kalari warriors began a daring display of equestrian skills, such as no one had seen the like of before. Firstly, the brothers spurred their horses on to a gallop. Then they jumped on and off each side of their speeding steeds.

As they landed with a light step on the ground, it was as if they'd got springs in their feet. For no sooner had they touched the ground on one side, than they sprang back into the saddle, and repeated it on the other. It was incredibly dangerous and few of even the most skilled horsemen in the world would have been able to attempt it. The crowd cheered them on enthusiastically.

Next, Lakshman set up an archery target to the side of the long gallop track, halfway down. Rama poised his horse at the start. He appeared to centre himself, eyes closed for a moment. Then he took his bow from off his shoulder, and held it with one hand. The other held the reins.

He spurred his horse on to a gallop. This time as he drew near level with the archery target, he dropped the reins. With practiced ease, he used both hands, one to load an arrow onto the bow, the other to pull it taut. He was still looking straight ahead.

At the very last moment, as he became level with the target, he twisted his body in the saddle to face it. He released the arrow and let it fly. It landed with a twang, right in the centre of the target. Bull's eye.

The crowd roared and cheered their approval of this ancient skill of noble warriors. The two brothers then dismounted and demonstrated their Kalari Warrior skills both with weapons and with bare hands.

Richard gave a running commentary.

'This is Kalari Payattu, the oldest martial arts in the world. It has been practiced in India since time immemorial. It was so effective as a means of defence, and the warriors so fearless and skilled, that the British Raj outlawed it. They hoped they could stamp it out.

'But the tradition was too strongly engrained in the culture and could not be completely eradicated. It continued in secret groups, being passed on from Master to disciple in hidden arenas, particularly in the South of India.

'Here you can see Rama and Lakshman engaged in martial arts combat. They are demonstrating extraordinary mastery over their bodies,. The oil on their bodies is said to ensure that they would slip through an enemy's grasp and so no Kalari warrior could be held down.

'In fact, it is said that under cover of darkness, they are the ultimate stealth fighters. All an enemy is left with if he makes contact is oil on his hands! In this demonstration set piece, you can see how supple their legs are, stretched as they move low to the ground. This skill allows them to pass through jungle undergrowth undetected.

'We can see the high leaps that Kalari warriors are famous for. They twist and turn in the air ensuring no enemy can touch them, or match their agility and strength. Their prowess makes the impossible look easy, almost as if they are levitating.'

The crowd went wild with delight, cheering as the noble brothers' performance came to an end. As the two brothers left the arena, the student novices were waiting in the wings. Kalari training had gained quite a following, and other students had joined, not only from Danny's school, but also from the Bhavan Classes in Manchester where Sita taught at weekends.

They included girls as well as boys, and although Urmila had preferred the traditional dance classes to the martial arts, Izzie had joined in with great gusto and showed real aptitude.

But it was Danny and Sandeep who excelled in the art, Sandeep having discovered in himself an unexpected aptitude for the discipline. He was fit and agile and trained hard. He and Danny were well matched.

Rama had seen their potential early on, especially Danny's. He had been hard on the boy because he knew what Danny would have to face in the future. He'd made him work late and pushed him to the limits of his endurance.

Rama had given him mental techniques to develop his inner Shakti power. But often Danny would feel he was getting nowhere and go home, dispirited.

Today was a demonstration of set pieces, stylised ritual fighting to show their skills and progress. Although Danny and Sandeep had been partnered with each other, the old rift was still there. They had agreed beforehand to set aside all past differences between them. But it was easier said than done. There was a pain in Danny's heart at his friend's behaviour that wouldn't go away. And Sandeep still couldn't understand how his best friend could have betrayed him.

And now it was their turn to fight each other. Urmila sat beside Sita on the rostrum, twisting her fingers and holding her breath.

Little did any of them know the mortal danger the two young warriors were about to face.

MORTAL DANGER AT HARTLAND ABBEY

DANNY AND SANDEEP gave the traditional bow of respect to each other as they began their set routine. They both wore the costume of the Kalari with its white top, dark baggy trousers and red cummerbund.

They were to display an advanced programme that showcased the whole range of the Kalari warrior skills: the wooden staff, the use of sword and shield, bow and arrow, the hand-to-hand combat.

At first they seemed well matched. But as he completed the practice moves some kind of inner energy took over Danny. He started to feel a surge in power that lifted him out of himself. It felt as if he was having an out of the body experience. It was very odd but exhilarating at the same time.

As his leaps in the air got higher and higher the crowd cheered him on. He felt invincible inside. *So this is what it feels like to have Shakti power.*

It was as they were nearing the end of their performance that disaster struck. It had all been going so well. Sandeep had just executed a spectacular leap high into the air. Unfortunately, he landed heavily on his right ankle and it twisted awkwardly under him. He lay on the ground groaning in pain and holding onto his foot.

Danny heard the crowd give a sort of gasp. He looked over at them wondering what they were shouting at. Sandeep was on the ground a little distance away. But the crowd were shouting at *him*.

'Look out. Behind you!'

'Run for your life, Danny. *Run!*'

Mystified, Danny turned to see what they were pointing at. A shiver ran down his spine and he stood rooted to the spot. He felt as if the blood in his veins had been blasted by an Arctic chill. For padding ominously into the arena was a massive male lion. And judging by the throaty growls it was making, it did not look pleased to find itself there.

It had every right to be angry. Maricha and his crew, dressed in white lab coats had posed as a veterinary team. They produced a report to the keeper that said the lion had to undergo emergency surgery.

After sedation it had been loaded onto the Safari Park's trailer and driven off with blue lights flashing. But the vehicle had taken a detour. It stopped right outside the underground entrance to the amphitheatre. The lion was given the antidote and forced to 'escape' out of the trailer into the tunnel.

From there, it was goaded and prodded forward by Maricha and his crew with long barbed poles. It was hardly surprising the creature was now beside itself with rage.

The two boys froze in mute horror, weighing up the aggressive beast's next move. Danny was some distance away, behind his friend. Sandeep Mithil lay on the ground, helpless. He was closest to the powerful animal, and was transfixed by the massive brute force facing him.

To the lion, here was easy prey. It fixed Sandeep with a mesmerizing stare. Then it snarled, revealing enormous meat-shredding fangs. It emitted a low menacing, rumbling growl. It was a primeval sound of wild, untamed power that sent shudders through the assembled onlookers. Sandeep's face blanched. He knew he was facing death, for sure. He tried to get up but winced in unbearable pain. This was it. He was done for.

Danny looked on in horror at his friend's helpless plight. Thoughts raced through his mind. *What should I do?* The crowd's words echoed in his ears.

Run!

Danny ran as fast as he could. But it was *towards* the lion. As he moved, he executed a high leap in the air that lifted him right over his friend's head.

To Sandeep's dismay he saw Danny was now between himself and the lion. All he could do was watch helplessly as Danny instinctively stuck out his arms and legs to make himself appear bigger to the predator.

'Mate,' whispered Sandeep through dry lips. 'What are you *doing*? Get away from here. *Run.* While you still can.'

'No!' Danny spoke firmly. 'I'm not leaving you. It'll have to get me first and then it'll lose interest in you. Lie still. Don't make a move.'

Something inside Danny had changed. His fear was replaced with a detached sense of purpose and duty. He then attempted the move that Rama had taught him one time. It was the Nataraj pose. It was incredibly difficult to maintain the posture without overbalancing and falling over. It should look like the Dancing Shiva outside Cern in Switzerland.

Danny stood on one leg. He bent the other leg at the knee and raised it to his hip height. He raised his arms in the correct position and centred himself. He breathed as Rama had taught him. He felt the power surge through him as he maintained the pose.

The lion paused. The movement captured his attention. He was diverted by this strange tactic. A new prey. But some sense of the integration of his prospective prey was transmitted to him at that moment. He hesitated.

Crack!

A loud gunshot suddenly ricocheted around the arena. General Maricha, now disguised as one of the security guards, had fired a rifle into the air. He intended to freak out the creature and spook it into attack mode once more.

The ruse succeeded. The shock aroused the ferocity of the lion, who transferred all the anger and frustration onto the target that was now Danny. He crouched low, ready to take the next few steps and pounce for the kill.

There was a slight noise behind Danny. An audible sighing breath came from the crowd. The teenager turned and saw Rama had leapt lightly into the arena. He now stood at a little distance, keeping away from the two boys.

Once more, the big cat's instinct kicked in causing its attention to be diverted. This new movement heralded further prey. People in the crowd were on the edge of their seats. They noted with great anxiety that Rama carried no weapon. Surely he wasn't going to use his bare hands to wrestle the lion?

Security guards were running in from everywhere but hesitated on the outskirts, fearful of escalating the situation. The crowd continued to shout instructions.

'Get him a gun!' someone shouted.

'Shoot the beast before it gets him!'

'He'll be killed.'

'It'll tear him to pieces.'

'Somebody help him!'

At that point Lakshman appeared at the far side of the arena. He held a hand up and spoke to the crowd with firm authority.

'There will be no need for violence. You will create even more tension and fear in the animal if you panic. Please sit still and be silent.'

That left the crowd little option but to sit and watch. They could see marksmen had taken up positions with rifles. But they were fearful of taking a shot for fear of hitting one of the boys or spooking the lion still further.

Everyone looked up to the Royal Enclosure to see what Raja Janak's instructions would be. He, in turn, looked enquiringly at his daughter.

'Father,' Sita said, her unwavering gaze fixed on the Kalari nobleman. 'Please let Rama deal with the situation.'

Everyone held their breath as the lion padded silently towards Rama. Rama stood his ground, feet apart, unflinching. And then to everyone's astonishment the elite warrior did something completely unexpected. He looked the lion directly in the eye and made a little *'chuffing'* noise from his throat.

Danny recognised the sound. It was what the expert zoo-keeper did when he was communicating with the big cats. But it was unheard of that an animal would take any notice of a stranger, much less when it was in a heightened state of anger and distress.

The lion, however, was riveted. It looked at Rama and did a strange thing. It *chuffed* back. What did it mean? Whilst never taking its eyes off the Kalari warrior, it began to slowly approach him.

The audience didn't know what was going to happen. Some groaned in anguish. As the animal got to within six feet of him, Rama extended his hand. He was now eye to eye with the mighty king of the jungle. Rama quietly spoke some words in Sanskrit. He made a gesture with the palm of his hand.

Maybe the lion recognised something in this courageous warrior. He threw back his huge mane and let out a mighty roar. The sound reverberated all around the amphitheatre and quivered through every nerve and fibre of the people sitting there.

It was a sound that encapsulated the lush green savannah from which the big cat had come. It was the call of the wild. It was a longing for his homeland. Yet at the same time he was answering with all his might that he was willing to submit. That he recognised a mightier power emanating from this noble human in front of him.

With that, he lay down at Rama's feet in quiet submission.

'Good boy,' Rama said softly. 'Well done.'

He gently touched the lion's mane with his hand. Immediately, a low rumbling sound erupted from the beast's throat. Danny looked on in wonder. Was that the big cat equivalent of a purr?

The crowd erupted into noisy applause, cheering and whistling. Lakshman however, strode into the centre of the arena. He held up his hand and put a finger to his lips for silence, gesturing to the two boys who were being attended to by medics and security guards.

Lakshman went over to Sandeep and asked to see his ankle. He produced some medicine and a salve from a bag slung over his shoulder.

'This will take away the pain,' Lakshman said. 'And if the x-rays show nothing is broken I will give you something to heal the ligaments. You must not put any weight on it until it is healed.'

Danny remembered that Ayurveda was part of the Kalari Code. To heal any injuries, however they were caused.

The police marksmen stood down, putting away their rifles with exclamations of amazement. The Safari Park's keepers entered and with Rama's help, ushered their charge back to where it belonged. There was no sign of Maricha and his crew.

As Danny was being escorted out of the ring, he glanced over to where Sita was sitting. Her gaze was fixed on Rama and there was no mistaking the love in her eyes. Danny looked towards Rama. He had turned before he left the ring to wave to Sita. There was a reciprocal depth of expression in his eyes.

There was no mistaking their feelings for each other and some deep intuition told Danny that here was an age-old destiny at work. This was a true match made in heaven of hearts and souls.

But with that realisation Danny's heart gave a lurch. He thought with dismay that the happiness of his beloved sister, Sita and that of Rama, his teacher, mentor and friend, hung in the balance. If Rama wasn't allowed to enter the Challenge tomorrow all would be lost. For tomorrow was the final and most difficult phase of the Challenge. It was a closely guarded secret whatever it was. It would be held inside the Abbey behind closed doors.

And Rama had not even been given permission to enter the contest. The Kalari Code of Honour required obedience to the Guru Master. A warrior was committed to carry out his mission without consideration of his personal feelings.

The consequences of this seemed dire. It now looked certain that Rama would not be given permission to enter the Contest and thus would not win beautiful Sita's hand.

Danny felt sick as he realised that opened up the opportunity for the hateful Dark Lord Ravana to enter the Contest. And if he should win ... The very thought of Sita with that loathsome monster, gave Danny the creeps.

If Ravana wins the Contest, Sita will give up her life and all will be lost...

8:00 am

The following day dawned bright and clear at Hartland Abbey. The air was vibrant with a carnival atmosphere as Danny, Sandeep and Hugo entered the grounds of the stately home. Bunting lined the routes and there were colourful tents and marquees dotted throughout the grounds.

Long queues of visitors had built up behind them, eager to see the final stages of the Challenge. People had arrived early, and were jostling to get the best viewing positions, including the outside broadcast crews from several TV stations.

People made their way to the cordoned-off viewing areas lining the route all the way up to the main house. Speculation among them was rife. All they knew was that today was the final and most difficult phase of King Janak's Challenge.

'This place is awesome,' Hugo exclaimed. 'It's a great setting for today's contest. Do either of you two know what it's going to be about?'

'No, mate,' said Sandeep. 'It's a closely guarded secret. Only Sita and my Uncle Janak know. It's going to be held inside the Abbey behind closed doors. Only special ticket holders like us will be allowed inside. Everyone else will be viewing the Contest on big screens in the marquees outside.'

'I hear Rama's still not been given permission to enter the Contest,' Hugo added. 'If nothing changes by this afternoon, he'll lose the right to enter it at all.'

'Yeah. We *know!*' Danny looked strained. 'But you don't have to rub it in, Hugo.'

Hugo looked at his friend curiously. Why did it mean so much to Danny?

While the three boys waited eagerly for the procession to begin, Urmila was already up at the big house helping her sister get ready. She'd invited Izzie to join her there.

Sandeep was using crutches to get around while his lower leg was in plaster. He sat on a chair near the entrance while Danny and Hugo procured them all a cup of tea and cake.

Suddenly a look of alarm crossed Hugo's face.

'Hey, guys, what's happening?'

A chill, eerie atmosphere had fallen over the park as if a storm were brewing. An ominous dark shadow fell over the turreted lodge-keeper's cottage. To the consternation of the security guards, the massive, studded gates opened of their own accord.

'Listen! What's that roaring sound?' Danny said, pointing to the road outside the gates.

'What a racket!' Sandeep said. 'It sounds like World War Three has broken out.'

Security men ran towards the gatehouse from every direction. A stream of menacing foot troopers entered the grounds wearing the black and red livery of Ravana. They carried a banner aloft which depicted a black raven with outstretched wings. In its talons was a blood red caterpillar from which emerged a dozen ferocious wasps.

'Look at their flag,' Hugo said. 'They've got the black raven of Ravana above the parasitic wasp of *The Aculeata.*'

The troopers' footsteps created a rhythmic thudding that penetrated into the onlooker's brain. A burly henchman with dark glasses shoved Danny roughly out of the way.

'Move it!' he snarled. 'Make way for the Black King.'

Hugo climbed onto the lower branch of a nearby tree to peer over the crowds.

'I can see a black stretch limo. It's flanked on all sides by dozens of motorbike outriders. That's what the noise is. They're revving their high-powered bikes up and making as much noise as they can.'

Minutes later the cavalcade swept into view on the drive.

'Hey, look!' Hugo said. 'See that main outrider at the very front? Him in the military uniform?'

'Jeez,' Sandeep had to shout above the noise. 'I see him. That guy - isn't he the one that came to the South American marquee that day? *Pedro*? He's a massive brute.'

'That's General Maricha,' said Danny. 'Ravana's right-hand man.'

Someone in the crowd shouted,

'The Black King's brought his own military bodyguard so they can intimidate the opposition!'

'Talk about gamesmanship!' shouted an indignant lady.

The motorbike entourage wore leather body armour, their faces screened by black visors. The foot division led the way, carrying shields and truncheons, which they beat loudly in a monotonous, menacing rhythm all the way up the drive.

But security had set up a second barrier. As the limo reached it, the chauffeur handed over his passenger's Contestant's Pass. The military guard was forced to a halt, albeit with the greatest reluctance. The Chief Security officer waved everyone away.

'The rest of your entourage may not enter any further,' he said. 'Only the contestants and VIPs beyond this point.'

As the limo passed by, the rear window was lowered, affording the onlookers a glimpse of its occupant.

'It's the President of The Aculeata Corporation,' a senior gentleman called out. 'They have branches all over the world.'

'Don't you mean a global network of corruption?' another called out.

The crowd started jeering and booing.

But soon after this, the carriages bearing princes and nobility from around the world arrived. The atmosphere changed completely. There was excited applause as the TV presenters announced each of the contestants, noting their country's flags and livery. Each entourage was afforded a warm reception as they passed.

But Danny kept looking for Rama. He was not among them. Where in heaven's name could he be? A whisper went round the crowd.

'Rama's not coming!' A man held his mobile up. 'I've just heard on the news that he's been detained in the city.'

'There was a bomb scare at the museum,' someone else checked their phone's headline news. 'Rama's had to stay behind to fight the terrorists and make sure it's all safe and secure.'

'I don't know who is spreading the rumours,' a woman called out. 'But it's all propaganda and lies. Look!'

Everyone gazed at the entrance gates. As they opened, a cheer went up from the crowd.

'He's here!'

'I knew he wouldn't let us down.'

A blue and gold carriage bearing Lord Belvedere's crest, came through the gates. In it, was Sage Vishwa-mitra. Behind him, on magnificent white horses, came Rama and Lakshman. A cavalcade of liveried horsemen followed, magnificent in their colourful outfits.

Both brothers looked resplendent, their gold helmets and breastplates gleaming in the sunlight. Lakshman carried the colours of the Order of the Kalari Knighthood. They paused while Sandeep was helped into the carriage with Vishwa-mitra. Danny and Hugo, dressed in their colourful tunics, fell in behind the procession.

The crowds cheered wildly as the procession made its stately progress up the drive. The coach drew to a halt at the entrance to the stately home. The contestants on horseback dismounted and climbed the steps to enter the building.

As the three friends were guided to the seating area in the Great Hall, Danny noted with a sinking heart that instead of going to the designated Area for Contestants, Rama had gone to take his seat in the invited guest's area with his brother and his Guru master.

Oh no! He's not been allowed to enter the contest. Poor Sita. She'll be devastated.

IN THE LUXURIOUS white and gold suite on the upper floor of Hartland Abbey, Sita sat patiently in a plush button-backed chair while the ladies ministered to her. In the traditional fashion, Urmila and Izzie were just finishing the task of intertwining her hair with fragrant jasmine flowers. Her cousins and other female relatives had decorated her hands and feet with beautiful henna patterns, as was the custom. Sita wore the traditional jewellery and the red, beaded and embroidered sari of a bride-to-be.

Urmila stepped back to admire their handiwork. 'Mmn. The flowers look good. And I must say, sis - you look fit to enact the legendary Sita who just stepped out of the pages of the Ramayana.'

'Well,' Izzie said admiringly. 'Even the flowers are cast into the shade by your sister's beauty. There won't be a man here today who doesn't fall over himself to win her heart.'

Just then Urmila's phone rang.

'Hi Danny,' she said. 'Thanks for letting us know.' She cradled the phone under her chin as she nodded at Sita. 'He's arrived.'

A look of relief flooded Sita's face. But it was short-lived. As she heard the next part of the conversation, she gripped the arms of her chair tightly.

'What do you mean?' Urmila frowned. 'He's not sitting in the Contestant's area? Where is he sitting then?'

She handed the phone to her sister.

'Sita, he wants to talk to you.'

'Danny - tell me *immediately*!' There was urgency in Sita's voice. 'What is happening?'

As she listened, she shook her head, not wanting to believe what she was hearing.

'Rama is sitting in the *Visitors'* seats? N-not with the Contestants? And the one they call the Black King has entered the contest? It's really Ravana? Oh no. Please don't say so ... Does it mean Rama is not entering the Contest at all?'

The phone slipped out of Sita's hand and fell unnoticed to the floor. She swayed as if she was going to faint.

Urmila was seriously alarmed. She'd always looked up to Sita for being so calm and cool. She'd never seen her so distraught before. She held Sita's outstretched hands.

'Oh, Urmila,' Sita said in anguished tones. 'Please don't say Rama isn't entering the Contest. He absolutely *has* to enter in order to win. I'll simply *die* if he doesn't.'

Kirsty O'Donnell and Richard Greenwood had been provided with a sound-proof booth inside the Great Hall. It had been positioned to give them a clear view of proceedings for their live broadcast.

'The majority of people,' Richard reported. 'Are in the marquees outside, including high-level politicians and noble family members of the contestants. There are large TV monitors, strategically placed to relay scenes of the Contest as they happen inside the stately home.'

'Richard and I are fortunate,' said Kirsty O'Donnell. 'To have been invited inside the stately home itself, where only Contestants and a very few select guests are allowed on this day of Raja Janak's Challenge.'

Cameras panned round the interior.

'Here you can see the Great Hall in all its splendour,' she said. 'A thousand candles have been lit and their reflections sparkle in gilded mirrors. There are wonderful statues and paintings by Old Masters on the walls. Beautiful crystal chandeliers hang down, glittering in the sunlight which filters through the domed skylight above.'

'In the centre of the Great Hall,' Richard added. 'The space is open to the high ceiling, whilst at first floor level, a stone balustrade runs all round the edge. It encloses the balcony where Sita and the other ladies will sit to watch the proceedings.'

'In contrast to the noisy excitement outside the building,' Kirsty said. 'Inside the hall here, there is a settled, calm ambience. We can smell the scent of fragrant incense and roses in the air. People are automatically speaking in hushed tones. There's an expectant feeling that is hard to describe. It's as if something momentous is about to happen.'

Richard fiddled with his ear-piece.

'I'm getting the signal that King Janak and all the contestants are about to arrive.'

A stirring trumpet fanfare played by royal heralds reverberated around the Great Hall as she spoke. King Janak's preceptor led the way, followed by the Chief Minister who carried the Royal Insignia. Raja Janak followed looking regal and dignified in his traditional State robes.

The Contestants followed behind in procession, each wearing the state robes or national dress of their country. The guests stood up respectfully as they passed. Kings, rajas, princes, sultans, Counts and Marquises, Dukes and Domos, Chiefs and Chieftains, leaders from all the world's noble families.

King Janak in his long purple velvet cloak took his own seat on the raised dais, and courteously gestured for the Contestants to take the elegant seat that had been prepared for them as befitted their noble rank.

'Congratulations to you all,' Raja Janak said. 'You have demonstrated that you are skilled and brave warriors, the leaders in your field, the cream of your country's nobility. You have shown that you are valiant warriors, skilled and knowledgeable in the noble arts.

'As honourable representatives of your own land, you have been invited to enter this Contest known as the Challenge of the Great Bow of Shiva. Today's challenge however, will search for something out of the ordinary. To say it will not be easy is an understatement.

'So now, without further ado, let me reveal Sita's incredible Challenge to you ...'

19
RAJA JANAK'S IMPOSSIBLE CHALLENGE

'In days of old,' Raja Janak said. 'There was a contest which was famed in an ancient legend known as the Ramayana. It involved an object known as the Great Bow of Shiva. This sacred artefact has belonged to our family since time immemorial. Attached to it is a prophecy.

'It states that one day a Knight will appear who embodies the noble Arya qualities of the ancient Vedic tradition. He will come during a time in history when values are in decline, when Truth has become distorted, when the Veda has been misinterpreted, repressed and almost lost.

'My Grandfather left this artefact to me in his Will. In it he stated only a true Kalari Knight would have the Shakti power to render him a match for Sita. He also said it is the Great Bow of Shiva itself that will ultimately choose the winner of the contest. So now, without further ado, let me reveal the terms of the Challenge to you.'

He gave a signal to his Chief Minister. The camera panned to a large oblong table in the centre of the room. It was covered over by a silken embroidered cloth. Soundlessly, the fabric began to rise up, attached by fine cords to a pulley system high in the atrium above the Great Hall.

And there it was, the museum exhibit that had once been identified only by the number *108*. Although it was still covered with a layer of grey ash, hairline cracks had begun to appear in the surface. Something glinted underneath. The revelation caused a stir amongst the assembled company.

'This,' announced Raja Janak, 'Is the Great Bow of Shiva. Whosoever can lift and string this Bow, shall be deemed to have won the contest.'

A ripple of relief spread throughout the contestants at what they perceived to be an easy contest. A murmur went round the Great Hall. One or two princes rose to their feet and eagerly called out, 'Let me have a try, honoured sir!'

'Gentlemen, please,' Raja Janak motioned for them to sit down. 'I have not yet finished describing the contest. This as I said, is no ordinary challenge. It has been designed by Sita and uses modern science to test the integration of your body-mind power.

'The Challenge of the Great Bow of Shiva will search for something more than mere physical strength.' He motioned to the Chief Minister who flicked a remote control in the direction of a computerised bank of instruments.

Immediately an array of laser beams sprang up, over and around the Great Bow. They crisscrossed it in such a manner that there was no way to walk through them. They effectively cut off access to the table on which the Great Bow lay.

'Please demonstrate to the contestants how it works, Chief Minister,' instructed the monarch. The Minister passed his hand through one of the laser beams and immediately a piercing siren went off.

'This is what will happen if you so much as brush up against one of these beams. They go off on contact and if they do, you will be automatically disqualified from the contest.

'The latest research into brain wave imaging shows that the power of the mind can be harnessed. A brain map will reveal the contestant's brain wave patterns on the big screen for all to see. The more orderly they are, the more powerful they are. If Alpha Waves are displayed, it will be an indication of coherent brain functioning. This will indicate a high level of consciousness.'

'Your Challenge today,' Raja Janak continued. 'Is to switch off the lasers using the power of your mind alone.'

There were baffled looks and much shaking of heads from the contestants.

'But that's impossible!'

'I never heard of such a thing!'

'This is the cutting edge of science,' said a scholarly gentleman. 'I've heard of its application in robotic arms to help paraplegic victims, but this ...!'

'We would need training to undertake this task. Who among us has this level of Shakti power?'

The Chief Minister ignored the comments and gestured to a seat.

'You will be asked to sit in this chair and put on this special cap. It is fitted with electrodes that monitor the electrical activity of the brain as designed by our university science labs.

'It is connected to the computer which is projecting the lasers. We will be able to see a 'map' of each contestant's brain waves on the large wall monitor. We will then ask you in your own time, to use your mind power to switch off the beams or render them ineffective.'

'Whosoever can manage this first part of the Challenge,' said Raja Janak. 'Will then have the opportunity to attempt the second part. And that is to lift the Great Bow of Shiva up from the table on which it lies. By doing this, the successful candidate will have demonstrated his worthiness to be pronounced the winner of the Challenge.

'Please be aware that my daughter Sita is now the custodian of the Great Bow of Shiva and hers is the final decision. Gentlemen, we wish you good luck.'

The Chief Minister spoke into the microphone.

'Ladies and gentlemen, may I have your attention please? We must have absolute silence in the hall for the contestants to be able to give this task their full concentration. Now, will the first contestant step forward please?'

For a moment no one moved as they weighed up the task in stunned silence. Each looked round the room wondering who would be the first to try their luck.

Finally, a African Zulu chief courageously stood up. He inclined his head respectfully to Raja Janak and took to the chair. Beads of sweat stood out on his forehead as he closed his eyes. With a supreme effort he managed to turn a couple of the laser beams off, but try as he might he could not turn off more. Several other contestants tried – all with the same result. Most had no success, and even the best could only turn off one or two of the beams.

A murmur of doubt rippled around the room.

'It's impossible.'

'No one is going to be able to do it.'

'What is going to happen if no one succeeds in Raja Janak's Challenge?'

'Surely there must be someone?'

Suddenly there was the sound of a slow handclap followed by a mocking laugh at the failure of the other contestants. The speaker was on his feet.

'*Losers!* All of you!' the Black King's voice boomed out across the Great Hall as he pointed and wagged his finger at them all. 'Watch and learn, people,' he jeered. 'This is how it is done!'

With a shudder of horror, Danny studied Ravana, the Dark One. In his youth he may have been good-looking, but now his jowls hung heavy and his eyes were bloodshot and puffy with indulgent living. He wore a black leather jacket studded all over with rubies. A billowing red cloak trimmed with black raven feathers hung from his massive shoulders. He wore gauntlets with diamond studs at the cuffs and leather boots with spurs that jingled when he walked. When he stood up, his huge frame towered over the other contestants.

He made a big show of swaggering to the chair and put the electrode cap on his head.

'I will show you how it's done by a *real* man!' he bragged, giving a contemptuous look at the other contestants. He flexed his bulky biceps in a show of strength and sat down. Once the electrodes were attached he closed his eyes and concentrated.

At first he managed to make two or three beams go out. Then others began to flicker and it seemed to the anxious onlookers as if even more might close down. But the results were achieved only by dint of the greatest physical and mental effort. The strain began to tell. Beads of sweat formed on his brow and trickled down his flaming cheeks. The veins on his neck bulged. He breathed heavily under the exertion.

Kirsty O'Donnell spoke into the microphone in hushed tones.

'We can see the Black King's brain waves on the screen right now. The increasing disorder in the wave pattern shows that his thinking is becoming more incoherent. He does not seem able to keep up that level of forceful strain. It appears – in spite of his boasts - that he's not going to be able to do it.'

Ravana appeared to come to the same conclusion. His face contorted hideously and he let out a primeval roar of unbridled rage. He ripped off the cap, leapt out his seat and strode purposefully to the control panel on the computer table. He yanked the electric plug out of the wall socket and all the laser beams disappeared.

Security guards rushed to restore the set-up and prevent Ravana from attempting to touch the bow. But Raja Janak intervened, holding up his hand to stop them.

'Let him try what he will.'

The Black King strode up to the table on which lay the Great Bow, a triumphant expression on his face.

'Watch this, people,' he gloated, sure of victory. 'This is how it's done.'

Confident that he had more than enough strength to deal with this paltry challenge, he grasped the Great Bow round the middle and attempted to lift it with one hand. It remained firmly on the table, not moving by so much as a millimetre.

Ravana tried again. This time he used both hands and gave it a strong yank off the table. Still it wouldn't budge. He tried a slow pulling-at-it approach. It stuck fast.

He began to realise that he might have misjudged the situation. He loosened his cloak and let it drop to the floor. He braced himself more firmly on the ground, feet planted wider apart, flexing biceps in a greater show of strength. With every sinew and fibre of his massive, powerful body he tried to wrench the Bow off the table. His torso heaved, the massive muscles on his thighs bulged and strained, and sweat ran freely down his face and body. Still the Great Bow of Shiva did not budge, not even by the smallest fraction of an inch.

The Black King staggered backwards almost collapsing with the exertion. A baffled look of disbelief crossed his face. It was followed by a flicker of fear. The reality began to dawn on him that there was a fundamental power of nature holding the Bow in place, which was beyond the normal force of gravity. It would not yield to him. It occurred to him that he was powerless before it.

With that thought came the realisation he had failed. And he'd done so in public, his pride dented in front of everyone. His face reddened, his temper mounted and he went berserk. He let out a mighty roar of frustration more animal than human. He shook clenched fists at the Bow, his face contorted like a hideous monster.

Gone was any attempt to bamboozle with charm or fake the result. He had suffered a massive humiliation in front of all these people. For once in his life, he had not been able to bully, bribe or coerce his way to winning the prize he needed more than anything.

In a state of blind passion, Ravana turned on his heel and stormed out of the Great Hall, shoving people roughly aside as he went. There was the sound of breaking china and smashing glass as he destroyed priceless antiques and everything in his path on his way out.

Ravana's chauffeur was waiting outside with the limousine. He scuttled to open the door for his seething master. Through the window, Danny and the others could see the vehicle being driven off at great speed with a screech of tyres and blue smoke.

As it sped off into the distance the occupants of the Great Hall sat in stunned silence, reeling from the scene they had just witnessed. Then everyone started clapping and laughing. There were jeers and shouts.

'Good riddance to bad rubbish!'

'Let that be a lesson to all braggarts!'

A plaintive voice piped up,

'But *who* will actually be able to accomplish this impossible feat?'

Raja Janak allowed a few minutes for the spectators' noise to subside. He looked grave. From his point of view, there was nothing to rejoice about. He looked round the room, his face set. His inner sight told him there was only one person in the room who had a chance of lifting the

Great Bow. And to Raja Janak's dismay he hadn't even entered the contest.

The Chief Minister asked Raja Janak if he should switch the lasers back on. The room fell silent. Every eye looked up at Sita on the balcony. She had covered her face with her veil so no one could read her emotions. Inside she was in turmoil. Was this the end?

She saw Rama still sitting in the Visitor's area. He looked so calm. Was he not even bothered she wondered? She hid her head in her hands, hardly daring to look.

Raja Janak made a last, desperate request.

'Are there any other contestants? If so, please step forward.'

Silence. No one moved. All eyes were on Rama, but he remained impassive. He had given his Master an undertaking to serve him on this mission. The mission involved upholding the Kalari Code of Honour. Rama would not break his word under any circumstances.

Danny knew how bad Sita must be feeling right now, and he desperately wanted to find a solution. He had been told it was his mission to somehow bring these two soul-mates together. But for the life of him, he couldn't think how it could be done.

He saw Sita's imploring gaze on him and her anguish was evident. She was silently willing him to think of something, as if he was part of the Challenge.

Raja Janak looked forlorn like a man for whom hope was fading. The only one in the room who was a match for his precious jewel, his beloved daughter, was not even going to enter the Contest. He silently remonstrated with himself.

How could I have let Sita persuade me to follow the instructions in Grandfather's Will? I've caused her to sacrifice herself for my honour. And now I am duty bound to keep my word, to let the Great Bow choose the winner for my daughter's hand. And if there is no winner, all will be lost.

But even as these thoughts seared through his psyche, fate was stirring in the hall. The Chief Minister called for a tea break to give everyone time for a period of calm reflection before the final call for contestants was given.

DANNY STEPPED OUTSIDE to get a breath of fresh air and to clear his head. He strode off through the grounds away from the bustle and noise. He headed for a group of trees some distance away. It had started drizzling rain and most people had gone inside the marquees. There was hardly anyone about.

Danny checked his watch and decided it was time to go back. But as he turned in the direction of the building a flock of ravens flew over and landed on the parapet of the Abbey. Their beady eyes watched him intently. He remembered other occasions lately when he'd seen ravens. There was that first fateful day when he'd received *The Aculeata's* warning; there was the occasion in the park. And now, here. Why?

Suddenly, the birds launched themselves into the air and came towards him as if on the attack. But at the last minute they stopped short and landed in a nearby tree. Their glassy eyes fixated on him.

There was something odd about them. It was partly the way the light glinted on their wings. Then it came to Danny with a jolt. *They were not ordinary birds!* They were metal drones, made to look like real birds so they could spy on the situation in the big house. But now they were locking onto him as their target of interest.

A small child was playing with a ball on the grass, not far away. Suddenly, one of the ravens swooped down as if to attack it. Without hesitation, Danny ran over to help, lashing out at the drone and fending it off with a stick, before it could harm the toddler.

It gave the mother time to run over and snatch the child up under her arm. She ran off to the safety of the nearby marquee. Having drawn Danny into the open, the raven retaliated by savagely pecking him on the side of his cheek, drawing blood.

Danny was sure he saw General Maricha through the trees in the distance. He seemed to have the control panel in his hands. The next thing Danny knew, there was a flock of half a dozen drone ravens circling above his head preparing to attack.

Danny knew from his father that Artificial Intelligence was

programmed into military drones so that they responded to each other with 'robotic self-actuating technology'.

In effect, it meant AI drones would lock onto their target independent of their handler. Once activated, they would pursue their quarry wherever he went until they brought him down.

Instinctively, Danny's hand went to the silver pendant round his neck. It was an experimental prototype that Sita had given him. It used the latest in brain wave technology to harness the Shakti power for its energy source. Sita had explained how to use it.

The Shakti power is there when you need it. Go within to summon it.

Danny unclipped the pendant from its chain. It was in the shape of a silver arrow, about the width and length of a pencil.

He held it in his palm and pressed two tiny buttons on either side of the barrel. A hinged segment flicked open at the bottom, doubling its length. Simultaneously, out of each side, concertina wings sprouted. The arrow tip formed into an eagle's head and the tail feathers fanned out wide. In appearance it was a silver eagle with outstretched wings.

Danny closed his eyes and summoned the Shakti power. The eagle began to emit a focused laser beam of silver light. With its drone-like capabilities, this was a sign that its internal programming was now activated.

As quick as he could Danny clutched the silver tail and slashed the air. His first strike sent a raven-drone hurtling to the ground, twitching where it lay. He put his palm under the body of the eagle and launched it into the air with all his might. It soared high above the ravens looking down on them.

The raven drones were not programmed to evade a counter attack. They were locked onto the soft target that was Danny. They attempted to fly higher. But wherever they went the eagle drone followed and caught up with them, blasting each one with its laser beam.

One by one, Danny's silver eagle picked off the raven cohort, cleaving through the flock like a hot knife through butter. Three of them fell to the ground, burned out. Twitching, Batteries drained.

The remaining three started to use their AI to regroup and prepare for another attack. But Sita's ingenious programming used Danny's alpha waves as the energy source. It allowed him to draw on his creative intelligence.

The silver eagle began to pulse with multiple laser beams from its outstretched wings. It locked onto the raven drones and dealt them a devastating blast, exterminating every last one of them.

A few hundred yards away through the trees, Danny saw General Maricha frenetically punching his mobile keypad. But it was no good. Try as he might, he couldn't regain control.

As the last drone lay still, Danny recalled his eagle drone and reduced it to its pendant size. He checked his watch and realized with dismay that the whole incident had badly delayed him. Would he make it back in time? He felt a mounting wave of panic.

His deep intuition told him it was essential for him to be there for the final call for the contestants. He started to sprint up the drive.

But just as he reached the Abbey the big wooden doors were slammed shut. All was lost if he couldn't get back in. He pulled out his mobile phone. But would Hugo or Sandeep pick up in time?

20
THE GREAT BOW OF SHIVA
CONTEST

DANNY STOOD on the doorstep gasping for breath. In desperation he hammered on the massive front door and beat its iron knocker. There was no response. His heart was beating like a hummingbird's wings. He simply *had* to get in.

Suddenly, he heard the bolts being drawn back. A stern-faced security guard appeared on the threshold. Behind him Danny could see Hugo looking pale and anxious.

'You're in luck, young man!' the guard said, softening a little. 'Your pal got your phone message in the nick of time and told me who you were. Get in quick before the session starts. It's nearly time for the final call.'

Sandeep welcomed his friend back as he took his seat.

'Mate, what kept you?'

Danny relayed the events of the drone attack.

'So you think Maricha was trying to delay you for some reason?'

Hugo added hopefully,

'Maybe it was because you've hit upon an idea to save the day?'

Danny shook his head miserably.

'No. Afraid not, pal. I've got absolutely nothing.'

An expectant hush fell over the hall as Raja Janak re-entered the room with his Chief Minister. Everyone looked towards the visitor's seating area, willing some miracle to happen so Rama would be able to enter the contest. But no one, including Danny, had the remotest idea how this could be achieved.

'Hear this,' said Raja Janak. 'This is the last call for any contestant who has not yet taken part in the challenge, to come forward.' The monarch looked hopefully at the noble visitors' seats. No one stirred. His face fell and he looked as if he'd aged by fifty years. His shoulders bowed under the weight of the sorrow he felt.

'Then I will have to declare –'

He was about to say, *'a void contest,'* when he was interrupted by the voice of Fate.

'Boy!' Vishwa-mitra's booming voice resonated throughout the Great Hall.

All eyes swivelled in the direction of the powerful Kalari Master. He leaned forward in his seat and beckoned for Danny to come over to him. Danny was incredulous.

'Does he mean *me?*'

'Yes, of course he does, eejit!' Sandeep whispered. 'Don't keep him waiting.'

As if in a dream, Danny got up and walked over to where the Kalari Master sat. He put his palms together and bowed low in respect.

Sita watched from the balcony above hardly daring to breathe as the Master continued.

'Young man. You displayed extraordinary valour on the Kalari battle-ground. In the face of mortal danger, you chose to protect your friend at great personal risk to yourself.'

Danny saw his father in a wheelchair near the back of the room. He appeared to have something in his eye.

'Therefore,' the sage continued. 'I award you, Danny Hanuman, the Order of the Kalari Knighthood.' He placed a ribbon around Danny's neck on which hung a gold medal.

'Now, I will grant you a boon. Name anything that you desire. Money, fame, success. Ask, and it shall be given to you.'

Danny had no need to think. There was only one thing he wanted.

'If you p-please, s-sir,' he stammered. 'May Rama be given permission
_'

The sage put his hand up to silence Danny. No further words were needed. It was as if the great seer had read Danny's mind.

With a gracious gesture to Rama, the Master indicated that the noble Prince of Ayodhya, had his permission to enter the contest. As Rama stood up and bowed acknowledgement to his Guru, Danny gave a deep, heartfelt sigh. There was a spontaneous burst of applause from the audience, showing their wholehearted approval. Sita let out her breath and gazed at Rama, love shining in her eyes.

Rama wore an embroidered white tunic coat and trousers. He looked incredibly handsome as he walked over to the computerised EEG equipment. He sat down in the Contestant's chair and paused a moment. He looked searchingly up at the balcony to where Sita was sitting.

She still held her veil over her eyes. Although filled with renewed hope she dreaded lest the task might prove too difficult for *anyone*, even this mighty warrior.

Rama didn't bother to put the electrode cap on his head. Instead, he held the terminals in his hands and closed his eyes. The computer monitor began to register his brain waves, which were visible to all on the big screen in the Great Hall.

There was a sharp intake of breath from the onlookers. Even to the untrained eye it was remarkable. But to the eminent scientists who were present, Rama's brain waves were nothing short of a revelation.

Professor Emerson, the Head of the Cambridge department who was monitoring the challenge, murmured something to Raja Janak who nodded in agreement.

The Professor went to the soundproof booth where Kirsty O'Donnell sat and handed her his notes. She read them out loud.

'Professor Emerson has asked me to tell you about this contestant's brain waves. They are the most coherent alpha waves he has ever seen. The left and right hemispheres are exactly in sync, the waves of the rear lobes and pre-frontal cortex are lined up. The professor likens this phenomenon to the focused, orderly waves of a laser beam as compared to the randomized waves given off by an ordinary light bulb.'

'Remarkable,' said Richard. 'We are seeing clear evidence of a most powerful mind. But it now remains to be seen, will Rama's Shakti power be able to turn off the lasers?'

On the balcony, Sita bit her lip and twisted her handkerchief into knots. Danny and the rest of the audience looked at the monitors in awe at this display of mastery of mind and body. But the question uppermost in everyone's mind was the same. *Could he do it where everyone else had failed?*

And even if he managed to turn off the lasers, would he then be able to lift the massive weight of the Great Bow of Shiva as the Contest demanded? After all, no one else had had the strength to do it, including the powerful Black King.

You could have cut the air with a surgical scalpel, it was so tense. Everyone held their breath, willing Rama to succeed. Moments passed and nothing seemed to happen.

But all of a sudden one of the laser beams went out, followed swiftly by another and another, until all of the beams had completely disappeared.

Rama rose from the chair and walked with athletic grace to the long table on which lay the Great Bow of Shiva. Another revelation was in store. The audience let out an involuntary exclamation. For, where once had been a dusty old bow, a transformation was taking place before their very eyes. The ash and dust of centuries had begun to crack and fall away to reveal a shining object beneath.

Kirsty O'Donnell's voice was barely a whisper.

'Oh my!' she exclaimed. 'We are witnessing an extraordinary sight. No wonder it was so sought after. We can now see the Great Bow of Shiva is made of solid gold. Not only that, it is studded with precious gems. They are catching the light of a myriad candles in the chandeliers. The whole thing appears to be vibrating with points of dancing light, like sparklers on bonfire night. The way it catches the light forms a rainbow arc over the Great Bow.'

Rama stood before the Great Bow of Shiva for a minute in contemplation. He then walked around the table clockwise without taking his eyes off the object. Finally, he stopped. He reached out his hand and grasped the bow firmly in the middle. There was another tense moment. Was he going to be able to do it? Could he really lift this massive weight?

And then with just one hand, Rama effortlessly raised the bow off the table and held it aloft for all to see.

The room fell into an uproar. Everyone was on their feet, laughing and applauding. Conches, bells and drums were being sounded everywhere. Flower petals showered down from the ceiling atrium. Even the other contestants gave Rama a standing ovation. Sita was beside herself with tears of inexpressible joy rolling down her cheeks.

Kirsty made the announcement for all those in the outside marquees.

'He has lifted the massive weight of the Great Bow of Shiva with just *one hand*! Prince Rama has won the Contest. Raja Janak is coming forward to congratulate the victor. Sita, the most virtuous of women, her beautiful eyes shining, descends the stairs carrying the Victor's flower-garland in her hands.

'Rama is smiling at her as she approaches,' continued Kirsty. 'I imagine any woman seeing that smile would go weak at the knees. No wonder Raja Janak looks so relieved and happy. He has found the ideal husband for his amazing daughter.'

LATER THAT EVENING the celebration party was well under way in the stately home. A sumptuous banquet had been laid out. There was a fireworks display outside. Music and dancing were taking place in the marquees in the grounds.

A select group had been invited to a private dinner, which was taking place in the red dining room, with its splendid Rubens fireplace, and ornate over-mantle mirror. It was hosted by the elderly, frail looking Lord Belvedere. His figure was stooped and his hair was white but he had an intelligent face with shrewd grey eyes that took everything in. He insisted Raja Janak and his wife, Devaki should take place of honour at the dinner table.

Those seated around the table in evening dress included Richard Greenwood, looking slightly uncomfortable in a dinner jacket. Kirsty

O'Donnell wore a turquoise satin evening gown, and with her blond hair loose to her shoulders, she looked stunning. Professor Plendergarth wore a dinner jacket and red bow tie. Major Mike Hanuman, although seated in a wheelchair, looked distinguished in his evening jacket, even though a blanket covered his legs.

As they ate together, the talk turned to the subject of the work at the museum. Lord Belvedere said,

'What fascinates me, Dr Greenwood - Richard - is how your research appears to show a tradition of Vedic culture amongst so many ancient civilisations. And it seems from your research, that this was not confined to India.'

'I agree,' said Professor Plendergarth. 'If we remove our 'westernised blinkers,' as it were, and then examine the ancient world, it is a treasure trove of knowledge and culture. Richard, in terms of your Quest, what can you tell us about the identity of the *Ancient Sea Kings?*'

'Dr Anjani's Notebook,' said Richard. 'Reveals several ancient civilizations that were much more advanced and cultured than history has given them credit for.'

'Am I right in thinking that mathematics and astronomy were the common denominators in their advanced knowledge?' Professor Plendergarth enquired.

'Yes, but it is more than that,' Kirsty nodded. 'We found societies as diverse, for example, as the ancient Sumerians, the Indus Culture, the Anatolians, the Celts, the Norse, the Slavs, Cambodians, South American cultures, all knew about stories from the Veda.'

'What is the Veda?' Mike Hanuman said.

'The Veda,' said Raja Janak. 'Is the collective name in Sanskrit for all the Laws of Nature. Dr Anjani maintained that all the most advanced of the ancient cultures knew of the Veda and had a great respect for it.'

'Some of these cultures,' Richard elaborated. 'May have acquired Vedic knowledge from widely travelled experts who were the *Sea Kings.* These *Sea Kings,* such as Viracocha, for example, brought with them knowledge of Vedic principles in such things as mathematics, science, building and agriculture. They were expert navigators over land and sea.

We have the evidence in the Almanac to show they knew of *longitude* long before it was known in the West.'

'There is significant evidence they practiced the principles of Vastu Veda,' said Raja Janak. 'And it is also clear in the layout of so many ancient cultural sites with an east-west axis.'

'Now that the Almanac has been returned,' said Professor Plendergarth. 'We must give it its correct title, *The Indian Calendar*. I have seen for myself just how truly remarkable the mathematics and astronomical knowledge of the Vedic Arya people of ancient India was.'

'I agree, professor,' Kirsty said. 'The Arya scholars used numerals with decimals to nine places; they worked out calculations of longitude thousands of years ago, not just on the earthly plane, but on planets such as Jupiter, the sun and the moon.'

'And we mustn't forget,' said Professor Plendergarth. 'That the invention of the decimal number system and zero came not from the Arabic, but from ancient India.'

'Yes, it's true,' said Richard. 'And it's thanks to the Arab scholars who were the first outside India to learn the *'Hindoo'* system, as they called it. In their treatises, they actually give credit to the Indian scholars for their 'ingenious' methods of calculation, including the numerals 1-9 and the essential use of *zero*. Without *zero*, modern mathematics and computing would not exist.'

'And the knowledge of zero,' said Raja Janak. 'Comes from the Veda itself in a very profound way. 'Zero' is the power of pure potentiality, contained in the empty space, for example, at the centre of the seed, or the centre of a galaxy. It is the interface between matter and non-matter. It is the Unified Field of Quantum Mechanics.'

'What impressed me' said Professor Plendergarth, 'were the insights the students came up with, especially Danny. They solved mysteries that have puzzled the academic scholars for years.'

'I agree,' said Kirsty O'Donnell. 'Danny's insights into such cultures as Tiwanaku have been extraordinary.'

'How has he done it?' said Professor Plendergarth. 'His understanding of the mythologies on which all pyramid cultures of the ancient world were built has given us much to work on for the future.'

'I was most astounded by Danny's revelations,' said Richard. 'The mystery of the figures in the Kalasasaya Courtyard has puzzled academics for decades. How did he guess that they are intended to look as if they are emerging from the foaming water of the Churned-up Ocean of Milk? It was inspired.'

'Yes, and the fact they are the *Sea Kings* of the legend,' said Kirsty O'Donnell. 'Is of great interest in terms of our quest.'

'Can you tell us who they are?' said the professor.

'The figure carrying the hinged and bound casebook,' said Kirsty. 'Represents Manu, the first man, the law-giver. He was the first to emerge from the Milk Ocean when it was churned. There is another figure who is holding the drum of Damaru. This represents Shiva who controls the beginning and end of time, '*Kala*' means 'time' in Sanskrit.'

'The third sea-king,' said Richard. 'Carries the Kalash vessel containing the Nectar of Immortality. He is called Dhan-vantari and is the giver of perfect health and longevity.'

'So, this adds up to a persuasive argument,' said Professor Plendergarth. 'For Tiwanaku being a Vedic culture right from its very beginning. Remarkable!

'All the students did a great job,' said Mike Hanuman. 'And I must say, Danny made good use of his mother's Notebook. There were clues in it that only he could have interpreted.'

'There is still more information to be revealed,' said Richard. 'After we've had time to study Dr Anjani's Notebook in further detail.'

'But what interests me,' said Kirsty O'Donnell. 'Dr Anjani refers to an even more important Notebook. 'She says it contains the 'Rosetta Stone,' which is a key to deciphering the ancient world. She believes it could unlock the secret code to many mysteries that have puzzled the academic world.'

'The problem is,' said Richard, his brows drawing together. 'It's missing. We've no idea where it could be.'

'If you're correct,' said Mike Hanuman. 'It would be imperative that we find the second Notebook before *The Aculeata* beat us to it and get their hands on it first.

'So we *must* find this second Notebook,' Professor Plendergarth reflected, cocking his head to one side. 'It is of paramount importance, Richard. We will place the resources of the museum at your disposal.'

'Thank you,' said Richard. 'We have a challenge ahead of us and the students are key players in it.'

'But the big question is,' said Major Hanuman. 'Will we be in time?'

'How do you mean, major?' queried Richard.

'Our intelligence,' the major said. 'Indicates that *The Aculeata* are behind the systematic destruction of the world's cultural heritage. And they are still at large.'

'I agree,' said Raja Janak. 'Those negative forces are hell bent on destroying indigenous people and wiping them off the face of the earth. Chopping down the Amazon Rainforest is just a fraction of their game plan. There are signs they are planning a worldwide 'ethnic cleansing' of indigenous people and their habitats on a unbelievable scale.'

'And with their loss,' said Kirsty O'Donnell. 'Will also go the ancient wisdom and knowledge of how to live in harmony with Mother Earth. If the Dark forces get their way, the evidence of mankind's cultural roots will disappear at an alarming pace.'

'Can't they be stopped?' Professor Plendergarth said.

Raja Janak looked grave.

'There's only one person I know who could do that ...' He fell silent for a moment as he mused, almost to himself. 'But now, with Sita by his side, there is a chance for the future.'

'So judging by the public's response,' Richard said. 'We can conclude the Challenge was a great success. Raja Janak, I take it you are happy we have a worthy winner?'

The Monarch beamed. All at once, his troubles evaporated.

'I am utterly delighted with the outcome. Those people are fortunate who find a match such as these two. A marriage truly made in heaven, you might say.

'I wanted to ask you what the saying means,' said Kirsty. '*Satyam eva jayate?*'

'It is a Sanskrit saying,' said Raja Janak. 'Which means *Truth Alone Triumphs*. The power of the Truth, the ultimate Reality, breaks the bondage of ignorance and sends it flying, like clouds which obscure the sun are dispersed by the wind. Truth, happiness and wisdom are the characteristics of the *Sat Yuga*.'

'Is that the Golden Age?' said Kirsty.

'Yes. A time of great joy for everyone.'

'Suppose it doesn't happen?'

'Then the Dark One will triumph and his powers will increase. He feeds off decay and decadence. He will go on to be the supreme ruler of the earth, using the powerful force of the Kali Yuga to bring about the total destruction of the planet and annihilation of humanity.'

IN THE GROUNDS of the stately home, everyone was preoccupied with firework displays, banquets and generally making merry. But even while the betrothal celebrations were in full swing, there was one who had a very different outcome for the bride in mind.

Anchored in a quiet bay off the South of France, a dark figure sat hunched over a desk in the sumptuous presidential quarters of his luxury yacht. He was oblivious to the turquoise sea lapping at the hull. Nor did he notice the brilliant sunshine streaming in through the windows.

The Dark Lord Ravana, although garbed in expensive silken robes, and surrounded by every material comfort, yet seethed with passionate hatred and jealousy. His once handsome features were now puffed and raddled by decadent living and corruption. His face was contorted with an obsession for getting revenge. Nothing was going to stop him from getting even, no matter how many lives it cost in the process.

But it was more than that. He had needed a source of Shakti power in order to regain his full strength. Normally those powers would be automatically conferred on him during the Kali Yuga era. But this Kali Yuga wasn't normal. It somehow had a glitch in the fabric of Time. It seemed to be trying to revert back to a Sat Yuga, the Golden Era when purity prevailed. And it was weakening his Dark powers.

Who was it that could alter the very nature of Time, itself? He knew the answer. Only Rama was capable of achieving that feat. And only

Ravana was capable of stopping him and maintaining the status quo, allowing the Kali Yuga to take its destructive course.

The Great Bow of Shiva would have conferred its powers on him had he been able to lift it. But he'd lost the contest. And he'd lost Sita. Without either one of these, the power of the Kali Yuga era was weakened, even starting to wane. Rama was the cause, so Rama had to be dealt with. And now the Dark One knew how it could be achieved.

Ravana peered intently at the computer on the desk in front of him. There were images of Sita from every angle, collected over a period of time. They included CCTV footage of her at work, at the dance class, at the contest. General Maricha was on the deck outside the open door. He could hear the chilling, obsessive mutterings of the tyrant, as he flicked through many images, which now included Rama.

'No one beats Ravana, or makes a fool of him. Rama, you will discover that The Contest is not yet over. Not by a long way...'

Maricha glanced through the window and saw there was an enlarged photo of Sita on the screen. Ravana stroked her cheek with his finger in a proprietary gesture. He spoke as if she were in the room with him.

'Now, I have found out Rama's weak point. It is *you*, my dear Sita. And it will also be *you* who will help me stop any more of the Vedic knowledge from being revealed by your young protégé, Danny Hanuman.

'One thing is for certain. The next round of the game my precious, will be played by Ravana's Rules ...'

THE NEWLY ENGAGED couple stood on the balcony overlooking the grounds of the stately home as the sounds of the last revelers faded away into the darkness.

Rama took Sita gently by the shoulders and turned her to face him. She was aware of the moonlight reflected in his luminous eyes, highlighting his handsome features as he smiled down at her.

'Sita, duty told me that I had to come here on a mission. But my heart tells me that Fate brought me here to find *you*. Now we're together, side by side, we can face anything the world might throw at us.'

Sita's eyes shone. 'Nothing can spoil our happiness.'

'There's something else I wanted to say,' Rama continued. 'I haven't got you a conventional wedding gift, but I do have something to give you. It's a promise.'

Sita's eyes widened.

'What is it?'

Rama said,

'Many people in this Kali Yuga promise to be faithful, loyal and true when they marry and then break their word, causing untold misery to the ones they love.

'Here is my promise – that *you* will be my one and only love from this day forward. I will not look on any woman with lust or desire even in my thoughts. I will always be true in my heart and soul to you.'

'Oh, Rama!' Sita felt as if she were floating on a cloud. 'And I will always be true to you, no matter what happens in the future.'

It was as well at that moment, that neither of them could foresee future events.

IN A SITTING room downstairs in the stately home, Danny and Sandeep were joking and laughing like old times, about light sabers versus phasers. It was good-natured banter, and this time it was Sandeep arguing for the merits of Shakti power techniques over physical weapons.

Urmila and Hugo were playing a laid-back game of chess, and Izzie was on her iPad.

'Hey guys!' she looked round to demand their attention. 'Listen to this. There's a mystery that's never been solved at – '

'Nooooo!' the others all shouted at once.

'Put a sock in it, Izzie,' Danny advised. 'We're having a night off.'

'Gotcha!' Izzie burst out laughing. 'I was seeing if I could get a rise out of you. And you fell for it, Danny Hanuman.'

He threw a cushion in her direction.

'You ol' Bossy-boots, Dalton!' he grinned at her. 'But whatever would we do without you?'

Through the open window, sounds of music carried to their ears from one of the marquees in the grounds. The DJ's voice boomed over the loud speaker.

'NASA liked this Beatles number that I'm going to play for you now. They beamed it out into space back in 2008. It must still be reverberating out there amongst the stars and galaxies.'

The lyrics and melody wafted through the warm night air.

> *"Limitless undying love which shines around me like a million suns*
> *It calls me on and on across the universe."*

Printed by Amazon Italia Logistica S.r.l.
Torrazza Piemonte (TO), Italy

48099782R00154